ROARING
OF THE LAMB

Jack Lange

They will make war against the Lamb,
but the Lamb will overcome them.

REVELATION 17:14 (NIV)

VMI Publishers
Sisters • Oregon

Inspirational Fiction

PUBLISHED BY MUSTERION PRESS
a division of VMI Publishers
Sisters, Oregon
www.vmipublishers.com

ISBN: 1-933204-08-7
ISBN 13: 978-1-933204-08-6

Library of Congress Control Number: 2005927698

Author Contact: jack@jacksgold.com

Contents

◇◇◇◇◇◇◇◇◇◇◇◇

1

Madeline

◇◇◇◇◇◇◇◇◇◇◇

M ADELINE SPICER SAT APPREHENSIVELY in Dr. Nambodak's waiting room. *He's only spending a few minutes with each patient,* she observed. *I hope he's not just rushing us through for the extra cash.* Her large dark eyes appeared to be focused at a pile of magazines on the coffee table in front of her, but she wasn't really seeing them. She was in a confused state of mind and was despairing about her emotional pain and the hopelessness of her future.

Four seats to her right sat Evan Hawkins. He tried not to make it too obvious that he was looking at her, but he was struck with the symmetry of Madeline's face and build. He stood, walked across the room, and picked up a magazine from the rack then sat down two seats from Madeline.

"Are you all right?" he asked, noticing her dabbing her eyes with a tissue.

Madeline, embarrassed a little, quietly replied, "Oh yeah ... fine." Then noticing the intensity of Evan's enquiring blue eyes, she added, "Well, not really. I guess that's why I'm here. What about you?"

"Diabetes—I'm here to get a prescription for insulin. You look a bit distressed."

"Yeah, things aren't too good. I'm just feeling rotten ... depressed."

"We haven't got much time to talk," whispered Evan, "but I've got a fantastic book that helps depressed people. Can I loan it to you? I'm Evan, by the way."

Madeline looked at him questioningly.

"I'm into alternative healing, and I often loan books ... to help people," Evan quickly added.

"OK. Thanks. I guess anything's worth a try." Madeline wrote her name and phone number on a scrap of paper. Just as she finished, her name was called.

She followed the nurse down a hall into a small room.

When Dr. Nambodak's bored eyes looked up from his desk to his new patient, they instantly became animated with interest. Despite her exhausted appearance, she was one of the most beautiful young women he could remember seeing in his practice.

"Sit down, please, Madeline. What seems to be the problem?"

"I'm not sure I can explain very well, but I ... I feel terrible. I don't enjoy anything anymore. And I'm ... fearful. I—"

"Fearful about what?"

"I ... I can't control my thoughts," Madeline sobbed. "They're strange. I'm frightened I might be ... going mad. Little problems that wouldn't have worried me before, now seem like ... real threats."

Nambodak came around the table and handed Madeline a tissue as he put his arm on her shoulder. "When did all this start, Madeline?"

Madeline leaned a little away from the doctor and he retreated to his chair.

"It's gotten worse the last couple of months since my parent's ... um ... fighting and arguing got worse. I love them both, but for a long time they've only been staying together because of the family. I know they really want to ... uh ... split."

Madeline avoided the doctor's unblinking gaze as she tried to gather her thoughts. "Then there's the matron at the hospital ward where I work. She's jealous of me because no one likes her. They come to me for advice, not her."

"Sounds as if life has gotten a bit tough for you. How are your personal relationships with men?"

Madeline looked at him enquiringly.

"Are things going smoothly there?"

"I wouldn't say smoothly. I just broke up with a guy. He's taking it pretty bad."

"What about yourself? How have you taken it?"

"Well, to be honest, I've had a few boyfriends in the last couple of years."

"Lovers?"

Madeline thought she detected an admiring expression on the doctor's face. "What's that got to do— Yes, but no one I wanted to stay with. What do you think is wrong with me, Doctor?"

Nambodak's casual slouch altered to a more professional upright position. "Clinical depression. You're mentally and emotionally exhausted. Your serotonin—your mood chemistry levels—are depleted. So mentally you're sort of dragging along at rock bottom."

The doctor leaned back in his chair, his voice becoming even more somber. "Madeline, have you been thinking about ending your life?"

Madeline's gaze dropped to her knees. "Yes," she whispered. "To end the pain. So much pain and … emptiness. Death seems like the best option sometimes."

"Do you take any drugs? Marijuana perhaps?"

Madeline paused before she committed herself. "Yeah. Grass. And speed."

"We'll have to get you off those—in due course."

The doctor asked a few more questions, scribbled on a pad, and tore off a sheet, which he handed to Madeline. "You're seriously depressed. Here's a script for anti-depressants. They should help you. I'll see you in two weeks."

Madeline looked at him blankly. *Is that all?* she thought. *A five-minute consultation to fix months of pain? Is there no counseling, no blood tests? He's treating me like a guinea pig.* She stared at the prescription in her hand. *If these don't work, I'm not coming back. I knew doctors couldn't help me. Maybe nobody can.*

A few days after Madeline's doctor's visit, Evan phoned her. "Hi, Madeline. It's Evan. We met at the doctor's office."

"G'day, Evan."

"How have you been?"

"Not many ups. Mainly downs."

"Sorry to hear that. But maybe I can help. I promised you a book, remember?"

"Yes. But I don't think any book's gonna do me much good."

"I think it will. Anyway, it won't hurt to just have a look at it. I'll drop it off at your place if that's OK. Will you be home about seven?"

"I suppose."

"What's your address?"

She gave it to him and agreed to see him at seven.

After hanging up, Madeline resigned herself to a meeting with Bert Stone, a local drug dealer whom she had found to be particularly repulsive. Not just because of his body odor, which matched his smelly apartment, but because he treated her with the same inhumane fascination that he held for a poker machine or a porn show. Other dealers had been reasonably presentable, even polite. But Stone's price for low-grade heroin was cheap, and Madeline was desperate.

She descended her home's narrow stairway, dodging the overhanging bushes. She turned the key of her old car and felt relieved when she heard the battery crank over the engine.

It would take twenty minutes to drive to Stone's place and about the same time for Platils, the sedative she had just taken, to take effect.

As she entered Stone's cottage, she grunted, "You got some deodorant for this joint?" she said half jokingly, using the blunt, gruff language she had always received on previous visits.

Bert gave her an indulgent grin. "I'll put deodorant on if I can kiss ya."

"Where's the stuff?" she asked impatiently.

"Got the cash?"

"Course I have."

When the deal was finished, she briskly walked away, the unpleasant encounter further fueling her craving for heroin. After driving home hurriedly, she parked the old Falcon sedan in a no-parking zone outside her cheap shared unit, forgetting to lock it in her hurry to attend to an urgent need. She noticed a pamphlet sticking out of her letterbox and grabbed it as she hurried up the stairs.

Within three minutes she was inhaling the smoke of a cheap-grade heroin, which she burnt on foil—enough to blast her into an unreal escape for a few hours.

Madeline lay on her bed and glanced at the pamphlet. Its title was: "The Mark of the Beast or the Seal of God. You Decide!" She read some of it, then sat up, crumpled the pamphlet, and threw it in the bin. Surprised at how much the pamphlet had disturbed her, she left the bedroom and turned on the television.

Evan Hawkins looked around nervously as he knocked on the old wooden door with the peeling paint. Madeline opened the door slightly. After seeing Evan, she invited him into her living area, its faded walls decorated with pictures of strange-looking rock singers and cute animals. In the center of the graying floorboards, a heavy, low-set coffee table sat on an old, thick, cream-colored rug. A number of old photos were scattered about on the half-empty bookshelf and the glass-fronted cabinet.

Evan's self-conscious inhibition surprised him. He thought he would feel confident in this situation. But instead he felt awkward. *Maybe it's because I know I can't get involved with a non-Christian woman, even though I am attracted to her.*

"Here's the book I promised," he said weakly.

"*The Bible and Mental Health*," mumbled Madeline. "You really think this will help?"

"I hope it will. It's helped others. But if you don't want it ..."

"Won't kill me. You may as well stay for a chat."

"OK," said Evan, surprised.

Madeline relaxed on her old vinyl couch. "I've got nothing else to do for a while, and I'm not feeling crash hot. I suffer from panic attacks and get a bit fearful—for no particular reason. Having company helps."

"I'm not sure I should stay."

"You're different from my usual run of friends. You seem a ... a bit of a thinker."

Evan talked intensely and rapidly about a wide range of subjects. As he calmed down, his speech slowed. When a fluffy white cat nervously jumped off the couch, he reached up to pet her.

"Your cat isn't very affectionate," Evan said.

"Puff's affectionate, but she's sensitive. She was my mum's, so she's kind of a link to my past. What sort of work do you do?"

"I ... uh ..."

"You don't have to tell me."

"I manage a Christian youth hostel." The words came out apologetically as Evan slouched a little into the sofa, shifting his eyes from Madeline to Puff, who sat on the mat between them. "That's why I feel a bit concerned about being here tonight, alone. I..."

"I'm glad you're honest. But you're being a bit hard on yourself, aren't you?"

Evan nervously straightened his shirt. "You don't know me. This isn't really me—what you've seen tonight."

"No? Well, who was it then?"

"Look, I don't feel comfortable talking about myself. Tell me about you. I would never have guessed a lovely girl like you could get so depressed. How are you coping with it?"

"Drugs."

"Drugs?"

"The bad ones. They're all I've found that works."

"But why in the world are you doing this . . . if you don't mind my asking?"

"I don't mind. I've tossed it around with my friends and my conscience often enough."

"It can be therapeutic," Evan said, awkwardly reaching out to pat

Puff, who kept her distance.

"You've shown an interest in me that goes deeper than the boy-girl thing," said Madeline. "Look, Evan, I'm not going to pretend I'm a victimized Miss Innocent and make excuses. But I tried the doctor's medicine and it didn't work. I'm desperate, man. It's not as if I sat down one day and said, *I think I'll become a smack addict.*"

"Smack?"

"Heroin."

"Heroin?" Evan asked incredulously.

"Yeah. I go off my brain when I can't get it."

Madeline vainly searched Evan's face for some slight expression of sympathy.

"What made you get started on it?" asked Evan, his voice slightly indignant.

Madeline sighed. "I cracked up. I'm a nut case. It's a long story. But the doctor prescribed drugs for when my nerves snap under the stress of it all."

"Come on, Madeline, a doctor wouldn't prescribe—"

"Of course not. What he gave me was anti-depressant stuff. But it was hopeless. I just became a mess."

"Why didn't you try something else or see another doctor?"

"If you knew what I've been through, you'd understand why I haven't got much faith in doctors and their drugs. My friends reckon I've got doctor-phobia."

"I know a couple of people who believe antidepressants have helped them almost miraculously."

"Yeah, well maybe, but it's a bit late now, isn't it?"

Evan noticed Madeline's sad, contemplative expression as she picked up Puff, hugged her for a moment, then put her down again.

"One night when I was stoned on grass," Madeline said, "a mate's friend gave me some smack, and the nightmares lifted a bit—a lot, actually. It was crap stuff, but it was a fix. Now I'll do anything to get it."

"It can't be that hard! Just be strong. What happens if you don't take it?"

Madeline laughed. "Nothing much. Only diarrhea, violent stomach pains, nausea, and I vomit all over the place. Not to mention bizarre suicidal thoughts. I'm not sure if I take smack more now to get rid of the depression or to avoid the withdrawals."

Evan's eyes danced in animated enthusiasm for the correction he was about to offer.

"That's a bit of a cop-out, isn't it? I mean, come on, you could have gone to a clinic, or the Salvos, and gotten help."

"Counselors? I watched them wreck my parent's marriage." She paused and bent down to fondly stroke Puff. "Besides, I haven't got a clue how I can get off it now." She sighed resignedly.

Evan impatiently tried to grab Puff, but she sprang away.

"You need God in your life, Madeline. You can get off drugs. You just need to get into the Bible. Do you mind if I read you something?"

"Yeah, I suppose. Go ahead."

"Revelation chapter 14 says, 'If anyone worships the beast and its image, and receives a mark on his forehead or his hand, he shall drink the wine of God's wrath, poured unmixed into the cup of his anger.'"

Madeline, there isn't much time left for you to learn how to avoid getting the mark of the beast. You have to get ready."

Madeline slowly shook her head with a slightly bemused expression.

Evan stood and the cat's eyes widened as it tensed further. He put the Bible back into the half-empty bookcase. "Pity it's not the original 1611 King James Version, but it might do for a beginner."

"I'm not a beginner, Evan. I used to go to church."

"Why'd you stopped going?"

"It's a long story. There was a fair bit of bitching and gossip going on."

"Well, that shouldn't keep you—"

"No sermons just now, please."

"All right, then. Guess I'd better be going. Please read the book."

Evan wanted to linger in Madeline's beautiful presence, but he resolutely made for the door. Peering cautiously out the doorway, he bent low to avoid the overhanging bushes and quickly walked to his vehicle. As he drove home, his thoughts were conflicting. He was intrigued by the mysterious quality in Madeline's expressive eyes, which at times flattered him with their wonderment and intense interest. However, he was searching for a strong Christian woman, and Madeline fell far short. He resolved that if he ever spent time with Madeline again, it would be to prompt reform in her life.

2

The Singer

◇◇◇◇◇◇◇◇◇◇◇◇◇

As soon as Evan left, Madeline swallowed a couple of Platils, then flicked through the first few pages of Evan's book. After a few moments she put it away. She opened the Bible, skimming over some passages until she settled on a highlighted passage in Psalm 139.

"Lord, you have searched me and know me. You know when I sit and when I rise; you perceive my thoughts from afar. You discern my going out and my lying down. You are familiar with all my ways."

If God knows all about me, she thought, *what chance do I have?*

She kept reading: "How precious am I in your thoughts O God, how vast is the sum of them."

I used to almost believe that. Instantly she was distracted by other thoughts. *Where can I go tonight? I hope I've got enough smack.*

As Ami Dobson wearily climbed the stairs of the apartment she shared with Madeline, she tried to ignore the rubbish thrown under the bushes by partygoers. Ami was studying psychology in her final year at Newcastle University and was struggling financially. She'd thought about leaving when Madeline began to use harder drugs. But since her studies had taught her to be sympathetic with addicts, she had stayed on.

Ami dropped onto the couch, exhausted, while Madeline told her about Evan's visit. "OK, so he's a nerd, but at least he's good looking. And maybe he's right about God and all that. Listen, Madeline, I haven't gone to church or prayed for quite a while, but I do remember that when I prayed about my problems, it sometimes helped."

"It's been a while since I've been to church too," replied Madeline.

"Mum used to take me quite a bit. I stopped going since I came to town." Ami thought for a moment, then continued, "Why don't we both go to the church down the road tomorrow? Something different for a change."

"I don't feel like it. But if you want to …"

"Let's check it out. Might do us good."

Ami woke Madeline late the following morning. "C'mon, Maddy, we've only got half an hour to get ready."

"Ami, I'm feeling rotten," Madeline murmured groggily. "Don't want to go. Too boring."

"I'm already dressed and I feel like going somewhere radical. C'mon, get up!"

"Well, if I'm going, I'm gonna suck some smack in first. But I'm not gonna get dolled up. I just wanna hide in the back."

Madeline and Ami arrived a little late and sat in the back row. The loud beat of the music seemed a welcome distraction from their timidity. "Boy, they're playing some up-tempo music," whispered Ami.

"This place is like a religious disco." Madeline giggled. "There's nothing holy about this joint. Look at those girls wiggling to the music."

"You haven't been to church for a long time," said Ami. "That's how they do church these days."

Madeline studied the assortment of faces up front. "The singers seem a bit fake to me. I bet they're not that emotional normally."

"Shh, they'll hear you."

"I'm trying not to think about my next smack hit."

"Shh."

When they introduced Owen Boyd, a tall, fair-haired young man of around thirty, he calmly stepped out onto the stage, picked up the microphone, and sang.

"Boy, he's a great ballad singer.," whispered Madeline, glancing at Ami. "I wonder why he's wasting his talents in this tin-pot church." After the service, as they walked outside, Madeline mumbled, "That preacher was high-brow—really out of touch. Do you believe in that scary last-days stuff?"

"Yep, I do. It's all in the Bible. In the book of Revelation."

Madeline looked around her as if looking for someone. "Hang on. I want to say something to that singer guy."

Madeline walked over to Owen Boyd, trying to look casual. "Excuse me." "I heard you sing. You're really good. You ought to be singing professionally."

"Thanks. I'm not known much around these parts, but I've done a bit of singin' up north. I've only been livin' in Newcastle for a few weeks. Is this your first time here?"

"Yes. We just thought we'd take a look."

"I'm glad you did. I'm singin' at the Leagues Club tonight. Would you like to come? When I've finished singin', we can get to know each other."

"Thanks, but I … I don't think I can make it tonight," Madeline replied.

"Sure we can," said Ami cheerily. When Madeline gave the slightest nod, Ami made arrangements with Owen.

The girls dressed in casual jeans to suit the atmosphere of country night at the Leagues Club. Madeline ran out of heroin and was suffering minor withdrawals, so she took twice her normal dose of Platils to try to compensate. They sat at a table, ordered a beer, and listened to Owen Boyd sing. Madeline noticed sweat marks on his hat and stains on his boots.

"Bit of meaning to his songs," observed Ami.

"Yes. The one about the farming family who pulled together during a drought—he wrote that himself. Pretty good, eh? Interesting clothes. Bit of a bushwhacker I'd say."

After his set, Owen casually walked over to the girls' table, sat down, and ordered a beer.

"Love your voice." Ami smiled.

The conversation centered on Owen's cattle station life for a while, but Madeline was in a philosophical mood. "That song you sang… 'A Different Kind of Loving' … It made me think about why we go to dances and clubs. I don't think it's just to have a good time and flirt around. I think deep down we're looking for someone to love for life, not just till the next good sort comes along. Really, people are looking desperately for love. You could call it their god." Madeline paused to organize her thoughts. "If love's their god, and God is love, then—"

"I don't think that's quite right," Ami interrupted. "You could say that God loves, but you can't say God *is* love."

"But people value love above everything else."

"I like this," said Owen. "You girls are thinkers."

"And what do you think?"

"Oh, I'm staying out of this. I don't want a fight on my hands." He laughed.

As the night progressed, Madeline realized that a song in the background was overworking her imagination and she became nauseated. She stood giddily and only just managed to reach the bathroom before vomiting. She didn't have any heroin left so she took two more Platils and hoped for the best. They were sedatives she had been taking for her severe anxiety and panic attacks.

Ami's curiosity surfaced. "Owen, what did you think about the preacher's comments about that mark of the beast thing this morning?"

"Well, I hadn't planned on getting into anything heavy tonight. But I didn't agree with him on some things. He thinks people will escape getting the mark by joining some political and spiritual unity movement or something. But I think it has more to do with walkin' with God."

"But won't people be marked on their hand or forehead? Hasn't this got to do with chip implants forced on people?"

"That could be part of it, but the main deal's about following Jesus. We shouldn't just guess what the mark of the beast means. We should let the Bible explain itself. The toughest warnings in the Bible are against the mark of the beast, so you'd think the Bible would make it clear what it is."

Madeline came back from the bathroom. Her mental condition was rapidly deteriorating. She was weakened by her heroin withdrawals, and her drugged imagination was inducing an uncontrollable nightmare effect even while she was awake.

As she listened to Owen describe the terrible deeds of Revelation's beast, hallucinations of weird creatures threatened her. She was partly aware of what was happening to her and became very distressed. In an effort to separate herself from her bizarre anxiety, she stood. "Thanks for the evening, Owen, but I've gotta go. I'm not feeling well. See you."

"Hang on, Maddy," said Ami. "I need a ride home."

"Sorry about the heavy beast stuff," said Owen. "Can I see—?"

But Madeline was already out of hearing range, with Ami close behind, looking back apologetically. Owen was glad he had Madeline's phone number.

Owen Boyd woke up the next morning with Madeline on his mind. He took a quick shower, got dressed, and drank a cup of coffee to clear his mental fog. Then he picked up his guitar, his hat, and some clothes he had carelessly left on the floor the night before. Instead of doing his routine morning music practice, he phoned Mathew, an old friend from Townsville.

"G'day, Matt. It's Owen."

"G'day, Owen. How's things in Newcastle?"

"I've met this incredible girl."

"Yeah?"

"She's beautiful."

"What's she do?"

"I'm not sure. But I'll find out."

"Did you meet her in church?"

"Yeah, but she doesn't go to church much."

"That's a bit of a worry. I thought you weren't going out with non-Christian women?"

"Well, she's good hearted and seems open to truth, but she said something about taking some sedatives or something."

"Did she seem OK?"

"Yeah, till it got late. Then she got crook suddenly and went home."

"You really like her, huh?"

"Oh, yeah. When she gets interested in something, she looks real sweet and animated. She's gentle, and you know I like that. But there's something about her that's crying out for help. Something's worrying about her. I think she's in some sort of trouble."

"What kind of trouble?"

"Maybe I've been led to help her."

"Be careful, mate," Matt warned.

"Should I phone her today?"

"Mate, I'm no expert."

"She left in a hurry last night. I'm not even sure if she likes me."

"Take a risk!"

"I'll do it."

After hanging up, Owen opened the glass door leading to the small veranda of his small second-story apartment overlooking Newcastle Harbor. He sat on a cane chair, stretched his long legs onto another chair, and dialed Madeline's number. "Hello, Madeline," he said, trying to sound relaxed. "It's Owen. How're you doing?"

"I'm OK, thanks. Better now. I must have had too big a day yesterday."

"Sorry if I came on a bit heavy with that prophecy stuff last night. It was just that—"

"I enjoyed last night, Owen. I just became a bit crook and had to go. And listen, it's a shame you only sang a few songs."

The rapport of the previous night flowed as they talked on.

"Madeline, could I see you next weekend?" asked Owen.

"Why don't you come over today?"

Madeline remembered that the scrap of heroin she'd managed to find would wear off by the afternoon. "It will have to be this morning. Can you come over soon?"

"I'll be right there," said Owen.

After she put down the phone, Madeline spread newspaper on her bed, then pulled the drawer out of the dresser next to her bed. She dumped the contents of the drawer onto the paper. Success! She managed to find a gram of old heroin powder.

She burnt it and inhaled all the smoke she could. Then she entered the living room, where Ami was finishing breakfast. "So, what did you think of Owen?"

"Nice. A friendly, easygoing cowboy. Seems genuine."

"Yeah, he's no film star, but he's real fit looking."

"He was certainly giving you some eye contact." Ami grinned.

"He's a bit heavy with the religious thing. But you know, with all my hang-ups, maybe I need someone like Owen."

"Well, I've gotta go. See you later."

Owen drove slowly down Madeline's narrow street, searching for her address number. He noticed terraced houses on one side of the road and the rear entrances to old shops and warehouses on the other. Some garbage cans had been knocked over, and the shrubs and trees looked unkempt.

He found her street number on a letterbox that stood on a rotten fence post outside some dense shrub that obscured a high-set house. Parking his four-wheel-drive Toyota truck, he took a deep breath to calm his nerves. Ducking under the unkempt bushes that crowded Madeline's stairway, his lanky legs took two steps at a time. He noted empty bottles and cigarette packets alongside the steps and under the bushes. Owen gave a confident knock to hide his mild apprehension.

He relaxed a little when Madeline gave him a quick welcoming hug and offered a cup of coffee. "You don't mind if I finish my breakfast, do you?"

"Makes me feel at home."

He watched her share her breakfast with the cat and laughed. "I see you like animals as much as I do. How're you feeling this morning?"

"Oh, better thanks. I've learned to live with my … health problems. What brings you to Newcastle?"

"I left the family cattle station up in North Queensland to do a bit of singing in the cities around here."

"Oh, that's right. You told me that last night. —Sorry. I forgot. Ever sing at the Tamworth country music festival?"

"Yeah, I did all right there."

"You won?"

"Yeah."

"Best male vocalist?"

"Most promising, actually."

"That's great."

"Maybe I'll get better known 'round here eventually. Takes time."

Owen broke the silence. "How long have you been crook, Madeline?"

"Oh, it started after Mum and Dad split. You don't want to hear the depressing story.

"What'd your doctor say?"

Madeline rubbed her fingers. "He prescribed antidepressants, but they didn't work. So I started to drink more…smoked more joint."

Madeline had a sad, faraway pained look in her eyes.

"It all became too much for me, I became desperate enough to take heroin." Madeline wondered why she was telling Owen.

"That's heavy stuff."

Puff moved to Owen's lap and started purring. Owen ran his fingers over her soft coat. Madeline looked earnestly at Owen, as if she wanted her words to sink in. "To be honest, Owen, I'm very sick—clinically depressed."

Owen studied Madeline's face, trying to comprehend but only partly succeeding.

Madeline's expression was of a little lost girl, searching for relief and comfort.

"I haven't got the answers, Owen. No one has."

"Madeline, you shouldn't give up on doctors. My auntie was cured of depression with the right pills. So have lots of other people."

Madeline had heard that advice before. "Maybe they had the right pills back then …but it's a lot more complex now." Her shoulders slumped as she stared at the carpet. "Smack's the big worry now."

"To be honest, Madeline, I'm a bit surprised. And … "

Madeline looked up. "Disappointed?"

"You don't seem the type."

A feeling of hopeless despair swept over Madeline. "I get terrified at what might happen to me. It's like I'm being forced into a dark cave from which there's no escape."

Owen noticed her tears and prayed silently as his heart went out to her.

"I'm real sorry about what you've been through. I couldn't even guess what it's like to be crook with depression. But there's a way out and that's for sure. Can I read you something from the Bible?"

Madeline nodded.

"It's in John chapter 14, verse 14—Jesus' words: 'You may ask me for anything in my name and I will do it.' Do you believe in Jesus, Madeline?"

"Well, I used to go to church."

"He claimed to be the Son of God and that all his words were true."

"I suppose that'd be right."

"So he wouldn't lie to us, would he?"

"I guess not."

"Well in John 14:14, he's saying that if we ask him for something and it's best for us, he'll do it. Do you think he'd want you to be free from drugs?"

"Yes, I'm sure he would. But my faith is pretty weak."

"That doesn't matter. Jesus said all you've got to do is ask, and he promised he'd do it. Why don't we ask?"

"I wouldn't know what to say. I'd feel kind of strange, praying."

"That's OK. What if I pray and you just thank him for healing you?"

"But—"

"Don't worry. Just say, 'Thanks, Lord, for healing me.' "

"OK."

Owen placed his hand on Madeline's arm. "Lord, thanks for your promise to hear our prayers. We know you want to help Madeline stop wantin' drugs, so we're askin' you for it. Help her depression as well, and help her to love you with all her heart. Amen."

A brief silence followed. Madeline sobbed quietly.

"Madeline, just say, 'Thanks, Lord.' "

"Thanks, Lord," Madeline said between sobs.

"You'll be all right now," said Owen, hugging her. "You know, when Jesus was being tortured on the cross, it wasn't the nails or the bleeding that killed him. His heart broke from taking our punishment so that we could have our sins forgiven and have eternal life. We can believe that we're saved. You were spot on last night when you said, 'God is love.' "

"But I've got to be good enough, don't I?" Marilyn asked. "And I haven't been leading much of a Christian life."

"None of us are good enough. We're not saved because of our good works, but because we believe in Jesus. The reason we can believe we've got eternal life is that God isn't unfair. He won't punish us the second time."

"The second time? What do you mean?"

"Well, you've already been punished for all the sins you've ever done or are ever likely to do."

Madeline said nothing.

"When Jesus died on the cross it wasn't the nails that killed him. He died of a broken heart. It was the pain and guilt of your sins that killed him. He died instead of you."

"So I can't be punished for my sins again?"

"Not if you trust him."

"But it sounds too easy."

"Easy for you, but it wasn't easy for Jesus."

After Owen left, Madeline threw the rest of her Platils in the rubbish bin. She thought for a moment, then retrieved them. She went to the fridge, picked up a half-empty bottle of wine, and flushed it down the toilet with the Platils.

3

Valley of Promise

◇◇◇◇◇◇◇◇◇◇◇◇◇◇◇◇◇◇◇◇◇◇◇◇◇◇◇

T WO WEEKS LATER, Evan Hawkins parked his beige Subaru in the church parking lot. He brushed some specks from his dark grey suit, straightened his black tie, and looked at his watch. *Good. That terrible guitar music song-service should be almost over by now*, he thought. Carrying his large black King James Bible under his arm, he waited in the foyer for the last song to finish before he walked in.

As Evan sat down he was astonished to see Madeline Spicer standing in front of the microphone. She was relating her past drug addiction and telling how Owen had encouraged her to seek Christ's power to free her from it.

This is amazing, Evan thought. *Maybe what I told her did some good. Seems a bit soon for her to be giving testimonies about being freed from drugs. Yet she looks so happy and bright ... and even more beautiful. Perhaps it's OK for me to try to win her, now that she's coming to church. Strange. I thought Owen Boyd was too liberal to be able to help her. He might even drink alcohol for all I know. What incredible willpower she's got. She must have been just making excuses for taking drugs, when all the time she just needed to put her mind to it. Maybe what I told her did some good.*

Later, outside the church, Evan approached Madeline, somewhat apprehensively. She saw him coming and her warm smile removed his fears. "Evan, it's so nice to see you. I didn't know you were in church. Did you hear my story?"

"Yes. It's terrific. I never knew you had it in you."

"It wasn't in me. It was the Lord."

"I'm surprised to meet you here."

"This isn't exactly my idea of a good church. It's a bit too liberal for me. But I come sometimes. It suits Owen more."

"Oh, I think Owen is sincere."

"Owen is a nice bloke, but…anyway, I'm glad he helped you. Madeline, I meet with a small group in a friend's house where we do some *serious* study. They don't do much here. You might like to join us sometime."

"I'd like that."

"Great. I'll let you know when it's on next.

Madeline, I've got a property with a beautiful creek running through it, in the Wattagan Mountains. Would you like to see it?"

Madeline flashed her perfect white teeth. "Sounds like an adventure."

As they walked home, Ami noticed Madeline's bemused look. "Who was the handsome guy?"

"That was Evan, the bloke who visited me and loaned me that health book a couple of weeks ago."

"Oh, so that's him! If he got rid of his old suit, he'd be a bit of a knockout."

"Yeah, he's a bit different. But he sticks up for what he believes in—he's not wishy-washy."

"What happened to Owen?"

"Oh, didn't I tell you? He phoned. He had to go back to his parents' property up north."

"Bit sudden, wasn't it?"

"His parents needed him on the cattle station. They're going through a terrific drought because the wet season failed."

"How long will he be away?"

"He couldn't say for sure, maybe weeks or months. I'll miss that guy."

Evan Hawkins drove the youth hostel's van through the main street of Newcastle to pick up a load of organic vegetables from the railway station. He was thinking about Madeline. He'd only met her twice, but his imagination was trying to recapture the beauty of her smile.

It was only mid-afternoon but semi-darkness had settled in as turbulent storm clouds rolled in from the west. Evan turned on the vehicle's lights and windshield wipers as torrential rain began to fall. Lightning flashed through the eerie darkness and monstrous three-dimensional clouds churned like moving, multi-headed black mountains. Evan steered his car in the direction of the youth hostel, admiring the forbidding sky. He wasn't worried—he enjoyed a spectacular thunderstorm.

Suddenly, something hit the van's roof with the force of a sledgehammer. Chunks of ice the size of oranges smashed onto the road in front of him. Something huge crashed through the van's windshield and landed on the passenger seat. Horrified, Evan saw a jagged hailstone the size of his cap.

With the windshield shattered, Evan could barely see the road. He slammed on the brakes and the van skid sideways. Gripping the steering wheel, he braced himself as the vehicle skidded to a halt in the middle of the road. Evan grabbed the huge hailstone from the passenger seat and jumped out of the car. He threw it through the windshield on the driver's side to clear the shattered glass so he could see.

Before he could shelter in the vehicle, a large hailstone struck him behind his left shoulder, sending him sprawling to the ground. Bruised and frightened, Evan leapt into the car and sped off, searching for shelter.

He thought about driving under the awning over the sidewalk until he saw that the missiles were crashing right through the canvas.

The deafening pounding on his van increased in intensity and frequency. Fearing that the roof would no longer protect him, he accelerated for home, forcing the van to dance and shake over the giant hailstones. Evan didn't feel safe until he found refuge in the parking lot under the hostel.

He ran up the basement stairs to his room, turned on the radio, and fell exhausted onto his bed. The announcer said the hailstorm was the worst in recorded history and had stretched to almost as far Sydney. So far, eighty people had been admitted to hospital and nine had been killed.

Evan knelt and prayed out loud. "Oh, Lord, I thank You for making me worthy of Your protection and counting me among Your righteous children. Please protect the unworthy and help them realize that this is a warning sign of Your coming wrath. And Lord, may this be a wake-up call for our church members who are in apostasy. Please protect my fruit trees in the mountain refuge that you have prepared for me. Amen."

A few days later, Madeline Spicer sat beside Evan Hawkins in his Subaru, enjoying the adventure of exploring the mountains. When the dirt road became steep and boggy, Evan locked the transmission into four-wheel drive and carefully avoided the soft edges of the tight corners. Madeline noticed the boxes of plants on the back seat. "What are those for?"

Evan's eyes lit up. "They're medicinal herbs to plant around the cabin. According to the book of Revelation, the time is soon coming when we won't be allowed to buy or sell anything if we don't accept the authority of the beast. I won't be able to buy any insulin for my diabetes, but I'll do quite well on this."

"I didn't know there was an herbal substitute for insulin. Besides, you have to be careful with herbs. They can have side effects in strong doses."

Evan's correction came swiftly. "Don't worry. These herbs work all right. But drug companies don't want anyone to find out about the healing properties of herbs, or they'd go broke."

Frustrated, Madeline changed the subject. "You're really getting wound up about this mark of the beast thing, aren't you?"

"It's very close," replied Evan smugly. "That hailstorm must have been God's warning that the seven last plagues will soon fall—just before Christ returns. According to Revelation 16, one of the plagues is hailstones as big as hay bales."

"So you feel Christians should be making preparations for Christ's return physically, not just spiritually?"

"Yes. That's why I bought the land—it's within easy reach of the city, but still remote enough to lead a lifestyle free from interfering government agencies. The soil's great, and I'm planting an orchard and building dams."

Madeline smiled. "I remember watching a documentary about religious extremists in America who lived in the mountains and armed themselves. When the cops came, there was a shoot-out and people were killed."

Evan's tone became even more serious. "They might've been a bit extreme but they were trying to protect their religious rights."

They drove off the dirt road onto a side track through steep, rain-forest-covered hills. Madeline watched in awe as they hugged enormous sandstone cliffs and passed between giant boulders. "How could you grow anything out here?"

Evan steered along the deteriorating track without answering. Before long they were driving slowly into a narrow, lightly forested valley with a rocky stream running through it. The track crossed the shallow stream several times, and eventually they came to a rough split-log cabin in a magical setting under scattered gum trees on the creek bank.

As Madeline stepped out of the vehicle, the forest's musky perfume inspired her to take a deep breath. "This is a beautiful place!"

"And it's all mine!"

"It's truly enchanting," Madeline said as she absorbed the beauty of the lightly timbered, brilliant green paddocks that sloped up to the towering escarpments. "How in the world did you find this?"

"Luckily ... or, rather, providentially ... I looked in the classified adverts in the *Green's Choice* magazine."

Madeline admired the music of the running waters, punctuated occasionally by the shattering call of a whip bird or the fairy-like tinkling of bellbirds. The pristine stream gurgled past the cabin, its current split by moss-covered rocks and fallen logs. There was a deeper pool near where she stood. It was a calm backwater sheltered by an enormous upstream log. She noticed moving shadows in its depth. "Look, Evan! There are fish down here, so you wouldn't starve."

Evan pointed at the paddock on the sunny slope, which was studded with dozens of young fruit trees. "Actually, there's our future food supply. We won't eat my little friendly trout. Genesis 1 and 2 says that in the beginning God gave us plants for food, not flesh. We've got to get back to God's original plan if we're going to be ready when Jesus comes."

"That makes sense, now that you mention it. God did give Adam and Eve a vegetarian diet. But Jesus ate fish, so it couldn't be that bad."

"Well, the Bible says he cooked them for the disciples, but it doesn't say he ate any."

"I think he would have. Eating meat was part of their religious culture."

"OK, he might have. But Jesus said, 'Be ye perfect as your father in heaven is perfect.' We have to be perfect or we won't be ready when Jesus comes back. Eden's diet was perfect so we have to be vegetarians too."

"I'm sure that being a vegetarian is probably better for your health. But you seem to be making it a religious issue. In that text Jesus was talking about accepting him wholeheartedly and putting him first. Evan, you make me feel as if there are hundreds of little issues in my life that need changing. It's a bit discouraging."

"Madeline, if I can do it, you can too."

Evan showed Madeline his organic garden. "I haven't used one drop of poisonous spray. It's all natural, just like God created."

"Wow, that's great. Organic foods are so healthy. And look at the size of those pumpkins!"

"By keeping my body free from impurities, I'm getting ready for my translation to heaven."

"But our sins are forgiven. Isn't that enough? Besides, there's got to be plenty of good Christians who eat veggies that aren't organically grown. Would you call that sinning?"

"We enlightened ones have a special responsibility to glorify God even in the small details of life."

Madeline followed Evan into the one-room cabin. It had no electric lights or lanterns, only candles. Not even a fireplace. Thin foam mattresses covered the double bunks. There were no paintings on the wall, no decorations of any sort. The few books on the shelf were mainly on alternative health subjects and last-day conspiracies.

"It would be rather cold here in winter, wouldn't it?" she asked, looking around.

"I've got blankets, but I'm trying not to get too comfortable. We need to get toughened up for the persecution and isolation ahead," replied Evan, gazing out the window at the towering sandstone escarpments.

Madeline noticed the bare cement floor and gaps in the walls. "It's better in here than in a tent, that's for sure," she said, then added, "Just being in these mountains is a spiritual buzz. Nature is God's beautiful canvas."

"Yes, it's good to have faith, and fasting strengthens it," said Evan with conviction.

"Fasting? Going without food?"

"And water, preferably—that's how we get to deserve his blessing."

"Perhaps God wants us to shave our heads and wear old bags for clothes. Maybe that will earn some points with him?" Madeline half teased.

"Now, that's being ridiculous. I don't think we should go to extremes," said Evan.

"I was only joking."

"It's not really funny. There's value in fasting. Speaking of food, are you hungry?" Evan produced some heavy homemade bread, apples, and shelled walnuts. "I rarely drink anything but water. It helps me spiritually. Let's eat by the stream over there."

Evan sat by the deep pool and rested his back on the huge fallen log that spanned half the stream and created a protective barrier for the pool. He threw some bread crumbs into the water and watched some small rainbow fish rise to nibble on them.

Madeline sat close to Evan. She had been through a lot of changes over the past few weeks, since her day of miracles. Owen would be away for a long time. Evan valued her new spirituality and obviously liked her. She was in the mood to appreciate some affectionate male attention. Apart from his symmetrical face and dark wavy hair, she admired Evan because he acted out his convictions courageously, even though she was confused about some of them.

All morning Evan had been preoccupied with his desire to share his spiritual convictions with Madeline, but the closeness of this lovely creature in this peaceful setting drew out romantic impulses. They were entirely alone in a totally isolated place.

Madeline was wearing a light cotton top with a delicate lace that decorated her graceful neck and enhanced the softness of her shoulders. Her shorts exposed her shapely legs, which stretched out over the soft green grass curving down to the water's edge. Delicate maidenhair ferns decorated the grass and caressed her slim ankles. Evan could feel a warm flush all over his body and his pulse rate lifting. He couldn't deny that the beauty of her new, sweeter character enhanced Madeline's physical loveliness and that he was infatuated with her. But he was looking for a wife, not a just a temporary girlfriend. He sensed himself weakening, so he thought of a strategy that would divert his infatuated emotions into the arena of sobering reality.

"I've got people all around me at the youth hostel where I work," he said. "I meet people at church, but I still get lonely. There's something missing in my life. Up until a couple of years ago, I thought I would stay single. But I've come to realize that I'm the marrying kind after all."

Madeline studied Evan to see if there was any hint of what he really meant.

His serious eyes looked into hers. "It's hard to find a good Christian woman who is fair dinkum about following her convictions. Some of them go to church, but when it comes to commitment ..."

Madeline didn't want to risk spoiling the day, so she decided to discourage his line of thought. She stood up and pretended to look at the fish in the pool. "That trout down there is really big. I reckon I'd throw a line in if it was my land."

With difficulty, Evan ignored her controversial comment. He had been thinking hard and long before he decided to confide his secret plans to Madeline, and his admiration for her overcame his caution. He gave the broadest and most enthusiastic smile Madeline had yet seen him give. "I've got a surprise for you," he gushed with a fresh enthusiasm that surprised Madeline. "There's an important part of my project that you haven't seen yet. It's a fair way up the valley. Jump in the car, I'll show you."

After a short drive, Evan parked the car where the track ended at a wall of dense rain forest. They walked into a dark, shaded world where the sunlight only touched the leaf-covered ground here and there. They stepped over the long, thick fig tree roots that snaked their way around like dinosaur tails. Their trunks were as thick as a car and soared to great heights. Thick vines hung from their interlocking branches, adding to the mystery of the forest.

Evan was determined to enjoy Madeline's suspense and gave no hints of the destination. They came to a smaller tributary stream and followed it into a narrow gorge until it became a waterfall and couldn't be followed any farther. At times they had to get on their hands and knees to penetrate the thick undergrowth. After a long, tiring scramble and climb, they came to a sandstone cliff face.

Madeline collapsed onto a rock to rest, breathing heavily. "I think I've had enough," she gasped. "This had better be good. What do you want to show me?"

"It's only up there a bit farther. We've got time. Have a breather, then we'll go on. This is good for you. It'll toughen you up for the tough times ahead."

After a short rest they scrambled up a steep gully to the top of the escarpment.

"Watch out for loose boulders," cautioned Evan.

As they broke through the tree line, they came to the top of the escarpment. The panoramic view surprised Madeline who flopped down to rest. "I'm not going any farther. I had no idea it would be so far!"

Evan laughed. "It's just a stone's throw away now."

Madeline caught her breath as she briefly admired the layers of distant blue mountains. Then Evan led the way down into a secluded valley about the size of a football field. It was tucked away in the top of the range and was hemmed in on all sides. Once they scrambled down to the floor of the heavily forested valley, they began to round the bend of a steep rock face. Madeline flopped down and rested her back against a boulder beside a small pool of water. She was seriously concerned now and glared at Evan. He grinned at her.

'That's it! I'm not going any further," Madeline pronounced.

"I'll go ahead," said Evan. "You rest where you are for a couple of minutes. Just around the corner I'll show you my ... uh ... project."

A few minutes later, Madeline plodded around the contour of the cliff, but she could not see Evan. "Where are you?" she called out.

For a moment there was no answer. Then Evan's nearby laugh startled her. She spun around in the direction of his voice but couldn't see him. He laughed again and suddenly emerged from behind thick scrub growing against the cliff. "It's in here. Come on in." He gave a theatrical flourish.

Madeline squeezed between the bushes and was surprised to see the entrance to a cave. "So this is the surprise you've dragged me to."

It was narrow at first, about the width of a small car, but as Madeline stooped to enter, it opened into a house-sized cavern. She gazed about in wonder. She saw some foam mattresses on the sandy floor, a few light aluminum folding chairs, and a rough table that had obviously been built in the cave. Some boxes were stacked neatly at the rear of the cave. A shaft of light penetrated from somewhere above.

Enjoying Madeline's obvious wonderment, Evan exclaimed, "When I found this cave, I knew it was a sign that I had to buy the property."

"How in the world did you find this little valley, let alone the cave?"

"It took me a fair slice of my holidays, mind you. It was raining when I found this valley and I noticed two rock wallabies dart behind these bushes. Out of curiosity, I investigated, and there it was."

"But why do you need a cave?"

Evan sat down on a chair, enjoying Madeline's reaction. "When the persecution comes, the caves will be a safe hiding place, don't you think? And we will certainly be safe from the hailstone and the heat plague."

Evan spoke with a new earnestness. "Madeline, you are one of the few people I've even mentioned the caves to. I've seen you change and I trust you. Don't tell a soul about these caves. You never know who might turn against us."

Madeline dropped exhausted onto a foam mattress on the cave floor and enjoyed some water and a handful of dates from Evan's hoarded supply. *Maybe he's onto something. A cave hide-out makes sense. Maybe Evan's a step ahead of us all and there's more to the Christian life than I first thought.*

4

Distant Thunder

◇◇◇◇◇◇◇◇◇◇◇◇◇◇◇◇◇◇◇◇◇◇◇◇◇◇◇◇

EVAN'S FATHER, SIMON HAWKINS, lived with his wife, Sarah, in a small waterside cottage by Lake Macquarie near Newcastle. It was the largest saltwater lake in Australia. Since he had become blind a few years previously, he spent much of his time fishing from his small private jetty, where he loved to decipher the varied sounds of the pelicans and seagulls, the surface stirrings of fish, and the laughter of holiday people. He could usually feel what sort of fish was nibbling at his bait, how big it was, and if it was going to drop the bait or swallow it. He didn't associate with his church much these days, because his blindness had made him bitter toward God.

His eyesight had faded rapidly, until one morning he had woken up to find he was blind in both eyes. The loss of his eyes had devastated him and made him question God's providence. Sarah cared for him faithfully, and she and Evan tried in vain to encourage Simon to go to church and regain his faith.

Simon had been a strict disciplinarian when he was younger, to the point where some of his friends thought he was overly harsh in raising his children. Evan respected his father but rarely felt close to him, although he had absorbed his father's strict religious views, even taking them to a stricter level. Evan had floated around a number of churches but settled on forming a small home fellowship of his own with other disenchanted Christians, one of whom had secretly invested in Evan's mountain property.

Shortly after Evan took Madeline to his cave hideout, Simon was sitting on his jetty one day but his thoughts were not on fishing. He had an important decision to make. He and Sarah had read of a visiting American TV evangelist who had a reputation for having the gift of healing.

"This Ron Noble seems to be working real miracles under God," Sarah had said. "A while back he even healed a blind man."

"These TV guys claim to have healed lots of people, but do they stay healed?" Simon had responded.

"Well dear, I've seen lots of supposed healings on TV and some of them did seem a bit suspect. But Noble has doctors do checks before and after the healings."

Simon rubbed his graying head. "Why would God want to heal me when he could have prevented my getting blind in the first place?"

"There could be some reason we don't know about, and it wouldn't hurt just to go. At least you would have tried."

Simon was thinking about all this as he sat on his jetty. He hadn't even bothered to re-bait the hook. He reeled in his line when he finally made his decision.

Just then he heard the familiar sound of Evan's Subaru flat-four engine at his front gate. He stood and cautiously felt his way in Evan's direction, his cane in front of him.

Evan met him near the front gate and they shook hands in a formal manner. Simon ran his hand over the Subaru's bonnet. "There's no hail dents on your car," he said. "You were lucky."

"Yes, but the hostel's van copped it. It's a write-off," replied Evan.

"Come on in, Evan."

"How are things, Dad? Are you still eating those fish?"

"C'mon, Evan. Fish have important fatty acids that are good for the heart."

"This lake's full of heavy metals from the smelter."

"If I have to stop fishing, I may as well kick the bucket. Nothin' else to do."

"You can study the Bible like you used to and get ready for the coming of the Lord."

"If the Lord wants me, he can have me as I am."

"You shouldn't talk like that. We have to be perfect by the time he comes."

"That's a bit hard when you're blind, and you've got time to let your thoughts wander. I tend to imagine all sorts of things that I guess wouldn't be perfect. Speaking of blind, your mother has talked me into going to a healing service run by an American fella called Ron Noble."

Evan turned on the steps and faced his father. "You can't be serious! That guy's only been out of jail three years for siphoning the saints' offering money."

"I gather he's put all that behind him now."

"You don't know what he was up to just because he's gone low key. I read that after jail he never went back to his wife, who'd waited for him. He got himself a young girlfriend."

"Well, I don't know about that. He did some good stuff for the poor in India, and apparently he's into anti-abortion demonstrations. I heard ... Look, Son, it won't hurt me just to go. I don't think I'll get healed either, but what harm is there? I'm going. It's on Wednesday night."

Simon and Sarah Hawkins sat at the front of the auditorium where Simon could hear what was going on. He listened carefully to what Ron Noble had to say and how he said it. "I think he sounds like a bit of a con man, Sarah," whispered Simon. "Sounds to me as if he's acting."

"Oh, that's just his personality, luv. Bit of an extrovert, I suppose."

"He's spending a lot of effort pointing out how much God will bless our giving to his cause."

"I'm worried your attitude might hinder your healing. It costs a lot of money to run these concerns, and he does help the poor in India."

"Yeah, and I bet he drives a Merc or a Jag!"

"Your cousin Bert drives a 'cedes."

"Yeah, a '76 model, and he gets parts from the wreckers."

Ron Noble called for children to come forward, and about twelve came. Noble walked up and down the stage with his head down as if praying silently. Then he explained that it was Jesus, not him, who healed. Waving his arms about with aggressive gestures, he prayed with a commanding tone.

"Can't imagine Jesus carrying on like that. You'd think this guy's doin' the healin,'" mumbled Simon.

"Shh. Wait to see what happens."

A small group huddled around a young mother and her child. The mother was weeping out aloud when suddenly the preacher yelled out, "Halleluiah! Praise the Lord!" He stepped over to the mother and held the microphone to her. "What was wrong with little Billy, ma'am?" he asked.

"Billy can hear now!" she exclaimed.

Sarah used her most self-effacing, tactful tone. "Did you hear that, luv? That little kid's been cured."

"Could be," replied Simon.

When the adults were called forward, Sarah led Simon out. "I feel like a goose out here," he said.

"You've come this far—can't turn back now, luv."

The preacher paced in front of Simon as if in an agitated trance. Simon could sense his agitation. Noble threw his arms forward as if to spiritually embrace the sick and called out, "In the name of Jesus, I command you to be healed from whatever infirmity that binds you!"

Instantly, Simon felt a strong, warm glow over his face and head, and he sensed a strange tingling sensation around his eyes. He thought it felt a bit like the vibration of an old-fashioned electric shaver.

Sarah looked around her. Some seemed to be quietly praying, and a few were weeping, but no one seemed to be experiencing an instant miracle. Then she glanced at Simon. His mouth was open in astonishment and his moist eyes looked at Sarah. He threw his arms around her and sobbed, "I can see. I can see!"

Noble hurriedly stepped over and jabbed the microphone under Simon's nose. "You can see? Were you blind?"

"Yes. I've been healed!" Simon exclaimed as he looked from side to side, testing his eyes.

"Praise the Lord!" shouted Noble as he skipped a little dance. The crowd roared, and others began to praise the Lord because they too had been healed. Simon was so overwhelmed with emotion that he couldn't take any more. After weighing the risk of appearing ungrateful, he and Sarah stepped off the platform and quickly left.

﹡

Owen Boyd sat on the bank of the Burdekin River that bordered his parents' Queensland cattle property, which two generations ago had been named Jardine Station after a famous explorer. It was not large by Queensland standards, covering only about three hundred square kilometers. That much land was needed to feed eight hundred head of Brahman cattle in poor country. In the wet season, there was normally abundant grass, but during the long dry season, there often was barely enough feed.

This year there had been no wet season at all apart from a couple of brief thunderstorms, which had only settled the dust. This had never happened before in the history of Jardine Station, and the family could see no human solution to the crisis. The cattle had run out of grass weeks ago and were trying to survive on the lower branches of shrubs and trees, plus what was occasionally hand fed to them. About sixty head had already died, and the rest were weak and gaunt.

Normally, in the dry season, there were intermittent deep pools of water in the river, and some of the large dams held enough water to last till the summer rains. But as Owen sat on the river bank, he couldn't see a single water hole. He'd brought in an excavator to dig down to the water level, meters below the dry river bed. He had then connected a pump to pipe water to a truck that carried a thousand-gallon water tank. This was then empted in water troughs around the property.

Owen hadn't seen Madeline for some weeks, and he was missing her. But he tried not to think of her too much. He had real problems on his mind. As Owen drove around the property, the sickly sweet smell of decaying kangaroos, wild pigs, cattle, and other animals wafted through the vehicle. The animals had crawled into the shadiest places they could find to die. Even the resourceful dingoes were struggling now.

Black crows and giant wedge-tailed eagles, Australia's vultures, were among the few creatures that were coping with the drought conditions. They were carnivores, and cruel ones at that, who routinely obtained moisture from the eyes or blood of dying animals. Large goannas were also doing well, as they were expert at crawling deep into a carcass for food and moisture. But as the carcasses were now dehydrated, even the crows began to migrate to the coast.

Owen's parents, Gordon and Joan Boyd, were resting in the shade of their veranda after a hard day's work. They watched Owen park the truck in the machinery shed and were grateful for their son's help, especially as he had put his music career on hold to help save the station. Being young, he could handle the extremely hot weather better than they could.

Gordon went inside and came out with another jug of cold juice and handed a glass to his son. "I've never known heat like this before. It's been around fifty-two degrees centigrade in the shade. That's about six degrees hotter than it's ever been."

Owen took his work boots off as he spoke. "I couldn't even touch the river sand today without getting burnt. I saw a lizard tryin' to cross the river bed and he died before he got halfway across the sand. Dad, I'm sorry, but I had to shoot two more of the young bulls today. They were in agony."

"Well, I thank the Lord that things aren't worse. The neighbors have lost half of their cattle. And I read that some other stations farther north have packed it in." Gordon sighed.

Owen took off his shirt, then tipped water over his head and the lean, rippling muscles of his back and chest. He sipped his third glass of juice. "Sure would be cooler down south in Newcastle," he said.

Joan remembered what she had seen on the news that afternoon.

"Maybe it's just as well you weren't there. They had a terrific hailstorm."

"Oh, they get 'em down there all the time," said Owen.

"Yes, but not as big as rock melons!"

"You're joking."

"People were killed, and the hospitals are overcrowded with the injured. Thousand of homes had their roofs smashed to pieces, and the rescue people didn't have enough tarps to go around."

"What?"

"Too right. A state of emergency has been declared by the prime minister," said Joan.

"I can't believe what's happenin' around the world," said Gordon. "Much of California was devastated with fires they couldn't put out. Russia has turned into a deep freezer with minus 70-degree temperatures. And what about the tidal wave that submerged some of the Solomon Islands last week? Record heat is shriveling up the top half of Australia, and now we've got hailstones that kill people! The world's always had calamities, but nothing like this."

"And you haven't even mentioned what terrorists have blown up in the past few weeks," added Joan, wiping her forehead with a damp towel. "Makes me wonder what's going to happen next and how close the Lord's coming must be."

"The drought's really brought it home to me," Owen said. "The Lord's trying to tell the world something with freak hail storms and freak heat in the same country at the same time. I'm not saying that the Lord's doin' it, but he's allowin' them to happen for a reason. It seems to be leadin' up to what Revelation 16 says—how the seven last plagues will bring shockin' heat that burns God's enemies and drops giant hailstones as big as hay bales on 'em."

"God loves people and he's allowing the droughts and floods to wake 'em up—bring ' em to their senses and turn to him," Gordon said as he fanned himself with his stained felt hat.

"He's warning 'em now because when the plagues fall it'll be too late to repent," Owen reasoned.

Joan lifted her big ginger cat off her lap because it was making her hot. "Well, I think this drought seems to be awakening a need in Sally Macleod. She came over the other day and we had a real good yarn about her kid's plans to go to college and how they need the money. But this drought's wrecked all their plans. She's never been interested in spiritual things before, but she asked me to pray for them."

"I hope my friends in Newcastle are all right," said Owen.

"Worried about your girlfriend, are you, Son?" Gordon chuckled.

"Madeline's not my girlfriend, Dad."

"But you'd like her to be, right?"

"I could do worse."

Joan put her arm on Owen's shoulder. "What about Suzy? You've been seeing her for a long time now, and she loves the outback life. You two get on so well together. If you can't make a go of it with your singing career down south, you could always run the farm for us with Suzy. She loves you to death."

"Suzy's a great kid, mum, and maybe if I hadn't met Madeline … I've never felt that way about a girl before."

As the evening cooled a little, Owen finished his simple evening meal of steak and baked vegetables and entered the large family room with its high ceilings and old-fashioned board walls. A large oil painting of a cattle muster hung over the piano. The ceiling fan was a bit noisy but he had become used to it. A huge brown-and-white tanned steer skin gave a cozy look to the polished floorboards. Owen sat in front of the TV and flicked through a few channels to the news, but his mind was somewhere else. He went into the office and turned on the computer to draft an e-mail.

Hi, Madeline. I just found out about the hailstorm. It must have been pretty amazing. Are you all right? It's been very hot here and we are frying and are battling to save the cattle, but we believe the Lord will see us through. And what about your hailstorm! Read Revelation chapter 16. It tells us that giant hailstones and burning heat will be part of the plagues just before Jesus comes. I'm not suggesting this is it, but is it leading to it?

Madeline, I am so impressed with what the Lord has done in your life and I am praying for you. Satan will be on your track, so when you get discouraging thoughts or trials, just remember how much Jesus loves you and that he will help you. I'm really looking forward to seeing you again. I still can't say when that will be, but I hope it's not too long. How is nursing going? I've told Mum and Dad about you and they're impressed. How is Ami?

Take care.

Owen

Later that night Madeline's reply came:

Hi, Owen.

I really miss you too. You took off just as we were getting to know each other. That wasn't fair!

That was some hailstorm. Our joint survived all right, but some of the trees lost their branches. You should see the car. It's a mess but it still drives. I had to give up my day off for emergency duties at hospital. I had to work a double shift because of all the injuries from the hail. People came in with shocking bruises. One poor old fellow had a fractured skull. But when you think of the size of the hailstones, it's a wonder more people weren't killed.

Owen, I have got no desire for drugs anymore. Not a bit. Sometimes, when I feel overstressed, I can feel some mild depression creeping back, so I have to be careful not to overdo things. I feel like I am me again. I realize, though, that there is more work to be done in my life before I am ready for Jesus to come back. He said that we should be perfect like our heavenly Father is perfect. That worries me a little because when I look at my lack of love, I realize that I have a long way to go.

I have been getting some help from Evan Hawkins, who seems to know his Bible well, though he does have some challenging ideas that I'm not sure about. A while back he showed me his mountain property. It's a bit of paradise up there. He is growing fruit trees and a garden organically.

Owen turned toward his mother, who was reading nearby. "Oh, no. She's been out with Evan Hawkins!"

"Bit of competition, dear?"

"This legalistic guy's taken her to his mountain hideout. I think he's beginning to brainwash Madeline, judgin' from what she said about her not being ready for Jesus' return. Of course she's ready! If we've given our lives to Jesus, we are ready."

"Never mind, Owen. If it's meant to be, it will work out."

Owen read on.

Ami has started to study the Bible with me and is enjoying it. She often talks about you, and wonders how you are doing.

I just had a look at Revelation about the plagues, and it makes you think, doesn't it? Evan was caught in the middle of the hail and feared for his life. He reckons we should all be getting out into the country to escape what's coming.

Nice to hear from you. Love to your folks and to you. I am forever grateful to you, Owen.

Madeline

Owen left the computer and flopped down beside his mother on the couch.

"She sounded friendly enough, but somehow that Evan guy's come into her life. I've gotta do somethin' about it."

"Just be your own dear self and you can't go wrong."

"Thanks, Mum. But she needs protectin' from Evan's way-out ideas."

During the time that Owen was away, Pastor Samuel Edwards, the youth pastor at Owen's and Madeline's church, was driving through central Sydney with his wife, Joy. He had been at a youth congress all week in Brisbane, and Joy had picked him up at the airport. He always chose the tunnel freeway under Sydney Harbour, as it was quicker than the bridge, and the novelty of it never failed to fascinate him. It was a calm, sunny autumn day, and they were looking forward to the country drive where the freeway bridge spanned high above the wide Hawkesbury River and passed through a spectacular mountain range. Sam often daydreamed about the tiny island in the river and the fishing cottages that decorated the narrow forest between the river and the mountains. But the river was over an hour's drive away and he was still in heavy city traffic.

They were about two kilometers from the Harbour Tunnel entrance when they felt the car shake as an underground tremor surged around them. At the same instant they heard an enormous explosion, which seemed to come from the bowls of the earth, threatening the stability of nature. Fear such as can only be produced by the terrifying unknown gripped their hearts.

"It's an earthquake," cried Joy. "Pull over!"

Sam steered to the safety lane and braked hard. Other cars were either pulling up or accelerating wildly, trying to escape the mysterious terror.

"It must be a great earthquake," Sam said as he looked around, trying to make sense of what was happening.

"Sam, look!" Joy pointed toward the harbor, where the sky was rapidly filling with a gray smoke cloud.

"What could that be?"

"I don't know. But earthquakes can cause fires and ... The shaking's stopped."

Sam saw fear in his wife's eyes and embraced her.

"I've never been in an earthquake before. I didn't know they could just explode like that. Will we be all right, Sam? Are we safe here?"

"We're not under any buildings or bridges. Let's just wait here till we find out what's going on."

The radio music was suddenly interrupted. "This is an important announcement. It has just been reported that there has been an underground explosion in the vicinity of Sydney Harbour. All vehicles should avoid the area. It is unknown—"

Just then several fire engines screamed past, their sirens screeching like an air raid warning, drowning out the radio. An enormous mushrooming cloud had grown and darkened the sky.

They heard the words "possible terrorist attack" come over the radio as ambulance sirens sped past.

Sam started his car, its wheels spinning as it U-turned, bouncing over the concrete center strip.

"What are you doing?" asked Joy.

"I'm getting out of here," Sam cried, his heart racing and adrenalin surging.

"Careful, don't panic!"

"Sorry, Joy. I'll try to be calmer."

"You're going the wrong way!" Joy squeezed Sam's arm.

Police cars vainly tried to bring order to the chaotic traffic. The radio announcer continued. "The harbor tunnel has been blown up. There has been massive damage and horrific casualties. It is unknown exactly what has happened because of a lack of witnesses. Flooding has occurred over the low-lying harbor shore from the force of the explosion."

"Let's take the bridge," said Joy. "But phone home first to see if it's safe."

"Are you crazy? Remember the Twin Towers? The second tower was blown up fifteen minutes after the first. Fifteen minutes after that tunnel explosion we would be right on top of the bridge!"

Joy started weeping. "We've got no way of getting home."

"I'll double back and take the freeway. That'll skirt the inner suburbs. It's longer, but it'll get us home."

When they reached the freeway, traffic was almost at a standstill.

Joy phoned home. Karen, their twelve-year-old daughter and eldest child, answered the phone.

"Karen, there's been a bombing. Have you heard?"

"Yes. I tried to phone you but couldn't get through. Thank God you've rung! Are you both OK?"

"Yes. We were on our way home but got stuck."

"I'm so happy you're safe."

"We were about to go into the tunnel. We could have been down there. The Lord saved us."

"I saw pictures of the harbor from helicopters. The water is full of wrecks. And a tidal wave drowned heaps of people. When will you be home?"

"It's bumper-to-bumper traffic. We've been stopped by police at three different search points. Don't expect us home until late tonight."

"I can't wait to see Dad. I'll tell Brady and Josh. They're watching TV."

Once Sam and Joy left Sydney behind, they listened to the latest radio report.

"The Harbour Tunnel no longer exists. An estimated two thousand people have lost their lives. The explosion had been timed for peak-hour traffic. Over three hundred others have drowned from the resultant twenty-foot wave that capsized two ferries and many other craft and flooded the shores. The final death toll could be almost as high as September 11. There are no survivors among those who were under the harbor at the time of the explosion. Some survivors who were in the tunnel approaches were rescued when the force of the blast bulleted vehicles out of the tunnel, some backward. Federal police believed the force of the explosion is evidence that this was the work of trained terrorists. Probably a truck full of explosions was detonated. Just minutes prior to the explosion, motorists phoned police to report that an abandoned truck was blocking the inside lane in the tunnel. Possibly they were picked up by a backup vehicle and made their escape. Al Mugniyah claimed responsibility for the attack and warned of even more serious attacks to come.

5

The Debate

◇◇◇◇◇◇◇◇◇◇◇◇◇◇

TAKING ADVANTAGE OF OWEN'S ABSENCE, Evan invited Madeline and Ami to the home-church meeting at Victor and Betty Zinski's house. Victor suffered with minor chronic fatigue syndrome, and with Evan's encouragement had been avidly researching alternative medicine. His food intake was restricted to raw vegetables and fruits. He would not use any soap in his cold or lukewarm baths because he believed it washed away natural healthy body oils. He ate half a clove of garlic daily plus a combination of special herbs. Since adopting this new regime he had become even thinner, had a yellow complexion, and developed some nervous depression. Evan assured him this was due to the toxins coming out of his system and that he would become better in the long run.

When they arrived, Evan introduced Madeline and Ami to Victor, who welcomed them and introduced them to Maude Smith, the morning's discussion leader. The proceedings began with a long prayer by Victor. Next they opened old black hymnals and sang three hymns that Madeline had not heard since childhood. Each hymn exhorted obedience and heart searching. Victor explained that these hymnals had not been corrupted like most Christian song books.

Zinski then preached his sermon, the topic being "How to get ready for the Lord's return." He taught that belief in forgiveness of sin often leads to presumption, and that true Christians are made right with God through obedience, which merits their salvation.

"We must be as holy as Jesus in every respect," preached Zinski. "God expects far more of the last generation of true believers than previous Christians. Like sinless Elijah of old, they will be taken to heaven and never experience death."

Zinski cut his sermon short and reclined on his couch. "My energies have failed, brethren. Perhaps Sister Maude can guide our testimony section."

Maude Smith stood and eyed her small audience solemnly. She had been attending these meetings ever since Evan invited her to come about two years previously. She still hoped that one day he would reciprocate her romantic interest. She looked at Madeline and Ami with a disapproving eye. Ami surveyed the tall, angular young woman, noticing her bonnet and her long, loose cotton dress, which reached halfway between knees and ankles. Ami turned and smiled slightly at Madeline, but Madeline appeared not to notice.

"Is there anyone who would like to thank the Lord for mercies great or small?" Maude enquired.

Victor raised himself on one elbow. "I have always worried about my tendency to irritability, fearing it would keep me out of heaven," he weakly croaked. "Yesterday my dog barked at the mailman again, and I resisted the temptation to shout at it like I had done in the past. I praise God for the victory."

Ami put a tissue to her mouth to hide her amusement.

"Anyone else?" asked Maude. There was a long silence until Madeline spoke. She briefly described how Jesus had helped her overcome depression and had taken away her cravings for drugs. She expressed her desire to be ready for Christ's return.

"Thank you," Maude responded. "Anyone else? No? Well, do you have any comments on what Brother Victor preached, then?"

Evan stood. "I appreciated what he said about overcoming every weakness and character fault to be ready when Jesus comes. This is our special message to the world," he said solemnly.

"Amen," the group responded.

"I thought Christians should be confident in being saved and be concentrating on giving the good news to others, and not just on their own preparation," said Ami, surprising Madeline with her forthright remark.

Evan quickly turned the pages of his King James Bible. Tapping with his forefinger on Revelation 14:4, he read it emphatically.

"These are they which follow the lamb whithersoever he goeth ... and in their mouth was found no guile; for they are without fault before the throne of God." He continued. "This passage describes those who will be ready for Christ's return. Notice they follow the Savior's example in being absolutely faultless. This is what is required of us as well."

"But if they followed Jesus in everything," said Ami, "that would mean they followed his example in being happy and secure in God's love.

Jesus doesn't want us to be continually worried about whether we are good enough."

Madeline barely heard Ami's remark because Evan's comment had triggered some insecure thoughts. She felt far from faultless—in fact, she had been increasingly aware of her selfishness compared to Jesus' selflessness.

Maude straightened her bonnet. "The King James Bible says, "Be ye perfect as your father in Heaven is perfect." So Evan's right. It's only when we're perfect that we can know we're saved."

"Were the disciples so perfect?" countered Ami.

"Well, no, they weren't," mumbled Maude. "They weren't saved yet."

"But Jesus told them that their names were in the Book of Life. That's being saved, isn't it? Yet they weren't up to your standard of perfection."

"But they weren't getting ready for Jesus' return, like we are."

"Then why did Jesus tell them not to worry because he had prepared a place for them in heaven and would take them home with him?" reasoned Amy.

"I think we've discussed it enough. Let's move on," Maude mumbled.

Evan drove Ami and Madeline home after the meeting and parked his Subaru outside their place. Madeline looked at Evan until he returned her gaze, then smiling gorgeously, thanked him for taking her to the fellowship meeting. Evan's pulse raced and he felt a warm glow of excitement. No woman had ever had such an effect on him before. He felt helpless to change the overpowering feelings that he realized were predominantly motivated by infatuation and promised himself that he would not go inside with Madeline.

"Would you like to come in for a while, Evan?" Madeline said sweetly.

Evan's struggle was strong but brief. "Sure. But just for a while. Thank you."

While Madeline was preparing a snack for Evan and herself, Ami changed clothes and left for the university. Madeline went to the refrigerator got out some cold chicken and yogurt and placed them on the table. Then, remembering that Evan was a vegetarian, she put them back in the fridge. She made up a salad, thawed out some frozen whole-meal bread in the toaster, and poured two glasses of fruit juice. When she noticed Evan avoided using butter, she found some olive oil for the toast.

"Madeline, you're a health reform inspiration to me. If everyone at church was as conscientious as you, we'd all be healthier. I have to be so careful with my diabetes."

Madeline searched for a suitable hot drink and found some herbal tea.

"Would you prefer dandelion or peppermint?"

"Dandelion is better for the nerves and therefore the soul," said Evan.

"I remember an article written by a Buddhist who believed that dandelion tea was excellent for meditation and the soul, as it calmed the stomach nerves that interact with the brain."

"Buddhism?" Evan replied quietly. "Buddhism is a pagan religion. I'm sure they have a different reason for drinking dandelion."

"Actually, they're pretty health conscious But I guess their motives aren't Christ-centered like yours," Madeline said, sensing Evan's attempt to suppress his indignation.

Evan picked up a photo album from under the coffee table and opened it. "Do you mind if I look through your pictures?"

"No, that's fine. I'll just get changed."

Madeline came back into the room wearing form-fitting jeans and a top. Evan started to say something but thought better of it. He believed it was just a matter of time before she adopted more suitable attire— something like Maude Smith wore. Meanwhile he felt that it wasn't his fault he admired her physical charms—she chose to dress that way.

Evan turned a page of the photo album.

"This your mum and dad?"

"Yep."

"They look like nice people. Your mum looks like you. She has your gorgeous smile and hair."

"Thanks, but her frown can be powerful too." Madeline laughed.

"Who is this guy with you at the party table?"

Madeline sat beside Evan on the couch for a closer look. As she did, Puff, her cat, woke up and briefly stared at Evan, then headed at Madeline. Avoiding Evan, she jumped to the floor and leaped onto Madeline's lap. Sniffing Madeline's salad sandwich, she shook her head and settled down to purr in her lap, facing away from Evan.

"That's Bob. He used to be my boyfriend. We were quite serious for a while."

"He's holding a smoke and a beer. How could you have liked him?" Evan asked stiffly, trying not to sound jealous.

"Oh, Bob was just a softy inside."

"Why'd you break up?"

Madeline paused. "To be honest, I got a bit bored. And I enjoyed dating other men."

Evan's manner stiffened further. "How could you?"

"I told you I was no angel."

Evan flicked to the next page and paused, his electrified emotions overpowering any weak impulses to turn the page away from Madeline's beach bikini shots. Conflicting emotions struggled desperately within him, but he finally managed to turn the pages, barely noticing the rest of the photos.

Moments later his emotions settled down, and through the filter of his confused brain, his feelings consolidated. How could he let Madeline go? Despite her faults, her attractiveness overwhelmed him. He had been praying for a wife, and she had come into his life under extraordinary circumstances. He didn't believe in long romantic courtships. He believed in divine guidance that could produce rapid results.

Evan was confused, because with his conservative background he was rather inexperienced when it came to romancing women. He wasn't sure how much Madeline liked him, but remembering how she had rebuffed his words at the mountain stream, he decided not to express any thoughts of marriage.

He wondered if another approach might work in his favor. He was craving for her warmth, especially after seeing the photos.

Puff purred under Madeline's gentle, sensuous strokes, and Evan longed for the same affection. He trembled with nervousness and excitement as he slid closer to Madeline. It was up to her now.

At that moment there was a knock on the door. Madeline absent-mindedly placed the cat on Evan's lap as she stood. Puff tensed, spiking Evan with her unsheathed claws as she leapt away.

"Pastors Fletcher and Edward, please come in," Madeline said.

Evan quickly returned the photo album to its place and leaped to his feet, dusting his clothes as if wiping away traces of moral impurity. He had often complained that he'd never received a pastoral visit, yet he had never resented any visit more than this one. At first he felt that they were interrupting his life's destiny—certainly God had not sent them at such a crucial time. Then the thought flashed through his mind that maybe he had.

Evan pretended to walk toward the door from the direction of the kitchen table.

Sam Edwards was cordial. "It's good that you're here, Evan. It will save us visiting you later. Pastor Fletcher and I decided to join forces to visit church members today."

"I'm not a member," corrected Evan. "We fellowship mostly at Zinski's house."

"We're aware of that," said Sam as he touched Evan's shoulder. "But we count you as one of our most sincere brothers. Madeline, we are thrilled at your example to the young people at church. We notice your friend Ami is coming regularly now. Is she here?"

"She's at Uni. Please sit down."

They conversed for some time but Evan said little. He was suspicious of the pastor's beliefs and could not find it in himself to exchange ideas cordially.

"Pastor Edwards …" said Madeline.

"Call me Sam, please.

"I heard you had a narrow escape at the harbor."

"Yes. If we'd been just a few minutes earlier, we would have been in the tunnel when it exploded."

"It must have been terrible," said Madeline, handing out some fruit juice.

"We thought it was an earthquake at first, but when we heard the enormous explosion we realized it was more sinister."

"It would be terrible to have your life end so suddenly and not have time to confess your sins," said Evan.

Sam looked at him warmly. "Actually, Evan, I believe the Lord knows when our hearts are in the right place, even if we had forgotten to confess something. Otherwise it would be salvation by memory, or luck, rather than by grace."

Suspecting that Evan was about to defend his statement, Sam switched to another subject. "That terrorist bombing had a sobering effect on me. With the phenomenal increases in natural disasters, I've come to realize that Jesus' return is imminent."

Karl's smile was patronizing, "The world's always had disasters and wars. It's just that with modern technology we're more aware of them."

Evan shook his head. "You remind me of what the apostle Peter predicted—that in the last days there'd be people who would scoff about any talk of the nearness of Jesus' return, saying that world conditions haven't changed. What about the freak hailstorm and the record heat waves up north? It's all been predicted in Revelation."

Karl spoke with calm and friendly intellectualism. "The best scholars teach that Revelation's prophecies were only given for the day in which they were written, and not meant to be stretched out into our future."

Sam did not relish getting into a debate with his senior pastor, but he felt a principle was at stake. "It says in Revelation 15 that the seven last plagues are the final wrath of God just before Christ's return, so Revelation's prophecies certainly *do* apply to the end times."

Karl gave a benign smile. "At the end of the day, what counts is having a relationship with God. And we can have that without solving all the Bible's mysteries."

Evan feared that Madeline's young faith was being threatened. "Pastor Fletcher, I am surprised that you can't accept God's Word just as it reads."

Sam interrupted, trying to diffuse the situation. "I'm sure Pastor Fletcher understands that we can lean upon God's Word in any trials."

"Of course," said Karl. "But the Bible needs interpreting, and with modern educational tools and an understanding of biblical culture, we have the tools to do it. Taking the Bible just as it reads means we'd have to deny proven science—take evolution, for example."

Evan sat upright, slapping both hands on the table before him, his suspicions confirmed. "Don't you believe in a literal six-day creation?"

"I believe we can reconcile Genesis and modern evolutionary science in that God works *through* evolution."

"The interpretation of Genesis is best left to the Bible writers," countered Sam, shocked at Karl's remark. "When God wrote the Ten Commandments in Exodus 20, he included a *literal* creation. Likewise, Jesus believed in Adam and Eve as real people, not monkeys."

Encouraged by Sam's comments, Evan felt his zeal firing. "Evolution is not scientifically proven; it's just a leap of faith in a theory."

"We should give credence to the dating methods that date the earth at many millions of years old," Karl said.

"There are a lot of top scientists who have little faith in the accuracy of dating methods," said Evan zealously. "I've read about it in John Ashton's book *In Six Days*, which records the Genesis creation beliefs of about fifty top academics."

"No point in arguing," said Sam, trying to diffuse the tension.

"Evan," said Karl, picking up on Sam's tactic, "you must be so happy that God healed your father from blindness. How is he?" .

"He can see quite well. But what makes you so sure it was God who healed him?"

"Well, who else could have? A Christian preacher prayed for him and he was healed."

"I think Evan's right in being cautious," said Sam. "There are warnings in Scripture with tests that can be applied as to the genuineness of miracles in the last days. For example, let's look at Mathew 7:23."

Sam read, "Many will say to me in that day, 'Lord, Lord, did we not prophesy in your name, and in your name drive out demons and perform many miracles?' Then I will tell them plainly, 'I never knew you. Away from me, you evil doers!' "

Madeline finally spoke. "I see. These miracle workers thought the Lord worked miracles through them. But he didn't even know them."

"The point is they weren't genuine miracles," Karl pointed out.

"Jesus didn't say they weren't genuine," responded Sam. "But since these faith healers had sin in their lives, it must have been Satan's power that healed them. We're also warned about Satan's end-time miracles in Revelation 16."

Karl was getting exasperated. "We have to be careful not to deny God's power and attribute it to Satan," he warned.

"I've done quite a bit of research on Ron Noble since Dad was healed at his session," said Evan. "He's been charged with fraud three times and convicted and jailed once. He also has a history of womanizing."

"I think we have to be tolerant and grateful for your dad's eyesight being the fruitage of his ministry," said Karl.

Evan glared at Karl. "Dad's been listening to Noble's tapes and he's starting to believe some of the same lies you do. Maybe that's why the devil healed him—to make him believe lies."

Karl stood, his demeanor becoming official. "Well, Pastor Edwards, we'd better be going. We have others to visit. But it has been a very stimulating discussion."

When the pastors had gone, Madeline said, "I'm sorry, Evan. But I'm feeling exhausted by all that, and I need to get some sleep before my evening shift at the hospital."

The debate had replaced Evan's romantic inclinations with religious zeal. After saying good night to Madeline, he drove off, his mind churning with a vision of enlightening the sleeping church.

Madeline went to bed anxiously reflecting on the morning's meeting at Zinski's house. Was she no longer right with God? She felt that she wasn't progressing to holier living and had depended on the feeling of peace to assure her of God's acceptance. But now that the peace had diminished, she felt insecure. *Why am I feeling so down if I love God? I'll have to study and pray harder and share my faith more,* she thought.

6

The Supernatural Visitor

◇◇◇◇◇◇◇◇◇◇◇◇◇◇◇◇◇◇◇◇◇◇◇◇◇◇◇◇◇◇◇◇◇◇◇◇◇◇

PASTOR KARL FLETCHER had completed his PhD in religious philosophy at Newcastle University. As part of his research, he found that there were an increasing number of credible reports in prestigious magazines about prominent Christian leaders who claimed they had been visited by deceased saints such as the apostle John. In each case, these deceased visitors conveyed some sort of comforting message or spiritual teaching.

Karl was in awe of the leaders who were receiving these visits. He regarded it the greatest honor possible to be chosen in this way. Karl kept an open mind and wondered how this could apply to him personally. Hadn't he received special recognition for his studies? Had he not had articles published in theological journals? Were not his insights profound? He was envious of the scholars whose work seemed to have the stamp of approval from none other than the authors of the New Testament. Was it possible that he might receive such an honored visit? He sometimes felt frustrated that the sphere of his influence was too restricted as a small-church pastor and little-known author.

One night, not long after the debate at Madeline's place, he was alone in his living room watching TV when he clearly heard a male voice behind him. "Karl, you are a true servant of God. Do not be afraid."

With the voice came a shimmering white light that filled the room. In that instant many conflicting thoughts coursed through Karl's mind. He had no idea who or what was speaking to him. He jumped up from the recliner and spun around. His philosophy that a rational explanation existed for every mystery suddenly evaporated.

Brighter than any artificial light, it emanated from a mysterious being standing before him. Whoever he was, it occurred to Karl that he could not have entered through a door or window. Karl could only stare with profound fear, shock, and confusion.

The light modified into a warm glow, making it easier to see the form of the being before him, who began to speak English with a distinguished and unusual accent. "I am the apostle Paul, bringing greetings from the

Son of God and his disciples. You are in no danger, so please listen carefully to what I say."

Overwhelmed, Karl dropped to his knees in submission. The bright being smiled and took one step closer. He was dressed in a biblical robe, and he wore a beautiful tiara on his head studded with countless small white sparkling diamonds that seemed to reflect and intensify the mystical light emanating from him. His noble face shone with wisdom and intelligence such as Karl had barely imagined possible. The visitor held an ancient scroll in his right hand, and in his left hand he held a striking cross the size of a large book. It was made of gold but it had the shape and texture of rough timber.

The being spoke warmly. "Karl, my instruction, if followed, will prepare many for the Lord's soon return. It will solve the confusing problems of Christendom and other religions."

The warm, friendly aura of the visitor dissipated some of Karl's fear. With a noble gesture, the visitor raised the cross and the scroll above shoulder height and said, "Please get up, Karl. I am Paul, a servant like you. Only God must be worshipped. You should not be surprised that I now live in the Father's kingdom and serve him in this way. Here is the message you must pass on: First, all must believe the letter to the church at Rome that is now in the holy canon; namely, that there is salvation only in the cross of our Lord."

As he said this he moved the golden cross from shoulder to shoulder.

"Second, this generation has now entered the age of special miracles. Because of the confusion in interpreting the Bible, God has seen fit to confirm his truth through signs and wonders. All people must listen to the teaching of those whom God endows with power from on high. He will not enable miracles to be performed by those who teach error.

"Third, those who are preparing for Christ's return must live by the law of love, tolerance, and submission to God's international plan. The Ten Commandments have done their work and are no longer to be binding on the consciences of people. They are not acceptable to all religions, and the law of love and tolerance has replaced them.

"Last, everyone must live for the good of others and must not feel as if they can follow their independent conscience. Mankind is on a course of self-destruction and great wickedness and confusion. God has chosen some of the world's political and religious leaders for a united plan to save the world. Individual freedoms must be sacrificed for the good of the majority. There will be a new order of central government in the world."

When Karl saw the benevolent and wise countenance and the graceful gestures, and heard the golden voice, he was certain it was indeed the apostle Paul standing in front of him. His fear turned to awe and admiration. "I am overwhelmed with gratitude to God for your condescension in leaving heaven and entrusting me with this message. I now realize that I have been mistaken in putting Christ's return a long way off."

Paul suddenly vanished, leaving Karl to his astonished thoughts. Karl could not sleep—his mind was too active in preparing his most important sermon.

A few weeks later, Ami and Madeline were enjoying each other's company at home.

"I got another e-mail from Owen," said Madeline.

"What'd he say?"

She read.

Hi, Madeline. How are you and Ami going?

That tunnel attack has really rammed home to me what an insecure world we live in and how much we need Jesus to come and take us home. The drought is getting worse, and we will have to wait for the next wet season for rain, but it is starting to cool down a bit. We have managed to set up a water pump system that is saving the cattle. My brother Bill will be arriving in a few days to help Mum and Dad during his holidays, so I'll be able to come down to Newcastle again. I'm looking forward to seeing you.

The neighbors are pulling together because of the tough times. I sang at the rodeo barbeque last weekend and mixed in more gospel songs than I normally do at rodeos. People seem to be asking more questions. It reminds me of the religious interest that September 11 created in the United States.

It was great to read your e-mail. I'm glad you are enjoying work and meeting new folk at church. That was an interesting trip up to Evan's hideaway. I've heard it's a wild and beautiful place. As you know, Evan is a dedicated bloke, but he does have a few ideas on the gospel that seem a bit different. Maybe we can talk about it when I see you.

God bless you, Madeline, and Ami too.

Owen

"What do you think of that?"

Ami gave an exaggerated frown. "Not very romantic, but I reckon he's keen to see you and he's worried about Evan."

"What do you think he's worried about?"

"He can see that Evan likes you and he's worried about some of Evans's ideas, I guess."

"It'll be really good to have a long yarn with Owen when he gets back. It might help sort things out."

Normally, Pastor Karl spent a lot of time researching his sermons, but on this occasion he didn't need to. In his heart, soul, and mind a spiritual brew had been stewing that he couldn't wait to serve to his congregation. His fear of fundamentalist reaction had gone and he was willing to accept any consequences. He barely listened to the song service. His lips moved but his heart was elsewhere.

Evan sat with Madeline and Ami near the center of the church. He was disappointed to see Karl step up to the pulpit but he resigned himself to it. *He doesn't preach the Word but an intellectual philosophy.* "Well," he quietly told Madeline, "at least we can get some benefit from discussing what was wrong with his sermon afterward."

Karl began his sermon as one with a heaven-born mission—as commissioned by none other than the great apostle himself. "Friends, I have something very important to confess to you today. As you know, I have been skeptical about any suggestion that Christ is returning to this earth soon. However, I now know without a doubt that he is in fact coming *very* soon. We are living on the threshold of great and solemn events, and I have to acknowledge that I have been blind to this reality. My skeptical mind has led you astray. For this I am truly sorry."

The surprised congregation remained quiet, wondering what had changed their pastor's mind. Some of his avid followers had viewed him as their guru and they looked at one another in dismay. Was their enlightened intellectual faith in vain after all?

Evan Hawkins was shocked at the admission. "I can't believe my ears," he whispered to Madeline.

"Shh," Madeline whispered back.

Karl continued. "Most of you are aware from media reports that for some time now, some of our spiritual and secular leaders have claimed to have had visitations from heaven. Personally I have had some doubts about these encounters, but have tried to keep an open mind. However, much to my amazement, a few nights ago I myself had a visitation, which has changed my life forever."

Karl looked up, as if conscious of Paul's approving smile. "I saw the visitor before me as clearly as you can see me here today," he said solemnly. "He was none other than the great apostle Paul, sent by God with a special message for these final days. Yes, Paul, who has been in the Father's presence for two thousand years. He behaved and was attired as I have always imagined Paul would. It seems to me that God held back visits of this kind until this generation for the special task of preparing us for Christ's imminent return."

The congregation gasped. One elderly man stood, threw his arms in the air, and exclaimed, "Hallelujah! God has visited his people!" Many responded with amens while others looked at one other with bewildered expressions.

"He's possessed by a deceiving spirit," Evan hissed. "I must say something."

Madeline grabbed Evan's arm to restrain him.

Karl continued. "I will always remember Paul's words. He said we are entering the special phase of mighty miracles for the endorsement of vital truths. These teachings, coming from the lips and pens of those gifted with God's power, will clear up the confusion in Christendom—indeed all religions."

Tears moistened Karl's cheeks. They seemed to some like a special anointing—a baptism of truth and grace. He spoke with a broken voice. "We must be humble and accept any teachings that accompany these miracles. If the miracles are worked in the name of our Lord, we need not fear deception. Remember, the Lord himself was accused of performing miracles in the name of the evil one."

Among those rejoicing at Karl's message were Simon Hawkins, who had been healed from blindness, and his wife, Sarah. Karl leaned over and whispered, "It all makes sense to me now."

Simon's appreciative face encouraged Evan to exhort more fervently. "Remember that Jesus rebuked those accusers who attributed his healings to demonic power."

Wildly indignant, Evan could no longer control himself. Once more, Madeline tried to restrain him, but he loosened her grip and stood. Evan's bearing and his flaming eyes reminded Madeline of Moses, as played by Charlton Heston in the movie *The Ten Commandments*, when Moses received the law on Mount Sinai.

Evan pointed at Karl with trembling hand. His whole bearing was that of an indignant, accusing prosecutor. "How dare you relate your wicked deceptions to God's church! You're a false minister, masquerading as an angel of light but really teaching the doctrines of devils. All miracles are *not* from God. Revelation chapters 13 and 16 say there will be signs and wonders in the last days, but they don't come from God. Satan uses miracles to deceive the whole world into getting the mark of the beast. The Lord rebukes you!"

Adrian Sebastian, the head deacon, had been listening to Pastor Karl with rapt and reverent attention. He quickly approached Evan and said, "Please be quiet and sit down, sir. You are disturbing our worship."

Evan ignored him. "You substitute the Word of God with the doctrines of devils," he continued. "We have had enough of—"

Sebastian and another deacon grabbed Evan by the arms and removed him from the worship area.

"Persecution is upon us just as was prophesied," cried Evan. "It's no longer safe for us to live in the cities."

Once outside, Sebastian said, "Listen, Hawkins, I want you to stay outside until the sermon's over. Keep your nose out of there."

"I can't allow Fletcher to teach his heresy. You have no right to stop me."

Evan turned to go back into the church, but Sebastian grabbed him by the arm.

"You are under arrest, Hawkins, for disturbing the peace in a public place. I'm taking you to the station. Anything you say may be given in evidence."

Sebastian was not only a deacon of the church; he was also a police inspector.

Once Evan had been formally charged at the station, Sebastian took him aside. Sebastian returned Evan's stare for a moment, then spoke quietly. "Evan, we're both Christians, and there was no need for all this. But once you forced me to remove you from church, I had to charge you."

"It's not me you should have removed, it's the preacher. God struck down Nadab and Abihu for less than what Karl Fletcher did today."

Sebastian calmly sipped coffee. "A minister's got every right to preach his point of view and we can't all agree on everything."

"At least I gave them something to think about. If I'd said nothing, the sheep would have followed the shepherd blindly."

"If you feel so strongly about Karl's preaching, I suggest you go to church somewhere else. Then again, who would keep that new girl warm?"

"That's *not* why I go to church."

"Wouldn't blame you if you did. She's not bad. And I've noticed you're coming fairly often these days." Sebastian laughed, looking out the window. "Actually, I think she might be outside waiting for you now."

"Can I go now?"

"Yes. I'll notify you about the court hearing date. Don't worry, I'll be easy on you. You'll probably only get a slap on the wrist. But the next time you feel like tearing the pastor to bits, do it somewhere else, will you?"

7

The Lawman

◇◇◇◇◇◇◇◇◇◇◇◇◇◇◇◇◇

M ADELINE SPICER FINISHED READING her King James Bible. Inside the
front cover she read the inscription:

To dear Madeline,
May the Lord sanctify and enrich you from the pages of his holy book.
In Christian love,
Evan

She closed it and put it down, wondering why she wasn't enjoying
it like she used to, unable to work out what had changed. Not so long
ago, it had filled her with peace and hope, and when she had read the
promises, she knew they applied to her. She had read of the failings and
trials of Abraham, David, Peter, and John, and she had believed that just
as God had forgiven and strengthened them to rise above discouragement,
he would help her. Now those same passages seemed to condemn her. Her
religion had changed from one of hope and happiness to one of anxiety
and striving to gain God's favor.

Madeline often wondered if she should voice her troubled thoughts,
and finally decided she would. "Ami, Owen's been away for more than six
weeks now, but he'll be here any minute now and I don't want him seeing
me like this—depressed and not enjoying life much anymore."

"We all have ups and downs. You'll get over it soon."

"It's not like that. It's something deeper."

"When I feel like that, I read the Bible and pray," offered Ami.

"That used to work for me too. But now it just makes me feel
condemned."

"Why?"

Madeline sighed as she allowed her feelings to surface. "Because I'm not progressing like a true Christian should. I seem to be going backwards."

Ami stopped making a salad and turned toward Madeline. "But you've made a lot of progress."

"In a way. But I haven't got enough love for people, and I've got selfish motives, and I don't think God approves of me anymore."

"Maybe that's the trouble. Maybe you should analyze yourself less and focus more on Jesus."

"When I spoke to Joan Edwards, she told me I should lay my burdens at the foot of the cross. But that only made me think I must have a very hard heart not to respond to the cross more, and Evan pointed out that before Jesus comes we have to be perfect."

"You know, Maddy, I don't think Evan's got it all right. I mean, that outburst in church proves he's got to find some more tact somewhere. He's not so perfect himself, you know. But Owen's pretty balanced—he might be able to help you. That might be his car pulling up outside now."

Madeline peeked out the window. She saw Owen Boyd open the back door of his Toyota. He swept a bundle of rope away from a carton on the seat and wiped some dust off it.

"It's a long time since I've seen Owen," she said. "I'm a bit nervous."

"But excited too, right?" Ami smiled as she looked out. "Look at him, combing his hair for you. And he's got a gift."

Madeline opened the door. "Hello, Owen. Come in," she said warmly.

"It's so good to see you again," said Owen as he hugged them both. "I've brought you somethin'."

Ami opened the carton and lifted out two gift-wrapped packages, each containing a country gospel CD and a beautifully carved boomerang.

"They're made by an aboriginal artist from Townsville," Owen explained.

Madeline hugged Owen again, and he held her a little longer this time.

"Thanks so much," she said. "That's very sweet and thoughtful of you. We're about to have a bite to eat. Like to join us?"

After lunch the women related how Evan had been arrested.

"Oh, man, that's amazing. He's a funny bloke! I can just imagine Evan's reaction." Owen grinned. "I knew Karl's been on shaky ground, but I never thought he'd get sucked in that easily."

"At least Evan had the courage to say something," said Madeline. "Since the apostle Paul supposedly visited Karl, I've been reading 1 Samuel

28, where the spirit medium of Endor called up Samuel from the dead to give him a message for King Saul. Maybe it really was Samuel. After all, his message for Saul did come true."

"But God had warned Israel about witchcraft and talkin' to the dead," Owen said. "That's why the spirit medium didn't want to admit to King Saul who she really was. She was terrified he'd kill her on the spot."

"But didn't Saul recognize Samuel?" quizzed Ami.

Owen was adamant, "Yes, but it wasn't really him. It just proves what a con it was. Remember it was *after* God had stopped hearing Saul's prayers that Saul resorted to talkin' to the medium. Now, think about it—after God stopped listenin' to Saul's prayers, would he then talk to him through a way that he'd already banned? The story's a warnin' not to reject God's ways or we become open to Satan's lies."

Madeline grew thoughtful. "So Pastor Karl's been visited by a lying spirit?"

"Afraid so. And according to Bible prophecy we're going to see lots more of it before the end. But I'm glad you're readin' the Bible, Madeline."

Madeline poured three soft drinks. "Actually, just before you arrived, I was telling Ami that I'm not enjoying the Bible like I used to. It makes me feel condemned and not good enough. I've found out that we have to be perfect by the time Jesus comes back."

Owen put his drink down, his face expressing concern. "Madeline, there's somethin' you need to understand."

Owen spoke slowly. "You *are* perfect."

"No way. You're far too generous."

"It's not how you see yourself, or how others see you that counts, but how God sees you."

"That's what worries me. God knows how mixed my motives are."

"Sure, God knows you're not really perfect. But he counts you as perfect. He treats you as if you're perfect."

"So, you're saying that I can look at the dirty dishes and pretend they're clean?"

"A bit like that."

"That sounds too cheap and easy to me."

Owen shook his head. "It wasn't cheap—it cost the life of the Son of God. When Jesus was on the cross, he was treated as you deserve, so that you might be treated as he deserved. In other words, he was treated as if he was sinful, so you could be treated as perfect."

"Is that in the Bible?"

"Yep. Second Corinthians chapter five says that God counted Jesus as being sin for us so he could then treat us as if we're as righteous as God. That's what Jesus did for us on the cross. There's more in Romans 3 and 4 as well."

"I'm a bit confused. I'll have to think about this and study it up."

"Good idea. Maybe we can talk about it sometime too. I'm sure you'll get your peace back once you've sorted it out."

"Thanks, Owen. I guess it's hard to believe I'm right with God when I can't feel his presence or his peace like I used to."

"You can't trust feelings to tell you about your standin' with God. You've gotta live by faith in what he says, not by the way you feel."

"I hope it all makes sense to me one day."

"It will. I promise."

Inspector Adrian Sebastian was known as a fair but tough police administrator who preferred hands-on work rather than sitting in an office. Feared by other policemen as well as by the criminal element, it was hoped he would be a deterrent to police corruption, which had been a major problem in the area. Sebastian had been a key witness in corruption inquiries at Sydney, and widespread publicity in the case had shaped him into a controversial figure. His reputation had gone before him to his new appointment at Newcastle.

Not long after his clash with Evan Hawkins, Sebastian had been called to an urgent hostage situation. What began as a domestic dispute had snowballed into the threat of a multiple murder. Joan Cox had taken her three young children into a welfare shelter for abused mothers to protect them from Wayne, her drug-addict husband. He had become violent and had threatened to kill Joan if she left him. After discovering where she was hiding, he had broken in with a double-barreled shotgun and attempted to abduct the children. Staff had called the police who had been patrolling nearby, and they arrived quickly enough to trap him in the refuge. But Cox wouldn't give himself up, so they called Inspector Sebastian to use his considerable negotiating skill. Unfortunately Cox was so deranged by drugs, he seemed incapable of responding to any sensible appeals.

Using a phone, Sebastian tried once more. "Wayne, Joan was planning to bring the kids back to you one day. She was going to wait until you received the help you needed to get your health back together. You won't go to jail for this. You'll get expert medical care where your family can visit you."

Wayne Cox thought of the good times he used to have with his wife and children, and contrasted it with the hell he was going through now. He remembered the traumas of a criminal psychiatric unit and the promise he had made to himself that he would never go back. He looked at the fear on his wife's and children's faces, and a hopeless despair swept through him. "Look, mate," he responded, "you've got nothin' to worry about. And the family's got nothin' to worry about. It's all over."

Sebastian recognized the signals. "Wayne, no! Don't do it!"

Wayne Cox leapt into the bathtub, put the shotgun to his head, and pressed the trigger.

Inspector Sebastian had never become used to that kind of violence. It always emotionally drained and depressed him. He came home early, totally exhausted, and took his uniform off, hoping he could shed the day's stress with it. Dropping into his leather recliner, he opened a can of beer and reflected on the day's work. While he didn't admit it to colleagues, the rising crime rate was stressing him out. The future seemed bleak in a society where the cancerous spread of crime had created so much insecurity. He felt the answer did not lie in a better police force, but in some kind of drastic revolution within society itself. He was aware that drastic measures were being proposed in the US, and he was monitoring developments there.

As he sipped his beer, Sebastian watched the news on his super-wide TV. He learned that a record number of unusually severe tornadoes had disintegrated a number of communities in the US Midwest. Terrorist activity in Asia had halted all tourism there. The normally lush Papua New Guinea highlands were experiencing another freak drought, and food was being flown in from Australia to prevent starvation. The drug-related crime rate was almost out of control. A riot had broken out in a Sydney soccer match and seven British spectators had been killed by overzealous fans. *What is possessing people? Murder and sport don't go together.*

Sebastian muted the TV and looked at his wife, Brenda. "Take your mind back twenty-five years, love. If you were watching today's headline news back then, what would you have thought?"

"It would have seemed like a far-fetched movie," replied Brenda.

Sebastian swallowed some more beer. "We've become used to this rotten world because it's developed gradually, but something's gotta change."

He managed to relax and he drifted off into a troubled sleep. He woke fifteen minutes later, feeling groggy. The blurry image on the screen gradually sharpened into a recognizable person—Floyd DeCosta, Secretary General of the United Nations. He was addressing an assembly of national political leaders at a summit meeting in Berlin. Sebastian straightened his recliner and called to Brenda, who was in the kitchen. "Bring me my coffee, please, love. I don't want to miss this."

"What's happening?"

"It sounds like world leaders are finally on the ball. The United Nations leader seemed to pull it all together tonight, and the others seemed to go with him."

"I heard something about the world being in a mess—as if we didn't know."

"Yeah, he said terrorism is more rampant than ever."

"We all know that—look at the Sydney tunnel."

"Then he talked about droughts and global warming. Can you believe that over 120 billion dollars was spent last year for worldwide natural disaster relief?"

"That's big bikies!"

"He mentioned the recent new crop of previously unknown diseases."

"There's some new weird ones now, all right."

"Apparently big drug lords are almost running the economy in some countries—that was the main guts of it."

"Did he give a solution?"

"He said what was needed was more than just the existing United Nations. We need the cooperation of the world's great religions—a kind of spiritual UN."

Their youngest son, Brett, joined in. "Uni history classes taught that whenever a lot of the big brass get together and make rules for everyone, it spells trouble and a loss of freedom."

"But I would think that when leaders stop fighting and come together, good should result," Sebastian replied.

"Uh, no," corrected Brett. "Whenever religion and politics have joined hands, persecution and intolerance have taken over."

"Well, something's got to happen soon, or you kids won't have much of a life."

"It's all right for the political big shots to say religions should unite, but how in the world are non-Christian religions going to play along?" asked Brett. "How would the UN envisage Muslims cooperating with American fundamentalists, for example? I just can't see it happening when some of their leaders call the US 'The Great Satan.' "

Sebastian remembered how the apostle Paul had told Fletcher that mighty miracles would unite the religious world, but he didn't mention it. Later, as he lay in bed, he quietly pondered its significance.

8

The Barrington Retreat

◇◇

OWEN BOYD WAS DELIGHTED to have Madeline Spicer as his passenger as they followed a rough map to the church's camping retreat. This was to be their first extended date since his return. This year it was to be held in the remote northern end of the Barrington Ranges, a huge mass of rugged mountains covering more than two thousand square kilometers. Only four-wheel drives could negotiate the road as it snaked its way through spectacular wild and rugged mountains.

Madeline found the scenery absorbing as they circled the towering granite escarpments that fell to the valley floor almost a kilometer beneath them. A thin, white, snaking ribbon far below was a series of rapids and waterfalls.

The freedom of the drive and the anticipated adventure made her briefly forget about her spiritual troubles. She wished that both Owen and Evan weren't going to be at the camp at the same time, because she was fond of each of them and they were both attracted to her. In the past she had enjoyed it when men competed for her affections, and if someone was bruised emotionally, it was just part of the game—but she had changed.

As he carefully guided his utility vehicle over the slippery road, Owen felt he had helped Madeline to be a little more confident in being ready for Christ's return—she didn't feel so threatened by it.

"Ever read how Martin Luther discovered the good news?" he asked.

"Yeah, I've read a bit. He was the sixteenth-century reformer Martin Luther King was named after, wasn't he?" Madeline replied, her serenity disturbed a little.

"Yeah. Luther was raised real strict in a God-fearin' German home, and as a young bloke he couldn't find peace by tryin' to be good. He just felt he was too rotten and felt condemned by God. One day he was almost struck by lightnin', which sacred him to death, so he promised God he'd try harder to keep the commandments. He fasted and prayed but still found no peace, so eventually he joined a monastery, where he kinda punished himself and fasted until his health broke."

"Owen, I think I've been going through something like that."

"Luther thought he'd never make it, and at times he was so angry that he shook his fist at God. But one day he was contacted by a guy called Staupitz. I'm not sure whether he was priest or a lecturer, but he told Luther to stop punishin' himself for his sins because Jesus had already been punished in his place. He told him to believe his sins had been forgiven and God had accepted him. Well this blew Luther's mind, and he began to study Romans chapter three to five for himself. He found out that the righteousness he was trying to get by good works was already his as a free gift."

"I've been reading those chapters in Romans, and I think I'm beginning to understand. But I don't feel peace like I used to."

"Luther didn't feel peace straightaway, either, but he understood he was at peace—right with God. It's not a feelin' but a fact. Later, he felt good about bein' right with God."

"I'm beginning to see. Maybe I've been looking for the feeling of peace first, sort of putting the cart before the horse—Look out!"

Owen jerked the car to the left to avoid a large wombat, but he thudded into it anyway. The heavy, thick-set animal had run down a steep slope and onto the road.

"Oh, no! Hang on—I'll just park over in this clearin'."

Madeline frantically opened the door before the vehicle had quite stopped, then ran back to the bear-like creature with short, stout legs and the endearing face of a toy teddy. She hovered over the animal with the same concern that she showed patients in the hospital emergency ward. "He's badly hurt," she said.

"There's no vet around here. What can we do?"

"He's bleeding from the mouth and his chest has caved in. There's nothing that can be done. Poor thing's making pathetic little grunts."

Madeline's tears ran down her cheeks as she gently stroked the dying animal and examined its pouch to make sure it was empty.

Owen checked the vehicle for damage. "The car seems OK. You love animals like I do—I've often had to sit by dying animals on the farm. They can tell you're there for them."

When the wombat had stopped breathing, Owen wrapped his arms around Madeline, comforting her. She stayed in his embrace long enough to hint that she was in no hurry to separate. Finally Owen dragged the dead wombat to the side of the road and threw some branches over it.

Because of their cattle-raising and nursing backgrounds, both of them had trained themselves not to grieve over suffering for too long, so as they continued driving, the spectacular scenery absorbed their attention once again. Before long, Madeline's thoughts drifted to spiritual themes. "Owen, there's something that's been bothering me about Evan."

"What's that?"

"He's so strict on diet. He places so much importance on it. Almost as if you'd miss out on heaven if you didn't go along with his thinking. He won't eat any animal products at all. That's not taught in the Bible, is it?"

"The Bible doesn't teach that it's a sin for us to eat meat. But if you go back to Genesis chapters 1 and 2, you'll see that before sin entered the world, Adam and Eve only ate fruit and veggies."

"So is Evan right?"

"He's wrong in forcin' his ideas on others. Besides, after Adam and Eve sinned, God let people eat meat. And Jesus ate fish. I mean, vegetarian food must be good for you if God gave it in the first place, but if you turn it into a way of earnin' your way to heaven, you're in real trouble."

"Do you think Christians should be careful about their diet and health then?"

"Sure, as long as they're sensible and not legalistic about it. Like doin' anythin' else that's good, we do it *because* we're saved, not to *be* saved."

"I guess we should pray for Evan."

"You're right, he needs it."

Owen spotted the yellow rag that marked the track turn-off to the camping area. "I can see why they told us to take four-wheel-drive vehicles. Nothing else could make it down here," he said as he stopped the Toyota to engage the four-wheel drive. The track descended steeply, twisting its way through stands of giant gum trees and carving its way through granite cuttings and under cliff faces.

They crossed some clear, boulder-strewn streams that rippled their way through dense ferns, occasionally stopping to absorb the enchantment of the dense rain forest.

An hour later the track leveled out to meet the valley floor, which was dissected by a narrow, swift river. Owen got out and peered through the pristine water to check its depth. It was shallow enough to see the stones on the bottom, and tire tracks on the banks showed that others had safely crossed before them. Owen selected low range and slowly drove through.

As they followed the river upstream, it alternated from calm, deep pools to frantic, shallow rapids. Kangaroos grazed fearlessly on its banks—a sure sign they had never been shot at. Hundreds of parrots and giant yellow-tailed black cockatoos fed on the grasses and bushes that lined the river bank. An abandoned stand of wild quince trees suggested that miners or timber men may have lived there long ago.

When they arrived at the campsite, Ami greeted them and cheerfully introduced them to her new friend, Basil Dorf, whom she had met at university, where he was studying electronic engineering. Ami had invited Basil, an avowed skeptic, to the retreat, hoping he would be influenced toward spiritual things. While he appeared to be self-assured, Ami had perceived that it was just a veneer for his loneliness and troubled mind.

Basil had been living with his alcoholic father for several years and still struggled with his own drug dependency and poverty. He was surprised that this relatively conservative and attractive blonde woman had taken an interest in him with his long, drooping mustache and lip and nose rings.

Including children, about twenty campers were sitting around the welcoming campfires. The sun had set early because of the mountain range that towered around them. Basil had never been camping before, and he was captivated by the nearness and clarity of the stars that stood out against the deep blue night. The enchanting heavens seemed to be beautifully framed by the blackness of the towering mountains and enhanced by the musical notes of mysterious night birds perched near the gurgling stream.

Evan, who sat next to Madeline, was uncomfortable with Owen's cheerful and at times lively gospel music, which he considered worldly, so he didn't sing but just stared at the fire. He became more uncomfortable when he noticed Madeline and Owen occasionally smiling at each other. The jealously that surged through his soul alarmed Evan, and he desperately wished Owen wasn't there so he could relax with Madeline.

When it was dark, Pastor Sam Edwards read the story of the prodigal son to the other campers, whose faces reflected the flickering orange glow of the fire. When he finished reading, he said, "The ungrateful son had wasted his father's money and squandered his own conscience, but the father kept searching the horizon for his lost son. One day his loving father spotted him and ran joyfully to meet and embrace him, and he celebrated with a party. What can we learn from that?"

"The son was forgiven, treated as if he hadn't sinned, and we're treated by God the same way," said Owen.

"What if we've been Christians for a long time? Do we still need to be pardoned?" asked Sam.

Evan felt he had to speak up for the truth. "Being pardoned for our past sins is important, but we progress in holiness and need less and less of his forgiveness. We shouldn't need it at all by the time the Lord returns."

"Actually," Pastor Sam replied, "we'll always need to be forgiven in this life because we'll always be conscious of our unworthiness."

Sam shone his flashlight on Galatians chapter 3 verse 1 and read, "You foolish Galatians! Who has bewitched you? Before your very eyes Jesus Christ was clearly portrayed as crucified. I would like to learn just one thing from you; did you receive the Spirit by observing the law, or by believing what you heard? Are you so foolish? After beginning with the spirit, are you now trying to attain your goal through human effort?"

"The Galatian Christians made the mistake of believing that we begin the Christian life by trusting in Jesus, but continue it by trusting in our good character or works."

Evan felt that his very soul was being challenged, but to prevent a scene, he kept quiet. He had expected to hear teachings he didn't agree with and consoled himself with the thought that Madeline could be more easily influenced when they were alone.

Sam kept focused. "How would the forgiven son have related to his father's acceptance and love?"

"He'd be happy to follow his father's wishes," said Sam's wife, Joan.

"How can we know our heavenly Father's wishes today?" asked Sam.

"By keeping the Ten Commandments," Evan quickly replied.

Pastor Karl Fletcher remembered the apostle Paul's visit and instructions. "If we love one another and live with tolerance," he said, "that's all that's required. The Ten Commandments were only temporary. They are no longer valid for us today. It's a burdensome legalistic law."

Once again, Evan struggled to remain calm. He lifted a smoldering branch out of the fire and poked it into the coals.

Rohan Kent, an elder, joined in the discussion. "There's something in First John on this subject. I just read it recently. Ah, here it is—1 John chapter 5 verse 2: 'By this we know that we love the children of God, when we love God and obey his commandments. For this is the love of God that we keep his commandments and his commandments are not burdensome.' Clearly, then, living in love doesn't replace the Ten Commandments. Rather, if we keep the commandments, that's evidence we're living in love.

It's only a burden when we don't have the love of God."

Pastor Karl decided against an extended debate and did not reply. Since he believed that Paul had instructed him personally, he felt he could afford to wait for God to influence his flock in his own good time, perhaps with the promised miracles to come.

When the discussion ended, the campfire atmosphere prompted the campers to share their experiences. Ami's friend Basil left the campfire to smoke marijuana behind a rocky outcrop on the riverbank.

When he returned, he lay quietly on his sleeping bag beside the fire's warm glow, absorbed with the apparent infinity of the universe above.

"Amazing that a mindless evolution could be responsible for all that," he said, moving his extended hand slowly across the sky.

Ami patted Basil on the head. "Enjoying yourself, are you, Bas? Keep looking at those stars. They really speak to you."

"Yeah, they give out a lot of knowledge, those stars," Basil said quietly.

The raucous screams of the yellow-tailed black cockatoos woke Owen just before dawn. He lay in his sleeping bag, prayed, and waited for daylight. When he stepped out of the tent, the grandiose beauty of the valley captivated him. Refreshed, the invigorating morning had sharpened his appreciation of beauty. The coolness of the dawn kept the campfire smoke low as it wisped around the peaceful, scattered tents like a low fog. Nothing else stirred except a diving azure kingfisher and some distant rabbits skipping around their burrows.

Owen placed a fishing line and some lures under the seat of a large, green fiberglass canoe, then slid the canoe over the gravel beach to the water's edge. Next, he put some dry branches on the fire and went for a walk along the riverbank. By the time he returned, others were waking up.

"Comin' for a canoe ride, Madeline?" Owen asked. "We'll be back in time for breakfast."

"Great. Hang on. I won't be long. Can Ami come?"

"Yeah. What about her friend?"

"Basil? He didn't get to sleep till late, so we won't see him for a while."

Evan was still in his brown sleeping bag on the ground near his vehicle. "Mind if I come?' he called out.

"Not at all," replied Owen.

The four of them poled the canoe through the shallows, sliding and scraping over the smooth rocks until there was enough depth to paddle in.

The rapids emptied into a long water hole that disappeared around the far-distant bend. Evan pointed to a retreating family of small wallabies they had disturbed. "If we're quiet we might see a bit of wildlife," he whispered.

Madeline, sitting behind Evan, admired how the orange glow from the rising sun defined the contours of his iron-hard arm muscles and highlighted the waves of his dark hair. The first glimmerings of sunshine lifted the last traces of mist from the still water.

"What are they?" asked Madeline, pointing to some movement in the water beneath some overhanging leafy tree branches.

"Stop paddling," whispered Evan. "Those are platypuses—probably nesting in a hole in the bank behind those jammed logs."

"Wow!" said Ami excitedly, frightening the timid creatures which disappeared under the water. "I've never seen a platypus in the wild."

Arriving at the end of the deep water hole, they turned the canoe around to paddle back. Owen withdrew the fishing line from under the back seat, where he was sitting, and threw a lure into the water behind them.

"There's gotta be some big trout in this hole," said Owen.

Evan spun around. "You're not going to fish, are you?"

"Sure, why not?"

"This is like Eden, where there was no killing or eating little friends." Evan glared.

"Well, mate, this is the real world—not the garden of Eden."

"Isaiah says there'll be no killing in the new earth, and the lamb will lie next to the lion. We should be purifying ourselves for that time and subjecting our lust for killing."

"Does it really say that?" queried Madeline. "I get upset when I think of the pain we cause animals."

"I respect people for bein' vegetarians and all that, but being perfect is more about bein' lovin' … Oh, no, the line's caught a snag," Owen complained, frustrated that his heavy fishing line had halted the canoe. "Stop paddlin'. I'll just haul us back on this snagged line."

Owen gradually pulled the canoe toward the snag, then the "snag" started to move across the waterhole. "That's no snag," he cried. "What've I hooked? It's too cold for crocs down here."

Owen peered down into the clear depths with his glare-reducing polarizing sunglasses. "My goodness, it's a huge cod!" he exclaimed excitedly. He tugged on the strong line. The fish swished its great tail and began to turn the canoe around.

"Why don't you just let it go?" Evan protested.

"I couldn't if I wanted to, which I don't. The line is too strong to break."

"Here, let me cut it with my knife," said Evan, reaching into his back pocket.

"No way," Owen said. "It'll make a great barbeque tonight if we can land it."

"It's heading for those submerged logs," Ami warned.

"Grab those overhanging branches and hang on," directed Owen, almost shouting. "If it gets into those logs, it's gone."

The girls hung on to the overhanging tree branches while Evan concentrated on balancing the canoe, his taught face expressing moral concern.

"Just hang on. It's tiring." Owen gasped for air as he hauled the weakening fish close to the canoe.

"We don't want him in the canoe," Evan.

"Let's keep him for dinner tonight," Ami countered.

"Wow, must be fifteen kilos easy," exclaimed Owen as he grabbed the exhausted fish by its gill opening and pulled it over the side, where it flapped between his feet.

"Good on ya, Owen. That's the biggest fish I've ever seen caught," Ami said.

Since they hadn't had breakfast and were hungry, they paddled toward camp.

Evan said nothing on the way back, feeling grieved that his conscience had been compromised against his will.

The young adults among the campers were exploring upstream, where the river churned wildly through gorge country. Karl Fletcher's son Brett was extremely fit and almost ran along the narrow path, leaving the group behind. After a few kilometers, Brett came to a waterfall and stopped to admire the scene. The cascading water struck a protruding ledge as it plummeted down and became a raging white turbulence, spraying a fine mist and creating a small rainbow that crowned the wild scene. Green ferns grew profusely nearby, and root vines from above swept over the ledge, partly obscuring it.

As Brett rested his athletic frame, he noticed that the ledge penetrated under the waterfall and wondered if became a cave under the falls. He stripped to his shorts and carefully groped his way along the ledge. As he approached the cascade, he could see that indeed there was a cave under the waterfall. The ledge that barely supplied a foothold narrowed to almost nothing under the vines and ferns for a few feet, then widened again near the cave entrance. It was easily within jumping distance, but to land safely on the narrow ledge on the other side would be difficult.

The mystery of the cave lured Brett on. He reached up and grabbed hold of a vine for support. With his face to the rock wall, he leaped sideways. He landed safely, but broke the only vine capable of supporting him. He wondered how he would get back. He feared falling onto the enormous boulders way below—there was no deep pool to safely jump into. But he would worry about that later.

Brett crawled under the waterfall and stepped into the cave's entrance, only to be disappointed—the damp cave was just a few meters deep. He emerged and waited for the other hikers to catch up.

The others arrived shortly and heard Brett's call for help above the roar of the falls. Evan edged out onto the dangerously narrow ledge. He looked down and was gripped with the fear of plummeting to his death. A terrible dread of his imperfect condition before God and of being eternally lost possessed him, making him extremely tense and dizzy.

Despite his desire to impress Madeline, he turned and nervously edged his way back to safety, embarrassed and distraught. When Basil was out of Ami's hearing range, he quietly said to Evan, "What's the matter, mate? Got no God to help ya?"

Evan was alarmed at his own heated anger and his urge to throw Basil off the cliff.

"I wouldn't trust those thin vines, and nobody's got a rope," Brett called out to Owen above the roar of the waterfall.

"I might put that log over the gap," replied Owen.

"Bit risky."

"Can't think of a better idea."

Owen edged his way along the slippery ledge, closer to Brett. Holding a vine for support, he carefully placed the log over the gap. Brett let go of a supporting fern bush and grasped Owen's outstretched hand.

Then came the most dangerous part of the maneuver. Owen stepped backward to make room for Brett, who shifted his weight onto the unstable bridging log, then quickly stepped onto the secure ledge, where he was grasped by Owen.

There was a simultaneous cheer, but Evan sat on a log, feeling alone and dejected.

9

The Roaring Begins

◇◇◇◇◇◇◇◇◇◇◇◇◇◇◇◇◇◇◇◇◇◇◇◇◇◇◇◇◇◇◇◇◇◇◇◇

A S THE AFTERNOON COOLED, the campers lazed around the campfire, resting from the day's activities. Rohan Kent, the middle-aged church elder, read the latest *Behind the News* magazine, a commentary on international developments. On its cover was a striking picture of Harold Foreman, President of the United States, making a fiery speech. The feature article was titled "The Roaring of the American Lamb."

Rohan held up the picture to Pastor Sam, who was toasting bread on the other side of the fire.

"Hey, Sam, you should read what Foreman's saying," said Rohan.

"What's he on about?" asked Sam, fanning the smoke from his eyes.

"First he gives a reminder of how God has blessed America and how its pioneers formed their Constitution on religious freedom, which became the reason for America's prosperity and greatness. He reckons that's why the American government has a God-given obligation to support the Christian Power Movement's proposed legislation."

"The Christian Power Movement? That doesn't make sense! Aren't they promoting legislation that would restrict religious freedom?"

"You're spot on," agreed Rohan. "But they'd deny it, of course."

Sam scraped his burnt toast with his pocketknife. "That's scary stuff," he said, shaking his head in wonder.

"It's been in the wind for some time," said Rohan.

"Yeah, but this is the first time the president's publicly stated his support so clearly," Sam said.

"What areas of reform is Foreman talking about?" asked Rohan's wife, Mary, putting down her binoculars.

Rohan moved his chair away from the shifting smoke. "He's not specific, but he mentions stuff like the protection of religious faith and family values. However, the article quotes Gerald Hopkins of the Christian Power Movement. Hopkins sees the increase in natural disasters and internal strife as God's wake-up call for the government to protect the American family and restore its faith values. His solution is for the government to legislate a cure."

Evan had been struggling to hear the conversation, so he sat on a log closer to the fire. "Did you say *legislate* a cure?"

"Yeah. Hopkins feels that God's cause will be best served by laws that encourage a unity of all religions, whether Christian, Jewish, or otherwise. It seems there will be some sort of ban on finger-pointing at religious groups or identifying them as being enemies of God. Apparently there's a real possibility that when it fully takes off, a kind of united world religion will emerge, headed by Protestant leaders and backed by the Pope."

"Forty years ago, nobody would have thought it was possible," said Sam. "I've read how America was settled by Europeans who were glad to escape the oppression and persecution of the church back in Europe. America became a kind of safe haven from religious intolerance backed by political power."

"But why would the US government go along with the Christian Power Movement if they want to restrict freedom?" asked Ami.

"They imagine that God would bless the economy and save traditional family life—save the country," said Sam with a touch of sarcasm in his voice.

"If their so-called unity means giving up personal freedom, they can jump in the lake," exclaimed Evan as he aggressively poked a log deeper into the fire, causing a shower of sparks.

"It is radical, but they're desperate," said Rohan.

"I've always been suspicious of Americans," said Evan indignantly.

"Hang on, Evan. It's not the American people who are the problem— it's certain religious and political leaders who are misleading the people," said Sam.

"Yeah," agreed Rohan. "We owe a lot to the American people and their democratic way of life—it's been an example to the world."

"They protected Australia in the war. If it wasn't for them we'd be overrun with some foreign enemy by now. We owe them heaps," suggested Basil Dorf quietly.

"What about American movies? I suppose they've lifted Australian morals, have they?" said Evan sarcastically.

"It's not only Hollywood that's glorified sex and violence," reminded Ami. "Many American Christians have led the way in protecting their families from the influence of the media."

Pastor Karl had read the *Behind the News* article and was pleased with the latest trends in America. He had been listening to the others' remarks and was looking for an opportunity to state his point of view in a way that wouldn't provoke Evan too much. Karl remembered Evan's barrage in church and could only guess what his reaction might be when outdoors. Avoiding eye contact with Evan, he reasoned gently, "In a sense we've already given up some religious freedoms without any qualms of conscience. For instance we don't have the freedom to go into Muslim mosques to burn the Koran. They haven't been able to pray in schools. Yet many Christians haven't complained too much about that. Are the new proposals so different, when they're for the common good?"

Evan began to speak but Basil interrupted. "I don't believe in all this religious gobbledygook. There's no God anyway, but logic tells me that you're asking for trouble by telling people how they can or can't believe or worship. History tells us that America drew immigrants from Europe like a magnet because people wanted to escape religious intolerance and persecution. Now it looks like they might have to face it in their own country."

Evan managed to speak. "What are they going to do about the First Amendment, which is the foundation of their democratic government? How does it go? 'Congress shall make no law regarding religion or freedom to exercise' or something like that."

Karl poured another glass of wine. "It goes on to say, 'And no religious test shall be required for public office,' if I remember rightly. But many legal experts are debating the interpretation of the first amendment, feeling that its meaning is not that clear and that it doesn't preclude church and state uniting in legislating for a common good."

"How in the world do they expect that non-Christian religions are going to cooperate in all this?" asked Mary.

"Christ used the persuasive power of miracles, and he'll continue to do so," Fletcher reasoned. "Ultimately, the Vatican and all the world's great religions—Buddhists, Muslims, the lot—could be persuaded by a miraculous outpouring of the Holy Spirit, endorsed by miracles."

Evan's warning glare persuaded Karl from naming the apostle Paul as the authority that was behind his assured manner.

Mary picked up her husband's magazine and scanned the controversial article. "This is unbelievable," she declared. "For years they banned prayer in schools, and now they're not only going to permit it, they're going to *enforce* teaching religion in a way that's compatible to almost all religions. Teachers will be trained how to do it."

"Don't you think it's a good idea to teach about God in schools?" Karl asked. "Millions of kids know little about him."

"Yes, but not if it's forced. We'd be back in the dark ages!" Mary said.

"Where's Owen?" Pastor Sam asked, looking around him.

No one knew, but Evan noticed that Madeline was also missing. His stomach tightened as he imagined the possibilities.

"Can you imagine Jesus going around trying to fix Israel's problems with political legislation?" asked Rohan. "Well, he's not doing it today either. I think it's just a matter of time before a ban will be placed on speaking out against this new system."

"I'm glad I'm not living in the States," said Evan as stood. He dragged a large log onto the fire and looked around, hoping to see Madeline.

Basil had been cooling his beer supply in the cold stream and had just returned with his fourth can in an hour. "Don't worry, mate," he said. "We're hot on their tail. I saw some Australian bishop spouting forth, praising the United Nations secretary for pushing a combined world religion thing. We'll be next to follow. What do you reckon, Ami?"

Ami shrugged; she had been quietly pondering the significance of what she had heard that evening. An anxious foreboding told her that her future would be more complicated than she wanted it to be.

Sam opened his Bible to Revelation chapter 13. "That magazine article implied the lamb was the United States leadership. That's interesting, because Revelation 13 describes a lamb-like beast or nation that roars like a dragon and forces people to worship the first beast described earlier in chapter 13. That first beast is apparently Satan's agency on earth."

"We know who the dragon symbolizes," said Evan. "Revelation 12 says the dragon is Satan, and he's going to use miracles as his secret weapon of deception."

"Yes," said Sam. "And we know that a lamb represents Christ, so a lamb-like power with two horns that plays a role in the last days of earth's history would represent a present-day Christian country, so it could certainly fit the United States with its Christian heritage. The two horns could stand for its democratic government and its religious freedom."

"So a superpower with a Christian tradition is going to give the lie to its profession and do the dragon's dirty work," suggested Rohan. "Maybe the author of that magazine article knows something."

Karl was unhappy with the way the conversation had steered. He said something about Revelation's prophecies only applying to the prophet's generation. Feeling sleepy from the wine, he retired to his tent and lay down. He tried to imagine what the apostle Paul was doing in heaven at that moment.

Evan was relieved when Karl left the campfire, but the day's events still left him with two major problems to consider: how could he win Madeline, and how could he perfect his character enough to be ready for the imminent Second Coming.

Madeline and Ami were relaxing, eating the last of the cod. Ami noticed that Madeline was looking in Owen's direction. "I see you're keeping an eye on Owen," said Ami with a grin.

"Nothing better to look at."

"Except Evan. Now, he's something worth looking at," teased Ami. "Although he'd be relieved no one videotaped him at the waterfall this morning."

"Guess he just thought before he acted. He wasn't chickening out. He just realized he couldn't do much without a rope."

"I love that about you, Maddy, you always see the best side of people. Though it could land you in trouble if you don't see a man's weaknesses until it's too late—after you've married him."

"Don't worry, Ami. I'm a bit *too* cautious." She stood. "Looks like Owen's getting ready to go fishing. I might join him."

"At least Owen likes fishing as much as you do, not like poor old Evan."

"Maybe he's right. Though I hope there's fish in heaven. Maybe mango- or chocolate-flavored fish, with no feelings."

"Can I come fishing with you guys?" asked Ami.

"Then Basil will want to come and we won't have any peace."

"Hmm, that's a good point. Better put your perfume on," teased Ami.

Madeline on put a sweater and walked over to Owen's tent. "Mind if I come along?" she asked.

"I was going to ask you. Can you carry the guitar and fishing bag? I'll need free hands to catch bait."

"Looks like you're going to fish for a while. There's a rug in the bag."

"They bite better at night, and there's a big moon."

They followed the kangaroo track along the river till they came to a low grassy bank. Owen turned some old logs over along the way, grabbing any black crickets hiding underneath.

"They're better than grasshoppers," explained Owen.

"Yeah, they're a bit small for cod, but great for perch."

"Oh, you know a bit about fishin', Madeline?"

"Love it."

Owen peered into the water, making sure it was deep enough to fish in. While he baited the hooks, he thought about how he and Madeline shared similar interests that went beyond their common spiritual interest. They both liked fishing, country music, four-wheel drive vehicles, horses, and cats. Owen cast the bait close to some submerged logs, where he guessed the fish were most likely to be feeding, and leaned the fishing pole against a log. He sat on the rug next to Madeline, who was gazing at the mountains across the river, her pretty face enhanced by an expression of carefree enjoyment.

Owen had resolved that he would never get serious with a woman unless he had known her for quite some time. Now his resolve was weakening. There was a transparent openness and genuineness about Madeline that he respected. She seemed unaware of the loveliness of her delicate and subtle facial expressions. A gentle femininity shone unconsciously out of her lovely mannerisms, which matched her physical charms. Owen found the combination almost irresistible. He decided to ignore any lingering caution and take a chance. One way or another, he would let her know that evening how he felt about her.

Owen rested his back against a fallen tree. The sun had long disappeared over the tops of the mountains, leaving the valley in deep shadow. It was the time of day when birds and other creatures were feeding. Kookaburras and kingfishers darted to the water to catch fish, barely disturbing the glass-smooth surface. Little zebra finches danced fearlessly on the branches only feet from where they sat. The couple was totally alone in their ethereal waterside grove. It seemed as if nature was communicating with them through the quiet stillness.

"It's great how God's creatures come close when you keep still in a place like this," observed Owen. He picked up his guitar and quietly sang "How Great Thou Art" in his country style.

"Perfect words for this place with: 'lofty mountain grandeur' and 'birds singing sweetly in the trees.' Now I know how Eve must have felt in the cool of the evening in the garden of Eden—*before* she blew it, of course." Madeline laughed as she looked up at the climbing bright moon. "Owen, I've been thinking about something and I've made a decision today."

"Yeah?"

"A couple of weeks ago I was nursing Alice Beckett, an eighteen-year-old—a pretty girl, and talkative! Yakked to me for hours about her past.

She's a bit different—uneducated but searching—can only just read. She tried to overdose. That's why she was in hospital."

"Poor kid."

"She told me the weirdest story. Her parents had raised her on a pig farm in a remote area of western NSW. They're kind of hillbilly fanatics, with extreme views about society, who see the government and the churches as their enemy. They're ignorant and poor, and her father beat her when she was a teenager."

"They homeschooled her, I suppose?" asked Owen as he looked around to see what caused some movement in the water.

"They didn't school her at all. She either worked hard on the farm or roamed about with a gun and her two wild brothers."

"Is she a believer?"

"Sort of. She likes Christians. She's cute—she's got the enthusiasm and mannerisms of a twelve-year-old."

"What's her mum like?"

"She's had a few men in her life, and she's not married to Alice's father. I don't think she can read. Didn't know how to look after kids either."

"It's hard to believe people live like that.."

Madeline watched a cloud drift across the moon. "She sees me as her best friend now. That's why I've had to do some hard thinking. I've decided to take her home with me."

"For a few weeks?"

"For as long as she needs. She can't go to her parents."

"That's a big commitment. But I think it's great."

"It won't be easy. She's a bit of a mess and wears me out trying to keep up with her thinking processes."

Madeline shifted closer to Owen. "I wasn't going to take her home, but you made me change my mind."

"I did?"

"When you were away I became confused. Evan talked about having to become perfect, but I felt far from perfect. I didn't know if I was still on Christ's side or not. I was getting really worried, and the depression started to come back, and I was thinking about myself all the time. I was in a state where I couldn't possibly have helped anyone like Alice. But when we were driving here, you convinced me that I was already perfect—perfectly forgiven and right with God. Now I can think about helping other people again."

Madeline began to speak more slowly and gently. "You reminded me about Jesus when I lost sight of him. You brought me back to him when no one else could get through to me."

Madeline took Owen's hands in hers, looked at him with moist eyes, and kissed him on both cheeks. "Thank you so much," she quietly said.

Owen noticed the fishing line moving, but ignored it. "I noticed you haven't been wearing any makeup," he said.

"And I noticed you haven't shaved." She laughed.

"A beautiful woman like you wearin' makeup is like tryin' to improve a rose by paintin' it."

"You're very sweet."

Owen picked up his guitar. "Wanna hear a great song?"

"OK."

Owen sung the sweet ballad "And I Love You So." His lighthearted tone become serious as the song progressed. From the way he looked at Madeline, she could tell he was describing his feelings for her.

"That's an incredibly beautiful song. Do you think it's got a hidden meaning ... about God's love?"

Owen gently put his arms around Madeline and kissed her tenderly. She melted in his arms.

Owen saw Madeline's lovely warm smile in the moonlight.

"I don't think I've ever been kissed before by someone who really cares about me," said Madeline.

"You know I love you, don't you, Madeline?"

"Have you known me long enough to be sure?"

"I can't imagine lovin' anyone like I love you. I didn't know I *could* love someone so much. It might be too fast, but for what it's worth, that's the truth."

"It's a real honor, Owen. Thanks. I trust and admire you very much."

Madeline loved Owen but couldn't say she was in love with him. Even though he was a few years older than she, she could evaluate things more logically and less emotionally.

After they had talked for some time, Owen said, "I guess we'd better join the others." He wound in his fishing line, wondering how many fish he might have caught if he had paid attention to his fishing. He guided Madeline back to camp in the semi-darkness. He made another campfire near his tent, and he and Madeline talked for hours as the moon brightened overhead, sending silver reflections onto the sparkling river rapids.

Ami could see that were preoccupied with one other, so she left them alone.

The rest of the campers were all talking and laughing around the campfire—except for Evan, who felt distressed and cheated. *I've come so close to winning Madeline. Am I losing her now? I've spent so much effort in winning her and teaching her biblical truth, and now this liberal is stealing her affections with his worldly music and the unnatural excitement of fishing.*

As he glumly stared at the campfire coals, he prayed fervently that God would give him Madeline and protect her from Owen's liberal ideas.

10

Deluge

◇◇◇◇◇◇◇◇◇◇◇

EVAN SLEPT ON THE GROUND near his vehicle, unaware of the darkening, turbulent clouds overhead. When a raindrop fell on his face, he suddenly sat up. He looked at his watch. It was 5:45, but the darkness of the surrounding mountains made it seem much earlier. As he crawled into his cramped Subaru for shelter, it started to rain steadily, and by the time he was secure in his sleeping bag, it was coming down in torrents. While he lay there waiting for the rain to stop, he lifted his thoughts to God.

I thank thee, O God, that thou hast protected your servant from living foolishly and sinfully like so many other church members, and I ask you for strength to overcome the last remaining vestiges of my carnal nature. Keep Madeline safe until, if it's thy will, she becomes my wife. Lord, thou knowest that I would not have come to camp among the tares and goats except I have come to deliver your daughter Madeline from the subtleties of Owen Boyd and Karl Fletcher. Please purify me from any liberal influences that I may have unwittingly succumbed to while here. And please stop the rain.

The torrent of rain continued. The seriousness of their situation dawned on Evan and he scrambled out of his vehicle and called out, "Wake up! It's raining and the river's up its banks. We'll be flooded!" He threw a raincoat over his head and ran around to every tent, shaking them as he yelled his warning.

"Go back to sleep, Noah," Basil called back. "There's still 119 years left before the flood!"

Evan ran to Madeline and Ami, who were peering out from under the tent flap in dismay. "The water's over the banks, and we've only got a few minutes to shift to higher ground," he warned.

"We may as well pack up and go home," said Ami. "That rain doesn't look like it's going to stop anytime soon."

"We can't go home," said Evan. "The river's too deep to cross, and it's the only way out of the valley."

"What?" Madeline scowled. "We could be here for days!"

"Just start collecting your gear," directed Evan. "We can put your stuff in my car and get your tent up on that high ground."

As the deluge continued, everyone shifted to higher ground, huddling and shivering in their wet tents. Pastor Sam suspended a thirty-foot tarpaulin between some trees. By saturating firewood with diesel fuel, he lit a fire under the highest edge of the tarp so the smoke could escape without damaging the tarp. Before long, all the campers were gratefully drying themselves by the fire, which lifted their spirits remarkably.

As the rain continued, Pastor Karl explained why he believed the flood of Noah was not a worldwide flood but was restricted to the Mesopotamian valley. His views created a debate on how the Bible should be interpreted, and Evan retired to his Subaru, upset.

After finishing his lesson, Karl made an announcement to the campers. "Even if the rain stopped now, it could take two days before the river drops enough for us to drive across. Most of us only brought enough food to last till this evening. This means we will have to ration our food somewhat."

One of the high school boys spoke up. "I saw some wild quince trees down the river, but their fruit is only half grown."

"We could boil them with sugar," suggested Mary Kent.

"I should be able to catch some fish," said Owen. "They still bite in muddy water."

Evan, who had returned, said, "The Lord will provide. We won't have to displease him by eating his creatures."

Basil bowed toward Evan and said sarcastically, "Let us hear and obey the wise words of the prophet, and the dainties of heaven shall be ours."

"Drop it, Basil," whispered Ami. "Don't push him too far."

After breakfast, Madeline and Owen sat close together by the fire.

"I'm going to go looking for bush tucker," said Evan, "so don't worry if I'm not back for a while."

"Maybe you should wait till it stops raining," cautioned Ami.

"I've got nothing better to do," replied Evan, buttoning up his raincoat and striding off with his soggy felt hat pulled down over his eyes.

While crossing a small clearing, he came across a patch of wild raspberries and filled two small plastic bags. As he hiked back, he decided to keep the berries for himself. Berries, although sweet, had a low glycemic index, which suited diabetics because they released sugar into the system slowly.

When he reached the campsite, Evan collapsed into his cramped Subaru and rested, feeling unwell. He ate a few more berries and stored the rest under the car seat.

That afternoon the clouds cleared and the campers hung out damp clothes and blankets to dry around huge fires. They relaxed in the sunshine once more and drank hot drinks to quell their hunger pangs. Pastor Sam talked to the group on the subject of Christian family life. He concluded by saying, "A loving Christian family is a more powerful witness for Christ than any sermon."

While Sam was speaking, Basil was thinking about his childhood. His religious father had been an alcoholic, and Basil remembered his verbal abuse and violent outbursts. He remembered the smashed furniture, the fear, and the poverty. "From my experience," Basil said with a touch of bitterness, "some of the worst abuse and behavior comes from Christian homes. You're better off being raised by atheists who don't believe all this bull about God and who don't torment their kids with outdated standards and impossible ideals."

Evan became indignant. "Listen, mate! You knew we were Christians when you decided to come here. You didn't have to come. Who do you think you are? If you were a Christian, you wouldn't be in the mess you're in."

Basil's reply was swift. "What's the matter, Noah? Are you upset because I didn't drown in your flood? Where were you today while people were struggling to help each other under this miserable tarp in the rain? Been hiding up on Mount Ararat, escaping the rising waters?"

Ami leaned over and whispered, "Basil, you smell of whisky and something else. Have you been smoking dope?"

"So what?" Basil said loudly. "God made the herbs for the healing of man, and wine to make the heart merry. Would you like a smoke and a snort, Evan? You look pretty sad."

Evan was furious. "I wouldn't touch your devil's brew. If I did I might turn into an idiot like you!"

"You're right, Basil," said Owen calmly, shifting his chair to avoid the smoke. "Religious parents with no love in their hearts really hurt their kids."

"My old man was just like that. And Noah over there reminds me of him. The old mongrel used to lock me in my room if he thought I was making too much noise on church days, while he drank grog and gave

Mum a hard time. I'll be glad when old mudguts kicks the bucket."

"We won't treat you like that, Basil. You can come and visit me anytime. And if you ever need a hand with anythin', just sing out."

"Thanks, mate. You're a good bloke, like Ami. Would you like a joint?"

"How about we have Milo instead?"

"Yeah, I'll have one of them. Sure you won't have a drop of the good oil too?"

"No thanks."

"I don't think Evan would be easy to live with," Ami whispered to Madeline, who smiled knowingly.

"That's for sure," replied Madeline. "But he's had a hard day, and he's a diabetic, which can make anyone a bit wonky. I guess that was just his way of trying to stick up for the truth in front of the kids."

"Maddy, I'm glad I live with you," said Ami. "You don't seem to see my faults either."

The following morning, the river level had dropped sufficiently to allow four-wheel drive vehicles to cross, and the campers were able to leave. Madeline went with Owen, while Evan drove home alone.

11

The Miracle Retreat

◇◇◇◇◇◇◇◇◇◇◇◇◇◇◇◇◇◇◇◇◇◇◇◇◇◇◇◇◇◇◇◇

A LTHOUGH MAHOMMET AZIZ WAS TIRED from his long journey over the
rugged, steep terrain, there were moments when he felt like skipping
with joy at the good news he was bringing Ayman Atef. Atef was the world's
most wanted terrorist and was leader of the notorious Al Mugninyah
organization. For years he had been hiding out in the isolated mountains
of northwest Pakistan, waiting for an opportunity to strike his most deadly
blow yet against the United States. His organization had been formulating
a plan to destroy much of Washington and the White House with it.

As Aziz approached Atef's cave, his pace quickened with excitement.
Calling out the designated password, he was immediately met by two of
Atef's guards and ushered to the cave entrance. On seeing Atef, Aziz ran
and embraced him then fell prostrate to the ground out of deep respect.

"Brother Atef," he said excitedly, "I bear good news. All is ready for
Washington. Allah's nuclear instrument of destruction has been smuggled
successfully into the United States, and our men have possession of it,
waiting for your—"

"Praise Allah!" exclaimed Atef loudly. Without waiting to hear more
he retreated to a dark corner at the rear of the cave, where he fell prostrate
to the ground and wept as he prayed. "I praise you, oh mighty one.
Your right hand has helped your servant Ayman to be your instrument
of vengeance on your enemy the Americans. For years you have brought
together many agencies to bring about this desired end. You have given
inspired men knowledge to manufacture this bomb and have given courage
to those willing to sacrifice their lives in honor. You have hid your servant
in your mountains so that they could not find me. Now I beg you, let me
live long enough to see Washington and the White House destroyed. May
your name be vindicated and justice carried out."

As Atef left the cave, he embraced his messenger once more. "Now the 'Great Satan,' America, will pay for its alliance to our enemies and for sending its soldiers to trample the holy ground of our motherland. Allah is a miracle-working God. I saw in a dream last night that he will soon work mighty miracles to defend his cause—not just the miracle of the nuclear bomb, but other miracles of a mysterious nature."

"When will the great day of vengeance arrive?" questioned Aziz.

"It will take two or three months to finalize plans, but meanwhile we will attack in a smaller way," replied Atef wistfully.

"Oh, brother Atef, we have lived for this day," exclaimed Aziz. "We have lived for the day when the smoke of American destruction shall ascend to the heavens as a sweet-smelling offering to Allah. Now the world shall see that Allah is on our side. May the miracles of which you dreamed come true. May Allah's miracles put terror into the hearts of his enemies."

As Atef lay down that night, he expressed his conflicting thoughts to Aziz. "You know, Mahommet, I have been very excited at our success in smuggling the nuclear bomb into America. Millions of our enemies will die. But some of them will be worshippers of Allah, and no doubt some others are just ignorant sheep. I pray that the generous and loving Allah will help me stop thinking of them. I must confess that for months now I have been asking myself if there is a better way. Does this surprise you?"

"No, Ayman. I must confess that I have at times been troubled about the same thing. But we must remember that we are destroying the Great Satan for the furtherance of Allah's work on earth. Long-lasting peace and a true worldwide faith can only be built on the foundation of the deaths of our enemies—even if this means the suffering of some innocent ones. In paradise they will be regarded as martyrs."

"Thank you for your faithful and comforting words, Mahommet. I shall sleep better now. Death to our enemies and glory to Allah."

The healings that occurred under the ministry of American evangelist and healer Pastor Desmond Piona became increasingly spectacular, and his fame spread internationally. During the same period, Dr. Ian Felberg became famous as a Christian prophet, and his spiritual insights and predictions were recorded in a best-selling book. Both men were using their influence to promote the Christian Power Movement and an international union of churches. It was advertised nationwide that Desmond Piona and Ian Felberg were meeting for a special TV interview. Piona would interview Felberg regarding his recent sensational vision, which reportedly would affect the future of the citizens of the United States and other countries.

At the scheduled time, Piona commenced the interview with several broadcast cameras aimed at him. "Welcome, Dr. Ian Felberg. It is indeed a pleasure to have you here with us this afternoon. I am speaking on behalf of countless Christians across the world, I'm sure, when I say thank you for your Christ-centered ministry, which has affected the lives of all of us."

"Thank you, Desmond. It is an honor to be here with you. All glory and praise be to God for giving his prophetic light to his people."

"Brother Ian, would you briefly describe how you first realized God's intention to use you as a last-day prophet?"

"It began some years ago. One night I was at home praying, when a sense of the suffering and confusion of God's people seemed to crush me, and I was overwhelmed with concern and pity for them. Suddenly, I could see right into the throne room of heaven, where sat the Father and the Son with veiled glory. Jesus then stood and spoke to me, saying, 'I have appointed you to give special messages to my people to prepare them for my coming. I will give you many visions, which you are to convey faithfully, no matter what suffering comes to you as a result.' I dropped face-down to the ground and pleaded with Jesus to send someone more capable and worthy than me. Then the Father stood, saying, 'Go, and you will receive all the help you will need. If you stay faithful till the end, you will receive the crown of life as your reward.'"

"Praise God!" exclaimed Piona. "The rest is history. Your many visions have been a source of inspiration and enlightenment to us. As you know, millions of Christians are with us in spirit right now, anxiously waiting to hear the most recent and apparently most important message that you have for us. Could you please tell us about it?"

"Certainly, Desmond. I would like to begin by saying that the vision concerns your ministry."

"Mine?"

"Yes. The Lord has seen your humble faithfulness in bringing miraculous healings to so many. He has shown me that through your gift he will do a work on this earth such as people have not even dreamed of. In thirty days' time, God is going to work miracles through you that will shake the very foundations of people's beliefs around the world, and prepare them for the return of Christ. The assigned meeting place for prayer will be in the Arizona desert."

On hearing these words, Piona dropped from his chair onto his knees. He seemed to be drained of strength. A camera focused on his trembling hands.

"I ... I too have had a vision," he said feebly as he looked up. "It is the only vision I have ever had. Last night I also saw the Lord, and he revealed to me the same message he revealed to you. As you said, the miracles are to begin in thirty days' time—the first of September. There will be three days of miracles. At the time of the vision, my wife and I were praying on our knees, and she told me later that I suddenly looked toward heaven as if in a trance. My eyes seemed to be fixed on a distant, glorious object. She waved her hand in front of my eyes, but I did not blink. I was in that state for ten minutes before I became conscious of my home surroundings again."

Piona gathered his strength and composed himself as he sat back. "Ian, tell your viewers more about what the miracles will achieve," he eagerly requested.

"Because the final miracle will be of a stupendous nature, even the most skeptical will confess to its genuineness. Millions will become believers for the first time. God's great desire is to bring all peoples of earth to a belief in his sovereignty. He wants all religions to cooperate in a special peace plan for the world under the auspices of a special governing body."

After a series of more questions, the interview concluded. "Thank you, Ian," said Piona. "I shall look forward to being with you on that great occasion. And I trust that the world will be tuned in on that great day."

Pastor Karl Fletcher stayed up late to view and tape the anticipated Piona-Felberg interview on his cable television. He could hardly contain his excitement as he played the video to his congregation at church. Afterward, noting that Evan was absent, he preached unrestrainedly about the visions of Ian Felberg and the anticipated miracle. He reminded the congregation that the message he had received from the apostle Paul included a prophecy of the arrival of an era of miracles that would change the world. Inspector Adrian Sebastian and Simon Hawkins stood and applauded, believing more than ever that the day of deliverance had almost arrived.

Pastor Sam and his wife, Joan, invited friends home for lunch that day, including Basil, Madeline, Owen, and Ami. Basil had come to Sam's church for the first time. After they were welcomed into the Edwards's living room, they were in no mood for small talk.

"What did you guys think about today's message?" asked Sam.

"Piona and Felberg have really stuck their necks out," said Owen. "If their predictions don't come true, they may as well pack their bags and join the dole queue. But if there's a miracle it would want to be a beauty."

"It reminds me of Elijah's challenge to the Baal worshippers on Mount Carmel," said Ami. "Elijah laid everything on the line and God rewarded him with fire from heaven. What if Piona gets a miracle of fire? Wouldn't it have to be from God?"

"No, it's different now," said Sam. "Satan has thousands of years' experience behind him to counterfeit God's fire from heaven."

"Would God allow Satan to counterfeit a sign that he once used himself?" asked Ami.

"According to Revelation chapter 13, he does," replied Sam.

In appreciation of the dramatic buildup, Basil slapped his hands rapidly on the couch's armrest, his wiry, tattooed arms conspicuous. "Those miracle guys either suffer from bipolar delusions of grandeur, or they'll rake in millions for TV rights and grow beards for disguise and retire filthy rich in another country. But one thing's for sure, there'll be no real miracles. A lot of people are going to be either greatly entertained and remain atheists, or become bitterly disillusioned Christians."

"There could be real miracles all right" said Sam, making himself comfortable on a bean bag, "but what worries me is that if the miracles do happen, atheists will believe, but for the wrong reasons."

"But if millions become believers, then that's good, isn't it?" said Madeline, letting go of Owen's hand to gesture her point.

"Not necessarily," said Sam. "Remember when the Pharisees asked Jesus for a miracle to prove his divinity, he refused to do it; he even said that a wicked generation looks for signs. The kind of faith that God appreciates is based on his loving character, not in some kind of miracle-working genie."

"Yeah, the miracle will happen all right," said Owen. "There are too many things pointin' to it. There's the supportin' visions of Piona and Feldberg, and there's Karl's spooky visitor who predicted super miracles too. For some time now there's been a buildup of healings by guys like Piona and Ron Noble, who healed Evan's dad. It's all been buildin' up, so I reckon somethin's gonna happen. The problem is the effect it's gonna have."

"So you really think that Simon Hawkins's healing was genuine?" asked Basil with an incredulous expression as he scratched his nose ring.

"No doubt it was real," said Owen. "But was it from God? Seems Evan did quite a bit of studyin' up on Noble and found he's a bit dodgy. But because people get healed, they believe what he teaches—stuff like love's in, but the commandments are a thing of the past. Can you imagine what would happen to a lawyer who said as long as we love each other it's OK to break the law of the land?"

"That's the Isaiah 8:20 test," suggested Sam. "It says something like, 'If they don't speak according to God's word, it's because there's no light in them.' "

"Why would God work a miracle through a fraud?" asked Madeline.

"He wouldn't," said Owen, "but the devil would. Remember, Jesus warned us about workers of sin who do miracles in Jesus' name, yet he doesn't even know 'em."

"This is all a bit mind blowing for me," said Basil. "I reckon I'll just sit back and see what happens. When is it supposed to be?"

"September 1, the first day of our spring or of America's autumn," said Ami. "That should be easy to remember."

"Normally I believe in supporting a senior minister," said Sam, "but I think Karl's gone too far in promoting this miracle thing. He hasn't approached it biblically. He should have opened God's Word and analyzed it from every angle first. It's dangerous to put supernatural phenomenon ahead of God's Word."

Madeline had just finished her night shift at the hospital and was glad to take her shoes off when she got home at 6:20 a.m. Her mind was still far too active to sleep, so she made herself a hot chamomile drink and turned the TV on to relax and unwind. As the picture sharpened, Madeline saw a man stumbling out from a wall of smoke, screaming for help. Except for a partly burnt torn shirt and one shoe, he was naked. He was grasping a small briefcase under one arm, and his other arm was dangling loosely by his side. People were running about, disoriented and shouting, but the camera remained focused on the naked man. He collapsed on the street, spilling money from his satchel as he hit the ground. He grabbed a few handfuls of notes and rolled over in agony, then managed to pull himself up and stumble out of sight behind a vehicle. The camera swung onto the burning and smoking chaos of what used to be an enormous building.

This is an incredibly realistic film. Or is it? It's too realistic—no, this is real footage of a war zone.

Then she heard the commentator. "You are watching a live broadcast of the devastation caused by an explosion that just ten minutes ago totally destroyed the Welcome Stranger Casino in Las Vegas. The explosion was so powerful that surrounding buildings were partially demolished by the blast. Little is known about the source or cause of the explosion, but it is certain that it was another terrorist attack. This is the third casino in the United States that has been blown up in the last thirty minutes, obviously due to an orchestrated assault. Heavy concentrations of police have been delegated to every remaining casino in the United States, and all casinos have been evacuated."

As Madeline watched in horrified astonishment, the cameras focused on dozens of bloodied and mangled bodies being lined up in the street. Those who were still alive were either being treated on the spot or loaded into ambulances. At times, the wind-driven smoke hid the scene from the cameras.

"It is unknown how many casualties there are from all three bombings," continued the reporter. "Estimates vary from four to nine thousand. We repeat, authorities believe this could only have been a coordinated terrorist attack. Further strikes are quite possible, and the country is on the highest terrorist alert."

Madeline had already seen enough blood and suffering at the hospital that night, so she turned the TV off. She was too upset to sleep, so she showered and had breakfast.

When Ami woke up and heard what had happened, she turned the TV on to hear the last part of US President Howard Foreman's address. "Because of today's terrorist attacks in our country, and the increase of these murderous attacks across the world, more drastic and aggressive steps need to be taken by our government to protect our citizens. Some may see these steps as restrictions on our freedom, but they are necessary for national security. Urgent negotiations will be made by this government, with political and religious leaders the world over, to lay plans for a concerted and revolutionary strategy against global terrorism."

Mr. President," a reporter called out, "could you tell us what the focus of these negotiations will be? How will non-Christian spiritual leaders be persuaded to join forces with what they may consider infidel religions?"

"While it may be difficult to see how that kind of cooperation can develop," said Foreman, "I believe that future events will prove to be a persuasive power in the formation of spiritual and political unity. That's all for today. Thank you."

Ami stretched, yawned, and stopped at the bathroom door as a thought came to mind. "Maddy, what's Foreman got in mind when he talks about 'future events'? Does he know something we don't?"

"I don't think he's just talking from a gut feeling," said Madeline. "Owen was saying that Foreman and his crew have been consulting with Catholic and evangelical leaders toward some united strategy."

"We are living in awesome times," said Ami. "Things are moving so fast, you wonder what's going to happen next. It's all a bit confusing."

On the first of September, more than sixty thousand people were camped in a desert basin well outside Phoenix, Arizona. Tens of thousands more commuted each day from the city to the advertised "Miracle Retreat," where a giant platform had been built for the occasion. The retreat was being viewed by hundreds of millions around the world. Interpreters were organized to translate proceedings into various languages through satellite TV. Special air-conditioned mobile units were brought in to house the sick who hoped to be healed.

There was an air of expectancy when, after a session of preaching and music, the acclaimed prophet Dr. Ian Feldberg took the stage.

"The reason this convention has been spread over three days is that the Lord revealed to me that there will be three days of miracles," he said. "The Lord wants me to emphasize that it is he, not Pastor Desmond Piona, who must receive the glory. I want to thank you for coming and for putting the confidence in the Lord that he deserves. Indeed this is a fulfillment of the prophecy recorded in Acts chapter 2. 'In the last days … your young men shall see visions, and your old men will dream dreams. … I will show wonders in the heavens above and signs on the earth below.' Christian friends, I welcome Pastor Desmond Piona to the platform."

The crowd applauded as Piona walked onto the stage, smiling at the ocean of faces. "Let it be known that today is the day of healing," he said dramatically. "We will not only pray for the infirm who are here with us today, but we have invited spiritual and political leaders of all nations to forward special requests for healing of their loved ones back home. I have here a few of the requests made by dignitaries who have a big enough need and faith for their prayer requests to be made public. Among them is a request from Archbishop Clive Jones from Canada, whose son has been in a wheelchair for two years since a motorcycle accident. Mr. Vernon Turnbull, Prime Minister of Australia, has requested healing for his brother John, who has liver cancer. Bishop Samson Mgundo of Tunisia seeks healing for his daughter, who suffers from epilepsy. The prime minister of Iran, who is, by the way, a Muslim, has requested prayer for his wife, who is terminally ill with cancer. Praise the Lord for their requests! What do you say?"

A mighty roar came from the crowd.

Ami, Madeline, Basil, and Owen were watching the Miracle Retreat live on TV. Alice Beckett, whom Madeline had taken into her home, was with them.

"Get a load of the size of that crowd," Owen said, then gulped some coffee to keep him alert, as it was well after midnight in Australia. "It'd put a football stadium full of fans to shame."

"Some of those sick ones look like they're on their last legs," said

Madeline. "This will be a real test."

"Yeah, but provin' what?" said Owen. "That it's a healin'? Maybe. But who's doin' the healin', God or the devil?" "We've gotta test miracles by the teachin' and the fruit."

☞

"I can feel the power of the Lord," proclaimed Piona as he walked up and down the platform with his arms outstretched. "The gift of healing is with us today such as I have never felt it before."

Feldberg jumped out of his seat, grabbed a microphone, and exclaimed, "Praise the Lord! I was shown that today God is going to heal many sick people of different faiths, Christian and non-Christian. This healing is to cross all denominational, religious, and cultural barriers. Praise God!"

Piona suddenly and aggressively gestured toward the choir behind him, and the singers collapsed backward like a pack of dominoes. "His power is so real!"

The choir members lay there blissfully, as if in a trance. "I can see the Lord," shouted one of them, pointed up. Piona ran to him, shoved the microphone near his mouth, and asked, "What was that?"

"I ... can see ... the Lord!" shouted the choir member once more.

"Where is he?" shouted Piona above the din of the appreciative crowd.

"He is in on his throne amidst the adoration of angels."

Dr. Feldberg sprang to his feet and grabbed a microphone. Pointing up, he appeared to be in ecstasy as he shouted, "I see him too. And there are large gaps in the assembly of the angels surrounding him in heaven. That's because they are here with us right now!"

The crowd roared its approval.

"I also see that the Lord is holding a bowl of his healing oil in one hand," continued Feldberg, "and the incense of his righteousness in the other. He is looking down on this assembly, about to heal."

Piona dropped to his knees and motioned for the crowd to be quiet. "It is now time to pray. As you can see, we have some of the infirm ones with us on the platform."

"Oh, Lord," prayed Piona as he stood with his arm outstretched up, "we thank you that the eyes of the whole world are upon you today. They are watching to see what the great God of the universe can do for his suffering children on earth. We do not presume to think that your children are confined within the walls of western Christianity. Stretch out your hand, O Lord, to heal the sick among those present, and also heal those loved ones whose names have been sent from other lands."

All eyes were riveted to the television at Madeline's place.

"Look at that guy on the far right of Piona," said Basil. "He's out of his wheelchair and jumping up and down."

"Talk about excitement!" said Madeline. "When people throw their walkers away, Piona touches them and they get knocked down again."

"Look at that guy," said Alice, pointing. "He looked half dead in the stretcher, but he got up and he's runnin' up and down the stairs. The crowd's gone berserk!"

"Can we be certain that it's real?" queried Basil. "Could they be planted, or fakes?"

"Nah," said Owen. "Medical inspections were done before the session. Look! That blind guy's leading his guide dog and runnin' through the crowd!"

"You mean he *was* blind," corrected Alice.

"It looks like Piona won't be joining the dole queue, Basil," said Madeline. "Maybe he'll get his fire from heaven after all."

After viewing the Miracle Retreat, Owen drove Madeline toward her place.

"How do you think Alice is comin' along?" he asked. "Do you think she's understandin' what the miracles are all about?"

"I think she's picking things up pretty good. Let's go this way." Madeline pointed toward the beach.

"What for?"

"I just want to forget about the miracles and dramas for a while and …spend a bit of time with you."

"I'll be in that."

Owen parked his vehicle toward the surf at Nobby's Beach. As he and Madeline walked hand in hand on the sand, in the moonlight, Owen looked at her and shook his head, grinning.

"What's the matter?" Madeline smiled.

"I've walked this beach a few times before, but tonight it's different. The squeakin' of the sand under our feet sounds like music."

"Oh, yeah? And why's that?"

"I'll give you three guesses."

12

Islam's Healing

◇◇◇◇◇◇◇◇◇◇◇◇◇◇◇◇◇◇◇◇◇◇◇◇

M OHOMED KAROUBI, THE PRESIDENT OF IRAN, sat by the bedside of
Shirin, his middle-aged wife, while their two young-adult children
were in the living room. All were watching the first day of the Miracle
Retreat on television. Mohomed was a devout Muslim who had a trusted
Christian friend with whom he had spent many hours discussing their
respective religious viewpoints. Through these discussions, Mohomed had
come to respect the Christian faith; however, he did not admit this to the
general public or to his political colleagues. His wife's cancer had spread,
so Mohomed had sent a desperate request for his wife's healing to Piona at
the prompting of his Christian friend.

Shirin was feeble and in pain as she lay in bed. Six months ago,
she had seemed healthy, though a little overweight. But then she began
to complain of intermittent pains in her abdominal region. These had
been misdiagnosed and passed off as due to minor ailments until a scan
revealed several cancerous regions. She deteriorated rapidly, losing weight.
Now, as she lay there, she looked the size of a child. She was expected to
die within weeks.

Shirin feebly propped herself up in bed a little higher, coughed, and
spoke slowly and feebly. "Mohomed, look how irreverently they worship;
they do not worship like we do. I do not think they can heal me, and your
political career will be ruined. All of Iran will think you betrayed your faith
by appealing to Christians. What will become of you?"

"My political career is not as important as having you with me, my
dear. I would rather retire with you by my side than lead the country
without you. But I am hopeful that you will get better. Our people know
you are very ill, and when you are healed, they will understand. I will
always stay a Muslim and would never convert to Christianity. I have only

requested prayer, and we both worship the same God of Abraham."

"But we have prayed to Abraham's God ourselves and I am still sick. If I am healed now, they will say it is through their Jesus."

"Yes, and maybe so. But Jesus is respected as a prophet by many of our people. If you are healed, you are healed. What can they say?"

"Soon now, they will call our name and pray. Mr. Piona is there now. Quick, help me to the toilet so I can get back in time and see what happens."

While Mohomed was helping Shirin back from the toilet, she paused and grabbed her husband's arm tightly as her whole body trembled. "I can feel great warmth of current going through my body. I feel as if something is surging within me. It feels like a deep massage. Oh, Mohomed, something is happening to me!"

"Let me help you into bed."

"No, wait! Can't you feel something is happening?"

"Yes, you are trembling all over."

"I can feel deep pressure within me. It is not hurting. Something … someone is at work, massaging and … I can't explain it."

The TV caught Shirin's attention. Pointing to it, she sat down on a chair. "What is the crowd screaming about?" she asked. "Look! That man has left his wheel chair and is jumping up the stairs!"

"Truly amazing," exclaimed Mohomed.

"Oh, I am feeling stronger!"

"Your voice is stronger."

"Don't help me. Look! I can stand up by myself."

"Oh, Shirin! I'll call the children and tell them. They—"

"No, wait. It's too early to—"

"Here comes Abbas."

Their son came into the bedroom, wide eyed and excited. "Have you seen what is—Mother! What are you doing out of bed?"

"I am feeling … something is happening!"

Maisun, their daughter, walked in. "Mother, what—?"

"I don't know. I'm feeling stronger … more energy. The pain is much less. No, it's gone!"

Shirin stood and embraced her daughter, then walked to the living room without any help.

"You are going to be all right, then, Mother?" asked Abbas.

"I think so. Yes." She wept and accepted her son's arms. All four of them huddled in an embrace, weeping.

"I am getting hungry," exclaimed Shirin, surprised.

"Hungry? You haven't been hungry for weeks! Praise be to God. You *must* be healed."

ᥴᣯ

Early on day two of the Miracle Retreat, Pastor Piona made an announcement. "Friends of God from all around the world, it is with great joy that I want to show you something on the big screen. Yesterday we prayed for Shirin, the wife of Mohomed Karoubi, the President of Iran. You want to know the results, I'm sure. I'll let Mrs. Karoubi speak for herself."

Shirin appeared on the big screen, formally dressed, smiling and standing without any help. Beside her stood her family and her doctor. The doctor introduced himself and said, "Yesterday, I was called to the Karoubi home and was astonished to see Mrs. Karoubi on her feet and markedly improved. Hospital scans showed that the recent large tumors in her internal organs have all disappeared. I can give no other explanation than that it was a miracle, which must have taken place yesterday."

With a beaming smile, Shirin spoke. "At the exact time that Mr. Desmond Piona prayed, I felt an incredible energy and warmth working inside me, and I felt my strength return. The pain left me and I became hungry for the first time in weeks. I thank God that he has given me my life back again."

The crowd's roar of applause was overwhelming, but quickly hushed when Mohomed Karoubi began to speak. "I would like to thank God and acknowledge that it was he who healed my wife yesterday. She was failing fast and beyond human help, so we were desperate. It was our last hope. Although we shall always be faithful Muslims, we have to acknowledge that God chose to work through the Miracle Retreat. I hope this shall be an effective means of creating better understanding and cooperation between people of all faiths."

The swelling crowd thundered their applause, which echoed off the range that circled the sea of faces.

As Karl Fletcher watched Karoubi's testimony at home, he stood in front of his TV and clapped along with the crowd. "History is being made today, Frieda. The world is watching what the God of the Christians ... of all religions can do. Millions of Muslims must be watching this. It's going to break down a lot of prejudice on both sides."

"Karl, my mind boggles just trying to understand the consequences of it all. Look at those demonstrators in the crowd, lifting that big placard. What's it say? 'I never knew you. Away from me, you evildoers! Mathew 7:23.' You wouldn't think they'd find anything to be unhappy about, would you?"

"We've got them in our church too."

Some in the crowd tore the picket signs in pieces and began to beat the protestors with the fractured timbers while many in the crowd cheered. Police quickly moved in and restored order, but several people were carried off on stretchers.

Evan watched the Miracle Retreat in the hostel's recreation room. When he saw the violence, he grabbed the cleaner, who was walking past, by the arm and pointed at the TV. "See that? That's what they are going to do to us—try to tear us to pieces."

"What in the world are you talking about?" muttered the cleaner as he walked away without waiting for an answer.

Evan ran down the stairs to the parking lot, threw a large towel in the back of his Subaru, and drove to an after-hours firearms dealer. He pressed a buzzer. The dealer warily inspected Evan through his double-barred shop entrance, then let him in. Evan surveyed the confusing array of guns on the walls.

"Can I help you, mate?" asked the salesman.

"I don't see what I'm looking for," said Evan.

"And what's that?"

"I don't see any automatic military weapons."

"Well, mate, you're too late. The automatics were banned ages ago. You been hiding in a cave or somthin'?" He grinned.

Evan looked at him in confused silence.

"What did you want one for anyway? Shootin' pigs? Crocs?"

"Uh, yes. Pigs and crocs."

"Ya headin' up north, then?"

"Uh, no. Not crocs. Just pigs—this year."

"Ah, mystery shooter, are ya? You got a license?"

"Sure do."

"I'll bring some good pig guns down for ya. What property 'ave ya got permission to shoot on?"

"My own, up in the Wattagans."

"Mate, there aren't any pigs up in the Wattagans."

Evan said nothing.

"Ya might get a few 'roos, but don't shoot any wombats or you'll be in strife. Now, here's a good .273 Remington for $950."

"Have you got anything cheaper with telescopic sights?"

"How much do ya want to spend?"

"Oh, up to a few hundred."

"Well, that only leaves ya with this old sports model .303 for $395."

"Will that kill large animals?"

"They were designed to kill people, mate. They're military."

"That will do me, then. And I'll take five hundred rounds of ammo."

"Five hundred? You off to war or somethin', mate?"

"The only war I'm in is spiritual," said Evan.

"Well, don't go shootin' any ghosts. They're protected." the salesman laughed.

Having satisfied his need for a resolute decision regarding his future security, Evan hurried back to watch the rest of the day's Miracle Retreat activities.

Piona was greatly emboldened by the miracles that had occurred so far. He called Ian Feldberg to the front of the platform. "Dr. Feldberg, could you please tell the audience about the vision you described to me this morning?"

"Thank you, Pastor Piona. I saw in my night vision a drought-stricken Muslim nation. Its people had been starving, dying of illness for years. Prayer was made on their behalf, and the God of all peoples sent rain, just like he did in Elijah's day. The parched earth was replenished, and much food grew. Many people were turned to the unity of all religions. I saw that religious leaders will put aside their differences and join hands, and God will pour out his Spirit on all flesh. "

"Thank you, Dr Feldberg. The world has seen the ravaging effects of the drought in Gambia. But before we pray, the choir will lead out in a song of faith, just like they did in Joshua's time, when praise brought down the walls of Jericho. Today the walls of drought will break down and allow the rain to gush in. We praise our God of all faiths in advance for his miracle, and he will honor our faith. "

After the choir led out in a triumphant song of thanks for answered prayer, Piona prayed specifically for the rain to fall in drought-stricken Gambia that very day, so that many lives would be spared. He prayed that this would draw the attention of non-Christian believers to God's great plan for spiritual cooperation under a common worldwide leadership.

It was late at night at Pastor Sam's home, and a few visitors had fallen asleep while waiting for the highlight of day two of the Miracle Retreat.

When Sam saw Piona call Feldberg to the microphone, he woke those who slept.

"Can you believe it?" said his wife, Joan. "He's expecting rain in a country that's been in a severe drought for three years now."

"The big dust storms shifted the topsoil across the country," said Owen, who had only just arrived after singing at a club. "People are droppin' like flies from the filthy, disease-ridden water. It makes the drought around Dad's property seem tame by comparison."

Madeline, who was still feeling tired from the afternoon shift at the hospital, sat up on the couch, trying to keep alert. "Has Satan got the power to make it rain, then?" she asked.

"Even scientists can make it rain to some extent," said Joan.

"Yes, but they need clouds to start with," replied Madeline. "And I don't think there are many clouds in Gambia right now."

"Remember the plagues of Egypt?" said Sam. "Satan gave Pharaoh's magicians power to make plagues of flies and blood, so rain-making should be within his reach too."

"But why would Satan want to send rain if he hates people?" asked Ami. "He likes to see people starve and die."

"He's the great deceiver," said Sam. "He's willing to do good in the short term if he can deceive people in the long term." He opened his Bible. "Ephesians 6:12 says, 'For our struggle is not against flesh and blood, but against the rulers, against the authorities, against the powers of this dark world and against the spiritual forces of evil in the heavenly realms.'"

"The programs switched to Gambia," Joan alerted, pointing at the TV. "And you can't see a cloud in the sky."

On the screen, a reporter was interviewing an Australian CSIRO scientist. "Dr. Rhoenfeldt," said the interviewer, "you've just seen the cloudless conditions in Gambia. Scientifically speaking, what would be the chances of creating rain in a country that has not seen rain in years?"

"With current technology, it's impossible to create rain on a nationwide scale. Any successful rain-making has been with silver iodide particles and is restricted to small areas and dependent on existing cloud."

"So if the drought were to break in Gambia in the next few hours, that would have to be a miracle?"

"If you're talking about nationwide drought-breaking rain, keep in mind that current satellite photos show very few cloud formations near Gambia, and it would take more than mere hours for them to develop. Put it this way: It would be outside the realms of scientific explanation."

"Thank you, Dr. Rhoenfeldt."

After waiting for another hour with no sign of even a small cloud, the visitors left Sam's place and went home. A few hours later, while it was still dark, Madeline woke from a restless sleep and turned on the TV. She saw a cloud-filled darkening sky in Gambia, and people were excitedly running through the streets of Banjul, the capital city. The screen flicked back to the Miracle Retreat, where behind the massive crowd the sunset was coloring the surrounding desert mountains with a reddish hue, while the choir sang "There Shall Be Showers of Blessing."

Piona looked exhausted from the long, exciting day. He picked up the microphone and said, "Tomorrow we will see the unprecedented power of God. You may wonder what kind of miracle the third day of miracles will bring. But the truth is, the Lord has not revealed it to us, except that it will be the most impressive miracle of all. We shall all find out in the morning, through the spirit of prophecy that is operating through Dr. Feldberg."

Next, the big screen showed some mud huts in Gambia. A mother was sitting outside her dwelling, smiling, and soothingly stroking the head of her young daughter, while brushing flies away from her face with her other hand. Both were pitifully thin and were the only survivors left in the family.

The woman was mesmerized by the sight of rain being channeled from a small sheet of plastic into a large earthen pot. Nearby some scarecrow-like children were feebly dancing about in the rain while their father lay prostrate in the mud with his arms outstretched in praise toward Allah.

Madeline went back to bed, wiping away tears. She was emotionally affected by the happiness of the Gambian mother, the exhaustion of the long night, and the spiritual warfare she found herself engaged in. She wondered why she had to face such conflict, change, and deception. Then she remembered how God had delivered her out of addiction and depression though Owen and others, and she felt comforted with the thought that she could leave her anxieties with her Lord. She drifted off into a peaceful sleep.

The phone woke her a few hours later. "Madeline, it's Evan."

"Haven't seen you for a while," she said groggily.

"Have you been watching the Miracle Retreat?"

"I've been trying to follow it. Amazing, isn't it?"

"How close we must be to the Lord's return. Madeline, so much has happened, and there's so much to talk about. Are you working on Thursday?"

"No."

"Are you free?"

"I'm not sure. I've—"

"I m going up to my mountain property, and I thought it might give us a chance to talk. We won't be there long."

Madeline had been undecided about making a break from Evan. She still found him attractive, but was growing fonder of Owen. Now she felt it was her duty to try to help him with his unbalanced ideas. "All right, Evan. It's a great drive and we can talk. I'd like to be back by lunchtime, though."

"Great. I'll pick you up around 8:30 Thursday morning."

13

The Dancing Opal
◇◇◇◇◇◇◇◇◇◇◇◇◇◇◇◇◇◇◇◇◇◇◇◇◇◇◇◇◇◇◇◇

THE MIRACLES OF THE DROUGHT-BREAKING RAIN in Gambia, and the healing of the first lady of Iran, made headline news around the world. It was a media bonanza. Religious and political leaders were interviewed for their analyses of the likely outcome of the miracles.

Pope Agapetus III was seen on the Miracle Retreat's giant screen. As usual, his eloquence was magnetic. "The breaking of the drought in Gambia is a miracle of peace. It is a sign to all people to put down their guns, dismantle their weapons of mass destruction, put away their religious prejudices, and pray for their spiritual leaders as they work toward a worldwide peace plan."

The Miracle Retreat crowd swelled to half a million from an influx of day visitors, and the nearby foothills were covered with spectators, some of whom had built small shrines. Scattered about on the fringes were uniformed and armed military personnel, who were supporting the police in case of a terrorist attack or an outbreak of violence. After a musical praise service, several religious leaders made speeches. They talked about how the miracles had opened their eyes to the need for cooperation in a world peace plan. One leader confessed with tears his previous prejudice against Muslims, but the Lord's solicitude in healing the first lady of Iran had changed his attitude. The crowd applauded when a Muslim leader spoke about his desire for a better understanding with Christians.

Dr. Ian Feldberg then spoke. "Fellow believers the world over— Christians, Jews, Muslims, or whatever faith you belong to. Last night I had a visitation from one who is respected by many of you as the father of your faith, none other than the patriarch Abraham himself."

Some people near the front jumped up and displayed a sign with the words, "Devil Worship!" But they were quickly hustled away by police for their own protection.

"He told me," Feldberg continued gravely, "that God had chosen him as his messenger for the occasion because he was the common father of Muslims, Jews, and Christians. His message to me was that it is time for a renewed faith in his God—the God of the New International Order. He said that the next miracle will be of such a startling nature that even the most skeptical person will not deny it. Abraham's eyes were moist as he related how his fatherly heart has been saddened by the centuries of religious conflicts, hatred, and bloodshed among his spiritual descendants. However, he was encouraged with the expectation of the fruitage of tonight's miracle."

The mountains echoed the tumultuous response of the massive crowd, which stretched out across the plains. A camera focused on several hundred protestors who were positioned on the foothills behind the main crowd, which was jeering them.

When the noise subsided, Feldberg continued. "I beg you for your patience. I have been shown that the miracle will take place shortly after sunset tonight. We will endeavor to provide an entertaining and profitable program for you till then."

Owen and Madeline watched day three of the Miracle Retreat at Madeline's place.

"Feldberg just said somethin' that should make every Bible student nervous," said Owen. "It's clear as a bell that those miracles are of the devil. He's even talkin' to the dead—somethin' the Bible speaks against—even if it is supposed to be Abraham he's talkin' to. He's really stuck his neck out by promotin' spiritualism because there are plenty of Christians out there who don't believe in it."

"Maybe they will now," suggested Madeline. "What do they do at spiritualism meetings anyhow?"

"Why are you grinning?"

"When you snuggle close to me like that, I have trouble concentratin' on this deep stuff."

"Sorry! I'll be good."

Owen's grin widened. "That's better. But only for a while. Spiritualists get messages from dead people—often relatives or famous people. But they're really evil angels impersonatin' them and teachin' lies."

"Do they actually see and recognize them?"

"Sometimes. That's why people fall for it."

"Where does it condemn spiritualism in the Bible?"

"It's in Leviticus, chapter 19 verse 31. 'Do not turn to mediums or seek out spiritists, for you will be defiled by them. I am the Lord your God.' "

"Pretty clear, eh?" said Owen. "And first Chronicles chapter 10 verse 13 comments on King Saul's sin of consulting the dead—it was serious enough for God to allow him to get killed."

"Makes you wonder how Christians can get sucked in so easily when the warnings are so plain in the Bible. Are there any other places where it's mentioned?"

"Yeah. King Hezekiah was called evil in second Kings 21 verse 6 because he sacrificed his own son in the fire and practiced spiritualism. And the apostle Paul predicted Satan's end-time delusions in second Thessalonians 2 verse 9: 'The coming of the lawless one will be in accordance with the work of Satan displayed in all kinds of counterfeit miracles, signs and wonders.' "

"Oh, boy!" Madeline sighed. "Then Satan's going to have a shot at deceiving the world tonight?"

"Do you realize that you just quoted scripture?" asked Owen.

Madeline looked at Owen quizzically.

"Look. Revelation chapter 14 verse 14: 'He deceived the inhabitants of the earth.'"

❦

The sun had behind the blazing ochre-tinted Arizona Mountains, framed by large, billowing, bright red clouds that contrasted with the deep blue of the sky. The glorious sunset and the old-style gospel music of the band combined their praise and encouraged the crowd to join in the singing.

When the sun had faded and the moonless sky became dark, Piona picked up the microphone. "When Elijah was on Mount Carmel, he asked God to reveal his miracle-working power as a sign that he was the true God. Suddenly fire from heaven devoured the altar, turning the hearts of his people back to God. Will God answer with fire tonight? We shall soon see."

Piona knelt and stretched out his hands toward the bright stars above. "O God of all religions and cultures, we thank you for your mighty healing hands and for your power over nature, which was exercised so compassionately yesterday. Tonight we ask for the final and greatest miracle—the sign of your own choosing, which shall turn the hearts of all mankind toward faith in your New International Order. We wait upon you."

As soon as Piona finished praying, he looked up and searched the night sky. Then he pointed up, shouting, "Look! It is the fire of God!"

The crowd saw only a small and distant glow at first. The powerful lenses of the TV cameras focused on the bright object, which, through digital enhancement, was projected onto the big screen, revealing a fiery glow of great beauty. The awed crowd saw the glowing object slowly advance to earth. It appeared to be a moving and dancing exchange of brilliant hues of red, yellow, blue, and purple.

Piona fell to his knees and exclaimed, "It is the symbol of Pentecostal power—a sign given by the God of Elijah and Abraham, the God of Mohammed and Buddha. May his children the world over open their hearts to his purposes!"

The mountains echoed the approving roar of the crowd. The fire drew closer until the crowd could see it plainly with the naked eye.

The TV commentator struggled to give a worthy description. "It is breathtaking in its beauty and resembles the constellation of Orion, with all its spectacular color, pattern, and motion, except it is much brighter and seems to be mixed with fire. It is like a beautiful black opal, alive with dancing colors."

Madeline and Owen sat transfixed. Deep questions posed themselves to Madeline. "That doesn't look like some cheap, low-level miracle like I expected from Satan. It seems to be coming from the depths of the universe."

"I wouldn't have predicted it'd be as spectacular as this either. Satan's really done a good job of it."

"They said it was from Orion. Is Satan allowed to go that far up?"

"Actually they didn't say it was *from* Orion, only from the *direction* of Orion. Remember, Satan is the prince of the power of the air."

"Owen, this is so real! Can you blame people for thinking it's all from God?"

"You're not havin' second thoughts, are you?"

"No. But it makes you think."

"Jesus said that even his true followers would be in danger of bein' deceived. I can see why now."

The fire descended, hovering and adding an ethereal glow to the desert, and the mountains reflected its changing glory. Beautiful, enchanting music from some invisible source matched the mystery of the changing colors of the fire, which danced above the desert.

As Pastor Karl watched the TV, he was too overcome to speak, and could only moan. His mind was filled with a glorious vision of the future. He visualized happy leaders of all the world's great religions working together toward peace on earth. He imagined terrorists hugging their enemies. He imagined wars, hunger, and sickness disappearing under the auspices of a new world religious order. He pictured a world under the wise guidance of visiting apostles.

The music and the fire hovered even lower above the Arizona Miracle Retreat. "The music of the angels! Heaven is here with us," proclaimed Piona, trying to control his weeping.

The dancing opal of fire spread outward and took the form of a spectacular hovering cloud, full of changing color. Some spectators became frightened and began to move toward the parking lots, but a deafening thunder froze their movements and in terror they sank to the ground. Four tornadoes of fire materialized from the glorious cloud and descended to the four sides of the valley that housed the crowd. Overcome, the entire assembly, including Piona and the camera crews, were compelled to fall prostrate.

Madeline huddled fearfully in Owen's arms. "That is really scary."

"Never thought it'd be like this," said Owen. "Imagine what it must be like to be there! Don't be scared. God's with us, so let's just keep watchin."

Offshoots of fire exploded from the tops of the four fiery tornadoes. They flew across the sky and blazed words of fire across the sky: *"I am the God of Abraham. Listen to my servants Abraham and Piona."*

Slowly the music from the sky and the fire faded, leaving the worshippers awe-stricken.

14

Religious Seduction

◇◇◇◇◇◇◇◇◇◇◇◇◇◇◇◇◇◇◇◇◇◇◇◇◇◇◇◇◇◇◇◇◇

EVAN HAWKINS DISMANTLED the old .303 rifle and meticulously cleaned and greased each part. Sealing each box of ammunition separately in airtight plastic bags, he stacked them neatly inside a plastic carton. He put one box of bullets in the Subaru's rear trap-door compartment. He would use this ammunition to sight in the rifle and practice some shooting.

He assembled the rifle, wrapped it carefully in an old towel, and placed it in the luggage area of his vehicle under a tarpaulin. Loading some boxes of plants and some other goods, he drove to Madeline's place. Evan's excitement about seeing her was tempered by being unsure if she still had any romantic feelings for him.

Madeline heard the distinctive sound of the flat-four Subaru motor and went out to meet Evan, who hugged Madeline for longer than she wanted. Evan looked tired and drawn as she got into his car. "How have you been?" she asked.

"I'm good. But my mind has been working overtime. I can't help thinking about the devil's miracles and how quickly the world has gone after them. You've been following the news, no doubt."

"Who hasn't?"

"I always knew the final movements would be quick, but nothing like this." Evan pulled out from the curb. "Did you watch the interview with our prime minister last night?"

"No, I was working."

"I've never seen Vernon Turnbull so fired up about anything, let alone religion. Yet it's understandable—his brother's liver cancer was healed by Piona. Turnbull thinks the miracles have changed the face of politics and religion across the world. He reckons the miracles will make terrorism a thing of the past."

"Really?"

"Yes, because of the healing of the Iranian leader's wife and the breaking of the drought in a Muslim country. And, of course, the common ancestor, Abraham, spoke out of the fiery cloud, telling everyone that all religions should cooperate in the new radical peace plan."

"But these terrorists are total fanatics. Why would they change?" probed Madeline.

"Well, they might be fanatics, but fanatics have always been impressed by the miraculous, and they see how the miracles soften the attitude of the Christian West toward the Muslim world too."

"I see. Their reasons for fighting the west are being undermined."

"Yes. In a way they feel as if Allah has intervened and done the work for them. They don't usually work independently, either, so if their leaders back off, they follow suit."

"I guess that'd be right."

"They'll feel that their God and the Christian God are one and the same after this."

Madeline prayed for the courage to confront Evan. "I want you to know something," she said tactfully. "I have always thought of you as a very sincere and courageous Christian. But your ideas about getting ready for heaven aren't … quite right."

"I was worried you'd think that after talking to Owen."

"For a while I really believed what you said about being totally perfect before the Lord comes. But I knew I wasn't perfect, so I lost hope."

"We don't do it by our—"

"Evan, Romans 3 and 4 taught me that the only way God sees us as being perfect is because he forgives all our sins and doesn't see us as sinners anymore—we're perfectly forgiven."

"Then we can live like the devil and sin away because God forgives us." Evan's voice betrayed tension and frustration.

"That's not what I believe. If we realize that God accepts us, unworthy though we are, we'll want to keep his commandments."

"Madeline, I believe that the only righteousness we have is in our character and obedience."

"I know what you believe, Evan. But if it's true, then according to Romans 3, we'd all be lost because no one's good enough."

"You've come a long way in quoting Scripture Madeline. I've got to hand it to you."

Madeline was getting frustrated. "Don't you ever feel that compared with Christ you're a sinner and need forgiveness? You remind me of the

Pharisees. They trusted in their own good works and didn't need Christ."

"But I *do* need Christ for power to obey." Evan was getting emphatic.

"That's just the point. Christ should mean more to us that just power. He's our very life. He wants to cover our unrighteousness."

When Madeline saw she wasn't getting anywhere, she changed the subject. "By the way, what did you mean when you said you wanted to talk to me about your sin?"

Evan stopped the car. He was already shaken by Madeline's rebuke, and this conversation was too important not to give it his full attention. He took a deep breath and sighed. "Madeline, we both have sinned ... you more than me—when you were on drugs, I mean. But you've shown you can overcome. And you can keep overcoming. We can strive together until we're ready for the Lord's coming."

Evan paused, then continued. "Madeline, I haven't told you this before, but ... I love you. If we were to get married and become perfect together, then we wouldn't have to worry about our sins of the past. I—"

"You think we haven't been forgiven?"

"Not fully. If we got married, we could live in the cabin. We could shelter there. We wouldn't need to be forgiven anymore."

Madeline looked at Evan with pity and compassion. But Evan saw the tenderness in her eyes and mistook it for romantic love. He drew her close to himself and tried to kiss her.

Madeline turned her head away. "Evan, you've got it all wrong. I—"

"Madeline, I've got food stored up here and ... herbs. When things get too tough, we've got the caves."

Madeline leaned on the car door and took several deep breaths. "Calm down for a minute, Evan. You're getting carried away. You're talking about marriage, yet you believe the Lord's coming is just around the corner. Why marry then?"

Evan paused. "Good question. I'm a bit embarrassed about this, but there will be no marrying in heaven, and ... it's something I've wanted to experience before it's too late. I know it's crazy and confusing, but that's why I ...oh, never mind!"

Evan spoke imploringly. "Can't you see it? We could encourage each other to be perfect and healthy, and we might become good enough one day."

"I feel secure in God and his love *now.* I wish you were too. Jesus will be my Savior in the trials ahead, just as he is now. He's coming back to take me to heaven—not to condemn me for any imperfections. Look, Evan, you're a great guy, but I could never marry you. I don't feel that way about you."

Evan sank back into his seat for a moment, shattered and resigned. "It's Owen, isn't it?" he asked hoarsely. "He's got you where he wants you with his easy Gospel."

"What?"

"That's right. He plays at worldly pubs, watches sinners destroy themselves with alcohol and the devil's dancing, and goes home, where it's so easy for him to ask God for his cheap forgiveness and go to sleep peacefully."

"Is that what you think? Evan, Owen only plays good, decent songs and mixes gospel with them. He talks to people about Jesus and he doesn't drink anymore. He's even given up beer—and not to earn salvation."

Evan started his car. "Well, when the persecution starts, you'll all be coming up here to escape it. We'll know then who's on the right track. Maybe you'll think differently about things then."

As they drove to the cabin, Evan remained quiet and despondent. When they arrived, he started to empty the luggage area of his Subaru. He felt disoriented and was fighting back tears at Madeline's rejection. While he was unpacking, Madeline picked up the bundle wrapped in a towel in one arm and a box of plants with the other. The oiled rifle slipped out from the towel and fell to the ground.

"I thought you didn't believe in killing animals," said Madeline.

"That's not for hunting."

"What's it for, then?"

"When the enemy comes looking for us, I can protect us," Evan said weakly.

"With a gun? Do you think guns will save us? Evan, I can't understand you. You talk about faith in God, but you trust in bullets to protect you?"

"Well, *they* will be using bullets, and it might give us time to escape. God can work that way. When the Waldensian Christians were being hunted by their enemy in the Alps of Europe, they rolled boulders down at them. And it worked, I might add."

Madeline changed the subject. "Have you tried your herbs yet? I mean, in place of the insulin.

"No. The first lot of plants failed, and these are still small, so it'll be a while before I have a good supply. But I'm confident."

"Don't you think you should make some more now, before it's too late?"

"Oh, Madeline, where is your faith?"

After checking his plants and transplanting some herbs, Evan picked up his gun and ammunition. Resting the .303 on a log, he aimed and shot at a large can thirty meters away, grazing it. A flock of galahs flew from a nearby gum tree, screeching.

The strength of the recoil surprised Evan. Gripping the stock more firmly, he found it hard not to flinch and shut his eyes as he squeezed the trigger. He fired half a packet of bullets to get used to the rifle and to sight in the telescopic sights.

Later, as they drove back to town, Evan was quieter than usual, dejected that he was losing his romantic and spiritual influence over Madeline.

ᕦ

Shortly after Evan dropped Madeline off and drove home, Basil Dorf arrived with Ami. Basil was uncharacteristically subdued. "I watched the miracle action the other day. Made me think. I could tell the Iranian president's wife wasn't lying. There's no way a prominent Muslim would confess publicly to something that would give credit to Christians if it wasn't true."

"So you think there might be a supernatural force?" asked Madeline.

"I know there's a supreme being now. There's no other explanation. Every move of that evangelist Piona and his cohort prophet Feldberg have been scrutinized by the media and science, and there's absolutely no evidence of a fake. Even the leader of the skeptic's society reckoned he would resign."

Alice Beckett spoke up. "Did ya see the miracle of fire on the last night? Oh, boy! That freaked me out."

"Piona couldn't have faked that even if he had all the technology of the world at his disposal," said Basil. "The tornadoes have even left burn marks on the desert! It turns out that truth *is* stranger than fiction."

"I reckon there's a God for sure now," said Alice. "Ami's been talking about it for a while, but I've seen stuff with my own eyes. Everyone I know believes there's a God."

"Atheists are extinct," Basil agreed thoughtfully.

"What about how that bloke's prayer sent rain to that African joint?" said Alice.

"That was another reason for the Muslim world to sit up and take notice of the Christian God," said Basil.

"Or for the Christians to take notice of the Muslim God," replied Ami. "Whichever way you look at it, those miracles don't prove God was behind them. They only prove the existence of the supernatural."

"Then, who *was* behind them?" asked Basil.

"There are other supernatural forces around—fallen angels that can work miracles," said Ami. "Revelation 12 tells us that one third of the angels of heaven joined forces with the devil and they're at war with our planet. It's a war of deception and lies, and they have terrific power when God allows them to use it."

"What makes you think the devil and his angels were involved in those miracles?" scoffed Basil.

"Would God be behind miracles that reinforce a worldwide conspiracy against God's people?" asked Madeline. "Would you like me to ask Pastor Sam to study the topic with you?"

"No, thanks I've always said seeing is believing. I'll just keep looking."

Pastor Karl put down his phone and chuckled. "That was Graham Britton, Frieda."

"One of your bosses?"

"The big boss. He's giving directives to every minister under his jurisdiction in Australia, but he's already e-mailed us and sent us faxes about the same thing."

"About what?"

"He wants us to educate the flock about the significance of the miracles—spiritually and politically. How could he possibly imagine that I wouldn't have already done it?"

"How do you think it will go?"

"It's such a hot topic that if I spoke about anything else, the church would be disappointed. There's been nothing but miracle talk on the media. I don't believe that anything else has effected such rapid and dramatic change in world history like the miracles have."

"Fancy being alive at such a time," replied Frieda.

Pastor Fletcher walked behind his pulpit and surveyed his congregation. It seemed unusually restless and eager for divine direction. Evan was noticeably absent, but even if he had been present, Fletcher had no intention of toning down his message, feeling that he now had all of heaven's authority behind him. He preached a stirring sermon on the role of miracles in the Bible and history, then invited everyone to attend his afternoon seminar on "The Miracle Retreat."

Although Evan and Maude came to the afternoon meeting, he kept to his outline and went over each of Piona's miracles in detail. Using his considerable knowledge of theology, science, and astronomy, he explained why he believed the miracles were genuine.

Karl finished his speech by saying, "The prayers of peace-loving religious
and political leaders the world over have been answered. We have longed
for a spiritual governing body that would work toward healing religious
divisions—divisions that have been responsible for wars, hostilities, and
terrorist attacks. It is only as religions unite in concerted cooperation that
solutions can be found. We have had a United Nations political organization,
but we haven't had the spiritual equivalent, and it has been like trying to fly
a jet without wings. But at last, God has given the recent miracles to provide
the necessary impetus to unite the religions of the world."

The youth pastor, Sam, responded, "Pastor Karl, the miracles are
undeniably of a supernatural source. But why assume that God is behind
them? There are many warnings in Scripture about satanic delusions. It
is my view that God would not work miracles that accompany dangerous
and unbiblical teachings."

"The great majority of Christians would disagree with you," Karl
responded calmly. "They don't see Piona's teachings as unbiblical.
Remember, when Christ worked miracles, he too was accused of using
Satan's power."

"Christ didn't work miracles to encourage errors like communicating
with the dead or that the Ten Commandments are irrelevant," reasoned
Sam. "Christ's miracles upheld the Word of God, and he always quoted
Scripture to support his actions and teachings."

Karl assumed a dignified and confident manner. "I have recently had
messages from a New Testament writer—Paul himself—and they have
enhanced my spirituality. How can I deny my experience?"

"Experience shouldn't come above Scripture. You said that Paul told
you the commandments have been done away with and they are replaced
by a code of love. However, that contradicts his writings. For example, in
Romans 7, he says, 'The law is holy, just and good.' And in Romans 3 he
asks, 'Do we nullify the law by faith? Not at all, rather we uphold the law.'
Therefore it couldn't have been Paul who spoke to you."

An elderly female parishioner stood. "I'd like to read from Revelation
chapter 14," she said. "Verse 12 tells us how we can avoid getting the mark
of the beast: 'This calls for patient endurance on the part of the saints who
keep God's commandments and remain faithful to Jesus.' It would seem
that keeping the commandments is the only safe course to take. In fact
Satan is out to destroy those who keep God's commandments according to
the last bit of chapter 12."

"She's dead right," said Owen. "We keep God's law not to *be* saved,
but because we *are* saved."

"It's the devil who's behind Piona's miracles," Evan blurted out.

A murmur of displeasure went through the church, and Evan's father stood. "Was it the devil that healed my blindness too?" he asked indignantly, pointing at his son.

Pastor Sam responded before Evan could. "Simon, that's something for you to work out from the Bible."

Inspector Adrian Sebastian walked out and put his arm around Karl's shoulder. "I support Karl 100 percent on this," he said. "I'm just amazed. I expected everyone to be over the moon about the miracles—look at the way they've made the world leaders pull together for a change. My advice to everyone is not to get paranoid about anything. Let's just be grateful for the miracles, and wait and see what happens."

Encouraged by the support, Karl said, "Why can't everyone see that God is pouring out his Spirit in these last days? There's a danger of rejecting God's Spirit through unwillingness to change."

"Undoubtedly God is pouring out his Spirit," Sam responded. "Every day tens of thousands around the world are learning to trust in Christ alone, and not in some political-religious amalgamation. And why wouldn't Satan want to counterfeit this genuine movement of God's Spirit? You can read every chapter in Revelation, and nowhere does it say that miracles are to be the test of God's power. To the contrary, we are told that the greatest miracles will be worked in the last days by Satan to deceive the world. Here's Revelation chapter 13 verse 13: 'And he performed great and miraculous signs, even causing fire to come down from heaven to earth in full view of men. Because of the signs he was given power to do on behalf of the first beast, he deceived the inhabitants of the earth.' In this case, miracles are the tool of—"

"Sam, you just read 'fire from heaven' was going to be the devil's great miracle," interrupted Owen. "That's exactly what happened at the Miracle Retreat—fire from heaven. If the Bible predicted it, why are people suckers? Couldn't Piona's fire be a counterfeit of Elijah's fire or the Pentecostal tongues of fire? Maybe God knew that Satan would work this way."

"Good questions, Owen," Sam responded. "If it's miracles that trick the world into worshipping the beast, then the greatest danger facing Christians isn't the microchip or plastic card, it's not blatant witchcraft or the occult—it's the greatest masterpiece of deception of all time."

"The thing about counterfeits," said Joan Edwards, "is that it's only in the minor detail that you can tell the fake from the genuine."

Karl maintained his assured bearing. "I would think that getting the mark of the beast has more to do with not cooperating with the light given through miracles and visitations."

Evan sprang to his feet. "I've always suspected it, but now you've said it. This New World Order is being fueled by those miracles, and it's going to blame nonconformers like me and brand us as having the mark of the beast. True?"

"It's not for me to brand anyone," said Karl diplomatically. "But I think if you study trends, people will be making life difficult for themselves if they don't go along with the only possible solution to the world's ills."

Owen had his Bible open and ready. "According to Revelation chapter 13 verses 3 and 8, the entire world's going to follow the beast, so it's going to be a real big deal. And chapter 14 verse 14 says, 'They are the spirits of demons performing miraculous signs as they go out to the kings of the whole world to gather them for the battle on the great day of God Almighty.' Don't you think that's amazing? The big shots of the world will be sucked in by miracles. We're seeing this right now, with world leaders cooperatin' with the New International Order. Even the Chinese and North Korean leaders have had a complete turnaround."

The church organist stood, looking distressed and indignant. "I have been listening carefully to everything that's been said and I think we should support Pastor Karl on this. He's a learned and respected theologian, and it's sad to see that Pastor Sam disagrees publicly with his senior pastor. But it's not just Pastor Karl's opinion. The church leaders and government agree. So who are we to say they're wrong? The country's in a mess, the crime and drug use rate is soaring, and we're all afraid of the terrorists. At last some sort of solution is being offered, but some of us don't want to give it a go."

A murmur of approval and some clapping followed. Maude Smith looked around the room, then whispered to Evan, "You're gettin' some dirty looks, ya know."

Maude straightened her hat before standing. " 'Scuse me. I don't mean to be rude, but that's why I don't go to this church. Everyone just wants to go with the crowd and not think for themselves. The music this church plays sounds like a disco, ya dress and look no different to the unbelievin' world, and ya wouldn't recognize the devil if 'e kissed ya! I hope ya all wake up before it's too late."

Maude sat down, trying to suppress an egotistical feeling of victory that swept over her.

"I'm proud of you, Maude," Evan whispered in her ear.

15

Pobjik's Welcome

◇◇◇◇◇◇◇◇◇◇◇◇◇◇◇◇◇◇◇◇◇◇◇◇◇

ALICE GENTLY STROKED PUFF, Madeline's cat, as she lay purring on her lap. She looked at Madeline, who was lying on the living room floor, reading. "You know, Maddy, they tried to teach us how to fill out forms and sign our names and stuff in class today. It's hard to learn at my age—I'm only eighteen."

"Need any help?"

"Yeah, for sure, but not now, though. I've been thinkin' about other things."

"Like what?"

"Oh. about Mum and the old man. I used to hate 'im for beatin' me up and that. But now that I've learned a bit about God, I don't hate 'im anymore. An' poor old mum, she's like a slave around the joint. She's good hearted, but she didn't know much about carin' for kids, an' she can't write an' read or anythin'. I've been thinkin' I wouldn't mind seeing 'em and tellin' 'em about what you've taught me about God 'n' the Bible. What do you reckon, Madeline? Would you take me? Owen could come if he likes. He'd get on all right with 'em. He's a farmer too."

"Do you think I'd be safe?"

"Yeah, you'd be all right. But bring Owen. You're pretty, and ya never know with my brothers, especially Josh, what he might try if he's been drinkin'."

"I'm sure Owen will come, though it might take a couple of weeks for us both to get time off work together."

Owen's Toyota wound its way down the western slopes of the New England Range. The eucalyptus forest gave way to more sparsely timbered terrain, and farm houses became more scattered. The larger towns had been left behind, and there was just the occasional village.

Alice plucked up the courage to speak her mind. "Owen, you seem to be leanin' on Madeline a bit too much. Do ya mind hangin' on to the wheel with both hands goin' around these corners?"

"You're a great back-seat driver, Alice," said Owen, grinning. "Maybe you need someone to lean on you to keep your mind off my drivin'."

"Sounds good. You find me someone!" Alice laughed.

"You sure your parents won't mind me coming? From what you told me about your dad—"

"You'll be all right. He don't hurt people for nothin'. He only belted me when he wanted work done. Not far to go now."

They turned off the highway and followed a narrow dirt track for a few kilometers.

"That's our joint over there."

"You mean those old sheds?" asked Owen in disbelief.

"They're not sheds. They've got beds and a fridge and a kitchen."

"I see a cow milking shed."

"That's the main house. And there's Mum comin' out. She'll like my hair." Alice excitedly ran her fingers through her clean and shampooed long brown hair.

Owen pointed at a late-model Ford Fairlaine that was parked under a rusty corrugated iron shed. It had chrome horns mounted on a chrome bull bar and chrome wheels and chrome striping on the doors.

"Have they got some fancy visitors?" asked Owen.

"No. That's Ron's pride 'n' joy. He likes to keep up with the latest Ford."

"Looks like it's worth more than the house. How could he afford that?"

"Me brothers grow weed. The old man hits 'em heaps for a cut."

"What's that smell?" asked Madeline, screwing her nose.

"Might be the pigs," said Alice. "They're just behind that tin fence over there. There's about a hundred of 'em. Should see how fat they are. Josh and Daniel feed ' em plenty of 'roo meat, goats, anythin' dead— they're good shots, me brothers. They don't skin 'em, they just throw 'em in and the pigs rip into 'em."

"Have they ever shot at people?" asked Owen, still feeling a little apprehensive.

"Nah, not ta kill 'em, just scare 'em."

"Oh, thanks!"

Alice stepped out of Owen's car and ran toward her mother. "How ya doin', Mum?"

"Oh, Alice, ya look real pretty in those clothes. Let me give ya a hug."

"Where's ol' Ron?"

"Yer stepdad's fixin' some pipes out the back. He should have heard ya. He won't be long. I've got somethin' ta tell ya later."

"Where's Josh and Dan?"

"Oh, your brothers are probably over at Henry's joint, talkin' to his new house maid, I bet. Who's your friends?"

Alice looked proudly at Madeline and put her arm around her waist. My best friend Madeline and her boyfriend Owen—he's a farmer just like you and Ron. This is Rose my mum."

"Pleased to meet ya," said Rose. "Come in. And mind your head, young fella. Gee, you're tall. You must be seven feet!"

"Closer to six."

"Your mum must have given ya lots of pig meat and milk, I bet," said Rose.

As they entered the house, Owen ducked under the edge of the rusty corrugated-iron roof and noticed spider webs dangling from the rough bush timbers. Two of the windows had been repaired with scratched plastic sheets, and a wood-burning stove had a large, black kettle on it. Madeline stepped around some stacked wooden boxes, which were being used as a storage cupboard, and sat on a musty couch with collapsed springs, covered with an old blanket to hide the foam protruding through the torn vinyl.

"I'm learnin' to read and write a bit, Mum," said Alice proudly.

"Won't hurt ya, but I got along all right without it," said Rose as she scratched her nose with her long, bony finger. "Well, Madeline, she's lookin' real smart all dressed up, so you're doin' a good job of lookin' after her. Oh, here's Ronnie, her stepdad."

The old wooden slat door squeaked and scraped the torn linoleum floor as Ron Pobjik pushed it open and stepped into the room. He looked apprehensively at his visitors, who stood to greet him. He nodded, sat, and looked at Alice. "G'day, Alice. Haven't seen you fer a while. I heard you're stayin' at Newcastle now." He poured himself a beer.

"Yeah, Ron," Alice answered quietly, without a smile. "I'm stayin' with my friend Madeline here, who's lookin' after me."

"When are ya comin' back home? We need ya here to help with the pigs. Those loafer brothers of yours don't help much. If I had—"

"She's stayin' in the city to get some learnin'," Rose interrupted, "so she'll be away a long time."

"Well, I want ya home soon. You're only a young 'un, and you'll do as you're told, ya hear?" Ron glared at Alice, with both hands on his knees and his elbows poking out.

Alice avoided Ron's glare.

"Now, Alice," Ron persisted, "if ya don't come back soon, I'm comin' to getcha!"

"Don't listen to the poor old fella," Rose said. "I've been wantin' to tell ya somthin' that's changed everythin'. We saw somethin' on TV—a miracle—a *real* miracle."

"Yeah," said Ron. "They played it over 'n' over. Did ya see it?"

"You're talkin' about the miracles in the Arizona desert?" asked Owen.

"My oath! They healed our prime minister's brother, and that Arab lady, and then that African rain came, and—"

"An' what about the fire from the sky?" added Rose, waving her arms at the ceiling. "Real gorgeous like."

"Give a man a chance to finish what he's sayin'! Anyway, we thought and thought about it, and now we reckon there *must* be a God ta work them miracles," declared Ron, slapping his thighs for emphasis.

"I saw God before I saw any miracle," said Alice.

"Oh, bull!" scoffed Rose.

"It's true! I saw him in my friend Madeline here. Mum, I got real crook in hospital, and I just wanted to die. But they wouldn't let me. Madeline was my nurse and she spoke to me real nice. I couldn't believe it when she said she'd take me to live with her. She bought me clothes and taught me stuff and took me to a kind of school for grown-ups where I'm learnin' to read stuff. All her friends like me, too, and they all talk about God, and he's become real to me."

"Well, you can imagine God in people," muttered Ron, nodding his head, "but I saw him in the miracle o' fire and he spoke. I heard 'im."

"All them churches just take your money," said Rose. "So we never ever thought about God, only how to live and get by and raise you kids and feed ya and clothe ya and teach ya."

"Yeah, and how to beat the cops and meat inspectors." Ron laughed. "I shot at the inspectors one day. They came around a few years ago and shot some o' me pigs—reckoned they were too sick to sell. So next time they came around, I fired some shots with me shotgun."

"Now, Ron, stop that bull. When we saw their truck pullin' up out at the gate, Ron played smart. He hid in the little shed with the shotgun and fired some shots in the air. They heard 'em and backed out through the gate and took off! Thought Ron might've been shootin' at them. But he never shot at 'em. He's pretty smart!"

Ron laughed long and loud as he slapped his hands on his thighs.

Owen picked two flies out of his glass of water. "Did they call the cops?" he asked.

"What for? They couldn't prove nothin'. Nobody saw me."

Ron laughed louder as he rocked in his chair. Then he suddenly became serious again. "Now, about this 'ere God. Now that I know he's real, everything's changed, and I've been askin' him for me own miracles. I think he might make me chest pain better without me havin' to stop smokin'. What do ya reckon?"

"Well, Ron," said Madeline, "God can do those things. But his best miracle is to change our hearts—make us more like Jesus."

"Nothin' wrong with my heart, luv. I love me wife and I could love you too—just quietly, let me tell ya." Ron grinned, exposing his missing teeth. "But I live a good life and don't hurt nobody, and I'm happy just the way I am. You seem to know a bit about God. How do you get 'im to work miracles if you want somethin'?"

"You have to get to know God as a friend from reading the Bible. Oh, I forgot, you can't read. Well, you could go to church and hear about him."

"Couldn't drag me to church in a million years, what with all those fancy hypocrites," grumbled Ron.

Rose got excited. "We've been askin' for a miracle. Ron'd like the latest Fairlaine, and I'd like a house with pretty curtains and an electric stove. What would you like, Madeline?"

"I'd like to see Alice learn to read and write better and get a job. But I'm not sure if there's enough time left."

"Sounds like the boys are pullin' up in the truck," said Rose. "They'll be wantin' dinner."

Joshua staggered through the doorway, bending his huge frame, with Daniel close behind. He halted in astonishment when he saw the visitors.

"You boys been drinkin' again?" asked Rose.

"Henry brews his own. Since we help 'im a bit, we get some."

"Who's this pretty little chick?" asked Joshua, grinning.

"That's Owen's girlfriend, Josh. Don't get any ideas."

"You're real pretty, Madeline. I think I'll give ya a welcomin' hug."

"You're drunk, Josh. Go to bed and sleep it off!" Rose tried to pull his arm in the direction of his bedroom.

"Owen won't mind, will ya?" said Joshua, shrugging her off.

Madeline stepped behind the couch to avoid Joshua, but he lunged and grabbed her with both arms.

"You're harder to catch than an old sow, but you're a lot prettier. I just wanna friendly hug." Joshua grinned as he forced Madeline to himself.

Owen grabbed Joshua from behind. Kicking Joshua's feet from underneath him, Owen flung him to the ground. Joshua stood groggily and swung a few stray punches. He grabbed a broom and swung it. Owen ducked and threw a kitchen chair, which hit Joshua in the head, stunning him. He slumped to the floor.

"Let him be, mate," Daniel warned, his hostile eyes glaring at Owen. "Give us a hand, Ron, and we'll carry the poor blighter to bed."

Shortly after, Madeline examined Joshua's face as he lay in bed, snoring. "He's OK. Just some bruising."

"Want to go home?" asked Owen.

"I brought a picnic lunch," said Madeline. "Let's all eat together and we can leave on a nicer note."

"You'll have to turn a blind eye to Joshua," advised Ron. "He's not a bad bloke. But when he's been drinkin', he's got a weakness for women. Can't say I blame him with your girlfriend, though. Where'd ya learn ta fight like that?"

"On the station. We have to throw cattle. You learn to knock 'em off balance."

"That's hard work, mate. We don't throw pigs; we just shoot 'em when we want a feed," said Ron. "Now, gettin' back to this God business, I liked what the American president said the other day. He and some of them other big fellas reckon things will be better in the world from now on, after the miracles. They'll all work together, and it'll fix that terrorist stuff and crime."

"Didn't you know about God before?" asked Owen.

Ron put a cigarette in his mouth. "Never gave it much thought, mate."

Owen slid away from the collapsed end of the couch. "That's why Jesus came—to show us what God is like. Everything he did was teachin' us that God loved us and that his way of life is the best."

Ron lit his cigarette. "I don't know much about Jesus. But these miracle workers don't care whether you follow Jesus, Buddha, or Elvis, as long as you fall in line with their thinkin'. Makes it easy, don't it?"

Daniel put down his empty beer glass and burped. "Never thought the old man would get religious. Never thought he'd be thinkin' politicians could help us much, either. He's been knockin' 'em all his life."

"I *don't* like ' em," said Ron, slapping his thighs. "We came out here to get away from the interferin' tax-collectin' bludgers. Take pigs. Now, they bring good money in the butcher's shop, but we only get peanuts for 'em 'ere. The government's gettin' it all, and they let pork in from overseas, and we can't get a decent dollar for 'em."

"Now you've got Ron stirred up," said Rose. "He hates the government, the unions, and the councils."

"I do," muttered Ron. "But I hope the miracles straighten everythin' out."

16

The Lamb Strikes

◇◇◇◇◇◇◇◇◇◇◇◇◇◇◇◇◇◇◇◇◇◇◇◇◇◇◇◇◇◇◇◇

O WEN WAS DISTURBED by what he read in the email, and was about to dial Madeline's phone number but changed his mind. He printed out the e-mail and put it in his shirt pocket, its disturbing contents weighing heavily on his mind as he drove to Madeline's place.

Madeline was surprised at Owen's distracted manner and the briefness of his kiss.

"What's up? You look as if you—"

"I just got some troublin' news from the States. The writing's been on the wall for some time, but I didn't think it would happen so soon."

"Hang on, Owen. Slow down. What's happened?"

"I just got this e-mail from my old mate Lloyd Sanders in the US. He's from Queensland, but he's doin' the rodeo circuits over there. Have a listen to what he wrote:

Owen,

I've just seen the latest news and it's freaked me out. President Foreman's secretary was talking about the bad state of society. You know, increased crime, family breakdowns, and stuff. He said that church leaders think God wants certain laws and changes made before he can fix the problems. He talked about the huge stir the Piona miracles made and how they have made Americans think differently. Owen, we've both known for a while now that the US government has been pressured by the Christian Power Movement. But get this: The government has finally given in to what they want and made these new laws all across the country. I taped what was said so I could give you some sort of true picture. Here is a rough list of the new laws.

Any teaching that promotes disbelief in the existence of God is not allowed in educational institutions or media broadcasts.

All our educational institutions must teach the existence and power of a supreme being. Teachings that are shared by the main religions, such as love, forgiveness, etc., are encouraged, but any teachings regarded as destructive to interfaith unity are forbidden. One of those teachings is (get this!) the Ten Commandments.

Religious groups will not be allowed to have displays in public places. (Whatever that means!) I think it boils down to avoiding offending other religious groups.

We all have to belong to this religious unity movement and go along with the idea that the church and the government can join hands in making laws of their own choosing.

No one is allowed to knock the religions that are in this united movement. If a person thinks he has rights to freedom, but those rights oppose the new laws, that person has to give up his personal rights.

Here it is, practically word for word:

A person's conscience must now be directed to the good of the majority rather than individual freedoms. Although the best interests of the country were once served by tolerance to all religious and political views, because of the present urgent needs and the changes in our society restrictions on freedom must be made.

And here is the scariest part. The plan is to microchip everyone who cooperates within twelve months. They want to sort us all out!

Owen, anybody who doesn't go along with this new plan will not be allowed to buy anything, sell anything, or swap anything. Sound familiar? They are allowing a sixteen-week period for people to adjust and then penalties will be dished out. Big protests are being organized. Watch the news.

We all knew it was coming, mate, but praise God anyway, because it shows Jesus is coming soon. I thought I'd let you know as soon as I heard it. I've been getting some good prize money lately around the circuits. I'm cutting my trip short to come back to good old Queensland in a couple of weeks. Say hello to Madeline. It will be good to meet her. She sounds better all the time!

Lloyd

"We've been expectin' it, but it still just about blew my mind to read that," said Owen.

"Boy, that's scary," said Madeline. "When will it be our turn?"

"Oh, I think it's pretty clear that these changes will hit us soon. It makes me think that the lamb-like beast of Revelation 13:11 probably does refer to the United States government, just like we suspected." He grabbed a Bible and read.

"Then I saw another beast which rose out of the earth; it had two horns like a lamb and it spoke like a dragon."

"This power reckons it's Christian or lamblike," explained Owen, "yet it promotes Satan's methods of force. Verse 13 says it uses mighty miracles to deceive the whole world—and we've already seen that. Then in verses

16 and 17 it says the same power enforces the mark of the beast and the 'can't buy or sell' penalty for those who don't obey."

"Bit mind boggling," said Madeline.

Later that evening Madeline opened a tin of mackerel and gave some to Puff. She put a plastic lid on the open tin, which she put back in the fridge. Then she made herself a hot drink and sat in front of her TV. A demonstration was taking place on the streets of New York. The placards in the agitated crowd read "Death of the First Amendment," "Give Me Liberty or Death," and "Welcome to the Dark Ages." Effigies of George Washington and Abraham Lincoln were being burnt on stakes next to a placard with the words "Matches and gas courtesy of the White House." A student acted out the part of Christ with chains and manacles. One camera focused on the Coast Guard arresting an eccentric character in a small boat that carried explosives. He had tried to approach the Statue of Liberty. When arrested, he cried out repeatedly, "The White House sent me!"

"I've never seen American demonstrators so stirred up," said Madeline.

"They've called in the military, calling it a state of emergency," said Ami, who stopped washing dishes to have a closer look. "I can't get over those water cannons. Have you ever seen that in the States before?"

"No, and this might be the last demonstration they'll allow," observed Madeline. "What would you do if you lived in the States?"

Ami put down the dishcloth and faced Madeline. "Just off the cuff, I don't know. But we'd better do some hard thinking because it won't be long before we cop it here."

Owen noticed an attractive blonde woman who sat alone at a front table of the Leagues Club while he sang. She had hardly taken her eyes off him. But apart from feeling a little flattered, he didn't think too much of it. After his performance, he sat at a table alone to unwind before he went home. The tall blonde swayed over to his table, smiled at Owen, and said sweetly, "Hi. I'm Sandra. Do you mind if I join you?"

Owen looked at his watch. "I'm just about to leave."

He downed his drink.

"I noticed you sang kind of a message song earlier. So you're a Christian?"

Owen tilted his Akubra hat a little. "Sure am."

"I wanted to ask you something. Um … I have a problem."

"OK. Well, sit down if you like."

"I'm not a churchgoer or anything like that, but I feel as if there's something missing in my life. When I heard you sing, you seemed to have a confidence about you, as if you know where you're going in life."

"How come you're here alone tonight, Sandra?"

"That's part of my problem. Lately my friends want to do crazy things all the time. So I thought I'd have a quieter time alone tonight—do some thinking. I'm hoping you can help me."

Owen came to the point. "Sandra, are you searching for truth? Do you know what meanin' there is to life?"

"Is there meaning to life?"

Sandra looked around at the other tables. "It's so noisy in here, it's hard to think. Could we go outside…maybe down by the beach, where it's quiet?"

"Well, it's pretty late. Maybe we should—"

"I won't keep you long."

"OK, then."

Owen shifted some coiled rope off the passenger seat to make room for Sandra, drove a few blocks, parked in a lit-up area facing the surf at Nobby's Beach, and turned off the engine. The sound of the breaking waves lapping onto the sand added atmosphere to the moonlit ocean. On the horizon, the lights of several cargo ships winked above the waves.

"Thanks, Owen. It's nice and quiet here."

Owen looked at Sandra and wondered about her sincerity. Her eyes seemed to be sparkling with enthusiasm and she didn't look depressed.

"When a person feels empty inside," Owen explained, "it means God's creatin' a need that needs fillin'. He never meant us to feel happy when we're livin' without him."

"I've always believed there was a God, and everyone's been talking about those miracles."

Sandra slid a little closer to Owen. Her voice softened and she spoke gently and quietly. "Owen, we all need a good friend—someone with confidence and direction you can trust."

Owen was confused. He looked at Sandra, trying to work out her motives. *This attractive woman wants to be alone with me. She thinks I'm special, which makes me feel good, but there's something unhealthy about this situation and it's making me feel uneasy. Then again, maybe I should give her a chance. Maybe she's just had a few drinks that are making her a bit free with her affections but she really is seeking for truth. Lord, help me not to trust my own strength here.*

"Sandra, have you ever given your life to Christ?"

She leaned a little toward Owen. "I don't really know what that means. But I think you're the one to teach me."

Evan Hawkins often went jogging around the lamplit avenue by the beach at night. He recognized Owen's Toyota four-wheel-drive vehicle with its distinctive spotlights mounted on the roof, and he stopped behind it. Walking closer, he looked through the rear window. He had always suspected that Owen's easy Gospel was a breeding ground for secret sin hidden beneath his religious exterior. He was still upset, feeling that Owen had stolen the love of his life. Hadn't he warned Madeline about Owen's liberal ideas? It seemed a providential opportunity to get hard evidence to reveal the truth. Evan withdrew into the shadows.

Sandra leaned her head on Owen's shoulder. "You're a true blue country man, a real man."

Owen leaned away a little. "Now, Sandra, I thought we came out here tonight because you needed help."

"I feel kind of lonely tonight. We could go to your place and talk."

"Oh, I get it. First it's the quietness away from the club, and now it's my place. Are you sure it's a counselor you're after?"

Owen sat upright and started the engine.

"Don't you want to help me with my problems?" Sandra protested, trying to sound helpless.

Owen engaged first gear and put both hands on the steering wheel. "Where do you want to be dropped off?" he asked firmly.

"It's a bit lonely to go home by myself."

"Then I'll drop you back at the club. And I'll give you Pastor Edwards' phone number. He could help you better than I can."

"Somehow I don't think he's the one."

The next day, Evan awoke feeling as if he had a special mission.
He phoned Madeline.

"How are things going, Evan?" she asked.

"Good, thanks. Uh ... It's hard for me to tell you this, but ... Madeline, I've always had your best interests at heart, and I ... I think there's something you should know. I know this will hurt, but it's best for you to know the truth when your whole future can be affected."

"What is it?"

"Late last night, when I was jogging, I noticed Owen's car parked at the beach. I stopped to say hello and was shocked to see that he was ... um ... he was alone with a blonde girl."

"Come off it, Evan! You're imagining things. Owen's in love with me. There's no way he'd do that."

Evan spoke quickly with the emphatic manner of someone with indisputable evidence. "I saw it with my own eyes, Madeline. Have you ever known me to lie? If you don't believe me, ask him yourself."

"Sometimes jealousy can make us see things."

"What, me, jealous? Goodness, no! I just want to help you."

"Look, I'll talk with Owen, but I'm sure there'll be some explanation."

"I hope so, for your sake, Madeline. But I know what I saw."

Madeline was shaken a little. She picked up Puff, stroked her soft long hair, and sat down to think.

I'm confident of Owen's love and loyalty. There's got to be some explanation. Evan's probably jealous and he's just exaggerating. But entertainers do get targeted by infatuated fans, and Owen is a red-blooded male after all.

Owen came to visit Madeline that night. He cheerfully hugged her as he stepped in her doorway.

"Owen, what do you normally do after you finish singing for the night?"

"Oh, I just go home if it's late, or I might hang around a bit. Why?"

"What about last night?"

"I sat down to unwind."

"Evan phoned this morning. He said he saw you last night in your car with a blonde by the beach."

"Evan saw me? Oh, no! He'd tell anybody."

"Tell them what? It's true, then?"

Owen saw that Madeline was upset, so he paused, took a deep breath, and tried to explain carefully and slowly. "Yes, I did have a blonde lady with me in the car on the beach. She said she needed God in her life."

"Why didn't you admit to it right away when I first asked you?"

"I didn't want to upset you. Would you have understood?"

"I don't."

Owen sighed deeply. "Nothing happened—nothing!"

"Evan implied it was more than that."

"I did my best to stop her. She put her arm around me. I backed off—took her back to the club and went home. That was it."

"But you said she wanted to find God."

"That's what she said, but I realized later it was just a bait to get me alone. Madeline, I'm not interested in anyone else. You're the only one I love. I'd be crazy to chase anybody else. Why would I?"

Tears ran down Madeline's cheeks.

Owen put his arms around her and held her. "She sat at my table and said she needed a quiet place to talk. I guess I was a bit naïve. You trust me, don't you?"

"No worries, Owen. I'll get over it."

As the sun was setting, Karl Fletcher walked his fox terrier through the park near his home. He was thinking about his congregation, wondering how he could persuade everyone to believe in the agenda of the New International Order. He was especially concerned about his associate, Pastor Sam Edwards, who was openly opposing him on the issue of the miracles and the mission of the NIO. Karl was particularly pleased with the new US legislation, feeling it was just a matter of time before Australia would follow.

As he strolled under a stand of trees, Karl noticed a strangely dressed man walking toward him. As he drew nearer, Karl became intrigued by the person's unusual dress. Then it dawned on him who it was—he recognized the old scroll and the rugged gold cross. It was the apostle Paul. Karl was so filled with reverential awe that he had to consciously restrain himself from kneeling.

While Karl searched for appropriate words, Paul majestically lifted the scroll and the cross and said, "Karl, you are most privileged among men. I come with wonderful news from the courts of the Alpha and Omega. Much progress has been made since we last spoke. The miracles have done their work, and millions have turned to him who has no beginning and no end. You, Karl, have been specially commissioned to preach and write about my visit, proclaiming the wisdom imparted to you. Just as I was commissioned an apostle to the Gentiles, so I commission you to proclaim my teachings. It will be your duty to cooperate in the punishment of those who frustrate God's plan for the last days and who ignore the divine plan of unifying the world. The deluded ones will insist on following what they see as liberty and freedom, but which in reality is rebellion against God—in bondage to the restrictions of the Ten Commandments. The time has come when millions will once again behold the Lord healing the sick. So, Karl, prepare yourself and others to stand firm in the truths of these revelations."

The supernatural visitor suddenly vanished before Karl's astounded eyes.

In a daze, Karl looked around at the stand of large trees, tinted with the warm glow of the setting sun. To him it became a hallowed spot— the very grass under his feet seemed sacred. As no one was in sight, Karl knelt and asked God to strengthen him for what he felt was his divinely appointed task.

Several weeks later, Owen and Madeline were at Owen's apartment, watching a report on the latest legislation in America. Owen was fitting a new string to his guitar and Madeline was stirring some coffee. Both stopped what they were doing, alarmed at what they saw. Hundreds of believers who had been peacefully demonstrating for freedom of worship were being taken away in police vehicles to a huge holding compound.

"Did you see the anger and disgust on the faces of the cops?" said Madeline. "You'd think those poor people were murderers or something."

"I never thought I'd see it in the States," replied Owen.

The scene changed to an interview with a family in Cleveland, who were packing to leave for the country.

"Why are you leaving town?" asked the interviewer.

"We can't stay any longer. We sold our home just before the 'can't buy or sell' laws, and bought a small farm in the country. We're getting out while we can."

"Why don't you just go along with the laws of the land?"

"My grandfather came to the States because of the religious freedom. I can't go against my conscience and join something I don't believe in. The worst thing the government ever did was to give in to microchipping."

"How will buying a farm help?"

"At least we'll be able to live off the land, grow our own provisions, that sort of thing."

"What about buying fuel and medicine and seeing a doctor?"

"I've already sold our car. The Lord will take care of us. And this will give us a chance to get back to nature and a simple lifestyle. We'll ride the storm out till the Lord comes."

Owen shook his head. "Every day we see things gettin' worse over there. Did ya notice that the family didn't seem frightened or sad?"

"The Lord's giving them strength. It's inspiring to see them sticking to their guns. Yesterday they showed a guy who's refusing to leave his home even though they've shut down his water, power, and gas. He said he'd rather starve than give in to 'em. Great courage. But why doesn't he clear out? Didn't Jesus say if they persecute you in one place, go somewhere else?"

"Yep, in Matthew," said Owen, reaching for a Bible.

"We ought to be thinking about country living, too, sweetie. From all reports, the Australian government's going to follow the US. Have you thought of moving to your parents' property?"

"It's too far out in the sticks. We wouldn't find many people to reach for Jesus out there. Here's that text. It's Mathew 10:23: 'When you are persecuted in one place, flee to another.' "

"Might have to do a bit of that."

17

Making Apocalyptic History

◇◇◇◇◇◇◇◇◇◇◇

OWEN LOOKED SERIOUS as he stared through the front window of his apartment at the busy street outside. "Madeline, there's something we need to talk about. You know I love you very much. And the Lord's comin' back soon. And uh … um … we don't know … uh …"

"What are you trying to say, Owen?"

"Well, we were talkin' about country living, and I think now's the time to look around. But I don't want to do it alone, without you."

Madeline looked at him questioningly.

"As long as I've got you and the Lord, that's all I'll need."

"But you haven't got me, Owen. I mean, not really."

"You told me once that you weren't in love with me."

"I did say that—a while ago."

"Have things changed?"

"Of course. When I said you haven't got me, what I meant was that we aren't married."

Owen sat next to Madeline and embraced her, kissing her tenderly on the lips. "I would've married you months ago. I'd marry you tomorrow if I could."

"OK," she smiled.

"What do you mean, OK?"

"Let's get married tomorrow."

"Tomorrow?"

"I mean soon." Madeline laughed.

"Then we can find a place in the country together. Won't that be exciting?"

"It's excitin' just to be with you. You're the most excitin' person I've ever met, by a long way. Sometimes I wish the Lord wasn't comin' so soon. I'd like to spend a lifetime with you, raising our kids and just lovin' you."

"Well, don't get too excited. We're not married yet." Madeline smiled.

Owen's expression turned serious. "Does it worry you that we won't be able to lead a normal married life? Who knows what we might have to go through."

"It won't be normal for anybody from now on. But we want to be with each other. We can forget about having kids, of course. Life will be tough enough without them."

"I go along with that. What about we get married in a couple of weeks?"

"Hang on." Madeline laughed. "It'll take a bit longer than that to get organized."

After they had watched the latest developments in Australia, Owen turned off the TV. "It's depressin' to see so many people getting sucked in by the New International Order," he said. "I feel as if I'm not doin' enough to warn them. I've been thinkin' of visitin' homes and sellin' Bibles and videos, that kind of stuff."

"Wow! That'd be a big change. Do you reckon you could make a living?"

"The Lord'll see to it. Anyway, money will be worthless soon."

"What about your music career?"

"Oh, I'll keep doing a bit of gospel here and there, though I'm not gonna be very popular soon, the way things are goin'."

Since Evan had stopped attending Madeline's church, he and Maude Smith had drawn closer together. They were on their way to visit her parents, who lived in Western New South Wales, and had stopped at the small town of Narrabri so Evan could make a phone call. The phone outside the post office was out of order, and they drove around for a while without finding another phone, so they asked an old aboriginal man for directions. Evan had been brought up in the city and had met very few aboriginal people, especially full-blooded aboriginals like this man. The dignified old dark-skinned man with the cowboy hat and gray beard was walking slowly along the path beside the road.

"Hey, mate," called Evan from the driver's seat. "Could you tell me where there's a phone booth that works?"

The old man walked over to the car and looked at Evan through the side window, pointed and spoke quietly. "Turn right down there, then right again, then take the second street on the left. It's near the little shop. You can't miss it."

"Thanks," said Evan, somewhat dubiously. He drove off and noticed a man weeding his garden several houses away, parked the car, and walked over to him. "Excuse me, sir. Where can I find a phone booth? The one at the post office doesn't work."

The gardener stood and pointed. "Turn right here, then right again, hen the second street on your left. It'll be outside the only shop there."

"Thank you," said Evan.

The old aboriginal man, who was now across the street, called out to Evan, "Now you've got it in black and white!"

Evan was speechless. As he and Maude drove away, Maude asked, "Gee, Evan, you've got a lotta stuff in those caves of yours. Do you really need that much?"

"You've seen the persecution in America. It'll be us next. And if the gardens fail, I'm stocking up just in case."

"I noticed you've got some women's clothes with your stuff in the back of the cave."

"Well, I hope I won't be hiding alone."

"Could I hide with ya?"

"Well, if there's a few other people, that would be all right, I suppose."

"What if there's just the two of us?"

"I'm not sure if that would be right."

"But it could be a matter of life and death if I get caught."

"The Bible says to avoid even the appearance of evil. I wouldn't want to risk God's displeasure at that late stage."

"Well, I reckon it would appear pretty evil if they shot me because I couldn't hide anywhere!"

"Maybe we could find you another cave."

"I'd be all scared alone. Evan, we've been friends for a long time. And we won't wanna be alone then."

Maude took a deep breath and spoke slowly and gently. "We could get married. Then no one could say anything about appearances."

Evan spun around to catch Maude's expression. "You're serious?"

She gently touched Evan's arm. "I've loved you for a long time now. Can't you love me too?"

Evan realized time was running out and there were few women who held religious views similar to his own. And Maude, though plain, wasn't without her charms.

"Sure I do, Maude," he said seriously. "I've always admired you."

"I mean as a woman."

"You're a fine-looking woman, Maude." Evan put his arm around her shoulder as he drove along the country road. "Time is short, Maude. We need each other."

"Oh, Evan, I'll make you a real good wife," Maude said, unable to suppress her excitement.

Evan smiled. "You will, Maude. I think you will."

The world had never seen anything like this summit meeting of the New International Order. Leaders of every major religion had gathered. Dominant among them were Pope Agapetus III and Phillip O'Connell, the Archbishop of Canterbury. There were also various evangelical leaders, including Gerald Hopkins from the Christian Power Movement. Many leaders of non-Christian religions were also present, as well as a number of delegates from the United Nations, including Secretary General Floyd DeCosta.

The appointed chairman, Johanus Zamsi, was from Ghana. He had initially studied law and later attended a United States theological seminary before he became a prominent evangelist. Zamsi, a man of great intellect and presence, stood to speak. "Brothers, we have been meeting for two days of discussions and prayer, and I shall now give the consensus report that we have hammered out. We have all recognized that we are here largely because of the miraculous signs that God has graciously given us. At first, it was the Piona miracles. Since then, there have been others. God spoke to us through the miracles in a way that none of us can deny, and this historic meeting is the result.

"Over the past decade the people of the world have been subjected to unprecedented levels of violence, natural disasters and calamities, sickness and economic turmoil, and mass starvation. We have recognized that this is the outcome of God's blessing being withdrawn from the world, and through this suffering God has taught us that we have gone astray from his will. We have displeased him and have asked for his forgiveness. But now we have taken the following resolutions to restore God's blessing and introduce an era of peace and prosperity.

"All religious conflicts and bitter disunity must cease. Although we can follow our individual faiths, from now on we must work together, not against each other.

"God has been displeased at the apathy toward cooperation between religious and government organizations at international level. We have changed that and are now clasping hands with the United Nations."

All the delegates stood and gave a standing ovation. Zamsi continued. "God has also been displeased at the insidious teachings of atheism. This organization of united world religions has agreed to ban any teachings that promulgate atheistic ideas at academic institutions worldwide, and instead actively promote belief in divine sovereignty. No longer will there be a godless society."

The delegates clapped loudly.

"Any narrow views that pertain to one's particular faith that may offend people of other faiths will be discarded. For instance, there will be no denouncing of the name of Jesus Christ, and he shall be respected as pivotal to the Christian faith. We shall all remember that the miracles have endorsed that great name. Likewise, the names of Mohammad and Buddha shall be respected and due credence be given to their teachings. There shall be no dogmatic adherence to the Ten Commandments in a way that would compromise harmony with other faiths that hold a variant view of God's will. Tolerance is the great doctrine we all hold high above all else.

"Any organization or individual that attributes miracles to any other source than God will be regarded as the enemy of unity and spiritual progress. Where there is a conflict of interest between one's individual spiritual benefit and the good of the majority, the individual benefit must yield. Freedom of conscience must yield to the good of the worldwide community.

"To facilitate the regulation of these decrees, we have decided that every individual in the world should be microchipped as soon as practicable. The refusal of microchipping shall be regarded as a rejection of the above decrees. We do not expect opposition at a national level, but if any nation, group, or individual does not cooperate, they will be placed under economic embargo and sanctions. In this we have the benefit of the new measures taken by the global economy.

"Ladies and gentlemen, this is what you have decided on as a newly appointed body. We can only expect world affairs to improve from now on. Thank you for your contribution. Let us pray."

A small group eagerly gathered at Pastor Sam's place to view the momentous NIO meeting. When it was over, Sam said, "Well, there it is. We've been expecting it. But now that it's here, it's quite daunting."

"Can we be certain the NIO is behind the mark of the beast?" asked Ami.

"Sure looks like it," said Sam, opening his well-worn Bible. "Let's run through the main points of Revelation 13. Verse 8 says, 'All inhabitants of the earth will worship the beast.' The word *worship* suggests that the beast is an international religious authority, which the NIO is, and it's got worldwide control.

"Verse 14 says, 'Because of the signs he was given power to do on behalf of the first beast, he deceived the inhabitants of the earth.' It's the miracles that have set the NIO up to where it is. Piona and the others involved with the miracles have always promoted the NIO as being the answer to the world's problems.

"Verse 17 says, 'No one can buy or sell unless he had the mark.' Well, the NIO is doing a great job of pushing that law.

"Note that another 'beast' puts its weight behind establishing the first beast. It's in Verse 11: 'He had two horns like a lamb but he spoke like a dragon. ... He exercised all the authority of the first beast on his behalf and made the earth and its inhabitants worship the first beast.' This lamb-like beast fits the US government and church leaders that have turned their back on their heritage of freedom and influenced the world to follow the NIO."

"Could anything else be the lamb-like beast?" asked Basil.

"It bases its government on lamb-like—Christlike—ideals. But at the end, this superpower becomes dragon-like ... aggressive. Can you think of any country that fits better?"

"No, I can't," said Basil, wide eyed. "But I—"

"It couldn't be any clearer," interrupted Rohan Kent. "They want to use economic embargo to punish dissenters. Isn't this what's been happening in the United States and spreading?"

"But there are lots of good Christians in America," said Madeline. "How can they be called dragon-like?"

"It's not the people; it's the system," explained Sam, "the blending of church and state, that speaks like a dragon. Now notice how Revelation 14:12 describes those who escape getting the mark of the beast: 'This calls for patient endurance on the part of the saints who obey God's commandments and remain faithful to Jesus.' "

"The NIO is watering down the commandments, even calling them a burden," agreed Rohan. "However, those who escape the mark keep God's law—not to earn salvation, mind you, but because of their love and loyalty to Jesus."

"Well, it's all pretty clear to me," said Basil. "I used to think God was behind the miracles. But boy, is the devil clever!"

Most church members stayed away from Owen and Madeline's wedding because the couple was opposed to the New International Order. However, Pastor Karl came and mixed cordially and freely with the guests. Inspector Adrian Sebastian came, too, but appeared rather withdrawn.

Evan looked on glumly. He had resigned himself to losing Madeline, and he was surprised that the old feelings of jealousy and regret had surfaced again.

Alice was entranced as she watched Madeline walk down the aisle to the music of Owen's own composition: a beautiful, spiritual love song. She was proud that the beautiful bride was her friend. Ami was the bridesmaid, and Owen's brother Bill was the best man. The fragrance of Christ pervaded the simple wedding, and Alice felt that if she ever got married, she wanted a wedding like Madeline's.

"Madeline looks real beautiful in her white wedding dress, doesn't she?" Maude whispered to Evan.

"Yes, she does," replied Evan. "But I don't think she should be wearing white. She's probably no virgin."

"Don't be too hard on her, luv. Virgins are as rare as Tasmanian tigers these days. Just be grateful that you've found one."

Evan listened sullenly to the traditional appeal. "If anyone has a just reason for objecting to this marriage taking place, please voice it now or forever hold your peace."

What a stupid question, he thought sullenly. *As if anyone would speak up. I know God doesn't want Madeline to marry this worldly entertainer guy. If she had married me, I would have led her to the kingdom. But what's the use of saying anything now? It won't help, and I'd only make a fool of myself.*

When Owen kissed his bride, someone whistled and clapped especially loudly.

During the signing of the papers, Owen whispered, "Who was that couple in the way-out cowboy gear makin' all that racket?"

"Alice's parents. We must have left quite an impression when we visited them because they wanted to be here"

"You invited them?" Owen asked.

"How could I say no? They almost invited themselves."

During the reception dinner, Owen's parents, Gordon and Joan, sat at a table with Madeline's separated parents, Gregory and Barbara.

"I never thought they'd prepare for the wedding on time," said Barbara.

"Yeah, same with us," said Joan. "Wasn't easy on such short notice. But once Owen's made up his mind, he just goes ahead."

Barbara smiled wistfully. "Madeline and I always dreamed of an elaborate wedding taking months of planning—not like this simple wedding. But I don't think I've ever seen Madeline look happier, and I guess that's the main thing."

Greg beamed proudly. "I only met Owen today, though Madeline's been talking about him for some time. Barbara and I aren't very religious, but somehow, religion has made Madeline much happier. Owen's certainly been a good influence on her."

"It's the miracles—they've made everyone stop and think," said Barbara. "We've all changed a bit. The churches in town are packed now. I can't say that I used to think too much about religion, before the miracles."

"Deep down, how do you feel about God?" asked Gordon, looking at Barbara and Gregory.

"I must admit, lately I've been trying to find out more," said Barbara.

Alice's parents, Rose and Ron, approached the wedding table. They had been drinking cheap red wine on the way to the wedding and were in an exuberant mood. "Good on ya, Mr. and Mrs. Owen," Rose blurted out, slapping Owen's back. "You're the nicest pair we've ever met. Ya came all the way to our joint to say g'day, and we luv ya for it."

Rose leaned over the table and grinned at Owen, who drew back a little. "Ya look real smart all dolled up. I wouldn't mind swappin' places with Maddy here."

Ron roared with laughter and dropped a large gift-wrapped bundle on the table in front of Owen. He took off his wide-rimmed white western hat as he bowed. "That's yer present. Now, open it up."

All eyes were on Owen as he opened the damp gift wrap. He tried to hide his dismay when he exposed a large leg of raw pork.

"Thanks very much, folks," said Owen politely. Rose grabbed him from behind and kissed him on the cheek.

"Now I'd like to kiss the bride," said Ron as he groggily bent over, half tripping.

Madeline ducked his slobbering attempt, and Ron slipped and crashed onto the table. "Nearly kissed me own pig!" He roared with laughter, grabbed Rose, and attempted to dance with her. "You'll do, Rose, me luv," he said as he staggered to his own rendition of 'Waltzing Matilda.' "

People laughed, but Alice was embarrassed. "I'm not gonna say anythin' to 'em," she told Ami. "It won't do any good. Anyhow, I'm glad Madeline's taught me better."

When Owen had relaxed again, he poured Madeline a sparkling drink.

"You look like a magical dream in that white dress, Mrs. Boyd," he said.

"I'm glad you like it," Madeline whispered.

Owen looked at Madeline lovingly. "When you came back to Jesus, the old Madeline disappeared. You're a fair-dinkum virgin all right."

Madeline's mother wondered about the tears in her daughter's eyes.

18

Transient Paradise

◇◇◇◇◇◇◇◇◇◇◇◇◇◇◇◇◇◇◇◇◇◇◇◇◇◇◇◇◇◇◇◇◇◇◇◇

"YOU'RE GOIN' LOOKING FOR LAND?" asked Alice Becket, smothering some toast with thick jam. "Who's gonna look after me if ya find land? I've got nowhere else to go. Ever since you got married, I've been worried what's gonna happen to me."

Madeline smiled and hugged Alice. "You can live with us if you like."

"Thanks, Maddy. So, ya reckon the cops will be comin' for ya?"

"Not yet. We just think things will get too hot for us in the city soon, and we won't be able to buy stuff, so we'll have to learn to live off the land. Owen, how far out of town should we look?"

Owen put down his guitar. "Not too far, an hour or two at the most. We need to be able to witness and we can't do that if we're hermits."

"Are you sure your parents are going to lend us the money?"

"Dad's talking about *givin'* us some money now."

"Really?"

"Yeah. He reckons money won't be worth much anyway."

"That's kind of them."

Owen and Madeline spent several days looking for suitable land without success. One afternoon Owen heard a knock on the door of his apartment.

"G'day, Evan. Come in. How's things?"

"OK, thanks. I heard you haven't had much luck with land."

"The prices have skyrocketed."

"I always knew other Christians would need somewhere to stay when things heated up. You can both stay up on my Wattagan property."

"Mate, that's really great," said Owen, unsure of Evan's motives. "Would you let us build a shack up there?"

"Sure. There's heaps of timber and you can grow your own stuff."

"I'll have a chat with Madeline about it when she gets home. Thanks, mate."

"Don't thank me, thank the Lord. It's his land and he wants us to be sharing as part of our spiritual preparation."

"How much land can we have?"

"Couple of acres should be enough. There's plenty of water in the creek, but there's no fishing or shooting, rock 'n' roll music, jazz—any secular music …"

"Can I play my guitar?"

"Only if you keep it to yourself and play slow stuff, nothing jazzy or show-offy. No stuff like worldly magazines or books, miniskirts, rowdy friends, alcohol, smoking, unbelieving relatives—"

"There aren't any unbelievers anymore—since the miracles."

"Oh, yes. I forgot. No meat eating."

"We won't be able to buy meat anyway."

"Don't worry, it'll be good for your health. I know your parents raise animals to eat, but there won't be any of that in heaven, so we may as well get used to it down here."

When Madeline came home that night, Owen explained Evan's offer.

"Evan letting us stay on his land? I can't believe it! Why? Does he think he'll earn merit points?"

"Don't be too rough on 'im. He seemed fair dinkum."

"Well, we've looked everywhere without any luck, so maybe it's God's leading. What about Alice? Will he let her come?"

"Forgot to ask, but I'm sure it'll be all right."

"When do we go?"

"No big hurry. No laws have been passed yet. But I wouldn't waste any time. I'm buildin' a cabin up there soon and I want to take plenty of diesel fuel for later. I'll need to drive to Newcastle to witness and I won't be able to buy fuel soon."

"That's a good idea. It's exciting but I can't help being a bit scared"

"Scared?"

"Yeah. About the persecution."

"Me too. But I read something that helped me. It was a parable about a bloke who was tryin' to get to heaven, but when the track became too narrow, he left his horse and cart behind. When the track became narrower still, he had to carry his gear on his back."

"What does that mean? Do we have to be prepared to leave all our earthy possessions and support behind?"

"Yep. The track became so narrow as it went 'round a cliff that he even had to leave his backpack behind. He just hung on to a rope that dangled from above as he eased himself around the cliff. The rope was like our faith; that's all he had left to hang on to."

"That'll be us?"

"Yep. And the rope won't break. God's promises are sure."

Owen and Madeline inspected their new home site. It was right at the head of Evan's valley, where it narrowed between the mountains, and was surrounded by grandeur. There were giant cedars and gums on the slopes on one side, with a towering sandstone escarpment on the other side. The stream's rapids gurgled out of dense rainforest, cutting close to the escarpment and running by a small, raised, grassy flat on the western bank—a perfect building site less than a kilometer from Evan's cabin.

Owen was experienced with a chainsaw, and with Basil's help it only took him a few weeks to build a rough three-room cabin.

Sam Edwards and a friend camped there for a few days and helped as well. They also built an outside toilet and attached a small bathroom to the cabin. The roof was made from second-hand corrugated iron, and they poured a thin layer of concrete for a floor. They installed an old wood-burning stove and some windows and doors that they found at a recycling section of a rubbish dump. They next built a rough shed that could store enough drums of diesel fuel to last a couple of years, and they attached a chicken coup and a cow shelter to the shed.

Madeline and Owen went to an auction sale and bought some cheap furniture as well as some paintings, rugs, and other goods.

When Evan inspected the cabin he frowned. "Getting a bit too comfortable, aren't we? Settling down for quite a while?"

"Hard to say, mate. It's only cheap stuff; anyway' And you've got to keep the women happy," Owen said cheerfully.

"Make them tough rather than happy, I say. According to Revelation 13 there'll be difficult times ahead, so we can't afford to get soft."

Owen threw another log on the heap. "Daniel goes on to say that every believer will be delivered. Anyway, if things get too hot here, you've always got your caves."

"Caves? What caves?"

Realizing his mistake, Owen replied sheepishly, "Yeah, I know about 'em."

Evan spun around, his face reddening with anger. "Madeline told you?"

"Now, take it easy, mate. I haven't told a soul."

Evan glared at Owen, then looked down at the ground, exasperated. "She promised me!"

Owen was emphatic. "She's kept her promise. No one knows but us. You've got nothing to worry about."

"Look, the only reason I let you pair up here is because I hoped I could trust you."

"You can, mate."

Evan's jaw jutted out and his lips grew tight. "I don't think I'd feel comfortable with you living up here. You might have to look somewhere else."

"What? It's too late now. There's a thousand man hours gone into the place."

"Madeline should have thought of that before she broke confidence with me."

Owen felt himself getting heated, so he breathed deeply before he spoke. "Evan, look, we're both better off supporting each other during the tough times ahead. We're all here for the same reasons. Why would we blab about your caves?"

"You might switch sides and join up with the likes of Fletcher."

"But Madeline could tell 'em about the caves anyway, so you're no worse off by me knowing."

Evan sighed. "OK, OK, I guess you're right. Just don't tell anyone else."

"There's no way I would," said Owen, beginning to wonder if he'd made a mistake in accepting Evan's land. "By the way, did you watch the news yesterday?"

"I don't have a TV. Don't believe in them," Evan replied proudly.

"They're expectin' the senate to pass the new laws anytime now," said Owen, continuing to stack wood.

"We're going to have to have the spirit of martyrs, but I'm ready."

Owen stacked the last log and turned to Evan. "You remind me of Peter sayin' he'd face anything with Jesus—the night before he let him down."

"Just keep quiet about the caves, Owen."

A few weeks later, Pastor Sam called a meeting at his home for the small group who opposed the new laws.

"Some of you have been phoning me and asking about the meaning of the new Australian legislation and its implications," he said. "I thought it best to clear things up. First, let me confirm that it's been approved by the senate and it's now law in this country. It's practically identical to the laws in the United States, and we can expect more of the same outcomes here. The only difference is that the period of grace is a shorter—we've only got about eight weeks before the 'can't buy or sell' penalties apply. Microchipping starts in just two weeks. What upsets me is that practically all our religious leaders are touting it as the best thing since the resurrection! Pastor Karl has been promoting these concepts in Christian and secular publications both here and abroad, and one of his articles states that people like us who reject the NIO get the mark of the beast. He's had more visits from his old mate apostle Paul. That's where he got that from."

"So what they're saying," said Basil, "is that you can't follow your own conscience whenever you want, even if it means breaking the Ten Commandments and Christ's teachings. You've got to go along with their superficial unity no matter what they believe or worship. You've got to believe in the teachings of the miracle workers, and also the dead people who come back with messages from la-la land. And you've got to get microchipped and say you believe in all this garbage."

"Spot on, Basil," said Sam.

"What do you suggest we do?" asked Ami.

"We've only got a few weeks. I think it's going to be impossible to survive in the cities anymore. Some of you have been doing the smart thing and you've found places out of town a bit. My family's going to stay with the Rileys out at Dunn's Creek. Look, before I forget, Karl and the others don't want us to worship with them anymore, and of course I'm no longer his associate pastor."

"So they've finally given up on us, eh?" asked Owen.

"Yeah. But don't worry. We can meet here for the time being," suggested Sam.

"Do we quit our jobs?" asked Ami.

"There's no point just yet. But we should start selling things so we can buy whatever we need for the future. Definitely draw everything out of your bank and investments, because they'll freeze them soon."

"Wow, this is just like the movies," said Alice, glancing around at everyone excitedly.

"Except this is real," said Madeline.

"Start storing stuff in your country homes and keep witnessing," said Sam. "I've got heaps of literature here so people will see the issues about the mark of the beast clearly."

"Tell me again about this mark of the beast thing," said Alice.

"In a nutshell, people get the mark in these last days when they permanently reject what the cross stands for. They show this rejection by accepting man's laws over the law of God."

"What about the microchip?" asked Basil.

"They're using the chip as a test. But the mark has to do with rejecting Christ's truth and his character."

"And the seal of God is the opposite, isn't it?" asked Basil.

"That's right. We'll have to study Revelation chapter 7 and the early part of chapter 14 again to understand it better, but to have the seal of God is to follow Jesus no matter what. God can see when the cross has done its work in our hearts and minds, and he knows we won't turn back."

"You seem to think the true and false gospels are the main issues at stake," said Basil.

"Very much so. We believe in salvation by faith—it's of grace alone. The beast has set up a counterfeit man-made system of worship with political methods, which is really righteousness by man's works—a false gospel."

Sam looked around solemnly. "We're in the middle of a battle that's as real as any war that's been fought with guns—the battle of Armageddon. Could you look it up in Revelation 16, please, Rohan? Armageddon is not fought with earthly weapons, but with spiritual weapons. This is a battle between the power of deception and the power of truth; between the cruel force of tyranny and the power of freedom and love; between the power of darkness and the power of light. Armageddon is a battle for the minds and hearts of people—it's fought at a supernatural, worldwide level and it ushers in the coming of Christ. Everyone must choose between the compromise that miracles and deception impose, and allegiance to Christ's word and the Gospel. The stakes are high—eternal life or eternal death."

Basil gave a low whistle. "So that's what the battle of Armageddon is."

"It's in Revelation 16, verse 14," said Rohan. " 'For they are demonic spirits, performing signs, who go abroad to the kings of the whole world, to assemble them for battle on the great day of God almighty.' Then verse 16 says, 'And they assembled them at the place which is called in Hebrew, Armageddon.'"

"It's pretty clear that the devil uses the deceptive power of signs and miracles as his weapons," said Basil. "And the kings of the earth have certainly been deceived by them, including Vernon Turnbull, our own PM."

❦

The matron of Newcastle Shores Hospital wasn't smiling when Madeline entered her office. Madeline guessed what she had been called in for, and she just wanted the unpleasant experience over with.

"Madeline, you've decided not to comply with the new regulations regarding religious compliance, is that correct?"

"Yes. I don't want to be microchipped, and I honestly don't believe in the new laws."

"I'm sure you understand the consequences of your decision—you'll lose your job."

Madeline nodded. "Yes. But I like helping sick people."

"If you like helping people, why don't you help us all by cooperating? After all, it's in the best interests of everybody."

"But the Bible teaches us to follow our conscience."

"Conscience? Madeline, my conscience and the Bible both tell me to obey the government because it's been instituted of God. Wasn't Israel the most prosperous under Solomon's rule when it obeyed the king?"

"This is different. Israel willingly gave its allegiance to the king. But our government's enforcing a law based on fear and coercion, not God's law."

"I'm sorry you see it that way. I have to instantly dismiss you—without severance pay, under the new regulations. It's for the betterment of society."

❦

Owen walked down the freshly worn track and placed the shovel against the cabin's log wall. For several hours he had been digging, weeding, and raking the rich, dark soil under the hot summer sun. Tomorrow he would plant potatoes and pumpkins, but just then he felt like taking a shower. Rather than go to the trouble of lighting a fire under the primitive wood heater, he had a quick cold shower with water piped from the creek into an iron storage tank.

Madeline and Ami were planting strawberries in a sheltered plot on the sunny side of the cabin. Puff, her tail twitching, was stretched out on a log, absorbing the sun and occasionally taking a half-hearted swipe at a passing insect. As they had no fruit trees, they planted quick-growing berries that would provide them with enough fruit to bottle for winter use. They had already picked and preserved a few buckets of wild blackberries.

Alice Beckett was cheerfully decorating the tiny bedroom she shared with Ami. There was barely enough room for two single beds, an old dressing table, and their clothes, which hung from a rope in one corner. She had hammered nails into the rough walls so she could hang some paintings she'd picked up from a welfare store.

Alice had never felt happier in all her life. She was free from her father's oppression and the stigma of being almost illiterate—none of her new friends belittled her for it. Out there in the wilderness, she could indulge her passion for artistic freedom and the simple pleasures of life. She had even grown to be friends with Basil Dorf, who teased her unmercifully.

Basil was spending his nights on an old couch in the main room of Owen's cabin while he completed a tiny hut for himself along the creek bank. The narrow hut looked rather eccentric with its ladder going up to a second-story bed that was also the ceiling for the first floor. He could crawl from his bed out through the upstairs window, and sun-bake on an outside landing, which he had nailed onto an enormous gum tree branch. Attached to the roof was a bracket that accepted a satellite TV antenna. He could quickly put the antenna in place at night when Evan couldn't see it. A cable led to a small battery-powered TV set.

The sun came to rest behind the forested mountain to the west. Its red rays filtering through the trees was God's benediction over the day's work of his children. Everyone gathered inside the main cabin after washing off the day's sweat and dirt. Basil, believing in economy of action, had simply washed in the creek. He had dammed a pool for bathing with a row of huge boulders.

"It's like we're on a permanent camping trip," said Ami as she sprawled exhausted on the bean bag in the corner.

"Yeah, but this is no holiday. This is our life now—this is what we do," said Madeline, who had come in from her bedroom wearing a light tracksuit.

"There's no turnin' back now," said Alice.

"I wouldn't feel safe back in town anyway. People were acting strange to me at work—they'd changed," said Madeline, whacking a small spider on the floor with her sandal.

"Owen, do you reckon we've got enough food?" asked Ami.

"Just look at all those boxes stacked in the corner," replied Owen, lighting the kitchen stove.

"But there's no fresh greens in those cans and packets," said Ami.

Owen jerked his thumb downstream. "Evan's garden is big enough for about three families. Whatever faults he's got, he's definitely been good at preparin' for the crisis."

"We can't ask him for his veggies," said Madeline, preparing ingredients for a large pot of soup.

"No, but we can swap him our packaged stuff," replied Owen.

"OK, Husband, we'll trade. But when will our own veggies be ready?" asked Madeline.

"Radish and lettuce should be ready in about two or three weeks if we pick 'em young. Things grow fast in summer. Tomatoes, corn, and other stuff should follow a few weeks later. The soil's terrific here."

Owen stuck a chunk of ironbark log in the fireplace. "It's surprising how simple life can be—no stress, no computers or high-tech stuff, only a radio to hear the news and just good old simple work."

"Just as well you brought that truckload of fowl manure up here last month. It should last until our fertilizer factories start producing," said Basil with a straight face.

"Fertilizer factories?" queried Alice.

"You know, feathered factories that push cackle berries and organic fertilizer out of the same production slot."

"Oh, the chooks!" Alice laughed.

"Yeah, the fox food," said Basil. "We can't afford to feed another fox—we all forgot to reinforce the chicken wiring today."

"Oh, can you go and do it, please, Basil?" pleaded Ami. "I can't bear to think one of my pets might get taken tonight."

"Too late now, unless you want to do it. I'm not sexist—women are equal to the task."

"Oh, all right." Ami sighed. "I'll wire any holes together. Where's the wire?"

Basil pointed as he smelled the soup. "On the fence post. The pliers are near the door."

He stirred the soup and stoked the fire. "Evan seems to have accepted me staying here."

"Yeah," Owen said. "He grizzled about it, but deep down he's good hearted."

"He read me the riot act about no fishing, no fun, no nothin'." Alice laughed. "He didn't even like our cow. Reckons milk is only good for calves. But I reminded him that Genevieve's manure will be good for the veggies."

Alice's laughter was infectious. "He didn't think it was funny when I told 'im I had a pet pig called Evana tied up in the bush for when provisions grew short."

When Ami stopped laughing, she asked Owen, "How long do we live up here? Will they leave us alone for a long time—years maybe?"

"We aren't breaking the law by buyin' or sellin', so they'll leave us alone now that they've gotten rid of us. As I understand Revelation's predictions, things will get even tougher one day, but God will take care of us."

Owen didn't want to mention the predicted death decree. There was no point in alarming her prematurely.

⁊

Owen drove his four-wheel-drive Toyota slowly through the Wattagan Ranges in the direction of Newcastle. He had been door-knocking with literature one day a week ever since they completed Basil's Cottage nearly two months before.

Once more, he was about to enter a city that was familiar yet was part of a strange new world of control and restrictions—a world that was both visionary and hostile, where everybody spoke of the dawn of a new era. *How quickly everything has changed*, he thought. *Only a year ago I could freely sing the wonderful news of God's love. Now, I can't even get into a church, sing at a rodeo, or even buy a burger.*

Owen talked to God aloud as he drove. "I'm feeling scared today. I don't know what will happen or who I'll meet, so help me to forget about myself. I don't feel very lovin' and I wanna be back home, but you must have some people in town who need my help. Thanks for openin' up Flo Hopkins's heart last week. Show her what she should do and give her the strength to do it. How can I encourage her today? Open everybody's heart to accept the literature. Thanks, Lord."

Owen parked his car around the corner and walked to Flo Hopkins's place. She looked both ways to see if anybody was looking, and quickly ushered him in and closed the door. Owen spent almost two hours with her.

"I've been watching how terribly they've been treating brave people like you," said Flo. "It can't be right, no matter what they say. I was never very religious before, but now I want to find out more, and I'm not going along with what they want."

"Flo, why don't you come live with us? Sooner or later they'll notice you, and things could go bad for you here."

"I'm too old to run away. I'm just going to stay here and take whatever happens. I'm not afraid now that you've shown me God's promises, and I think Fred would've done the same thing—he died two years ago. Don't worry about me. There's lots of others to help. But don't go next door. They moved in not long ago, and they're a rough-looking lot."

After praying with Flo, Owen picked up his bag full of literature and left. Next door was a large old rambling wooden house with drawn curtains and unkept lawn.

Strange-looking joint with those fancy motorbikes in the shed. But I'd better go in—whoever owns them needs saving too.

Owen knocked on the front door. No one answered. He thought he heard someone coughing around the back, so he opened the rusty side gate and went through. A bald, middle-aged man sat on the back veranda steps, holding a marijuana cigarette and a bottle of beer. He wore black jeans with a dog-stud belt and had no shirt on. There was a tattoo on each shoulder: one a goat's skull and the other a black-backed spider.

"Can I help you, mate?" he said, startled.

Owen looked into a pair of wary, bloodshot eyes. "G'day, mate. I'm Owen. I'm just giving out Christian literature. Got a few minutes?"

The bikie looked Owen up and down. "Come in. I'm George."

Owen prayed hard. *Lord I think this is a bikie gang den I'm walking into here; I hope I'm doing the right thing.*

The stale smell of smoke and beer hung in the air, and empty beer bottles and pornographic magazines were scattered on the floor. A dirty sponge mattress lay on its side against the wall. One man was half asleep on the couch. Another slouched on a recliner, watching TV and drinking beer. Both had long beards, jeans, and black T-shirts. Their leather jackets hung on old wooden chairs. Owen was surprised that the smell of beer had already become unpleasant to him—he had only given up drinking relatively recently.

"This here bloke is, uh ..."

"I'm Owen."

"Owen wants to talk to us about religion," said George as he opened the fridge and withdrew another bottle of beer. "Have a beer, Owen?"

"No, thanks."

"Very wise. Bad for you, this stuff." George grinned. "We're all religious here, Owen, though ya mightn't think it."

"Good to hear," said Owen.

"Yeah, well, you'd have to be stupid not to believe in the big fella upstairs when you see what's going on these days—the miracles and all the big boys pushing for change and stuff. You saw the Harleys outside, didn't ya? Well, I used to belong to the Taipan Bikie Club—used to be a bit of Satan-worship goin' on there, but the miracles changed all that."

"You've given up on Satan?"

"Hell, yeah. Why wouldn't I after seeing those miracles? You believe in 'em, too, don't ya?"

"Well, they were real miracles, all right. I don't doubt that. But everything's got to be tested by the Bible."

George eyed Owen suspiciously. "But they were *good* miracles, weren't they?"

"I've got to be honest with you, George—I don't think they were from God."

George glared at Owen. "What sort of mongrel would dare not believe in those miracles! What does it take to convince you idiots! Last week my dead grandmother told me stuff about myself that only God could know about, and she reckoned the laws of the miracle guys are our only hope."

Owen tensed, feeling he had to be guarded in what he said. The other men had sat up, and their cold eyes bore into him. "OK, fellas," said Owen gingerly, "I guess we have to respect each other's feelings. I guess I'll be going."

George grabbed Owen by his shirt and eyeballed him up close. "No. I don't respect ya. It's scum like you that's gonna wreck things for everybody else. You've caused enough trouble—hasn't he, guys?"

The two other men walked behind Owen to block off any escape route. George kicked Owen in the groin. While he was groaning on the floor, he kicked him heavily in the back, ribs, and head.

"Keep your mouth shut or you're dead meat!" hissed one of the men.

But Owen never heard him; he was unconscious.

When he woke, his head and back throbbed. *Lord, help me,* he prayed silently.

George was thumbing through Owen's books. "Fancy you goin' to sleep on us. If we see ya goin' around givin' out this rubbish anymore, they'll find ya floatin' in the harbor," he warned. "Now, clear out. And if ya call the cops, your life's worth nothin'."

Owen tried to stand, but was overcome with pain and nausea, and fell down. After resting a moment, he crawled to a lounge chair and managed to struggle up. He leaned on the wall until he was no longer dizzy and edged his way to the back door. When the bright sunlight met his splitting headache, he vomited several times, then managed to stumble to Flo's front yard. Seeing that he was out of sight of the gang members, he groped his way to Flo's door and knocked loudly.

Flo gasped when she saw him and helped him lie down on her couch.

"Poor thing—you're in a bad way, luv. What happened? Was it next door?"

Owen nodded.

"Oh, I told you not to go there, luv. They're mean weirdoes if ever I saw one. I'll go and get some warm water for that head wound; it's nasty. You just rest. Is there anything broken?"

"Dunno. Nothing serious, maybe a rib."

"You're all blue. What did they do, kick ya?"

"Yeah. I'll be OK. Can I use your phone?"

"Sure, luv. I'll bring it over."

Owen's voice was thin and weak. "Could I speak to Inspector Adrian Sebastian, please?"

"Adrian," Owen continued, "it's Owen Boyd ... from church. I was giving out some Gospel literature, and some guys kicked me ... real bad."

"Where are you?"

"I don't want to involve the person helping me. What can be done?"

"Owen, you've got to realize that you've lost your citizen's rights. The law doesn't want me to defend you. You're not the only protester who's been beaten up."

Owen held his rib cage to try to ease the pain. "So anybody who wants to can beat us up?"

"Legally speaking, no. But there's a lot of strong feeling against people like you now. The best thing for you is to stay out of town. How did you get in anyway?"

"Oh, I had a little fuel left." Owen didn't want to tell him that he had a shed full of fuel.

"Use it to go home. I can't understand your ungrateful attitude. You know you're fighting God, don't you?"

"Thanks for the information, Adrian. Just thought I'd check. Bye."

Two hours later, Owen felt strong enough to limp to his car. He swallowed two more of Floe's painkillers and drove slowly south to the Wattagan Range, trying to avoid painful bumps on the dirt road with his stiffly sprung vehicle.

Owen woke when the sun rose over the ranges to the east and was renewing the life of the valley. Madeline applied some cold creek water fomentations to his bruises.

"Owen, I didn't want to tell you yesterday while you were sick, but Basil forgot to take his TV dish down, and Evan spotted it when he came out this way yesterday."

"Oh, no! What'd he say?"

"I'm afraid he's told us to go."

"What?"

"Well, you know what he's like. He thinks we've polluted his valley with the TV. He doesn't trust us anymore and feels that nobody can be saved while we're here. He just can't seem to understand salvation by grace. He thinks it's salvation through purification alone."

"Ouch! Take it easy, that's too cold."

"Owen, it's gotta be cold."

"He can't expect us to just go—go where?"

"What'll we do?"

"Nothin'. We're not going anywhere."

"But it's his land."

"Yeah, but he reckons it's God's." Owen smiled as he imagined Evan's reaction. "I'll tell him God let me know he wants us to stay."

"Owen! Is that honest?"

"I'm dead serious—God *doesn't* want us to go. Anyway, what can Evan do about it? The cops won't help him—they couldn't care less about his land rights. I'll talk to him later. If we promise to only watch stuff like news or documentaries, he might soften up."

Basil and Alice watched an American news report about the experiences of those who refused to cooperate with the NIO's new laws. It was called "The Marked Ones," implying that dissenters from the NIO had the mark of the beast. Cameras focused on the specially built compounds that held those who had dared to resist. Tens of thousands of dissenters had already left the cities and created quiet country communes. If they were lucky, a nurse or perhaps a doctor lived among them.

Schooling for children continued, but the subject matter revolved around practical subjects such as gardening, carpentry, Bible, and natural health treatments.

An interview was being conducted with Sergio Peron, a world-famous evangelist.

"Dr. Peron, Americans have been stunned at your decision. You have been very vocal in your opposition to the New International Order. Why is that?"

"My reasons are the same as those repeated by so many others. Our leaders have abolished the very thing that had set the United States of America apart as a great nation under God—religious freedom."

"Dr. Peron, because of your stand against the NIO, your work as an evangelist has been halted. Your freedom to travel and preach has been taken away from you. Wouldn't the Gospel cause have been better served if you had joined the NIO and remained an evangelist?"

"I believe the time has come to make a stand and accept the consequences. God can use my protests more than any compromised preaching. My message to every American is to stand firm in the cause of Christ and freedom, no matter what the consequences."

Basil sprawled out on his bed. "Good to see big guys like Peron take a stand," he said.

Alice had been watching from the outside tree-branch platform. She rolled onto her back and gazed at the upper branches. "What'll happen to him?"

"They'll throw him into a compound to rot."

"Sad, isn't it? They even locked Sarah Ashton up the other day."

Basil sat bolt upright. "The film star?"

"Yeah. She'd started to warn people about the miracles and stuff."

"Just goes to show we're not the only ones. Fancy, Sarah Ashton. Wow! I'll buy the joint next to hers in heaven."

"Basil!"

"Don't worry. It's impossible to flirt up there."

Ayman Atef sat quietly in a shepherd's hut that was within a short walk of his cave hideout in the isolated wilderness of northwest Pakistan. As the most-wanted terrorist leader in the world, he marveled that he had successfully avoided capture, and he believed there had to be a profound reason for it. He had been doing a lot of thinking, and for weeks his conviction was strengthening that Jesus was more than just a prophet. Once more, he read the prophecy in Isaiah 53 verses 5 and 6, which described the Messiah's work.

But he was pierced for our transgressions,
he was crushed for our iniquities;
the punishment that brought us peace was upon him,
and by his wounds we are healed.

We all like sheep have gone astray,
each of us has turned to his own way;
And the Lord has laid on him the iniquity of us all.

As he thought about the passage, Atef surrendered to the conviction that this passage, written centuries BC, could only be describing a suffering messiah—a description that could fit Jesus alone. Atef collapsed to the dirt floor of the tiny hut. The fingers of both his hands went white as they gripped a wooden beam on the ground with the same intensity that his anguished heart compelled him to pray. Every fiber of his being seemed to stretch out in an appeal to the one who alone could enlighten the deep complexity and distress of his soul. He promised God and himself that he would put aside preconceived ideas and any arrogant, egotistical views of himself and of his life-taking mission. Now, only one thing mattered to Atef—truth that would affect millions of lives and his own eternal destiny.

Never before had he prayed like this. Never had he even remotely experienced soul-hunger like this. Suddenly, hundreds of fragmented and challenging thoughts crowded his brain—thoughts that seemed to be painted into his soul by a covering divine presence. The fragmented thoughts flew around his head and settled into a pattern like a completed dream-like jigsaw puzzle. A superhuman, powerful conviction possessed him that Jesus was more than a great thinker and prophet—he was who he claimed he was: the Son of God!

The implications were at the same time horrendous and wonderful. An incredible remorse for sin instantly flooded his being. Overwhelmed with shame and guilt for the deaths of thousands of innocent people, he thought of the fragmented families, the homelessness, and the fear he had caused. He was conscious of a great cleansing and a miraculous transformation of heart taking place within. Still prostrate and weeping bitter tears, the terrorist asked Christ to accept and forgive him. A peace such as he had never before thought possible embraced him.

He gazed through the hut's open door at the rugged horizon in deep thought for a while, communing with God. He then walked up a steep, rugged track to where his assistant, Mahommet, was sitting, with his weapon by his side.

"Mahommet, I have been studying the holy writings for some time now," he said. "Only a week ago, you said that you wondered if Christ was more than a prophet. I knew then that you were becoming a Christian or you would have never risked your life in revealing your thoughts. Your questions angered me but drove me to study further. It will make you happy to learn that I have joined you."

Mahommet and Atef embraced as they joyfully laughed together.

With a hand gripping each of Mahommet's shoulders, Atef commanded him, "Make contact with the Syrian media. Tell them I will meet them at the Aksak market next week on Wednesday night. I wish to make a statement of great significance. Do not tell them what it is about. Do not tell our men at this stage. Tell the media that I will speak to them on two conditions. There are to be no police or military forewarned, and it is to be a live, unedited broadcast to go around the world."

"What if the police or soldiers set a trap for you?"

"Warn the media against it. Tell them I will send spies before me. They will be too frightened to do it. They know my ruthlessness well enough."

When the time came for airing the sensational live interview, the whole world watched in suspenseful anticipation. Owen and his friends crammed into Basil Dorf's hut, where Basil had extended the wiring to allow the others to watch his TV downstairs.

"You're brilliant, Owen—persuading Evan to allow us to keep the TV," praised Basil.

Owen laughed at the memory. "He actually made me sign a promise that we'd only watch it to monitor events. Why, I can't even watch a rodeo!"

Some of the delegates to the New International Order arrived for a meeting in Paris and gathered in a hotel lobby, eagerly anticipating the notorious terrorist's interview, speculating as to what he might say. Other terrorists had changed direction because of the miracles and were now supporting the NIO. The delegates cherished the possibility that Ayman Atef would do likewise.

The camera crew found a residence near the Aksak marketplace to conduct the interview. Atef had his armed guards posted around the building. The cameras were switched on and the interview began.

"Ayman Atef, as you requested this interview and the world is watching, no doubt you wish to get straight to the point. I believe you have an announcement you wish to make."

"Yes. As you know, I have been opposed to the Christian westernized world, and as its bitter enemy, have devoted my life to fight against it. However, in my mountain solitude I have had much time to study, pray, and meditate, and as a result, have come to a conclusion that will no doubt come as a surprise. Everyone should know that I have now become a follower of Jesus Christ, who has changed my life and direction. That is the reason I requested this interview."

"This news will have deep implications. Mr. Atef, did the Piona miracles have an effect on you?"

"Yes, profoundly so, especially because Muslims were healed and a drought was broken. The miracles turned my thinking upside down and gave me an open mind to Christianity. But that is not why I accepted Jesus as the Christ. I began to read the writings of Moses and the Prophets, and in Isaiah chapter 53, I found that the ministry and sufferings of Jesus were predicted centuries before they happened. He is the Son of God—the Messiah of the world."

As Atef spoke, his face glowed and his eyes grew moist with gratitude to God.

The delegates at the Paris NIO meeting looked at each other with great astonishment and delight.

"So now you give your full support to the New International Order?" continued the interviewer.

Atef looked intently at the camera and pointed at it dramatically. "No, I do not! The leaders of the NIO are crucifying Christ again in the form of his followers today, in the same way that the leaders in Christ's day crucified him for political and religious expediency."

"But Mr. Atef, you said that it was the miracles that first convinced you of Christianity. Yet you are opposing the NIO—those involved with the miracle movement?"

"Yes, at first the miracles convicted me and made me think hard about my position. But it was the Word of God that taught me about the real Jesus, who is very different from the NIO Jesus. Through the NIO, Satan wants to rid the world of the true followers of Christ and to establish his own kingdom on earth—a kingdom based on compromise, fear, and coercion, where the power of the minority governs the conscience of the majority. May God save us from the NIO!"

The NIO delegates looked at one another, horrified and stunned.

The Australian delegate, Richard Timms, was visibly shaken and upset. He stood and spoke angrily. "Atef must stand trial for his atrocities. He says he has changed his religion, but he still retains his hatred and insanity. He is more dangerous now than when he was as a terrorist! Every effort should—"

"Quiet," a delegate interrupted. "Let's hear more."

"Up until now I have been misguided in my fighting for the cause of justice for the Arab people, and I have sinned against God," admitted Atef. "Now I can see that because of the NIO, there is more injustice in this world than I ever dreamt of. But military weapons cannot conquer injustice, so it is time for all believers to use the spiritual weapons of prayer and Christ's love."

"Mr. Atef, what are your immediate plans?"

"I need to be brought to justice for my crimes against humanity. God has forgiven me, although most people will not. My punishment should suit the severity of my crimes. But I leave myself in the compassionate hands of Christ—may he have mercy on me. Unless you have questions about Jesus Christ, that is all I wish to say. The interview is over."

"Mr. Atef, I wanted to ask—"

"The interview is *over*," repeated Atef, standing.

Basil stood in his excitement and threw both hands in the air. "Wow! Ayman Atef is now one of us. Can you believe it?"

"Yeah, and he's fair dinkum about it too," said Alice.

"And he let the NIO have it with both barrels," exclaimed Owen.

"What a powerful witness for Christ," said Madeline excitedly. "Just think of all the Arabs watching—the world watching! It's like when the apostle Paul was converted on the road to Damascus and the Christians thought it was a trick. Ayman Atef? Unbelievable!"

Owen stood from his cramped spot and stretched. "It was amazing enough when the miracles convinced the Palestinians and the Jews to stop fighting over territory, but this tops it off."

19

Calm Before the Storm

◇◇◇◇◇◇◇◇◇◇◇◇◇◇◇◇◇◇◇◇◇◇◇◇◇◇◇◇◇◇◇◇◇◇◇◇◇

B ASIL DORF POSITIONED a small polystyrene float in the quiet water of
an inside bend behind some large boulders. He had cut a slot in the
flat float and fitted a miniature paddle wheel so that it was half submerged.
The current would turn the wheel, which was connected to a small electric
generator that he had found in a rubbish dump. He had repaired and
modified the generator and fixed the paddle wheel to it. He then ran a wire
to his hut on the stream bank and connected it to twelve-volt light bulbs
above his bed and also downstairs. Another wire ran to his TV set. It didn't
matter if the stream level rose or fell; the float would automatically keep
the paddle wheel immersed at just the right level.

Basil enjoyed watching the paddle wheel spin for a few minutes. After
making some adjustments to its position and depth, he was pleased to see
that the lights were working in both rooms. He turned on the twelve-volt
TV set and smiled to himself when it worked. Now he wouldn't have to
worry about batteries.

Evan's insulin supply ran out, and even though he had type-one
diabetes he wasn't worried. In fact he had been looking forward to using
the Besel wart herb that he believed would control his diabetes. He had
taken pride in the magnificent specimens he had lovingly cultivated and
which were now flourishing alongside his cabin wall.

A few days later, Evan visited his fiancée, Maude, who lived in an old
shell of a caravan a stone's throw from Evan's house.

"You look tired and drawn," Maude said. "How are you doin' on the
Besel wart herbs?"

"Oh, not too bad. A bit tired and shaky, I suppose."

— 173 —

"Maybe you should've tried the herb months ago, while you could still get insulin."

"Oh, I'll be OK. It's just the toxins coming out of my body."

"But yesterday you said you were feelin' great."

"I was at first, but now the stuff is starting to cleanse the system."

"Just be careful, darlin'. I don't want you sick for the weddin' next week."

"I still wish we had a proper minister to marry us."

"But you said it would be all right for Victor Zinski to marry us."

"Yes, but he's not … well, anyway, he's the best we can find."

"Of course, luv. And it's the promises we make in front of witnesses that count. All that signing papers rigmarole is of the world. I'm so excited, I can't wait."

"Basil upset me the other day. I spoke with him about getting married without a celebrant. You know what he said? 'Isaac just took Rachel into his tent, and that was it—they were married. Why don't you just do the same?' "

"Don't take any notice of 'im. He's just a stirrer."

"He sure is. The other day I saw him playing around with his water-wheel generator and I asked him to make me one. After all I've done for him, guess what he said?"

"'I'll do anythin' for you, you're so wonderful. Evan?'"

"Don't be silly. The blighter said he'd swap me a generator for four more hours of TV a week. As if I'd compromise myself to trade in sin! I told him he was lucky I let him stay on my property."

"What'd he say to that?"

"He said that by the time the year's over he would have so many useful inventions, just having him here would be an honor."

"The cheek! So will ya ever get one of those contraptions?"

"Who knows? I told him I wouldn't mind a spare battery if he found one, and he said he'd swap me one for six trout out of my creek!"

"What? He knows you don't allow eating meat."

"Of course he does. He always wants something sinful! How he expects to be ready for the Lord's return, I don't know."

Ami cooked the evening meal of boiled corn and fried tomatoes, and served it on the old laminated table. A tin of blackberries would be shared for dessert.

"When will the potatoes be ready?" Madeline fretted. "I'm getting a bit sick of corn."

"Every day I see steaks hopping around, but Evan won't let us shoot 'em," complained Basil.

"We agreed to the conditions," reminded Ami. "Anyway, I'm down to my perfect weight."

Alice spoke with a mouth full of corn. "You'll go down further yet, livin' out here. I was readin' that Jesus cooked fish, so why won't Evan let us catch fish? There's heaps of 'em!"

"We've been through this before," said Owen. "We can't change his mind and we're not starving. We'll just have to stick it out."

"You know what I miss the most out here?" asked Madeline wistfully. "Not being able to visit friends and relatives."

"I miss the steaks and burgers," said Basil, slicing the corn kernels off and mixing them with the tomato.

"And Coke and chips and ice cream," added Alice as she stirred some homemade tomato sauce. "Why don't those chooks lay more eggs?"

"They will soon, just wait," said Owen. "They don't like the hot weather."

"Fickle chooks," complained Basil. "First it's the fox trauma, then the rain, now it's the heat. There's always something to upset them. Leave me some of that sauce, Alice. What's on the menu for tomorrow, girls?"

"Baked corn, and boiled corn the next night," advised Madeline.

"And blackberries for desert," added Ami.

Alice was alone in the cabin one night while the others were watching TV at Basil's hut. She had blown the candle out and was lying in bed, dreamily thinking about what sort of wedding present she could give Evan and Maude. There was so little to choose from, and they had such strong likes and dislikes.

She was startled to hear a woman's voice coming from somewhere in the rooms darkness.

"Hello, Alice sweetheart. I've come to visit you now that you know Jesus. I have missed you very much."

Fear and amazement gripped Alice. Her sleepy state vaporizing as she sat up in bed. The voice was familiar, although she hadn't heard it for a long time. It was a voice that had often comforted her when she was a girl. When others had spoken to her in anger or ridiculed her, this voice had offered encouragement and praise. When other voices had remained silent and ignored her, this voice had been friendly and talkative. It was the voice of her late grandmother Violet, and it was the most pleasant childhood sound that she could remember.

"Don't be afraid, Alice. It really is me."

Alice had been warned how Satan had impersonated the apostle Paul and others, but this was different; this was someone she had known and loved personally. Conflicting emotions struggled within her, and sobering danger signals conflicted with her desire to speak to Grandma Violet.

Alice was confused. If she welcomed her visitor, she might be offering encouragement to a deceiving spirit. On the other hand, if she expressed disbelief, she may grieve her precious grandmother and lose a rare opportunity. She decided to say nothing until she lit her candle by her bed for a clearer view. She fumbled for the matchbox, broke the first match, and then, with trembling hand, lit the small candle.

With eyes wide open in wonderment and fear, Alice could see the indistinct form of a short, plump, gray-haired old lady in a light blue dress—Grandma Violet's favorite.

"You see? It's me after all, isn't it, Alice dear?"

"I … I can't see properly. Wait."

Oh, this really looks like my grandmother. I'll just light the big candle to make sure.

Alice lit the big candle, and the warm glow of the flickering light revealed the kind, wrinkled smile that she remembered so well. It was her grandmother's hair, her smile, and her twinkling, kind eyes. Part of Alice wanted to jump out of bed and hug her, but there was an ethereal, untouchable quality about her visitor that prevented her. She knelt on the covers, gazing in awe at the figure in front of her bed.

"Grandma? Is that fair dinkum you?"

"Who else, silly? I can't wait to hug you again, pet. But we aren't allowed to touch, you know, until you get to heaven."

"But you died three years ago."

"Don't be afraid of dyin'. We never die, luv. You know that now that you believe."

"But people don't come back. we don't see 'em. We—"

"I know, I know, Alice. But Jesus is coming back soon and I've been especially sent to help you. I want you to know, sweetheart, how much Jesus loves you and how he watches over you every day."

"Oh, Grandma, I *didn't* know, until Madeline showed me Jesus' love."

"I used to tell you Bible stories, so I planted the seed back then. Madeline is a good girl, but she's in great danger."

"Danger?"

"Yes. You and Madeline and your other friends—that's why I've come. God is pouring out his Spirit on the whole world with miracles and signs, and millions are coming together to serve the Lord as one. You're missing out by being on your own way out here, luv. You're really hiding from

God's Spirit. You've got to start believing the messengers that God sends to you; don't be afraid of them."

"I … I love you Grandma, but it worries me that the Bible says to have nothin' to do with spiritism stuff or talkin' to dead people."

"Yes, yes, spiritism is evil—stay away from it, Alice. They have meetings where wicked people call up messages from the powers of darkness. But remember, if there's a counterfeit, there's a genuine article too. This is the genuine; can't you tell? Can't you feel my love and goodness?"

"Yes, Grandma, I can feel love in this room, and somethin' smells nice."

"You see? That's God's blessing. So now, listen to what I say. Don't tell the others your plan. Go with Owen when he drives to town tomorrow. Pack a small bag with your essentials—no big bags, or he'll get suspicious. When you get past Broadmeadow railway station, ask him to stop so you can go to the toilet in the parking lot. You're close to Pastor Karl's place there. Walk to his place and don't look back. Owen won't know what's happened until after you've gone."

"But he'll be worried."

"Write a note in the morning explaining that you've decided to leave the valley. Tell them not to look for you. Leave the note beside the car seat. Owen will find it."

"Oh, Grandma, Madeline is my best friend. I don't want to leave her."

"You have Jesus and me to guide you now, my sweet. In a few weeks, you will meet a handsome young Christian man who will take care of you. He will marry you one day. Don't worry. I have to go now. I love you lots. Bye."

"Grandma!" Alice called out. "What about Madeline? How can she get away?"

Alice heard an indistinct voice that grew softer with every word. "You leave that up to us, Alice. Don't worry. I'll see you again soon."

Alice lay in bed and could feel her excited heartbeat. She lay still and enjoyed the presence and sweet smell of what she felt sure was heaven's love, wishing for it not to go away.

I wasn't imagining things—that was really Grandma. I can't go wrong in following her advice. I could always trust her, even as a child. Funny, I felt safe in this place, but I don't feel safe here anymore. I am so confused. I don't want to leave my friends. I wish I could be sure that was really Grandma. She said I'd meet a nice man. I hope he's nice as Owen.

For a long time Alice thought about the happy childhood times with Grandma Violet. Then she thought of Madeline's care for her, and her friends, and how she didn't want to leave them. Eventually she fell asleep.

In the morning, Alice mixed some fresh cow's milk with stale homemade bread for breakfast. "Good morning, Owen. See anythin' on TV last night?"

"They nabbed more of us in different spots around the world—actually, I'm sick of seeing it. I think you can get too much of it. I just want a peaceful life while it lasts."

"You goin' into town today?"

"I was, but just changed my mind." Owen looked at Alice curiously. "How'd you know?"

"Oh, I was just asking. You know how you told me it's wrong to talk to dead people like Paul and Peter and that?"

"Yeah."

"Well, what about talkin' to ordinary folk?"

"Ordinary folk? You mean dead ones?"

"Yeah."

"Didn't I tell you that we're warned about that too?"

"Don't think so."

"Why do you ask?"

"Oh, nothin', just wonderin' and learnin'." Alice changed the subject. "I can't think of what to get Evan and Maude."

"What are the choices?"

"I was thinking maybe a nice cake or pumpkin pie. I've also learned how to make nice big candles. And I've finished readin' that nice book, an' it's still new lookin'."

"What's it about?"

"It's not a true story, but it's got Christian morals and stuff."

"Evan won't read any fiction, Alice, no matter how Christian."

"Well, I'll cook him somethin' then. He hasn't been lookin' real good lately—looks a bit tired. Basil reckons he's changed his medicine or somethin'."

"In my opinion, he's crook—real crook."

The summer sun had risen well above the ranges, and the valley shimmered in its heat. The black-and-white magpies perched on high branches, their wings outstretched to try to catch the cooling breeze. Kookaburras dived and skimmed the stream with their feet to catch the spray. The loud buzzing of cicadas intensified as the temperature rose.

Madeline stood from weeding the rows of sweet corn and arched her aching back. She felt hot and tired, her clothes damp with perspiration.

She decided she had done enough gardening for the morning, so she went to the swimming hole to refresh herself. Alice was there, sitting under a tree, with her head on her knees, looking wistfully at the water. Her red eyes showed that she had been crying.

"Alice, are you all right?"

"Oh, Maddy, you frightened me."

"Sorry. What's wrong?"

Alice wrapped a leaf around her finger while she paused, wondering what she should say. "I wasn't goin' to tell ya, but I've gotta, it's worryin' me."

"You can tell me, Alice. We're friends."

"Last night Grandma Violet visited me and told me not to tell ya anything, but she wanted me to go to town with Owen today and then leave ya by goin' to Karl Fletcher's place."

"Did you *see* your grandma?"

"Yeah, she was right in my bedroom, when all of you were over at Basil's. I didn't know if it was her at first because of the devil's tricks and that, but she even smelled good and wore her dress and spoke the same. It was her, Madeline, I'm telling ya, it was her."

"What else did she say?"

"She said that Jesus loved me and that we're missing out by being up here and not joinin' 'em in town."

Madeline put her arm around Alice as she sat next to her. "Alice, the Bible says that we shouldn't try to talk to the dead. It says there's only one go-between us and God, and that's Jesus. He's the one to talk to. The devil tells lies through dead people who come to us—they're not real at all. That wasn't your grandma—that was an evil angel pretending to be her."

Alice burst out crying. "I was worried it might be, but oh, Madeline, it was just like Grandma. What'll I do if she comes back?

"If anything like that happens again, say, 'In the name of Jesus, get away' or something like that. Then pray to Jesus to protect you."

"Do you think Grandma ... I mean, the bad angel ... will come back?"

"I don't know. But if he does, don't argue with him. Just tell him to get lost in the name of Jesus. OK?"

"OK."

"Promise?"

"I promise."

"Let's pray about it now."

20

Fletcher's Trauma

◇◇◇◇◇◇◇◇◇◇◇◇◇◇◇◇◇◇◇◇◇◇◇◇◇◇◇◇◇◇

PASTOR KARL FLETCHER SHOOK HANDS with the last of the delegates. He stretched his tall, slim frame, yawned, and went over to the coffee machine. Now that the conference room was almost empty, he could relax. He felt good about himself, his career, and where he was headed in the society of the spiritual elite. His articles had given him eminence among those who counted, so he didn't care that he was not truly famous; it was the regard of the New International Order that mattered. He had been invited to attend the NIO meeting, where he received a special commendation for the articles he had written that supported their philosophical and theological views. He was particularly proud that he had also been appointed as an Australian consultant. The accurate predictions he had received personally from the apostle Paul had gained him immense credibility.

Fletcher gazed through the glass wall that overlooked Sydney Harbour from the twenty-third-floor conference room. He noticed that any damage done to the foreshores by the harbor tunnel terrorist explosion had been repaired. The view was entrancing, almost sedating—the quiet blue waters sparkled under the sunshine, and there was no strong wind to create white caps on the water's surface and spoil the charming peacefulness. But it was obvious to Karl that there must have been a breeze, for a number of tilting yachts added movement, color, and a decorative, festive atmosphere to arguably the world's most beautiful harbor.

Halfway to the opera house, a magnificent, enormous white ocean liner was moored, adding an extravagantly international flavor. The opera house glistened like a giant sophisticated clamshell in the distance, and Karl could see where the green lushness of Toronga Park Zoo on the far bank preserved some of the harbor's natural beauty. The strength and dignity of the Harbour Bridge spanned both shores with its imposing, high-curving arch. It reminded him of a steel rainbow, set to symbolize the peace and security that the New International Order promised the people of Sydney.

What a beautiful occasion in a beautiful city. God is surely bestowing this glorious day in celebration of our achievements.

The giddy excitement of the day had drained Karl, so he flopped into a luxurious chair near the glass wall and swiveled casually toward the view. *Ah, I can only climb heights of honor and success from here on. I've worked so hard and long—from pastor to PhD to NIO delegate. Thank you, Lord, for such honor, and for personally sending the apostle Paul to me, of all people.*

Karl put his feet up and relaxed. He was more tired than he had first realized, so he would just rest a while before the long, tiring drive home.

He felt a strange trembling through the building and his coffee shook in the cup.

A deep rumbling sound made him wonder if maintenance men were at work on the building, but he soon dismissed the possibility. Karl's mild apprehension dissipated with the passing of the rumbling. *I am God's man in a profoundly important meeting place. God would not subject me to danger at such a time,* he reasoned.

As he raised the scalding coffee to his mouth, a sudden movement made it spill and burn his chin and chest. He instantly leapt to his feet and held his damp, burning shirt away from his chest. The sickening, terrifying realization struck him that the forty-story building was swaying a little. Fear gripped Karl's heart and he desperately hoped the swaying would stop. But the movement intensified and the building leaned to one side at a frightening angle. He was sure it was leaning too far to recover and it must collapse, but it shuddered and trembled, then swayed back in the opposite direction in a terrifying motion, sending knickknacks flying across the room. Back and forth the skyscraper swayed. Karl became disoriented and nauseous and fell over, but somehow managed to roll out of the path of the decorative missiles.

Somehow, he managed to stand, despite the violent trembling, and brace himself against the glass wall. Karl forced himself to absorb the scene through his panic-stricken eyes.

What he saw increased his terror. The clam-like roof of the Opera House had split, and a low but ferocious wave was tearing through the harbor. The Harbour Bridge was twisting near its center, and several skyscrapers were either collapsed or collapsing along the foreshore. Numerous fires were breaking out above the reach of the tsunami, and a rapidly billowing column of smoke was forming a black, ash-filled cloud above the harbor. The earsplitting crunching of grinding metal and concrete amplified the horrendous cracking of the earth and the roaring of the terrifying wave.

Karl was relieved that his building was on higher ground. He had never experienced such fear of physical danger, but he was even more fearful of the spiritual implications of the earthquake.

The glass he was leaning on splintered. He dropped to the floor to prevent falling out of the building. Instinctively he rolled away from the gaping wall.

"Earthquake! Run!" someone shouted, while others screamed.

Karl, now running low with bent knees to gain stability, headed for the elevator. Then, chastising himself for his stupidity, he ran to the staircase. He sped past others down five stories, then jerked to a halt—some stairs had disappeared, leaving a menacing gap. His adrenalin-charged leap spurred him on to run for his life, but he came to a halt because hundreds of others had jammed the stairway in their desperate flight. Some screamed as they were trampled on. Karl used his tall frame to try to force his way through, but was punched and kicked to the ground by terrified and angry men. Managing to stagger to his feet, he kept to the rear of the compressed pack, which moved agonizingly slowly.

Every step delivered an excruciatingly painful jab to his side. He guessed he had broken ribs or bruised kidneys. An aftershock made the building tremble violently and sent people falling down onto the heads of those below them. Fletcher instinctively dropped down low and hung on. Choking smoke burnt his eyes and he gasped as he was drenched by the fire sprinkler systems.

When he finally reached the above-ground parking lot, he slumped into his vehicle, totally exhausted. After a moment's rest he headed for the Harbour Bridge, which was his normal route home. When he remembered that the bridge was destroyed, he decided to try Central Park, which was elevated and free from buildings. Weaving through chaotic traffic and fleeing pedestrians, he drove over the sidewalk and onto the grass, stopping near the center of the park. Karl briefly took in the scene of devastation, then turned on the radio. He reclined his seat and lay back, exhausted, his panting throat dry and burnt.

The announcer's voice was urgent: "The earthquake had its epicenter very close to Sydney Harbour and measured an astonishing 9.5 on the Richter scale. It is by far the most destructive earthquake to ever hit an Australian city, and much of the inner city has been destroyed or damaged, including the Harbour Bridge and the Opera House. At this stage, damage and loss of life is unknown, but is expected to be in the billions of dollars and many hundreds if not thousands of lives. A tsunami swept into the harbor and flooded the foreshores, and a harbor ferry was capsized against the jetty at Darling Harbor. The fire brigades were powerless to cope with the fires burning out of reach of the tsunami waters. We will give you an update as more information comes to hand. Meanwhile vehicles must keep away from the city area."

Karl slumped in his car. His fogged and panic-stricken brain struggled to think logically. It would be useless to phone for medical help, as all available rescue units had more urgent needs to attend to. But he needed treatment before he could drive home. He was in agonizing pain.

Should I phone Frieda? She would have heard of the quake by now. She probably felt the tremors too. She'll be worried. I'd better phone and tell her that I'll try to get checked at St. Vincent's Hospital. Thankfully, I've still got my phone.

Frieda had not heard the news and was shocked at Karl's report but relieved to learn that Karl was not seriously hurt. After resting briefly, Karl started the car and drove off, steering cautiously around rubble with his one sound arm. After weaving between chaotic traffic for a few kilometers, he screeched to a halt to avoid colliding with the rear end of a car sticking vertically out of a huge crack in the road. His thoughts raced. *I'd better not waste time stopping to check the driver; there'll be thousands of injured anyhow. I'd best concentrate on nursing my own injuries. .*

Karl reversed, turned around, and found an alternate route. Eventually he pulled up outside the hospital. There were about twenty ambulances unloading patients wherever they could find space. He found nowhere to park. *It's useless going in there. They will be too busy saving lives to help me. I'll just have to try to drive home with one arm.*

Two hours later Karl reached the outskirts of Sydney, but he was in too much pain to drive any longer. He pulled up alongside two teenagers who were walking on the sidewalk.

"Any of you guys got a driver's license?" he asked.

"Yeah, mate, what's up?"

"I'll give you a hundred bucks to drive me to Newcastle. I'm too crook to drive myself."

"I want two hundred—I've gotta get back again."

"OK, look, help me turn the car around, would you?"

"Man, you look like you've been in that earthquake!"

"I have—you sure you can drive?"

"Sure. Here's my license. Give us that cash now."

Karl checked the license. "Sven, I'll give you half now and half later."

"No way, man, I want it all now."

"OK, OK."

As Karl reclined in the passenger seat, he remembered he had some painkillers in the glove box. "Take it easy, no jerking or swishing around corners, please. I'm in pain."

"No worries, mate. You were in that quake, eh? They said more than five thousand people were killed. You were lucky, man!"

"More than five thousand?"

"Yeah, possibly seven or eight thousand, they said. Mate, it wiped out half the inner city."

"I just thank God I made it."

"Yeah, mate. Hey, it's funny how everyone hoped things would get better now that they've got those new religious laws, but look what's happened. It's like God's angry at somethin'."

"He might be. He might be."

"You a priest or somethin', mate? You've got that cross on your collar."

" I'm a pastor."

"Oh! Tell me, why are they forcin' everyone to join this international unity stuff and give up their freedom. It ain't right. It's a free country, mate."

"Well, Sven, we're uniting to make laws for a better country and a better life."

"Well, it ain't working. I think God's angry. He might be angry at the leaders who are making these laws, eh? I believe in God and I've been reading about Jesus, and these new laws just don't gel with me."

"You sound like the rebels against the system who've apostatized and gone to the hills and mountains."

Sven glanced at Karl. "Why'd they go there? To escape the new laws?"

"Something like that."

"How long they been up there?"

"Oh, a few months."

"Smart … brave. Where can I find them? Do you know?"

"They're in lots of spots. There's some in the Wattagan ranges. But I suggest you don't join them, there's no future for them. I can only see big trouble ahead for them."

Sven looked at Karl, grinning. "Yeah, well, I can see bigger trouble back in the cities. Will you draw me a map when you get home?"

"I don't see why not. I've got a rough idea of their location. But how will you get there?"

"I'll pawn a bit of gear. And I've got your two hundred—easiest money I've ever made. If I can't buy a car, I'll get a push bike!"

"You've been microchipped, I suppose, so how will you get on?"

"Easy. Just pretend it's not there. Who knows? I might be able to buy a bit of black-market stuff and sell it to the deserters." Sven laughed. "Might come in handy up in those hills."

Sven Melnik thought for a moment, then said, "Hey, pastor, you're a pretty bright-looking bloke. Why don't you join the deserters? They're the best people, eh? If they're goin' against all this unity crap because they believe in the Jesus freedom cause, then God'll be with 'em. You watch— they'll be on their way to heaven. I'm goin' with 'em. You comin'?"

"Sven, you're aware of the miracles that promote the NIO?"

"Yeah, they don't fool me, Jesus said to watch out for religious hot heads who work miracles, but they're really wolves dressed like sheep, and the devils trickin' everybody. You'd have to be pretty stupid to get sucked in by that. We've been warned, mate. No, I'm no sucker. I'm gonna tell my mates and my mum, and they might come with me up to the hills."

Karl found himself strangely charmed by this uneducated, extroverted, and forthright teenager, and he was surprised that he wasn't offended at his rebuke. Deep down he knew there was some truth in what he said, and the day's events had raised questions. Was God in fact sending judgments on cities because they were accepting the NIO and rejecting truth?

But as he thought of the disturbing consequences of changing course in midstream, he reminded himself of his career and the affirmations of his night visitor—the apostle Paul. He comforted himself with the thought that once he got home, he would be treated for his injuries, and life would become stable again. He would enjoy the fruits of his labors and aspirations.

Karl came up with a dismissive answer. "Each to his own, Sven. There's more than one way to get to shore from a shipwreck."

"Yeah? That doesn't sound right to me—I'd swim the narrow way myself."

A week later, Basil Dorf's quaint two-story hut, which bridged the upper branches of a huge tree, was packed with friends. They seemed mesmerized with the TV news broadcast about the week's unprecedented natural disasters. On the day after the Sydney earthquake, Washington DC, Montreal, London, and Vatican State were hit by earthquakes of unprecedented power. The next day Tokyo, Hong Kong, Cairo, Paris,

Berlin, and Nairobi were partially destroyed by earthquakes. Two days later temperatures plummeted to minus 70 degrees centigrade, freezing to death thousands in Moscow, Kiev, Warsaw, and many other cities. On the same day, thousands died in Rio de Janeiro, Buenos Aires, and Santiago as soaring heat waves of over 50 degrees centigrade scorched them. Floods drowned two million in various Asian countries.

Madeline shook her head in amazement. "The world's never seen anything like this. It's all happening so close together."

Ami sighed, and her faraway gaze looked sad. "Those poor, poor people in the Chinese river basins didn't stand a chance," she lamented. "Millions are just living on a sea of mud. There's no food, no building materials, and they won't get any international relief because it's every country for itself now."

Alice slid back into a corner of the tiny room to lessen the squeeze. "I don't think I'll watch TV anymore. It's too scary and depressin'."

Owen stood and stretched, as he had been rather cramped, sitting on the floor. "It was hot enough down here, but Brisbane hit 57 degrees in the shade! The roads were meltin'."

"What about your parents' farm, up in Townsville?" asked Ami.

"Wasn't so bad according to the weather report, around mid 40s."

"Why is God sending these earthquakes and stuff?" queried Alice as she stroked Puff, who gently purred.

Basil was quick to reply. "They're his alarm bells. He's saying, 'You're on the wrong track, world. I'm coming back, ready or not. I love you and have given you warnings before, but here's a bigger warning—it's bigger than a smack on the bottom now, so you'd better take me seriously.' "

"But that's not the way the NIO and its followers see it," reminded Owen. "Their leader, Zamsi, said last night that the disasters show God's anger at people like us who won't join 'em. He said we're backin' down on Christ's prayer to unite. It's pretty serious stuff, and it means that things could get a lot hotter for us."

Ami moved one step up the narrow stairway to make room. "Don't scare me, Owen," she said.

"But we've gotta be aware—do a bit of serious thinkin' about our next steps."

"What about your folks up in Townsville?" asked Ami. "They wouldn't have accepted that microchip biz, would they?"

"No way. No one's troublin' them up there yet. They're way out in the sticks. It'd be good to have a talk with 'em, though—it's been a while. I sent 'em a letter a few weeks ago, but I can't get any mail back, of course."

Owen opened his Bible to Revelation. "I've been tryin' to understand what all the earthquakes and stuff's been about, and I think there are some answers in Revelation chapter 7, startin' with verse 1. 'After this I saw four angels standing at the four corners of the earth, holding back the four winds of the earth to prevent any wind from blowing on the land or on the sea or on any tree. Then I saw another angel coming up from the east, having the seal of the living God. He called out in a loud voice to the four angels who had been given power to harm the land and the sea; "Do not harm the land or the sea or the trees until we put a seal on the foreheads of the servants of our God." ' "

Owen continued. "It's sayin' that God's angels are holding back the worst 'wind' or strife the world's ever seen until God's servants are 'sealed.' I reckon the seven last plagues would be part of that trouble. Once they're sealed, the angels will remove their protection to allow the time of trouble to fall upon the world. So these earthquakes and freaks of nature are God's warnin's us that the sealin's nearly done and the time of trouble's almost here."

"That's a bit mind blowing, Owen," said Basil Dorf. "So what's being 'sealed' mean?"

"Well, we know that gettin' the mark of the beast is acceptin' Satan's rule and rejectin' Christ's, so I reckon this is the opposite—it's about bein' loyal to Christ and acceptin' his character. These same sealed ones are in Revelation chapter 14 verse 1. It says they had 'his father's name written on their foreheads.' And in verse 4, 'They follow the Lamb wherever he goes.' Now, *name* stands for character, so these people are 'sealed' because they have the Father's character, and they follow Jesus at any cost."

"But aren't we are sealed with the Holy Spirit?" asked Madeline.

"Yeah. It's through the Spirit's power that we become more like Jesus," replied Owen.

"So, to be 'sealed' means to be under the control of the Spirit?" asked Basil.

"Spot on," replied Owen. "The sealed ones love the Lord and his truth so much that nothin' can ever make 'em change their minds."

Basil had been listening, occasionally taking a swipe at mosquitoes with a magazine. "What I get out of all this," he summarized, "is that God is using the earthquakes to wake everyone up. Once everyone has decided fully for or fully against the truth, things are going to get dramatically worse, and we need to stay faithful to Christ through it all."

21

City Meets Country

◇◇◇◇◇◇◇◇◇◇◇◇◇◇◇◇◇◇◇◇◇◇◇◇◇◇◇◇◇◇◇

E VAN AND MAUDE HEARD the loud exhaust noise some time before the
dilapidated, rusty yellow Toyota station wagon pulled up in the shade
of the large eucalyptus tree in front of their cabin. When the engine was
turned off, the quietness of the valley seemed overwhelming by contrast.

Sven Melnik had successfully found the valley from following Karl
Fletcher's map. He startled Evan with his appearance as he briskly stepped
out of the car, smiling broadly. "G'day! Quiet joint you've got here," he
said confidently.

Evan stared at the slightly overweight nineteen-year-old of average
height. His long black crew cut gave him an electrocuted look. He was
amazed at Sven's sheepskin slippers and black, broad-rimmed pilgrim hat
with a black feather in its rim.

Sven warmly shook Evan's and Maude's firm but unenthusiastic
hands.

"I heard you coming a mile off," said Evan dryly.

"Yeah, it's got no muffler, but goes like a rocket. We picked her up
from the wreckers for eighty bucks. The bloke thought we'd tow it away for
spares, but we just drove it home with no rego, nothin'."

"What about the police?" asked Maude.

"Anytime we saw a cop car, we just put 'er in neutral and sailed past so
they wouldn't hear nothin'."

Sven's friend, Eddie Blancho, combed his thin, long beard and covered
his shaved head with a baseball cap—one of many he had packed. The shy
seventeen-year-old slowly emerged from the car.

Evan's eyes focused on Eddie's T-shirt with a large imprint that said,
"Shut up and play Snooker." As he walked over, Eddie pulled his long,
baggy shorts up a little, but they still exposed three inches of his yellow

underpants with black polka dots.

"This 'ere's my mate, Eddie, and I'm Sven. We're deserters from the NIO. We don't believe in what they're doin' and we're wonderin' if we could join you."

"We're Evan and Maude. Join us?"

"Yeah. We're one of your mob and come to live with ya."

"Live? Uh, look, I don't think you're really suitable to be one of us. We're remnant Christians here."

Sven spoke with his typically quick style. "That's what I heard, mate. That's why we came—we believe in Jesus, too, and wanna escape those idiots like you do."

Evan gestured strongly to emphasize his point. "You don't understand—this is *my* land. I bought it and we're selective about who lives here."

Sven took off his hat and scratched his head. "How much land have ya got here?

"Oh, about five hundred acres"

"Five hundred acres? How many people live on it? Twenty?"

Evan folded his arms and stood stiffly. "Less. But what's it got to do with you?"

Sven bowed a little and swept his hand in a flourish. "We only need a quarter acre, mate, and we'll keep out of your hair. But we can buy stuff for ya—we're chipped."

Evan glanced at Maude, his courage feeding off their mutual displeasure. "Microchipped? You've got the mark? Then you *definitely* can't stay," he almost growled.

Sven used the polite, gentle tone he had found necessary at times to get a good drug deal. "Look, the chip don't mean anythin' to us. We got it before we knew better, but wouldn't do it now. Whatcha want us to do—knife it out? Listen hard, matey—we can get you food, medicine, gas, anything in town."

Evan looked at Maude's grim face for support and tried to sound aggressive. "You're one of them. You can't stay."

"We would have liked your OK, Evan brother, but we're stayin' anyway."

"You can't do that. It's against ..."

Sven's wide smile was friendly as he patted Evan on his arm. "Whatcha gonna do, Evan, shoot us? Call the cops? They're not on your side. Jesus told us to come up here, and he owns the thousand hills with the 'roos on 'em. Look, there's no way we're goin' back to Sydney, so where do we stay?"

"You can't! I'll find ways and means—"

"OK, we'll find our own spot." Sven used his final trump card. "But read the last part of Acts 2. It says something like, 'All the believers lived together and shared all their gear.' "

Sven paused and studied Evan's face for some evidence of softening, but saw none. He pointed at the Subaru. "That your car?"

"I suppose stealing cars is all right too?" Evan nervously blurted. "Well I won't—."

"No, mate. I got a present for ya."

Sven smiled sweetly as he opened the rear of his wagon. With Eddie's help, he lifted out four rusty cans full of gasoline and placed them at Evan's feet. "Here ya go. And there's more where that came from."

Evan made no obvious response. The door hinges made a painful grating sound as the visitors got in their overloaded car, and the engine gave a deafening roar as Eddie waved good-bye. "I like your dress, Maude," he shouted. "Just like in the black-and-white movies. Good one! See ya later."

Sven and Eddie drove toward Owen's cabin and selected a campsite near the swimming hole. Eddie gazed around with wonderment. "Gee, this is a real blast. "I've never seen chooks and a cow in real life before."

They pitched a large army tent they'd bought from a disposal store and stacked cases of food in one corner, then threw in two foam mattresses and some blankets. After unpacking, they dunked and splashed each other in the swimming hole. Their laughter and shouting carried through the quiet valley to Owen's cabin.

A little more than a week later, Ami was helping Madeline hang out her washing on a cord tied between two small trees on the river bank.

"Do you think the garlic will really keep the insects away from the tomatoes?" asked Madeline.

"So I've heard," commented Ami. "We'll just have to wait and see. Maude looked so happy at her wedding yesterday, didn't she?"

"She loves Evan a lot—just adores him. Evan didn't look crash-hot, though. I thought he looked a bit pale and worried. I don't think that herb he's taking is helping his diabetes."

"You know what Evan's like—he would have been happier if they'd been married by a proper minister."

"Evan's so traditional, although I don't know if that's the right word," said Madeline thoughtfully.

"He lives in fear, not love."

"His conscience is off the planet—he's frightened of being lost if he fails in some small thing."

Ami tightened the line to take the weight of her soggy tracksuit. "But he did look touched by Basil's wedding present. I don't think he ever thought he'd get a water generator. I had to laugh at the worried look on Evan's face when Sven got up to make that embarrassing impromptu speech—I mean, seeing Sven hardly even knows them. But in a way it was really spiritual."

"I hope they liked the book on marriage I gave them."

Ami's head spun around and her jaw dropped in astonishment. "You don't mean your book about God inventing sex? Maude would be mortified." She giggled, imagining Evan and Maude's reactions in private.

"Don't laugh—it helped me sort out a few hang-ups."

Ami became serious. "I guess I'll never need it. Too late for me," she lamented.

"What about Sven or Eddie?" Madeline succeeded in keeping a straight face.

Ami checked Madeline out for her expression. "Oh, Madeline,!" she exclaimed indignantly.

Madeline burst out laughing and ducked as Ami threw a wet face cloth at her.

<hr />

It was 5:50 a.m., and Sven Melnik couldn't get back to sleep because Eddie Blancho's snoring was keeping him awake. The first glimmerings of gray light were touching the valley, although it would still be more than an hour before the sun appeared over the eastern mountains. Sven never ceased to be surprised how the sharp tinkling of the tiny bell birds titillated his early-morning senses, inviting him to listen to his Creator's voice. The lyre bird wasn't imitating other sounds this morning—it gave a natural rendition of its own enchanting call, adding charm to the gurgling chorus of the stream.

Sven threw off the light army blanket and put on his jagged-edge Robinson Crusoe pants. Once outside the tent, he stretched and looked around him. He was awed at the awakening sounds of nature and the fresh, invigorating air that he had never experienced in Sydney. He dipped his cupped hand in the gurgling water for a drink and splashed his face. Then he walked past his freshly dug garden with a feeling of satisfaction.

He had already seeded it with corn and, surprisingly, wheat—he loved fresh bread.

He sucked in huge gulps of cool air as he hauled his unfit body up the slope, carefully picking his way in the semi-darkness to the edge of the tall tree line of the foothills. He sat on a large, flat, protruding rock. There was just enough dawn light to see the tiny outline of his tent way beneath him on the creek bank.

To Sven, the stream seemed an extravagant gift from his heavenly Father. *Millions of liters of water flowing past my tent just to give me pleasure,* he thought. He looked to his right and saw a thin wisp of smoke rising above the scattered tree line, and thought of the cute cottage nestled under the trees below that housed Evan and Maude. What a homey scene. *Lord, help Evan and Maude understand you better.*

He looked to the left, where the valley floor narrowed and rose, channeling the stream into a series of gurgling rapids. There the stream emerged from a mysterious rain forest world, where Sven suspected unusual creatures had their home. He spoke quietly to his God until it was light enough for the rooster to begin crowing far below. Then he went back to his tent and woke Eddie.

"Come on, Eddie. Someone wants to talk to you."

"Huh? Who?"

"God."

"God wants to talk to me? Oh, yeah, I forgot. But let me sleep a bit more first," mumbled Eddie.

"I want us to start early today because it's gonna be a real hot stinker. I'm goin' bush to use my toilet paper rations. Do you reckon you can get ready meanwhile?"

Later, Sven knocked on the rustic solid timber door of Evan's cabin. Evan emerged in his striped pajamas, his bleary eyes trying to focus on his visitor. "Yes?" he mumbled.

"Good morning, Evan! We would like to wash and clean your Subaru and put petrol in its tank."

"I'm not lending my car to anybody. Anyway, why don't you use your own?"

"Yours has a roof rack. We don't wanna drive it to town—we just want to get you some firewood."

"Firewood?"

"It's gonna get colder soon."

"The … the battery's dead."

"I'll put mine in. Thanks, Evan. Top of the mornin' to ya."

Evan looked back at Maude with a helpless, puzzled expression as she peered curiously over her blanket.

Sven and Eddie pushed the old Subaru from under the rough lean-to and brushed away the spider webs from inside and outside the vehicle. They installed their own battery and emptied one can of petrol into the Subaru, which only started after much cranking. They drove into the shallow creek and washed the dusty vehicle, then drove it to where dried timbers had fallen under the trees. They secured them on the roof rack with bungee cords. That morning they stacked about twelve loads near Evan's rear entrance.

Bewildered, Evan came out of his cabin.

"You look a bit crook, Evan mate, so I thought we'd save you some work," said Sven.

"Thanks," said Evan feebly. Then, feeling light headed, he went back to bed.

"Why are they doing this, Maude?" he muttered. "They must have something up their sleeves—they're not one of us."

"Maybe they're gettin' interested in the Lord, sweetheart," Maude replied.

"Can't see it myself. When they accepted the beast's chip, that was the point of no return."

"But remember, everyone's got the chip by now, and we're still prayin' for 'em to be saved before it's too late."

"No Christian would walk around with his pants around his ankles."

"You wouldn't think so, would ya? Still, it's kind of 'em, because the nights are getting colder now."

22

The Masterpiece

◇◇◇◇◇◇◇◇◇◇◇◇◇◇◇◇◇◇◇◇◇◇◇◇◇◇

PASTOR DESMOND PIONA had become a worldwide household name since the Arizona desert miracles more than a year ago. Since then he had been conducting healing sessions periodically from the same location that now boasted more than just a makeshift platform in the desert. The New International Order had voted to have an impressive international place of worship built there. It was an enormous building that was completed in six months and could seat fifteen thousand people.

The stage had a magnificent shrine built on it—a five-meter statue of Christ. The bronze Christ was leaning against the force of a hurricane, and his hair and robe were blown-back. In his arms he sheltered a lamb, and he was leaning protectively over the bronze pulpit.

Piona had called the international healing meeting because of a prophecy handed to him by Ian Feldberg, the visionary prophet of the previous Miracle Retreat. It had been widely publicized that Feldberg had predicted that this would be the most glorious healing service ever. The claim was outrageous in the minds of some, bordering on blasphemous, as it seemed to subjugate Christ's healings during his earthly ministry. However, so many people came that thousands could not be seated, and they had to watch on giant screens outside the building. Many pilgrims even took samples of desert sand home with them, counting it as sacred.

Piona's reputation with impressive miracles gave him a new, more authoritative and confident bearing. Overseas NIO delegates had flown in and brought photos of disabled relatives to be prayed over. Honored international political and religious dignitaries from a number of Christian and non-Christian nations were seated on the stage behind Piona.

When the leader of the NIO, Johanus Zamsi, was introduced, tumultuous applause broke out. His speech promoted the recent great achievements of the NIO and he outlined his vision for the future.

When Zamsi sat down, Piona spoke fervently of the Holy Spirit's power for a few minutes, then a choir was heard singing softly in the background, backed by beautiful harp and violin music. Puzzled, Piona looked at the choir and orchestra behind him, but they were silent. However, each time he looked around, the mysterious voices increased in volume until the voices of a mighty choir filled the building.

Just then, a mysterious luminescence began to fill the area around the stage, and a strange blue glow emanated from the bronze statue of Christ . TV cameras fruitlessly searched for the source of the music and the light. The awe-stricken multitude's astonished gasps became almost as loud as the unseen choir. The glorious brightness of the bronze statue intensified until it approached the brilliance of the living fire of black opal.

Suddenly the intense glory left the statue and materialized into a majestic being standing alongside it. He was more than seven feet tall and stood encased in the glorious light. His long scarlet robe was adorned with a golden girdle across his shoulder and chest. His medium-length beard and hair were fluorescent white. Majestically he strode to the microphone. As he did, Piona and those near him stepped backward in awe to join the terrified delegates behind.

The glorious being stretched out his hands in blessing, and his rich, melodious voice filled the building. His clear tones were endowed with compassion and gentleness: "My children, this is the moment for which we have all been waiting. For more than two thousand years, I have been weeping for your suffering and you have been longing for my return. I am the desire of all ages, the fulfillment of all your dreams. This is the moment that the prophets of old searched and patiently endured for."

As he spoke, the choir's voice and the glorious light faded somewhat.

Piona ran forward and called out, "Are you the Christ?" and he prostrated himself before the being.

"It is as you have said. Blessed are you among men, Desmond."

The crowd's reverential silence changed into an adoring roar. The being turned in three directions before the crowd, with arms outstretched, proclaiming, "Blessed are all those who have believed in me before this moment. Blessed are the poor in spirit, for theirs is the kingdom of heaven."

Over the next few minutes the Christlike being eloquently and fervently presented much of the Sermon on the Mount. The cameras captured close-ups of his compassionate, smiling face and his endearing gestures. The crowd was enchanted by the fresh meaning and pathos of the familiar words. Two angels appeared mysteriously, one on either side of him, bowing worshipfully. Then suddenly they disappeared.

Those who had enough space prostrated themselves or dropped to their knees in adoration. The Christ being finished his brief sermon, saying, "I am the same yesterday, today and forever, and I heal today just as when I walked by the Sea of Galilee."

This prompted some of the crowd to stir, preparing to come forward for healing.

"Stay where you are, my children," he continued. "There is no need to come forward; I can heal you where you are."

The Christ looked up and prayed, "Oh, my father, heal your children. I thank you that this healing is a foretaste of the time when we shall appear before you with new bodies and there shall be no more death."

Immediately, an excited tumult erupted as hundreds of people felt a surge of healing power, and the invisible choir sang once more. Those who had brought photos of sick relatives discovered later that their relatives had been healed as well.

The Christ then majestically raised his arms, hushing the tumult. He taught that the world should revere the New International Order because it was appointed by heaven. With exquisite eloquence, he proclaimed that the new restrictions were put in place to perpetuate genuine long-term freedom. In compassionate tones, he extolled the value of love and tolerance as having taken the place of the Ten Commandments, describing them as a temporary, burdensome law, valid only until the time of grace and love came.

Looking at a nearby camera, he tearfully appealed to any viewers who had rejected the recent communications of his original apostles and the laws of the NIO. Persuasively he taught that they were blaspheming against God, pointing out that the long-expected millennium of peace, with its freedom from death and suffering, was almost upon them. Only the newly converted world would enjoy this new heaven-sent era.

Suddenly, mysteriously, he disappeared, and the glorious glow returned to the bronze statue of Christ. The invisible angelic choir filled the building with musical praise, then gradually their voices faded in unison with the statue's fading glory, leaving the worshippers awe stricken and hushed.

All that transpired had been watched by hundreds of millions around the globe. Journalists struggled to adequately describe its impact upon the world.

Pastor Karl Fletcher and his wife, Frieda, were among millions of viewers in Australia. They had invited their friends, police inspector Adrian Sebastian and his wife, Brenda, over. Expecting to see a Piona healing service, they were totally unprepared for the Christ's surprise return.

"Oh, praise God, Christ has come back!" shouted Karl, breaking the awed silence and clapping his hands in delight. "I had my doubts at times, but we were always right!"

"I never thought he would come back so soon!" rejoiced Sebastian.

They hugged and danced around the room. Karl prostrated himself on the carpet, facing the screen, whenever the Christ praised the NIO.

"What will the blasphemous ones say now?" Sebastian laughed. "What will they say to this?"

"Seeing is believing," said Sebastian's wife excitedly. "The whole world has seen it now."

"He looks just like the description in Revelation chapter 1, but more loving. Did you ever see such a compassionate face! And that voice—so warm and kind."

"I don't think I'll ever worship half-heartedly again," Frieda said. "In fact, I'll never be the same again!"

Karl put his hands on Sebastian's shoulders and warmly shook them. "We're a privileged people, Adrian," he said. "Not even Moses or Abraham have seen what we've see today. I would've flown to Arizona if I'd known what would happen."

☙

Evan and Maude Hawkins had made an exception to their TV rule to see the special program. Basil had extended the wiring for the TV even farther so everyone could watch on the grass outside his crudely built hut. Maude had to drive Evan there, as he was getting weaker.

As they watched, Owen was flabbergasted. "That's ... that's the false Christ! That's the great counterfeit Christ we're warned about."

Madeline's emphasis matched her shocked facial expression. "If I didn't know better, I'd say that was really Christ. He looked *better* than Christ!"

"I have never ... ever ... seen anything more spectacular in all my life," pronounced Basil. "That is *so* convincing!"

"And that music was real," gushed Alice.

Victor Zinski spoke unemotionally. "I'm not getting taken in by all that. We were warned about the devil's tricks in Mathew 24. And Jesus couldn't have been plainer. There's only one way in which he will return— from the sky, where everyone will see him. And he's not coming back to heal the sick and then leave them behind on earth either. He's taking his followers to heaven with him."

"You're right," agreed Sven. "What a bunch of suckers that crowd was. Don't they know their Bibles? But you've gotta hand it to the devil—that was pretty cool. And Jesus warned us about looking for Christ in a desert place because he knew his coming would be counterfeited in the Arizona desert."

"I'm sure that crowd's read Mathew 24 too—they know what it says," said Owen. "But for them to admit that was a false Christ, they'd have to deny everythin' they've been taught about the NIO and the other stuff they've been believin'. So I think they *wanted* to believe that was Christ. People's characters are settin' hard like concrete now, and they prefer to believe a lie. It was predicted in second Thessalonians, chapter 2: 'The coming of the lawless one will be in accordance with the work of Satan displayed with all kinds of counterfeit miracles, signs and wonders, and in every sort of evil that deceives those who are perishing. They perish because they refuse to love the truth and be saved. For this reason God sends them a powerful delusion so that they will believe a lie and so that all will be condemned who have not believed the truth but have delighted in wickedness.' "

The group studied and discussed the familiar passages of Mathew 24 in a new light.

"You guys have church in different places," stated Sven after they had studied awhile. "Evan's mob goes to his joint and Owen's mob goes to his joint. You ought to be comin' together."

For a moment there was a strained silence, until Owen spoke. "I agree, Sven. Evan and his friends are welcome to join us."

"But we believe differently about some things," said Zinski. "For instance—"

Sven's interruption was emphatic. "Oh, come off it, man! We're just a small bunch surrounded by a world who hates us and blames us for everythin' and we're holdin' out, waitin' for Christ to come. We believe the same stuff, man! He died for us, made us, is coming back for us, plus a hundred other things the same. There's only a bit we don't see eye to eye on. We need to pull together or the devil's laughin'."

"It's not just that," explained Victor. "You see, we believe in dressing for church properly, not like for a ... a side show or the beach."

"Hey, that John the Baptist fella, he was cool with his camel clothes dyed in honey and the leather whip for a belt," said Eddie shyly.

"Yeah, man," agreed Sven. "We're desperados holed up in the mountains, and you're worryin' 'bout what gear we wear? Brother John the Baptiser even wore his camel gear to Jesus' baptism, so we're not doin' too bad compared to 'im."

"Another thing," said Owen. "Remember, we're all being blamed for all the earthquakes and calamities, so we've gotta have an escape plan for us all as a team. We've gotta stick together—none of this separatin' garbage."

"We can plan and worship together," said Madeline, smiling as she looked around.

"Who's willing to give it a go?" asked Sven, shooting his own hand up. "Great. We're givin' it a go then."

‹🦎›

Evan expressed no opinion until he and Maude returned to their log cabin and he flopped exhausted on his bed. "Maude, strangely enough, the compassion in Christ's eyes and his gentle voice really surprised me … and the way he commanded those quadriplegics to walk. Do you think maybe we should study it more? I mean, I'm not saying we've been wrong, but …"

Maude looked at Evan, surprised. "Are you thinkin' straight? A counterfeit's like the real thing, sweetheart. But don't worry yourself about it just now. You look real crook tonight. Your eyes are a bit puffy too. I wish we had some of that insulin." She stroked Evan's head gently.

"Have faith in God's herbs, dearie," Evan said weakly. "It's just the toxins comin' out."

"You've been saying that for a while now. I've been thinkin' I might talk to Sven about gettin' you some insulin."

Evan s head jerked weakly around. "Using that microchip? That wouldn't be honest—using the devil's tools. Anyway, you need a script."

"I don't like doin' it either, but if you get any worse … Sven could get you anythin', I think. You know, forge a script or buy through the back door or somethin'."

"Maude, I know you're trying to help, but … Sven? No way. Don't worry, I'll get better soon."

Maude peeled some vegetables for soup while Evan lay on his back, exhausted.

"Evan, I've been thinkin' hard about things. I've been asking myself, if the real Christ came tomorrow, would I be ready?"

"Of course you would be, Maude. I don't know anybody who lives a better life than you."

"How do ya feel about yourself, Evan?"

Evan paused before answering, wondering if he should open up. "Me?

If you'd asked me a month ago I would have said yes, I'm ready. But lately, since I've been off color, I've been thinking some strange thoughts, and I'm not so sure anymore."

"Strange thoughts?"

Evan's voice became soft and subdued, and almost broke up. "It's as if I'm looking at myself and seeing faults I never saw before. I'm not sure anymore if I'm good enough—if God accepts me."

"You'll feel better about yourself when your health picks up."

"I don't know, Maude. I hope so."

Two months later, Inspector Adrian Sebastian called a meeting at the Central Newcastle police station. "I have just been officially notified that some further developments in legislation have been introduced," he reported. "You've all heard about it on the news—we've been expecting it, and now it's here. You can read these copies later. As it has stood, the law stated that anybody who doesn't sign a declaration of cooperation with the NIO and receive the chip couldn't buy or sell. Now it's been toughened up. Dissenters will be liable for imprisonment for up to five years for the first offence."

"Sir," said Sergeant Bruce Fossey. "there are hundreds of 'em, and we know where most are. They're not armed, so it should be easy to round 'em up. But where can such a lot of 'em be held awaiting trial?"

"We'll only bring in small groups at a time, Bruce. There'll be no long waiting periods or fancy trials. We expect them to plead guilty, so they'll only need a brief appearance before a magistrate. Then they'll be held in illegal immigrant compounds until special family prisons can be built."

"Family prisons, sir?" asked Fossey.

"Yes. It's believed that families should be kept together. Read the legislation and we'll discuss it more later. For now, I want you and Constables Prior, Pierce, and Gooch to meet here with me at nine tomorrow morning. Come prepared for a search and arrest in the Wattagan Mountains—we're not expecting much resistance."

23

The Flight North

◇◇◇◇◇◇◇◇◇◇◇◇◇◇◇◇◇◇◇◇◇◇◇◇◇◇◇◇◇◇

THE CHRIST BEING made more sensational appearances in Jerusalem, Rome, London, and Cairo, where he healed the sick and urged allegiance to the NIO. He was urging severe punishments for dissenters.

In light of their new predicament, the Wattagan group decided to back Owen's plan of escaping to some remote area in North Queensland, which he had explored with his father some years previously. It was uninhabited range country several hours' drive west of Jardine Station, and Owen hoped his parents had already headed there.

Evan and Maude decided to follow their original plan of hiding in the cave.

Maude pleaded with Evan to allow Sven to buy some insulin. Although he almost consented, he eventually refused.

Sven and Eddie drove Owen's Toyota into Newcastle. Using Sven's microchip, and some cash, they purchased six cans of petrol. They also bought first-aid supplies and basics such as matches, candles, sugar, flour, rice, and a number of books from a Christian book store. They scoured the car wrecking yards and found a second-hand exhaust system and a few other parts for Sven's old Toyota. Then they drove back to Evan's valley.

Owen still had several drums of diesel in storage, and he strapped one in the back of his utility, then loaded their gear and provisions. They picked produce from the garden, including sweet corn and pumpkins, and packed it all into bags, which they stashed in the vehicles. They had to prioritize their personal belongings, feeling sad that they had to leave some behind. Basil grieved over abandoning his TV. The cow was untied and set free. Maude agreed to look after Puff, Madeline's cat.

They planned to leave at sunset, and after a huge meal of fresh roasted chicken, Owen and Madeline sat in the front of Owen's twin cab while

Basil, Ami, and Alice all squeezed into the backseat.

Madeline gave Puff one last tearful hug. After saying good-bye and praying with Evan, Maude, and the Zinskis Sven and Eddie drove off slowly.

Evan leaned on the cabin wall, and with arm around Maude, watched sadly as the vehicles drove down the two-wheel track toward the creek crossing. Through moist eyes, Madeline scanned the beautiful valley one last time. It had been her home over much of the year and she felt grateful to God for her stay there.

So much had happened since she met Owen about a year ago—so much change. She had changed. Now, though, it seemed to her that the future was totally unknown. Still, she believed God was leading her in a marvelous way.

The following day, Evan, Maude, and the Zinskis prepared to move to Evan's well-provisioned cave deep in the Wattagan Ranges. Victor Zinski had grown stronger since moving to the health-giving valley, and he and Betty were able to carry heavy loads to the caves. They tried to vary their route on each trip in an effort to avoid making a path that could be followed. Evan shuffled along laboriously, resting often along the way, too weak to carry anything.

Adrian Sebastian sat in the front police vehicle with driver Bruce Fossey as they made their way to Evan's valley.

"You've been a Christian for a while, haven't you, Adrian?" Bruce asked.

"All my life, actually. What about you?"

"Only since the first of Piona's miracles. They really shook me up and made me realize that God isn't just some theory."

"I've had some heavy responsibilities in church, and I've made some big arrests, but I feel as if today I'm giving the best service of my life. If we clean this mob up, things can only get better. What's the shotgun for?"

"Oh, I probably won't need it, but I heard that up north some of these guys were fanatics with guns."

"I know some of theses people personally. They went to my church. You won't have any trouble with them."

"What are they like?"

"One guy, Evan Hawkins, who owns the valley, is a bit weird. But the others used to be nice people, good Christians."

"Good Christians, eh? Strange they'd act this way. If everybody went along with the NIO, there'd be none of this hassle. We wouldn't have had the earthquakes, nothing."

"You'd think that now that Christ has come back, they'd wake up to themselves, wouldn't you? I mean, God comes down and says, 'Hey, I'm the one you say you believe in. You're going astray. Let me heal your sick and teach you the right way and follow me.' But no, they dig in and say they don't want any part of Christ or us."

"This lot's beyond me."

"When Israel got rid of that thieving Achan and his family, God restored his blessing to Israel. The same will happen here. But put that shotgun away; you won't need that."

The small police convoy slowly approached the valley. It crossed the beautiful stream several times and finally came to Evan's cabin. Finding no one home, they inspected the other huts but found them empty as well.

"Looks like they've recently pulled out," said Sebastian. "You can see where they've dug the potatoes out recently, and there's some fairly fresh tire tracks. I wonder where they got the fuel?"

"Must have stored some," said Fossey. "Great anticipation."

"They probably had a radio and figured we'd be after them. But where could they possibly go to? I was sure they'd still be here."

"Well, their vehicles are gone—they've driven out. So they're not hiding in the mountains."

"That looks like Hawkins's old Subaru—looks like he's abandoned it."

"I guess there's no point in bringing the dogs in."

"No. We may as well go home. But let's grab some of that ripe corn first."

Rather than drive through the city and risk meeting a roadblock, Owen' party decided to take the fire trail along the mountain ridges. They drove slowly, sometimes having to brake suddenly to avoid wallabies and wombats.

"Why do the animals hang around the roads?" asked Alice.

"The water run-off grows tender green shoots on the edges of the road," replied Owen.

They descended the mountains and emerged onto the New England Highway, which headed northwest and was the quickest route to North

Queensland. They listened to gospel CDs and sang as they drove.

"I can really sense the presence of angels more than ever," said Ami, leaning forward.

"I wish I felt the same." Madeline sighed. "I seem to be dreading something … the future … trouble—it's hard to explain."

"Finding it hard to praise God?" Ami asked.

"Suppose so," replied Madeline.

"What are you worryin' about?" asked Alice, putting her hand on Madeline's shoulder.

"What am I worrying about? " blurted Madeline. "We're being hunted like animals and we don't know where we're going to live, or even if we'll make it to Queensland!"

"It's just the devil temptin' you, Maddy," offered Alice, patting Madeline's shoulder "He does that to me, too, even though I know God's looking after me."

"That's part of it," said Ami. "But Madeline's been through a lot lately, and when you're exhausted with a history of clinical depression, you get those dark moods. It won't last, though, and it doesn't mean God isn't with you. You just can't trust your feelings."

"Did you pick that up in your psychology classes?" asked Owen.

"Yeah, some of it, but I've been through it too. Sometimes you just need a good rest and let time pass."

After they had been driving on the highway for a couple of hours, Owen cast a concerned glance at Madeline. "See those flashin' lights up ahead? I'd say the cops are stopping cars. If it's just a random check, I think they'll pull Sven over 'cause he's in front, and let us through. He's chipped; he'll be OK."

"Oh, I hope so," replied Madeline.

"We're prayin'," said Alice.

The policeman walked out in front of Sven's vehicle, waving a reflective stop sign in one hand and a flashlight in the other hand. He shined the light in Sven's face as soon as he pulled over. Owen drove past at normal speed and kept going. A second policeman with a device for reading microchips joined his colleague and inspected the passengers' faces. "I wouldn't worry about them, Mike. They don't look the type."

"I'll check him anyway. Hold your right hand out, please, driver. Hmm. Sven Melnik from Sydney, eh? You've sure got some junk in this old bomb. Where ya headed?"

"Camping, officer. We're goin' on a camping trip."

"Hope the old bomb makes it. You're carryin' more junk than my wife takes on our trips. You're good to go."

Sven drove off, relieved that the covering of darkness hid his vehicle's defects. "Whew! Boy, I thought we'd had it then. Thank you, Jesus!"

"Better catch up to Owen," Eddie suggested. "He won't be far ahead. Betcha he's pulled over, waitin' for us."

As Sven's vehicle took the lead again, Owen turned up the radio's volume and listened to the news broadcast: "More than one hundred twenty arrests have been made in the Sydney and Hunter Valley areas in the past week. Prominent among them was former Newcastle Pastor Samuel Edwards and his family. They will be held at the Beechton Detention Centre, awaiting trail. Edwards was wanted by police for harboring and assisting many rebels in the Hunter Valley to escape. His wife, Joan, was charged with a secondary offence of dogmatic homeschool teaching of the Ten Commandments and the superiority of her religious views over others. Another group in Coffs Harbour …"

"Oh, no. They've got Sam, Joan, and the kids!" Madeline lamented. "That overcrowded detention center is no place for anybody—let alone kids."

"Fancy being charged for teaching the law of God," said Ami. "Joan will give a terrific defense in court, though. She really knows her Bible."

The newscaster continued. "In Calcutta, hundreds of anti-NIO rebels have been killed in the streets by angry mobs. Angry locals blame their dissenting position for the recent destructive earthquake, which killed tens of thousands and left millions homeless. In the United States, where the economy is rapidly failing and unemployment has skyrocketed, the Christian Power Movement is pressing for the controversial death sentence for all those who persist in breaking the new laws."

"The death sentence!" exclaimed Alice. "They're gonna kill Christians over there? That's terrible!"

"They'll probably declare open season on 'em," said Owen angrily. "Hunt 'em like wild turkeys."

"You don't have to scare everyone," fretted Madeline. "I'm depressed enough as it is."

"I always knew we could get shot, or worse," said Owen. "We can't hide from reality. We wouldn't be the first martyrs."

"Do you have to be so negative?" asked Ami.

"We've gotta be prepared for anythin'," replied Owen, scanning the shadowy edges of the road for animals.

"Yeah, but try to be a bit more encouraging," Madeline chided.

"It's not my fault," replied Owen. "I didn't invent this whole mess,."

"I suppose it's God's fault, is it?" Ami was quick to reply.

"Of course not. Look, it's been a big day. Can we stop debatin'? It's wearin' me out."

Sven and Eddie were singing hymns along with the CD player.

Eddie laughed.

"What's so funny?" asked Sven.

"Nothing. I'm just happy. Won't it be great in heaven! Man, I can hardly wait. If they shoot me, they'll just be sending me to paradise a bit quicker."

"What triggered you off?"

"Oh, man, won't it be great, seein' the Lord face to face? I mean, he saved us with his grace, man! He'll be standin' right there, and he'll have a yarn with me."

"Hang on, Eddie. I don't think it's right to get all excited about dyin'. It's disrespectful."

Eddie laughed. "Next thing you know I'll be in paradise, and it'll be even prettier than Evan's valley, and it'll be excitin'—all kinds of fun things to do!"

"What makes you so sure you're gonna die anyhow? The Lord could turn up anytime."

"Oh, that'll be better still. Fancy not dyin'—I mean, what a ride! Flyin' to heaven and sayin' good-bye to this mongrel of a joint. Sorry for laughin', mate, but it just hit me how good it'll be. Hey, Sven, what's that steam comin' up under the bonnet?"

"Holy smoke! She's hot. I'd better pull over."

"Pull that hazard switch on so Owen'll see ya."

"No, might attract cops. They'd be sure to check us out. Owen's not far behind. He'll spot us. I gotta turn the engine off before I cook it."

Sven lifted the car hood and turned on his flashlight. "Oh, man. The top radiator hose is all split! You got a spare?"

"No. Maybe we can tape it up."

"Nah. It'll leak under pressure."

Sven put his hands on his hips and looked up at the stars. "We're in the middle of nowhere in the middle of the night. What are we gonna do?"

"Was that a prayer?"

"Dunno."

"Well, it shoulda been."

"Yeah? Well, it was then. Didya see that garbage dump sign a few k's back? There's usually some old wrecks in 'em. Owen can drive back and look for a hose we can make fit."

"Fat chance!"

"Did I or did I not pray?"

"OK, OK."

"*Big* chance then. This'll be Owen's car lights comin' up."

The party got out of the vehicle and stretched their legs while Owen and Sven drove back to the dump after removing the split hose. They checked some old wrecks. Finding that the only radiator hose there was too wide, they made a sleeve for it from the old split hose. Just then, the lights of a vehicle sped by.

"Oh, no ," said Sven. "That was a cop car."

"He might not have seen us," said Owen nervously. "He didn't stop. But he'll probably check the others out."

"So what do we do now?" asked Sven.

"Let's wait five minutes and drive up. If the cops are still talkin' to 'em, we'll just drive past and wait behind some scrub," replied Owen.

When Owen drove back there was no sign of the passing car, so he pulled up. "What happened to the cop car?"

"You mean the car that flashed past?" asked Basil. "That was just an RTA vehicle."

"Scared the daylights out of us," said Owen. "Anyway, we think we've found what we want."

"Thought you would," said Eddie, smiling, "I saw Sven lookin' up at the stars, prayin'."

❧

It was four a.m. and the two vehicles had penetrated deep into the dry, flat plains of North Queensland.

"I'm really cramped and exhausted," moaned Madeline. "Let's pull over and have a sleep."

"Don't be silly," replied Owen, irritated. "We've gotta keep goin'. There's still a couple of hours of darkness left. Then we've got all day to sleep."

"Owen, I've had it. I don't think I can go on any further. And they're terribly squashed in the back seat."

"Well, it's not as if we're on a holiday tour," said Owen impatiently.

"Yeah, but why kill ourselves?" said Madeline, trying to remain calm.

"Look, it just might save our lives if ... All right, all right. We just passed a side street. I'll turn around and we can spend tomorrow hidin' behind the scrub back there."

They spread an old large tarpaulin on the red dirt, dropped their blankets and sleeping bags down on it, and quickly fell into an exhausted sleep.

Just before dawn, the sharp crack of a nearby rifle shot shattered the stillness. Madeline clutched Owen's arm. "What was that?"

Three more shots followed in rapid succession, and bright lights flashed through the bushes around them. Gruff male voices came from the direction of the road.

Owen sat bolt upright. "I think we've been spotted," he hissed. "I was afraid this might happen. We've been lucky so far, but we've had it now!"

"Not yet, we haven't," Basil hissed indignantly. "Where's your faith?"

"Keep low and get behind the vehicles," ordered Owen as he ducked low and pulled out a .30 caliber Winchester rifle from under his car seat. Owen had left the small rifle there since Jardine station days. Sven, scampering on his knees and dragging his blanket, huddled behind his car next to Eddie, who, wide eyed, scanned the bushes fearfully.

Alice noticed Owen's rifle. "I didn't know you had that," she whispered.

"Where I come from, they come in handy," replied Owen, focused on the trees in front.

A few more loud blasts came from the road.

"Keep down!" hissed Basil, motioning with his hands.

"I'll let 'em know were armed," Owen whispered. Levering a bullet into the breach, he pointing the barrel into the air and fired off thee shots in rapid succession. Excited shouting responded from the direction of the road. Sven, running low, ducked down beside Owen. "Did ya see one of 'em?"

"No. Just lettin' 'em know we've got guns too."

"Good idea. They might think twice about comin' in."

A fearful voice rang out through the night, "Hey, quit shootin'. You might kill someone!"

"*You* quit shootin'," Owen shouted back. "And take off outa here before we come after ya."

"You crazy or somethin'?" came the panic-stricken reply. "OK, we're off. Just don't shoot."

"What are ya shootin' at us for?" yelled Owen.

"We *weren't* shootin' at ya. We didn't know anyone was around. We're off a cattle property, just spotlighting 'roos by the road."

"Do you reckon they're telling the truth?" whispered Sven.

Owen shrugged. "You guys get in your car and clear outta' here."

"OK, mate, were off. Take it easy!"

An engine roared to life. Gradually its exhaust note faded into the distance.

"I'll sneak around and make sure they've all gone," whispered Sven. He kept low, ducking from tree to tree, and checked out the nearby thick scrub before circling back to the camp. "They're gone. And there were two freshly killed 'roos on the side of the road. I reckon they were fair-dinkum hunters."

"I don't know who got more scared, them or us." Eddie burst out in nervous laughter. "Oh, man, those guys were petrified. They must have thought we were assassins staked out in the bushes."

Ami hugged Owen, relieved. "I didn't know you guys had a gun! What are you, Mafia infiltrators or something?"

Eddie laughed louder. "Oh, mate, this is so unreal—gunfight at 'roo coral!"

Owen rolled up his blanket and groundsheet. "I think we'd better take off and camp farther down the track where no one knows where we are."

An hour later, they set up camp behind a thick stand of trees, where everyone managed to get some sleep. Late in the morning, Sven was the first to wake up. He found some fishing line from among his tangled gear. He walked to the riverbank, catching grasshoppers on the way, and peered into the water. He was delighted to see some golden perch shoaling near the surface.

He had caught half a bucket full of fish before Eddie came over to watch. When the bucket was full, they cleaned their catch and brought it back to camp.

Owen looked in the bucket and said, "Good work, fellas. But did ya have to empty the river?"

"Well, matey, I know this is an overreaction to Evan's forbidden trout, but I'm gonna eat half of these beauties myself."

"Don't worry, we'll help you get rid of 'em. But keep the fire small," cautioned Owen.

After sunset, the two-car convoy headed north. Owen decided they should take an isolated dirt road to avoid any police roadblocks. Eddie and Sven followed in cheerful spirits. "Hey, Sven, these roads are rough. I'm getting shaken to pieces."

"Good for your digestion, Ed. We made guts of ourselves eating all those fish today."

"Do you think we'll ever eat a pizza or chocolate ice cream again?" asked Eddie wistfully.

"Not here. But up in heaven we might. Might have chocolate-flavored lemons up there."

"Well, they wouldn't be lemons, then."

"Could be. Could have mango-flavored lemons—Look out! Boy, that was close. Those kangaroos are brainless. Why do they suddenly hop in front of us like that?"

"What about those greenies who reckon 'roos might become extinct in Australia if we don't protect 'em from huntin'? I reckon there's more of 'em now than when Captain Cook landed in Australia. I've seen thousands of 'em just along the road tonight. How about you drive for a while, Ed?"

"I lost my license, remember?"

"Yeah, you've gotta be careful. The kangaroos could pull you over and ask to see it."

After Sven and Eddie changed places, Eddie said, "Just keep talkin' to me or I'll fall asleep at the wheel."

"Talk to yourself. I'm tired, man. I'm just gonna lie back for a while."

"Don't go to sleep on me," protested Eddie.

"I'm not sleepin'. I'm talkin' to God. I was just tellin' him how glad I was that all my rottenness is forgiven and he's takin' me home when he comes back. I've been a bit of a mongrel at times. It's just like he says in Romans 4—he justifies the ungodly."

"Yeah, and he says in Romans 5, 'How much more will you be saved from God's end time anger through me' … or somethin' like that."

"Hey! That being saved from end-time anger is a good one, man. You can go to sleep now, Sven. I wouldn't mind talkin' to him for a while too."

Maude slid down the creek bank and scooped a plastic bucket into the clear waters of a small rock pool. She was glad there were no cattle around to pollute the water, and she was grateful for the tiny stream that trickled into the pool over the moss-covered ledge. It had not rained for a few weeks, yet there was water seeping in from the surrounding sandstone escarpments—an encouraging sign that this was permanent water.

She filled the second bucket and put it down beside the first. She then looked around cautiously, stripped off her long, stained gray dress, and lay down in the shallow rock pool just below. It was warmer and she wouldn't pollute their water supply. She stood, lathered her hair and her body, and lay down again in the lukewarm water to wash the soap off—something she would never have done before they went into hiding. She reminded herself that the Lord was coming imminently, so pollution didn't matter so much.

After bathing, she dried herself and put on her clean, long green dress. She lifted a bucket of water in each arm and cautiously stepped from one sandstone slab to another as she made her way up the creek bed. After almost slipping and falling on a damp rock, she lifted the buckets and rested them on the banks of the creek. She grabbed some tree roots, hauled herself up the steep bank, and carried the buckets about fifty meters to the cave. "I'm gonna be pretty fit after a month of this."

Evan rolled onto his side to face her. "Thank you, my dear. Sorry I'm too weak to help you. I'll cook tonight."

"Boiling potatoes is about all you can do," Maude bantered cheerfully, trying to pick Evan's spirits up.

He sat up slowly and weakly flicked a piece of wallaby dung into a corner of the cave. "Here I am feeling sick, hiding in a cave fit for animals, and I'm asking myself why?" he lamented. "I realize we have no choice. They'd jail us as outcasts if they caught us."

"It won't be much longer, dear, and Jesus will take us home."

"I wish I could be as confident as you are."

Maude glanced at him. "Evan! You've always believed in the second coming."

"I don't mean that. I mean I don't think I'm ready—I'm not good enough."

"Don't think that, Evan. You live a good life."

"Good? Lots of people who are good will be lost. We've got to be *perfect*."

Evan stared at the ground and shook his head. "Lately, I keep thinking about the things I've done wrong."

"You're a good man, Evan. I couldn't wish for a better husband."

"I don't mean that. I mean ..."

Evan began to sob and Maude put her arms around him. He lay down on his foam bed and spoke quietly. "I always thought when this time came I'd be strong ... confident ... a warrior. But I'm not. I'm weak and falling apart inside. I don't feel saved. I'm scared, Maude ... scared of dying, scared of Jesus coming back."

"Stop worrying, dear. You'll be OK. You've led a good life. You'll be saved, you'll see."

Betty Zinski had been listening from the other side of the cave, where their bedroom was curtained off with a sheet. "Don't forget Christ died for you, too, Evan," she called out.

"My heart doesn't seem to respond, though, Betty. I'm not as good as you."

"You know what I think?" said Victor. "You're not thinking straight since you went off the insulin. Half your problem is that your diabetes is making you depressed."

"Maybe," Evan conceded. "But it's more than that."

Maude lit the firewood in the old kerosene-drum stove, and the smoke caught the upward draught, ascending to the natural gap in the cave roof. Betty sat contentedly on her folding chair and peeled potatoes. She reached down and pulled a smoking stick out of the fire and threw sand on it. "That sort of damp wood gives off a lot of smoke. We can't have too much smoke coming off the mountain or we'll be spotted."

Maude looked at her quizzically. "Whose gonna notice a bit of smoke?"

"I saw two choppers yesterday. They might be looking for us."

"You really think so?"

"If they're blamin' us for the all those earthquakes and floods, they'll be real serious about wanting to get rid of us, won't they?"

"Get rid of us? You mean kill us?"

"It'll come to that. Revelation 13 says those who won't worship the beast will be slain. And I heard on the radio that some of the NIO people want to go along with the US Christian Power Movement's idea of killing us remnant people so God can bless the country again."

"So it's happenin'. It really is happenin'. You afraid to die, Betty?"

"I don't like the idea, but it's worth it. Anyway, I'm not worried. I've always felt I'd be alive when the Lord comes. If we can keep hiding in these mountains, we might just sit it out till he comes."

Owen's convoy pulled off the little-used dirt road where it curved around a hill. He got out of the car, stretched his long, cramped limbs, then clambered up the rocky hill. Breathing heavily, he slowly scanned the horizon for familiar landmarks. Then with agile, surefooted steps he scurried down the slope to the cars.

"The country we're lookin' for is that way about 15 k's," said Owen, pointing to the northwest. "We should see a faint track soon, then we'll have to make our own track. Sven, you'll have to keep close and follow me through the scrub."

Owen cautiously steered the four-wheel-drive vehicle over the rough terrain, occasionally towing Sven's vehicle across the gullies as it bashed over rocks and logs.

After some hours of negotiating the raw terrain, Owen stopped at the upper reaches of a creek bed that dissected a small forested valley. "This will have to be it," announced Owen. "We're a long way from any road. We'll camp under that thick stand of trees by the creek, so it'll be hard for anyone to see us from the sky."

"What are we gonna live in?" asked Alice.

"We'll make some huts. There's plenty of bark around for walls and roofs. For now, Sven's got his tent and we've got some tarps. The wet season might not be quite over yet, so it could still rain, but at least we've got water in the creek."

"Bit muddy, though," observed Alice.

"It'll keep your skin clear," joked Owen.

24

Judas's Shadow

◇◇◇◇◇◇◇◇◇◇◇◇◇◇◇◇◇◇◇◇◇◇◇◇◇

SEVEN WEEKS LATER, the group was sitting around the campfire with Owen's father, Gordon Boyd. Owen had found him that morning when he investigated campfire smoke in the distance.

"It's amazing you're here with us, Dad. I had an idea that you'd be out this way somewhere. I remember explorin' this country with you years ago and we did some shootin' out here. God must have put this valley in both our minds. We might have even talked about comin' here to hide one day."

Owen was trying to sound positive. All the campers were distraught because they had heard that evening on the radio that Pastor Sam Edwards and his entire family had been executed. They had been shot together with many others at a Sydney military range and were buried in a mass grave.

Owen looked at his father and said sadly, "They were really nice people, Dad. Sam inspired me, and Joan and the kids were special too. They'll all be in the kingdom, I reckon, but I don't like to think about what the kids went through."

"From my experience at the hospital," Madeline remembered, "the kids faced death better than the adults did. The Lord gave them a simple faith and special strength when they needed it."

"I'll be honest—I thought I'd feel really strong and brave under heat, but I'm not," confessed Ami. "Sometimes I get scared."

"Me too," said Basil. "If it can happen to Sam, it could happen to us."

"There's something I fear more than being shot," said Gordon, shaking his head. "What really hurts me the most. I did my best with your mum and brother, Owen. I don't know why they changed. I feel terrible that they didn't make it."

Noticing Owen's head drop, Gordon put his arm around him to comfort him. "She was all right for a while. But when they started to jail people, she couldn't seem to handle the thought of it. She'd been visiting the church's ladies meetings every second week, but all of 'em went with the NIO—all of 'em. They talked her into joining ' em, Owen. I didn't realize what was happening at first. She'd come home and tell me what they'd talked about, and some of 'em were against the NIO at first. But Joan didn't tell me she was starting to believe 'em. She just talked about their reasons, and I tried to help her with it. It wasn't all that clear and easy for me, either, I can tell you. Her friends must have all become so convinced by the false Christ and his miracles that they got sucked in—and mum with 'em."

Gordon sobbed for a while, then said, "The sale of the farm helped her to buy a place in town not far from Bill's place."

"Why did Bill join 'em?" asked Owen, distraught.

"Well, you know what your brother's like. He was never what you'd call a strong believer. I'd hoped that these tough times would do somethin' for him. But they only showed up his weakness. He was easily led."

"If only he'd spent time with God's Word," Owen lamented. "I think he used to go to church more for the social life. By the way, Mum doesn't know where you're hidin', does she? I mean, now that she's with them, she could eventually talk."

"She knows I went bush, but she'd have no way of knowin' if I'd driven just over the range or gone interstate. The hardest thing I ever did in my life was to say good-bye to her." Gordon sobbed. "We hugged. She begged me to go with her—she actually got on her knees and begged. And I nearly did. I love her that much."

Owen and his father embraced and wept together. Everyone around the campfire was moved. Then Madeline suggested they all hold hands and pray for strength.

"I can feel the presence of angels," said Eddie, looking around as if expecting to see one.

"The Lord's right here with us 'round the campfire," said Alice. "I can feel 'im."

"I'll read you something from Psalm 33—that's helped me lately," said Ami.

> *"But the eyes of the Lord are on those who fear him,*
> *on those whose hope is in his unfailing love,*
> *to deliver them from death and keep them alive in famine.*

We wait in hope for the Lord;
He is our help and our shield.
In him our hearts rejoice,
For we trust in his holy name.
May your unfailing love rest upon us O Lord,
Even as we put our trust in you."

Owen picked up his guitar and sang the psalm to a simple tune he made up as he went along.

"What about the Hollins family and the Langmans, Dad?" asked Owen, resting his guitar against a log.

"They were chipped—all of 'em. I'm the only one who wasn't, from among the station people."

Gordon picked the tin can with the wire handle off the coals with a stick and poured the boiling water into his mug. "We're going to have to take special care camouflagin' the vehicles," he said.

"They're under thick tree cover," said Madeline.

"Yeah, but let's cover 'em with bushes from all sides tomorrow."

"What do you suppose the cops and army are doing to find us?" asked Madeline.

"They'll be depending on informers mostly," suggested Basil. "You know, property owners, miners, timber getters. If they spotted us, they'd be on the phone as quick as lightning. Planes are out at night looking out for fires, getting GPS coordinates, and sending choppers or ground crews in the next day."

"From now on we'd better keep our fires small and under a bark platform," said Owen.

"Won't the Lord just blind their eyes so they can't find us?" asked Ami.

"He might. But we've gotta do our part too," answered Owen. "When David hid from Saul he did everything he could to keep clear of 'im."

Gordon turned to Owen. "You got plenty of ammo, Son? What about you and me goin' shootin' tomorrow? You're all lookin' a bit skinny, and there's plenty of goats up in the ranges."

"Yeah, righto."

"I've gotta hand it to you all," commended Gordon. "You're great gardeners. The garden looks great."

"It's gotta be the Lord's blessing," said Madeline. "The soil's barely good enough to grow a toadstool, let alone veggies. And what keeps the 'roos and possums from eating them?"

Evan staggered to his feet and found Maude's hand mirror in a wooden crate on a rock shelf in the cave. He went to the cave entrance, where there was more light, and peered in the mirror. "Maude, I look ten years older, and I've got blotches on my skin, and my eyes are puffy," moaned Evan, shocked at his appearance.

"That's what I've been trying to tell you, luv. You're pretty crook, and it's not the toxins coming out. But you're better off than poor Sam Edwards was when he watched his family getting shot."

Evan made his way to his bed and lay down. "I've been thinking about Sam. I bet he died in peace, believing he was right with God. But I can't seem to find that peace. They've probably got heat sensors in those planes that fly over. It's just a matter of time before they get us. Maude ... I'm frightened to die. I'd be lost—forever lost."

"Don't think that way, Evan. Jesus loves you."

"Yes, he does. But I ... I don't love him back enough to be saved. I'm ... I'm a hypocrite, Maude, and God can't save hypocrites. At night I lie there and think of the terrible punishment of the hypocrites. I ... I need more time to get right with God."

"It's only Satan havin' a go at ya. Don't listen to him."

"Either way I'm trapped. If I don't get caught and shot, I'll die from my diabetes. And I'm not ready to die. Maude, I need to get some insulin—I can see that now. I should've got it before, when it was easier. Those herbs don't work. I've doubled and trebled the dosage and they just don't work."

Maude looked apprehensively at Evan's resolute expression, wondering what he was leading to.

"I'm going into town, Maude. I'm going to see Adrian Sebastian and tell him I'm joining them."

Maude's face paled. "You can't be serious!"

"What have I got to lose? If I stay here, I've had it both ways. In town, I can get the medicine, get better, find more time to overcome my weaknesses, and get right with the Lord. I'll even get chipped, but don't worry. I'll remove it later."

"Evan, no! You can't. It won't work."

"Don't worry Maude. And when I'm ready, I'll come back to you."

Maude's next words surprised even herself. "If you go, I'm goin' with you."

"No! I won't hear of it."

"You're all I've got, Evan. I can't go on without you." Maude sobbed.

Evan and Maude didn't tell the Zinskis about their plan. They waited until they weren't around and simply walked out of the cave. Maude struggled to help Evan down the rough, obstacle-filled path to the cabin.

Arriving at the cabin totally exhausted, Evan rested. From his bed, he instructed Maude how to rig up the water generator to charge the Subaru's battery. They drove to Newcastle at night to avoid detection.

After struggling up the front stairs of Inspector Adrian Sebastian's house, Evan pressed the buzzer and leaned on the wall, catching his breath.

"Well, well. If it isn't Evan Hawkins," said Sebastian, surprised and amazed. "You're the last person I expected to see."

'G'day, Adrian. I need to talk. Do you remember Maude?"

"Yes. You'd better come in and sit down. You look a bit wobbly," said Sebastian, trying to read their faces for some explanation

Evan flopped onto the nearest chair. "We want to join you, Adrian," he wheezed.

"Well, I must say I'm surprised, but it's not as simple as that. You're wanted people."

"But we're on your side now," Evan said desperately.

"How do I know you're telling the truth? Why'd you change your mind?"

"Please believe us," implored Evan. "We're willing to be chipped—to cooperate. I can't survive in the bush anymore. It's not working. If I don't get insulin soon, I'll go into a coma and die."

"So that's it—you're after insulin. Makes sense now. You realize you'd have to give your allegiance to the NIO and be willing to submit to the new laws?"

Evan nodded. "We've thought it all through very carefully."

"OK, you say you're serious. Where's Owen Boyd and his wife?"

"I don't know."

"Ha! I didn't think you'd cooperate," sniggered Sebastian.

"We really *don't* know. They left the valley some time ago, when they heard of the jail penalties. I think they were headed for Queensland somewhere."

"Where have you two been hiding out?"

"Near my property."

"That's pretty rough country. How could you survive up there? Where did you stay at night?"

"We stored food; I've been hoarding stuff for a long time."

"We've flown all over those ranges—we'd have spotted you."

"We saw the planes and helicopters, but you couldn't have seen us under that dense scrub."

"All right, Evan, come clean." Sebastian grinned, enjoying the upper hand. "What about Zinski and his wife? We know they were staying with you."

"I … I don't know where they are."

"Really? I didn't think you were fair dinkum. If you can't help me, then I can't help you. Look, here's the deal. I'm getting on that phone right now and have you both charged if you don't take me to Zinski. What's it to be?"

Evan looked at Maude, who was ashen faced. "Maude and I want to talk alone for a minute."

"No need to talk," said Maude. "We've gone this far. There's no turnin' back."

Evan slumped farther into the chair, his hands supporting his head. "OK. They're in a cave out back of my place."

"Cave, eh? You'll have to take us there."

Evan nodded.

"But he's too weak," protested Maude. "He should be in hospital for at least two weeks."

"No worries. We'll arrange that," agreed Sebastian.

Victor Zinski found Evan's .303 rifle and ammunition in the bottom of a wooden case on the cave floor. With Evan gone, he felt free to go hunting rock wallabies and other animals for food.

About three weeks after Evan and Maude disappeared, he was hunting in the escarpment country between Evan's valley and his cave home. Hearing voices approaching under the cliff beneath him, he lay down to avoid being seen. He then slowly crawled to the edge and peered down. Four men were climbing up the steep, rocky path, and when they drew closer he noted that three of them were carrying rifles. As they approached the bottom of the cliff, he was appalled to recognize Evan Hawkins. He was leading Police Inspector Adrian Sebastian and two other policemen, and they were less than thirty meters away.

Zinski felt an overwhelming sense of what he imagined was divine indignation and rage. He had never experienced such zeal before, and he felt prophetically commissioned, like he imagined Elijah felt on Mount

Carmel when he beheaded the priests of Baal. *What have you done, Evan my brother? After all we have been through together, how could you find it in your heart to betray us? Just as Judas betrayed Christ and met his punishment through hanging and bursting asunder, so this day, God shall execute his judgment through me.*

Resolutely, he picked up Evan's rifle, released the safety catch, and aimed carefully at Evan's head. He felt that the vengeance of God was burning within his righteous breast, compelling him to do his duty.

The loud report of the military weapon thundered and echoed around the cliffs. Evan Hawkins was dead before he hit the ground. The three policemen turned and fled in terror from the unseen and ruthless enemy who had taken advantage of the terrain. They slid and bruised their way down the rocky face in the direction of their vehicles.

Zinski hurried back to his cave hideout. The sick, empty feeling in his stomach was dominated by a victorious sensation. He imagined David felt that way after slaying Goliath.

He didn't tell his wife that day that he had killed Evan. He didn't expect she would appreciate the responsibilities of being an unexpected divine instrument of vengeance. Neither did he want her to be emotionally distracted from a quick escape to somewhere deeper in the mountains.

Fleeing the cave, they traveled though wild and precipitous terrain for three days, carrying what basic essentials they could. After crossing dangerous, steep-sided gorges and climbing towering cliffs, they finally reached a large, secluded cave. It was near a branch of the wild Nepean River headwaters, and the area promised enough fish and wildlife to provide food for a long time.

Inspector Sebastian stirred his coffee during his lunch break at Newcastle police station. "My job's taken on a new meaning now, Bruce," he confided. "Last year I was just doing the routine thing: catching crooks, serving on court cases, that sort of stuff. Now I feel like I'm on a divine mission. Talk about job satisfaction. I love it."

Sergeant Bruce Fossey looked up from his newspaper. "I'll be happier when we get rid of all the marked scum. We'll all be better off. Anybody who doesn't believe what Christ recently told us is dead meat as far as I'm concerned."

Sebastian was in a zealous mood. "We've implemented the death sentence, but we're still a bit behind the States. Over there, ordinary blokes are so indignant at the deliberate blasphemy of the rebels, every man and his dog are taking pot shots at 'em. Take a look at this character in the papers. He's showing off the seven notches on his gun. It's not legal, but nobody cares."

"Do you still think it was Zinski who shot Hawkins?" asked Fossey.

"Must have been," replied Sebastian. "There's no one else up there. He must be a ruthless mongrel, that one. Maybe they all get that way after a while. We'll have to be extra careful, seeing they've got guns."

"Yeah, well, I'm not sending any men up there just to get shot. We'll have to try another way, at least pretend to."

"Pretend to? No ideas, huh?"

"Yeah, but none of them are much good," Fossey laughed. "There's about three thousand square kilometers of rugged cave country in which to find two fanatics with a gun. I think we'll just leave 'em there, but don't tell anyone I said so."

"That country's so isolated that years ago they found a valley full Wollombi pine trees—supposedly extinct—and that was just by accident."

Owen Boyd was resting briefly from the exertion of dragging a log for firewood when he caught a movement from the corner of his eye. He kept watching some huge boulders on top of the hill overlooking the camp. Something moved again.

That looks like a hat. Someone's watching us. I'd better find out what's going on.

Not knowing whether the intruder was armed, Owen warily dodged up the slope behind tree cover. He saw someone carrying what looked like a pick and a gold pan running away in the distance, up the next ridge. "Hello," Owen called. "Can I help you?"

But the man kept running.

Owen hurried back to camp. "Some guy was spyin' on us from behind those rocks, Dad." He gasped. "When he realized I'd spotted him, he bolted."

"What'd he look like? Was he a cop?"

"He looked like he might've been prospectin'."

"Doesn't sound good, does it? Might've gone straight to his vehicle and gone to the cops. Then again, he might just mind his own business and keep prospectin' somewhere else."

"He was scared of us. He must have guessed who we were."

"Chances are the police will be out here to check us out, then. I think we'd better be shifting camp. We got much fuel left?"

"Heaps. I've got more than half a drum of diesel left and plenty in the ute. Sven's only got enough petrol in his Crown for about a hundred k's or so, though."

"I've got plenty of diesel in the Patrol plus a few spare cans full. I reckon we should pack up and leave—no muckin' around. We'll abandon Sven's old bomb, though. I'll fit the guys in the Patrol."

"Where do we go from here, Dad?"

"I know an isolated spot another eighty k's or so further west."

"That's no good. They'll be right onto us. I think we'll have to travel at night using back roads all the way north to the wilds of Cape York."

"That's real outback country, and it's a long way. Will we have enough fuel?

"We'll get close at least. Let's tell the others."

25

Plagues of Wrath

◇◇◇◇◇◇◇◇◇◇◇◇◇◇◇◇◇◇◇◇◇◇◇◇◇◇◇◇◇

FRIEDA FLETCHER WAS SITTING at her dressing table applying makeup while Karl reclined in his favorite chair, drinking beer and watching the news. "Come have a look at this Frieda," he called out. "This is a bit drastic. In the Solomon Islands they're driving the marked ones into the sea and drowning them."

"One second, Karl, I'm nearly finished," replied Frieda. She noticed a mark on her cheek she had never seen before. She covered it with powder but was alarmed to see some more marks appearing. "Karl, come quick!" she screamed in anguish.

Karl spilled his beer as he ran to the bedroom. Frieda turned to see ugly sores on his face. She put her hand to her mouth, shocked. She spun to the mirror—her spots had turned into ugly sores too.

They stared at each other in horror and confusion.

After packing the vehicles, Owen's convoy set off into the darkness. Madeline turned on the car radio and heard the broadcaster's strained and urgent voice. "An outbreak of terrible sores has spread quickly across Australia and throughout an unknown number of other countries. It appears that a new virulent strain of skin infection that breaks out in gaping, puss-filled sores all over the body has struck, causing excruciating pain. So far no relief has been obtained from antibiotics or painkillers, and laboratories have been commissioned to find a cure. Few people in Australia appear to have escaped it. The exceptions, strangely enough, are the captured rebels, who appear to be immune to the infection. Their claim that this is the first of the seven last plagues of Revelation has been ridiculed and dismissed by church leaders.

"We would like to thank Dr. Collin Henderson, lecturer on infectious diseases from Townsville's James Cook University, for a phone interview tonight, despite suffering from the infection."

"I'm in a lot of pain, Pete, and I know you must be, too, so let's get this interview over with quickly, OK?"

"All right. Dr. Henderson, is there any explanation for the rapid spread of this disease?"

"First let me say that this disease did *not* spread through infection. It hit simultaneously all over the country, and in many overseas countries too."

"What can you tell us about the nature of the sores?"

"Nothing much, except they're terrible and painful and we haven't seen them before."

"Doctor, can you give us any idea of how long the sores are likely to last?"

"Of course not. Don't ask such stupid questions! Look, I'm signing off now and getting back in the bath, where I'm getting some relief. But I just want to say this: Even a blind man could see that this plague has come from God. It hasn't fallen on dissenters, so that ought to tell us something if we had half a brain."

"Doctor, what is the—?"

"See you later."

"Uh, that was Dr. Henderson from James Cook University. Our next interview is with Archbishop John Henning, who is on the phone now. Archbishop Henning, thank you for sacrificing your time when you, like all of us, are suffering. You have consulted with other theologians. What is the consensus over the theological implications of the sores?"

"We see this plague as the culmination of God's displeasure at those who refuse to join us in our united efforts at world peace. Just as God's curse was upon all of Israel because of one Achan in the camp, so we must all suffer God's displeasure because of their blasphemy."

"What do you see as the mind of God on the issue, then?"

"For months, the NIO has promoted the idea of extermination of all its enemies, but governments have been too slow to act and we are suffering the consequences."

"So you believe greater efforts should be made to, uh, wipe them out?"

"It should have been our first priority right at the start."

"Thank you, Archbishop. We won't take up any more of your time. As more information comes to light, we shall notify our listeners."

Owen looked at Madeline with a shocked expression. "It's gotta be the first of the seven last plagues," said Madeline as she turned on the car's interior light and flicked through her Bible's pages. "Yes. It says, 'Painful sores broke out on the people who had the mark of the beast and worshipped his image.' "

Owen focused on the ribbon of dirt road dividing the darkness ahead. "If this really is the first plague, y'all realize what that means, don't you? It means probation is finally over for the human race."

"Probation?" asked Alice.

"There's no more chance left for people to accept Christ and repent," said Owen.

"But I thought God never gives up on people," said Basil.

"He doesn't," agreed Owen. "But God can't do anything with 'em if their hearts are set like concrete. The first plague doesn't fall until everyone has made up their mind to forever be on God's side or against him."

"You mean everyone's already taken sides and won't change their mind?" asked Basil.

"That's right," said Owen.

"I found it in Revelation 22.11," said Madeline. " 'Let him who does wrong continue to do wrong; let him who is vile continue to be vile; let him who is right continue to do right ; and let him who is holy continue to be holy.' "

"What makes you think the first plague falls after everyone's made their choice for eternity?" queried Basil.

"Give Basil your Bible, would you please, Madeline?" requested Owen. "Bas, have a look at Revelation 15 and 16. Those chapters show that the plagues fall straight after the events of the last part of chapter 14, where the harvest of earth's people becomes ripe."

"So you're saying that the plagues don't fall until everyone's character on earth is either ripe for going to heaven or ripe for destruction?" asked Basil.

"Yes. Christ said the wheat and the weeds—meaning good people and bad people—will grow together until the final harvest sorts them out."

Basil found Revelation chapter 15 verse 1. "It says here that the seven last plagues fall 'because with them God's wrath is completed.' And verse 8 says the plagues are 'filled with the wrath of God.' "

"That's right. It's never happened before," said Owen. "Up until then, God still pleads with all the deceived people. But once he sees that they're all ripe with evil, he pours his plagues on 'em. And during the plagues, none of the deceived ones confesses his sins or repents."

"You're dead right," said Basil. "Chapter 16 verse 9 says, 'They cursed the name of God because of these plagues but they refused to repent.' "

Basil was gazing out of the car window at the three-quarter moon racing through the trees and over the mountaintops. "Man, these are heavy times we're living in."

"It's a good feelin', knowin' I'm saved and won't go back on the Lord." Alice sighed as she rested her head on Ami's shoulder. "It makes me feel peaceful like."

"All of us in the car *must* be God's people. If we weren't, we would have got the sores by now," said Ami. "It's kind of strange knowing that everyone's made up their mind forever."

"I guess if Satan's in full control of the wicked, then we're in for it," said Basil.

"I don't think we've got too much to worry about," said Owen.

"What do you mean?" asked Ami, stroking Alice's hair.

"Why would God allow us to get killed now?" replied Owen. "Being a martyr wouldn't serve any purpose as a witness for Christ anymore"

"If it's all right with you guys, I'll read a bit of Psalm 91," offered Madeline. "It seems to fit our situation."

> *"He who dwells in the shelter of the Most High*
> *will rest in the shadow of the almighty.*
> *I will say of the lord, 'He is my refuge and my fortress,*
> *my God in whom I trust.'*
> *You will not fear the terror of night, nor the arrow that flies by day,*
> *Nor the pestilence that stalks in the darkness,*
> *nor the plague that destroys at midday.*
> *A thousand may fall at your side, ten thousand at your right hand,*
> *But it will not come near you.*
> *You will only observe with your eyes and see the punishment of the wicked."*

"Hey, that does fit, talkin' about the plagues and all," said Alice.

Sometime after midnight a bump in the road jolted Madeline. She woke up and looked around to see who else was awake. "Owen, I'd better drive now. Pull over."

"Thanks," replied Owen. "I wouldn't mind a snooze."

When they pulled over, Gordon's vehicle drew alongside and he wound his window down. "Everything OK?" he asked.

"Yeah, just changing drivers. Why don't we all stretch our legs a minute," suggested Owen.

"While we're all together," said Madeline, "I'd better tell you about an amazing dream I had tonight. It was different from any dream I've ever had—so clear and real. We were all camped together on a river, eating big silver fish. The bottom of the river was glistening with gold. And further downstream, a ribbon of gold stretched from the river to far up into the sky—as far as I could see."

"Palmer River! It was mined for gold along its entire length," Gordon said. "I've read a book on its history, called *River of Gold*. The big silver fish are probably barramundi—you'd get 'em downstream in the Palmer. And you said it was downstream where the gold went into the sky. I betcha it's pretty isolated there too."

"We've all been prayin'—must be the spot," agreed Eddie.

"Barra are great eatin'," said Sven.

Just before dawn, Madeline shook Owen. "Wake up," she said urgently. "Police roadblock—looks like four cops. What'll I do?"

Owen focused his blurred eyes. "They've seen us—just keep goin' right through. Don't stop."

"What?"

"Do it!"

"They're waving us down, Owen. They've got guns. What if they start shooting?"

"Look. They've dropped their guns and they're runnin' into the bush. Somethin's scared 'em. Just keep your foot down. That light barrier won't hurt the steel bull bar. Hang on."

"I hardly felt it!"

"Just keep going I wonder what frightened those cops."

"Do you think they'll follow us?"

"Doubt it. They were scared stiff. Put your foot down. Let's get outta here!"

An hour later, after turning into a track heading north, they pulled over. Ed and Sven sprang out of Gordon's car. "Yahoo!" yelled Ed.

Sven stuck his head through Owen's open window, his excitement spilling out. "You guys had glowin' passengers holdin' fiery swords riding on your roof. No wonder those cops took off! That was unreal!"

"You *saw* 'em?" asked Alice, grabbing his arm.

"Saw 'em? The brightness hurt our eyes! Wow! I've seen angels!"

"I wouldn't like to be on the wrong side of those bods," added Eddie. "They were fearsome."

Gordon opened his car door to get in. "Well, if the Lord saved us once, he'll keep savin' us. But we'd better keep movin' to find a spot to camp before it gets light."

Victor Zinski was lying naked on a bed of leaves his wife, Betty, had lovingly built for him under a sheltering sandstone overhang. With a pained grimace on his face, he rolled onto his side while Betty applied a moist rag to the dozens of weeping sores that covered his body.

"This pain is more than I can bear," moaned Zinski. "I think I have the curse of God upon me. Do you think it's because I killed Evan?"

"You've probably got an allergic reaction to some poisonous bush you brushed past. Don't think the worst."

"I can't help but think that the first of the plagues has fallen on me. If so, I must have the mark of the beast."

"That can't be. You refused to get chipped."

"I suppose you're right. You're very comforting to me, my dear. Oh, it hurts every time I move!"

Victor thought for a while, then said quietly but seriously, "You'd better hide the gun in case the pain gets worse. I don't think I can stand this much longer."

Owen gripped the sweaty steering wheel more tightly as he dodged the worst of the gaping potholes. On the dry ridges, the hot sun had already converted the track into dry dust in places. The four-wheel-drive vehicles left a long cloud of powdery dust that hung in the air for half an hour on that windless day. The dust was as fine as flour and penetrated everything inside the vehicles. The soft, deep dust camouflaged the deep ruts on the track and gave no protection to the cars that jarred over them, shaking and sliding.

The annual wet season had finished a while back, when meters of rain had been dumped on the waterlogged land. Peaceful streams had turned into raging, forty-foot-deep torrents that deposited enormous logs on the upper branches of trees. The floods routinely created enormous inland lakes that slowly receded into lush lagoons and became the home of myriad birds and fish.

All this life attracted crocodiles. Some were the smaller Johnson River variety, with their long, fish-eating snouts. Others, however, were the saltwater giants that could grow over six meters long and didn't care if they ate man or beast.

The vehicles drove through another night and into the dawn. They were well up into the huge eastern peninsula of Australia known as Cape York, and they were getting close to their destination. They passed Mulgrave Mountain, on which sat a fifty-meter rock sculpted by nature to look like a regal lion observing its kingdom. The dawn's glow warmed the lion-rock, making its orange coat stand out against the brightening eastern sky. A pack of wild yellow-coated dingoes fearlessly crossed the road and stopped to look arrogantly back through the long tropical grass.

Gordon shared some history with Sven and Eddie, who were absorbing the strange terrain through widened city slicker's eyes. "About eighty kilometers east from here, on the other side of the Palmer River, is a steep-sided mountain pass called Hells Gate. Thousands of miners walked the long trail from Cooktown on the coast, eager to find their fortune in gold nuggets in the Palmer. They had to risk Hell's Gate to get over the range. The local aboriginal tribes naturally resented the invasion of their land, which wrecked their hunting and fishing grounds, so they ambushed the miners, who carried heavy loads. Many of the poorly armed Chinese miners were captured or killed, legend has it, for food.

"Then there was a notorious white adventurer named Christie Palmerston. He was the terror of the Chinese miners on the Palmer River. He was practically raised with the aborigines, so he spoke their lingo and could hunt and fish with the best of 'em. The young warriors idolized him, and he led them on many raids on the Chinese to steal their gold. He was great with a gun."

"Sound like a legend all right," said Sven. "Wouldn't mind havin' 'im with us just now."

As the first glimmerings of light tinted the landscape with pale ochre, hundreds of strange mounds could be seen decorating the bizarre landscape. Most were thin and flat like porpoise fins, towering two to five meters high, with their edges always pointing north and south. Homesteaders crushed them into cement, which was then mixed with water to set like concrete and was used for building. Gordon explained that these anthills always faced the same direction to keep the internal tunnels in the nests at just the right temperature.

Eventually the vehicles turned off the track and had to make their own way through the bush with four-wheel drive engaged. Sometimes they had to tow each other out of swampy bogs, emerging covered in mud.

At times, they ploughed through water that reached halfway up the car doors. Finally, the vehicles pulled up about thirty kilometers from where the Palmer River ran into the mighty Mitchell River.

The party stared at the river in disbelief. "The river's red—pure red!" exclaimed Ami.

Owen walked to the river's edge and scooped some of the red liquid with a piece of bark. He examined it closely and smelled it. "This isn't red water; its blood. Look at all the bloated dead fish floating belly up. And oh, it really stinks."

"It's the second plague," said Basil, walking up to join Owen at the water's edge. "The rivers have turned to blood in revenge for the blood of the martyrs."

"It's the third plague," corrected Sven.

"Pardon?"

"The oceans turn red under the second plague and the rivers turn into blood under the third plague," said Sven. "Haven't you studied theology?"

"Dr. Melnik, I presume?" replied Basil sarcastically.

Madeline was tired and fretful. "Nature's gone bizarre. It's not the same world anymore. Why would God bring us here? I was dying to have a wash and rest, but I can't swim in blood and eat rotten fish. Maybe that dream wasn't from God after all."

Alice put her arm around Madeline's waist and hugged her. "God will take care of us. Remember the angels we saw? We can't see 'em now, but they must still be here."

"Well, there's nothing here for us," said Gordon. "Let's keep following the river for a while and see what turns up."

The off-road vehicles crawled around muddy bogs and giant ant nests, and crashed over grass-hidden boulders. Occasionally someone would point out a crocodile sun-baking on the mud flats.

"I don't wanna camp anywhere near those crocs," said Ami.

"We could thin 'em out easy enough," quipped Owen. "Anyone fancy croc steak for tea?"

"Depends what he was feeding on," said Basil. "I don't want recycled fisherman or rotten pig meat, thanks."

They drove over a ridge and approached a line of tall paper-bark trees and Pandanus palms. Owen got out of his vehicle and walked under the trees, then peered down at the quiet waters of a large, crystal-clear stream. He shot his arms in the air and smiled. "You beauty!" he called out to the others. "The water's deep and clear, and you can see big fish at the bottom."

Everyone hurried over to enjoy the discovery. Just above the tranquil waterhole were some rapids and smaller pools. Eddie, Basil, and Sven flopped into a shallow pool. Eddie blissfully dipped his hair and splashed his face, exclaiming, "Oh man, this is so cool."

"This will do me until the Lord comes," Sven blurted out.

Alice hugged Madeline. "Your dream was true, Maddy. I knew we'd be all right. Those angels are still with us, even though we can't see 'em."

After the dusty drive, it was a great relief for the campers to soak themselves in the pure mineral water that had its source in an underground spring. The tropical autumn sun quickly dried the clothes on their bodies. As they were all too exhausted to unpack, they lay down in the dense shade to rest and sleep. Basil observed Sven put a large knife on the ground beside him.

"What's that for?" he asked.

"Crocs."

"Givin' the angels a hand, are ya?"

"Yeah, just in case they sleep on duty."

At about the time Owen's party was setting up their new camp in the wilds of Northern Australia, an emergency meeting of the New International Order was scheduled for New York. Johanus Zamsi, the chairman of the NIO, was enjoying his long flight to New York, reading and preparing some speeches.

The announcement made by the captain sounded almost routine to Zamsi. "We are due to land in ten minutes. I hope you've had a pleasant journey. We've been advised that a record heat wave has been building up across the United States this morning, so passengers are urgently advised to seek air-conditioned accommodations on landing."

Zamsi kept working on his speech. The ugly red expanse of ocean beneath the plane had disgusted and shocked him at first, but as the hours dragged by, he had become accustomed to it.

Zamsi stepped out of the air-conditioned airport building into a sudden blast of heat that reminded him of his visit to an iron-smelting foundry. The temperature continued to soar freakishly, so he quickened his pace across the road, but the soles of his shoes began to stick to the melting surface. Cars were slithering and tires were beginning to smoke and melt with the soaring heat.

Zamsi staggered to the concrete pavement and attempted to get in a stationary taxi. "Quickly, can you drive me to—"

The driver, frightened and confused by the hot blast of air coming through the open car door, yelled, "Outa my way. We're not going anywhere. I'm gettin' out your side!"

The frantic crowd ran in all directions. Drivers abandoned their cars and ran toward the railway station, unaware that the lines had buckled hideously. Others desperately searched for air-conditioned buildings, but the air conditioners had overheated and stalled, and electricity plants had shut down. Pigeons dropped onto the pavement next to collapsed pedestrians. A fire engine siren screamed while firemen in heat-resistant suits tried to provide cooling water for the masses. But as their motors overheated and the pumps stopped working, fireman joined the rush to escape.

"This is hell," screamed one young woman as she staggered along, disoriented. "We're in hell."

"The sun's berserk and it's frying me," moaned someone as he tore off his suit and staggered in circles in his underwear.

Zamsi, a little more acclimated to extreme heat, eventually made it to the designated hotel, which he hoped was air conditioned. There he found some of the other NIO delegates sprawled out on the couches and on the carpet, dampening themselves with wet towels. Zamsi, drenched in perspiration, sank to the floor next to Archbishop Phillip O'Connell, who was lying down with his shirt off. The veins on his swollen and perspiring limbs were bulging, and he stared at Zamsi with glazed, bloodshot eyes. "May God be cursed for this injustice!" O'Connell panted, pointing at the sun, whose light had brightened to an intensity proportionate to its runaway heat.

Zamsi looked at him in shock. "Were we wrong about God all this time? Does he delight in torturing us?"

"See and feel for yourself, Zamsi. We are supposed to be his chosen elite and we are shriveling under his hatred. He mocks us in deception."

"Then we have deceived the world ourselves?" asked Zamsi.

"What does it matter?" hissed O'Connell. "The world is dying, whether deceived or not, and it's better that nobody knew this was coming. We flew over an ocean of blood to get here, and this is our reward."

Owen and Madeline were sitting on a log, catching fish in their spring-fed fishing hole. Though deep, the bottom could be seen as if through clear glass. Behind them lay a lifeless seventy-five-centimeter barramundi, stiffening as it dried, its chrome-like scales turning to lifeless gray.

They listened to the radio while they fished and were horrified to hear how the sun had scorched much of northern America, killing millions of people in one day. Some other countries had suffered as well. The most effective escape from the heat should have been the ocean, lakes, or rivers, but no one ventured into the putrid blood. All electricity supplies had been disabled, and water supply pipes had split and buckled. Bitumen roads had melted into slimy tar pits, and people dried hideously in overheated, stalled cars. Steel bridges buckled and became useless.

Madeline was awestruck. "It sounds like the sufferers realize that God's sending those judgments. But instead of repenting, they're cursing God."

"Yeah, it's happening just like it says in Revelation 16," agreed Owen. "The way they're actin' just proves their hearts are wrong, and yet they've been given every chance."

"Does each of the seven last plagues take place all over the world, Owen?"

"It doesn't say so in Revelation. I've never thought so or it would be just too much. For example, I think Revelation says that the plague of darkness takes place where the beast's power is concentrated."

"Makes sense. Do each of the plagues continue until the very end?"

"Don't think so. It doesn't say that in Revelation. In some parts of the world maybe one plague will end and another follows."

Madeline picked up a little green frog from the bait tin, looked closely at it, and when Owen wasn't watching, let it go and put a white witchitty grub on the hook instead. "It's incredible how God's protected the sealed ones in the death camps," she said. "They've been blamed for everything, but when the firing squads were brought in, the sun fried the soldiers but not God's people."

Owen spoke quietly, measuring each word. "Before the plagues, I thought we might die like Sam and his family, but now that the plagues are here, everythin's changed. God wouldn't let anythin' hurt us now."

"So why do I feel scared? I feel stupid for not rememberin' how we've been looked after so far. Over the past few months, since we left Evan's valley, God has sent a miracle to save us time after time."

Owen's fishing line began to move. He waited a moment to give the fish time to swallow the bait, then he tugged sharply on the line. The power of the startled giant barramundi jolted Owen's shoulder, and the huge fish leaped out of the water, shaking its head in a desperate attempt to dislodge the hook. Owen leaned against the massive fish's strength for a few minutes, gripping the line with a towel so his hands wouldn't get cut. He held on until the fish had exhausted itself, then he hauled it up to the bank and slipped his fingers under both its gills. Using all his strength, he heaved the massive flapping fish up onto the bank and dragged it well away from the water.

"What a beauty!" exclaimed Madeline. "It must be a meter long."

"We've got plenty for dinner now." Owen grinned. "I'll clean 'im over here, away from the water's edge, and bury its guts so it won't attract the crocs."

"When you've finished, why don't we go for a skinny dip together," said Madeline, grinning mischievously.

"Come on, Madeline. It's hardly private here."

"There's a secluded pool up above the falls."

"I'm in for that."

Madeline laughed and went to their bark hut to get her towel and treasured soap, while Owen sharpened a knife on a smooth rock.

26

The Real Lamb Strikes

◇◇◇◇◇◇◇◇◇◇◇◇◇◇◇◇◇◇◇◇◇◇◇◇◇◇◇◇◇◇◇◇◇◇◇◇

The famous miracle worker Desmond Piona and the prophet Ian Feldberg had been on a tour of Europe when the plague of sores struck. They were staying at a quiet health resort in Palmi, a southern Italian village on the Mediterranean, where they sought treatment. While there, Feldberg had a vision in which both he and Piona were healed from the plague's sores during a faith healing ceremony on a beach in that town.

Though Piona was aware that the ocean was now a mass of blood, he was obedient to Feldberg's vision. The media were informed, but only a thousand desperate sufferers came because the plagues had made most sufferers skeptical of God. Piona was hopeful, however. *God will not let me down if I call on his name for healing in public. Otherwise, it would disgrace his name.*

Piona's sermon was very brief because he was in pain, and every time he opened his mouth, it hurt the gaping infected cracks on his lips. Much of his hair had fallen out, and he had developed a stoop to relax his stomach muscles to take pressure off the huge sores on them. He stood just above the level of the bloodstained sand and delivered his sermon, explaining how suffering was followed by glory, miracles of grace, and healing. He pointed to the bloody sea behind him, predicting it would clear up—a fitting illustration of how their suffering would clear up once the testing time was over.

After he preached, Piona prayed for healing. Just then, a black cloud swirled in from the horizon. Piona praised the Lord for the healing energy he believed would come from the cloud. However, the thick black cloud grew and filled the entire sky. It became so dark that Piona could not see his own hands. The surrounding city was totally dark, for God had prevented even artificial lights from working.

The extreme darkness disoriented the weakened Piona. He lost his balance and fell backward into the bloody sea. As he rose, the blood coagulated and hung off him like thick red seaweed. He screamed with pain as his sores made contact with the salty, putrid blood. He heard Feldberg calling out to him in distress. As Piona stumbled toward him, they collided, and both wailed in pain. Car headlights refused to work, so motorists could only wait in their cars, distressed and confused.

Piona and Feldberg held hands, calling out, "Keep clear," as they groped their way to where they hoped the parking lot was. All around them people were abusing and blaming Piona and Feldberg. Trembling, the two religious leaders slowly made their way across the sand. A man bumped into Piona and grabbed his arm. "Your voice sounds like Pastor Piona. Are you Piona?"

"No, I'm Joseph Dean from New York," lied Piona, trying to affect a neutral accent.

"Just as well, Joseph. I have a knife in my other hand ready to slit Piona's throat. I didn't know what hatred was until I hated that man." He let go of Piona's arm. Piona panicked and ran into someone, and they both fell to the ground. Piona wiped the sand from his face. "I'm sorry. It is so dark."

The solidly built man recognized Piona's American accent and voice. He rolled on top of him, grabbing his throat, shouting, "There is only one voice like yours, Piona, so smooth and deceitful. But it shall lie no more. You deserve to die for your lies!"

He began to strangle Piona. The man with the knife quickly groped his way over to the voice and tripped over Piona's assailant. "Where is Piona?" he pleaded.

"I have him here, underneath me."

"Is this Piona's throat I feel under your hands?"

"Yes," grunted the big man who sat on Piona. "It's him."

"I have a knife; let me finish him off."

"No. I caught him. This devil is mine!"

Feldberg abandoned Piona, keeping silent as he felt his way from the beach along a handrail to the parking lot. He groped his way from car to car as he kept pressing his remote keypad and listened for the familiar click of an unlocking door. Finding his rented car, he rested in total darkness and listened to the radio. The broadcaster said that although little information had come in, the supernatural darkness had covered the whole of Europe and created total chaos.

After four hours of futile waiting, Feldberg became extremely frustrated, hungry, and cold. No one came to his rescue, so he decided to look for food. He smashed the windows of surrounding vehicles and opened their doors. He discovered a large packet of potato crisps and a bottle of lemonade. Feeling his way back to his own car, he started its engine and turned on the heater. For some hours, he alternated between sleeping and listening to the radio.

When the car ran out of petrol, he shivered in the extreme cold and was startled by a nearby male voice. He looked around and saw someone holding a large candle in front of him. The candlelight surprised him, but then he realized that hours had passed—enough time for candles to be found by a local. Feldberg called back, and a policeman came over and held the candle to Feldberg's face. He held out an apple to Feldberg's eager hands, but as Feldberg reached for it, he withdrew the apple.

"Don't I know you?" said the policeman. "Your face is familiar"

"No, no, I don't think so. I'm just a tourist," mumbled Feldberg, trying to hide his accent.

"Oh, I know! Your picture was in the paper. You're that prophet!"

"Prophet?"

"What is your name?"

"John Grant."

"I don't think so. Show me your ID."

"What for? Such petty details are inconsequential in this monstrous darkness."

"You are American. Your accent gives you away."

"No, no, Australian."

"No food or blanket for you till you show me some identification."

"It is against my conscience. That would be an invasion of privacy."

"You're freezing and hungry, yet you won't show me your ID? You must be that filthy prophet who deceived us."

"No, it wasn't me. You are mistaken."

"You promised healing but brought us this black curse. Probably it was your prayers that brought the sores and the blood!"

A terrible fear possessed Feldberg, and he quickly wound up the window and locked the car door. The policeman climbed onto the roof of the car, radioed for assistance, and held his candle up high. Soon another candlelight appeared out of the total darkness.

"This is the false prophet who came to destroy us," said the first policeman. "He refuses to show any identification."

"Look, prophet, open the door and show us something or we will take it by force."

"I don't have anything."

"Liar!"

The second policeman smashed the car window with his handcuffs and they dragged Feldberg out. They held up a candle to his wallet. "Aha! Ian Feldberg," he hissed. "Why did you send this murderous darkness?"

Feldberg's strained voice could only manage a hoarse whisper. "God … sent us to heal you … from the sores."

The policeman became furious. "If so, then God is evil, and so are you, his servant!" He viciously beat Feldberg on the head, rendering him unconscious. Using candlelight to guide them, the two men dragged him to the beach and waited for him to regain consciousness before they drowned him in the blood they believed he had summoned.

Sven Melnik tossed and turned on his mattress of sheet-covered, thick, dry grass. He woke up relieved that he hadn't really been forced to drink blood—it had only been a terrible nightmare. His mind was too troubled to allow sleep or peaceful thought, so he prayed silently.

Lord, I had to leave Sydney to go to Evan's valley in a hurry, so I hardly had time to ask forgiveness from those I sold drugs to. Have you forgiven me? Have I really repented? Maybe I am deluded. Maybe I still have a beastly, unrepentant character and don't really belong with your people. I still find myself showing off with my slick words, and I could be a lot more thoughtful of others. According to Revelation I'm supposed to follow you wherever you lead, yet I seem to feel more unworthy of your grace than ever. Lord, I guess I mustn't allow myself to think this way. I wish the morning would come so I'd feel better and think more clearly about all this.

Sven drifted off into a troubled sleep, but a mysterious light woke him up a few hours later. He blinked his bleary eyes in disbelief.

An angel enshrouded in light stood before him and was offering him a pure white robe. "This is all you need, Sven. This is all you need," said the angel gently and warmly. Then it disappeared.

It was almost dawn and Sven couldn't sleep, so he got up and sat by the fading coals of the campfire. He stoked the coals with a stick and added some dried tree limbs. Deeply moved, he pondered the meaning of the white robe.

At dawn, Gordon came and joined Sven by the fire. Sven told him about his dreadful nightmare, followed by the visit of the angel with the white robe.

Gordon shook his head in wonderment. "The Lord's sent you a

personal message, Sven. The white robe stands for the free gift of Christ's righteousness. God doesn't see your sinfulness because it's covered by Christ's perfect righteousness. Mate, he didn't only credit righteousness to you; he put it in your heart with his Holy Spirit. Satan knows he can't hurt you physically, so he was having a go at you through your mind, but the Lord wanted to encourage you with the angel's message."

"That's great, Gordon, but I don't *feel* righteous," said Sven.

"I think you'd be in strife if you felt righteous. The closer we come to Christ and see how good he is, the less we see that's good about us. Remember, Romans 7 says there's nothin' naturally good in us."

"But I thought you're supposed to get truth from just the Bible an' not trust visitin' angels and the like," said Sven.

"God sometimes sends angels, but we still have to test everything by the Bible. Sven, the message you got rings true. Hang on—I'll just get my Bible."

Gordon picked his way in the semidarkness around the heap of firewood and the giant gum trees. Stepping across a tiny gully to his bark hut, he picked up his worn Bible from beside his thin sponge bed and returned to Sven.

Gordon read a few passages in Romans 3 and 4 and finished with Romans 4.5: " 'To the man who does not work but trusts God who justified the wicked, his faith is credited as righteousness.' Sven, you may as well think of yourself as bein' counted perfectly righteous, because God does."

" I get it now. Boy, I must be pretty thick not believin' the angel, and needin' you to tell me."

That morning, Madeline was sitting beside the deep fishing hole, gazing at the water with tears streaming down her face. Owen noticed and came over. "What's wrong, sweetheart?" he said tenderly, sitting beside her and holding her.

"I'm not sure." Madeline sighed. "Guess I'm just so relieved it's almost over. My life's been incredibly tough at times. I've told myself that things weren't so bad—to keep battling on. Now that I'm leaving it all behind, I'm just so incredibly relieved."

The Palmer River group learned from the radio that the New International Order delegates unanimously concluded that God's plagues could only be appeased if they got rid of all the rebels immediately in a coordinated moment around the globe. Civilians and armed forces were to cooperate in an all-out effort to search and destroy, and the latest heat-sensing technology was to be employed.

The news of the intensifying persecution created a sober atmosphere in the camp. First they prayed for protection, then they camouflaged their camp. They decided to dispose of the vehicles because they had little fuel left, and the cars couldn't be hidden effectively. Owen and his father drove to the nearby river and parked on the banks of the deepest waterhole they could find. They engaged first gear in low range and drove the vehicles into the river. The men jumped out at the last moment and watched them slowly submerge in the foul-smelling blood.

"Your Nissan deserved it," quipped Owen, trying to lighten the mood. "But I never thought I'd do that to a good Toyota."

"Guess we won't need cars in heaven," replied Gordon. "Then again, if we do, I don't think any Toyotas will make it—they'd fall to bits."

A few nights later, the stars seemed especially brilliant to Gordon. It was as if, through them, heaven was communicating its intense interest in the affairs of the small group. Gordon lay back and enjoyed the spectacle of the universe. But when he noticed the blinking lights of a small aircraft, the comforting night sky suddenly changed into a menacing threat. He alerted the other campers.

"Basil, can heat sensors detect people who are hiding in the water?" queried Gordon.

"Probably not," he replied. "I think it's worth a try."

They doused the fire, and when the plane flew closer, they all submerged in a small pool, with just their heads showing. Shortly after, the plane passed overhead, turned, and made several more low passes before flying away.

After drying themselves and changing clothes, they all sat around fresh glowing embers. Beside them were buckets of water to douse the fire.

"They must have got a heat reading off us, or they wouldn't have made those low passes," reasoned Owen.

"What do we do now?" asked Ami. "Do we pack again? Look for a cave?"

"No. I'm sure the Lord will protect us right here," assured Gordon, expressing more confidence than he felt. "Anyway we wouldn't get too far. How could we hide from their heat-sensing gadgets anyway? I say we just sit tight and watch what the Lord does."

A large military helicopter was dispatched the following morning on a find-and-kill mission to the lower reaches of the Palmer River, where heat sensors had given a positive reading. Inside the chopper were five heavily armed soldiers. Two in the backseat were discussing their mission:

"With sores like these, I'd normally be in sick bay," complained one.

"We've all got 'em, so we've just gotta put up with 'em."

"Do you get used to the pain?"

"Nah. I didn't get much sleep last night. Whichever way I turn it hurts, mate. I just lie and think about the selfish slime out there causin' all this trouble. When we find 'em, it's not gonna be a clean kill. I'm gonna blast limbs off a bit at a time."

"This scum doesn't care if our kids' skin rots off their bodies, or if we crack up in the darkness."

"How far is it now?"

"Gettin' close—about five minutes."

"Can we be sure they're not just fishermen?"

"I doubt that. Everyone's been warned to keep out of the bush."

"Man, look at the river—it's a ribbon of blood. They say the rivers stink like hell and even the crocs are dyin'."

Eddie was the first to hear the helicopter, and he warned the others. As the distant speck in the sky grew larger, the group hid under thick tree cover, watching apprehensively. A moment later, rapid gunfire flashed at them from the helicopter. Branches started to crash around them, and bullets ripped into the earth.

They all dashed towards the thickest tree trunks for cover. Owen remembered a huge gum tree that shaded the creek higher up. Figuring it would be the best place to hide, Owen grabbed Madeline's hand and they ran toward it as bullets crashed all around them. The helicopter followed them, the hurricane winds from its swirling blades flattening out the tree tops. Desperately they ran from tree to tree.

"We can't make it!" cried Madeline.

"Keep running!" Owen shouted above the deafening gunfire and noise of the chopper. "The tree's just around the next bend."

Owen and Madeline ran desperately along the creek bank, where the tree cover was thickest, and disappeared into the hollow of the great tree, hoping they were not spotted, but fearing they had been. The noise from the heavy gunfire and bullets thudding into the tree was deafening.

Suddenly a strange darkness enveloped the area. Looking up, they were astonished to see that the chopper couldn't be seen. It had been swallowed by churning black clouds hovering just above the tree tops. It seemed as if the angry jaws of God's vengeance had swallowed the enemy.

The pilot turned around to try to escape the darkness. When he was near the camp again, he dropped the chopper lower and managed to get underneath the black cloud mass. The terrified soldiers saw a small florescent rainbow framing the camp.

From their hiding places, the rest of Owen's party gazed in wonder at the brilliant low-set rainbow that hovered mystically over their camp—a symbol of protection. Feeding the rainbow with a glorious aura was a spectacular multi-colored light stream descending from the heavens. A clear space of indescribable glory appeared between the high clouds.

"Look! Through that gap," said Owen excitedly. "It's glorious; it must be Christ and his angels."

Seeing the rainbow, the confused pilot fearfully veered away, accelerating through the darkness. But the thick blackness continued, so he decided to try to risk landing and wait for the cloud to lift. Horrified, he discovered that his lights weren't working any longer. He descended slowly, cautiously, hoping to avoid dangerous tree tops. He desperately hoped to land on solid ground, but it turned out he was landing on the river. The chopper's skid got caught under the protruding roof of Owen's car.

In desperation, the pilot attempted to lift, but the skid remained stuck. The helicopter spun and crashed into the congealing river of blood.

In blind panic, the soldiers fought for the half-submerged open doorway. It was like trying to swim in quicksand. They screamed and cursed God as they were being sucked down into their hideous bloody graves.

The campers heard the helicopter crash in the distance. The rainbow dispersed into a mellow light around them. In awe they knelt under the trees and thanked God for his deliverance. The promises of God took on a new and deeper meaning for them as they repeated them around the campfire, trying to renew their courage. Shortly after, when Madeline was alone with Owen, she hugged him tightly as if trying to gain some comfort. "I'm scared, Owen—real scared. Though I didn't want to admit it in front of Alice."

"Yeah, me too. We've just gotta keep believin', no matter how we feel. I keep thinkin' how rotten I am. Must be the devil temptin' me. I keep havin' to remind myself of the Gospel."

A few hours later, the earth beneath their feet began to roll like mighty waves of an ocean. The group lay flat on the ground. Some held hands, looking at each other in fear and astonishment. Then the dark clouds rolled up to the west like a giant scroll, and daylight returned.

Shortly after, they heard an indescribable noise that came from every direction and even from the depths of the earth below. The mountain range in the distance was rising and falling with the earth's convulsions.

"It's the earthquake of the last plague!" Basil shouted so he could be heard above the grinding of nature's forces.

For hours they desperately clung to each other, prostrate on the ground, feeling entirely helpless but in the hands of God.

As the entire surface of planet earth convulsed, the islands of the Pacific sank under the sea, but God preserved the islands where his people were hiding. Many of the great mountain ranges of the earth twisted and turned, and the steepest mountains collapsed, filling the valleys below. Great fountains of lava burst through the earth's crust and erupted for kilometers into the sky as fiery fountains of the deep burst forth to make lakes of fire. New mountain ranges were heaved up out of the bowels of the earth, where once deserts existed. Gigantic fountains of water burst out of the deep and flooded dry plains. None of those people who resisted the mark of the beast were harmed.

God shook violently the most evil cities of the world, and their tall buildings collapsed and burst into flames. Oceans broke their aged borders and spilled into cities. They broke their barriers and submerged the edges of the continents. Great lakes sank into oblivion as giant chasms in the earth yawned open and swallowed them. All of nature's forces conspired against the wicked inhabitants of the world, and they longed for death rather than face the ongoing horror of God's undiluted justice. Their familiar world had turned into an unfamiliar nightmare from which there was no awakening. They yearned for death with greater intensity than they once sought sinful pleasures.

Alice crawled under the blanket with Madeline, hoping the terror around them would pass, but not really expecting that it ever would. "The devil's in control of everythin'," she whimpered. "It must be him doin' it to scare us—he might get us."

Madeline did her best to hide her fear as she consoled Alice and soothingly stroked her hair. "It's God's anger at all the evil in the world, Alice. He's finally let all his anger loose, but he loves us and he's protecting us."

Dr. Karl Fletcher and Frieda were at home trying to ease the pain from their sores when the earthquake struck. Their house began to shake violently and tilted at a steep angle, causing the furniture to slide and crash forcefully into the walls.

They ran outside and were horrified to see the entire suburb twisting and rolling. Cars were sliding around like toys as the earth beneath them tilted, and tall buildings collapsed. The heaving elements and the sliding, grinding bedrock beneath them created an enormous roaring, which was intensified by a ferocious hurricane that made deadly missiles of anything loose.

"We'll be killed if we don't get away from these buildings," yelled Karl. "Jump in the car and let's go!"

"What's the point? We won't get anywhere," shouted Frieda, dropping onto the couch, sobbing.

"Let's go!" commanded Karl, forcing Frieda to stand. He dragged her to the door and helped her into the car.

Karl accelerated toward nearby King Edward Park, braking violently when he came to a yawning chasm in the road. He reversed, screeched a U-turn, and careered around the convulsing cracks in the road, his nerves tense and adrenaline racing. Finally he stopped on the elevated heights of the park and looked out at the city. The devastation was far worse than he had imagined.

"Oh, no," he screamed above the din. "It looks like it's been bombed. Everything's on fire. And look at Stockton! The mountainous waves have drowned it. Sebastian's place is gone! There's just a great chasm where their block used to be."

Frieda, frozen in fear, forced herself to look up from a fetal position. "Adrian, Brenda ... dead? It ... it must be the end of everything. What will we do?"

Karl slumped over the steering wheel hopelessly. "Nothing. Nothing!" he anguished. "Sit here and hope that the earth doesn't swallow us."

When the quaking finally stopped, Karl cherished a glimmer of hope that they might survive. He got out of the car, dazed, and looked around. Suddenly, an enormous object blurred through the air and slammed into the ground, its force causing the car to bounce. Karl leaped out of the car and stared in disbelief. "It looks like ice. Where did— Oh, my God! Look! There are more crashing down over there. Huge branches are being smashed off the trees."

Frieda clutched Karl's shirt. "Curse God before you die," she wailed.

"Why has the apostle Paul deceived me, his servant? I was so faithful." Karl wept bitterly.

Black and angry hurricane-driven clouds, streaked with an eerie dark green, dropped countless giant hailstones, which struck with bomb force. The barrage from the sky splintered trees and pulverized cars. Houses were flattened like matchboxes, and any remaining harbor craft sank with the force and weight of the ice.

Karl and Frieda didn't see the giant hailstone that flattened their car, killing them instantly.

Every city in the world had been devastated by God's undiluted wrath. But the plagues did not harm anyone who had the seal of God.

27

The Awakening
◇◇◇◇◇◇◇◇◇◇◇◇◇◇◇◇◇◇◇◇◇◇◇◇

A FTER THE HAILSTORM, A DRAMATIC CHANGE took place in the sky, which was seen all over the world. Through a rift in the clouds could be seen what looked like a bright star. It contrasted brilliantly with the forbidding gloom of the clouds.

As the world watched, the rift widened and the star's brilliance filled it and became a giant screen. A movie appeared, but it was not acted out; rather, it was a replay of Moses receiving the original Ten Commandments at Mount Sinai from God's own hand. Scene by scene passed before the astonished inhabitants of planet Earth. They saw the rebellious among Israel dance around the idolatrous golden calf at the foot of the mountain. Those loyal to the NIO became terrified because they were convinced that God identified them with the rejecters of God's sacred law.

Next, Christ's crucifixion was seen, and people could see God's magnificent love for sinful humanity with fresh hearts rendering clarity. They saw the enormous price Jesus and the Father paid to offer forgiveness and freedom to pursue individual conscience. This was seen in stark contrast to the repression of the NIO.

The deceived multitudes bitterly regretted suffering the consequences of the deception they had embraced, and this convulsed them in mental agony—not because they had a change of heart, but because they realized the enormity of the fate that awaited them. They gnashed their teeth, pleading to be hidden from the face of the Son of God—the one they had rejected and persecuted.

"It's like the angels videoed Calvary and kept it for us to see," said Sven solemnly.

Gordon shook his head. "Beats me why everyone don't love him."

"Actually seeing the cross ... Jesus' love is ... it's just too much for me to describe," said Ami with wonderment.

"Oh, man, I can't wait..." blurted Eddie.

"For what?" asked Sven.

"To see Jesus. Do you think the people on the other side of the earth could see that?"

"I guess so," said Basil. "I think everyone was meant to see it."

"How could they?" asked Eddie. "They can't see through the earth."

"Dunno," replied Basil. "Is anything too hard for the Lord?"

After some animated discussion, Alice and Madeline rested against the smooth bark of a large gum tree. "How are we all goin' to meet our friends up there when Jesus comes?" asked Alice.

"There's a really clear Scripture about that in Second Thessalonians," replied Madeline, quickly flicking to the passages. "It's in chapter 4 verse 15: 'According to the Lord's own word, we tell you that we who are still alive, who are left till the coming of the Lord, will certainly not precede those who have fallen asleep. For the Lord himself will come down from heaven, with a loud command, with the voice of the archangel and with the trumpet call of God, and the dead in Christ will rise first. After that, we who are still alive and are left will be caught up together with them in the clouds to meet the Lord in the air. And so we will be with the Lord forever. Therefore encourage each other with these words.' "

Alice read the words carefully, trying to absorb the full meaning. "It's saying that when Jesus comes back, he'll shout to wake up all the dead Christians, right?" she asked.

"That's right," replied Madeline.

"Then they'll be carried up in the sky to meet Jesus, right?"

Madeline nodded.

"And those Christians still livin' will be taken up in the sky to meet them, too, right?"

"Yep. And that's when they meet the raised ones."

"I get it. So Jesus doesn't land on earth at all?"

"Nope. Everyone meets him in the air."

Sven and Basil were both lying in their hut, resting. They were exhausted from all the danger and drama.

"Oh, man, nobody in the history of this world has ever been through anythin' like this," said Sven. "Why us—why *me*?"

Basil turned his head toward him, groggily. "Huh?" he grunted.

"I've been studyin' Revelation, and there's nothin' left to happen before Jesus comes."

Basil made an effort to listen. "I've had it, mate. I don't want any more miracles, deliverances, nothing. I just want Jesus to take me home."

Basil fell asleep while Eddie stayed awake, deep in thought.

"Basil, quick, come see this," said Eddie excitedly, shaking Basil and pointing up.

Basil stepped groggily out of the hut and looked up. As his blurry eyes focused, he could see a small, radiant white cloud descending through the widening gap in the black clouds. The cloud grew larger and brighter.

"Is that Jesus comin' to get us?" Alice asked solemnly but excitedly.

"Yeah, Alice, I think so," affirmed Owen quietly, in deep thought.

The party watched with increasing awe as the cloud came closer.

"They've gotta be angels, and that's gotta be Jesus," said Owen, moving alongside Madeline, conscious of a deep reverence he had never before felt.

"They're singing, and it's getting louder." Madeline smiled, putting an arm around Owen. "I hope we'll be still married in heaven."

Owen embraced her, his eyes moist. "If not, it'll be somethin' even better."

"I can't imagine what, sweetheart."

"I can't, either, but God can," said Owen, hugging Madeline more tightly.

A mighty voice reverberated through the sky. The voice's authority was absolute yet it was melodious and compassionate. They knew it was the voice of Jesus, the commander of the universe. "Wake up my children who sleep in the dust!"

The white cloud of angels shrank as millions of them left and blurred the distant sky on their flight down to earth. Shortly after, the white cloud of angels in the sky grew larger.

"Is that the raised ones goin' up?" asked Alice excitedly.

"It would have to be," answered Gordon, gazing steadfastly upward, his smile widening with anticipating joy. Any vestiges of unbelief and doubt anyone had were quickly vaporizing. Eddie jumped around as if he had just scored an important soccer goal. Everyone embraced one another joyfully, lovingly, for now they were certain that they were going home to be with Jesus at last.

Majestic angels dressed in robes of white landed beside the awestricken party. One of them smiled broadly as he approached Owen and Madeline. "Come. It is your turn to join the Lord and his people."

Madeline and Owen held hands, and an invisible power lifted them together with the angel. The mountains and river below shrank quickly, and they could see the circle of the earth's horizon. "I feel so safe, so peaceful," said Madeline, holding the angel's arm with one hand and Owen's arm with the other.

"Me too. We're not in heaven yet, but the way I feel I may as well be. Strange how there's no wind rushin' by, yet we're really movin'."

The angel grinned with the pleasure of his task, and Madeline was encouraged by his approachable friendliness. "Are my mum and dad safe?" she asked fearlessly.

The angel's expression changed to one of sorrow. "Madeline, sadly, you shall meet only your mother—she is safe. I will tell you the whole story later."

Owen embraced Madeline as she wept.

High above the earth, they joined a great multitude. People were hugging, talking, and weeping with joy. Angels were moving about, guiding people to their loves ones. Every person seemed wonderful and important to Madeline—not part of an impersonal mass, like they seemed on earth. She had never felt such love for people—strangers she had never met before all seemed like family.

"Most of these people must have been resurrected," she told Owen, laughing infectiously. "Their fashions are centuries old."

A familiar voice called her Madeline and she turned around. "Mum! You made it," Madeline said excitedly, embracing her mother, who was weeping with joy.

"I just knew I would see you again." She sobbed.

"Mum, you look so much younger and more beautiful. And that big mole on your cheek has gone!"

"I'll tell you what else has gone, Madeline, I don't feel jealous of all these beautiful women like I used to. I just love them. I love everybody."

"God has changed me, too, Mum. The power of love and truth is much clearer now. It's like scales have fallen off the eyes of my heart."

Owen wondered who the approaching beautiful young woman was. "Grandma! You look like your wedding photo again. What happened to your big nose and ears?" He laughed. "And Grandpa! You're young again too. You're walking straight and you lost a ton of weight."

After embracing, Owen's grandfather said, "I think you should call me John, now that my wrinkles have gone."

The angel that had stood by Pastor Sam Edwards and his family led them to Owen and Madeline, who didn't see them coming. Sam surprised them by bear-hugging them both from behind. They turned, and the entire Edwards family greeted them joyfully.

"Praise God you all made it!" Sam beamed. "We were praying for you the whole time we were in the compound."

Madeline was ecstatic. "It's so great to see you all safe together! When we heard you had been arrested, we prayed for you a lot. You must have all suffered terribly."

"Yes, it was hard," said Joan. "But it seems so insignificant now. The thing I remember most is how close Jesus was to us."

"Isn't he wonderful? Have you heard how Evan and Maude went?" asked Madeline.

"Yes, our angel told us," replied Sam sadly. "Evan never really trusted in Jesus, just the theory of truth and his own righteousness. Eventually he lost faith. In order to get insulin, he went back and joined Sebastian and Fletcher. Sadly, Maude went with him—she loved Evan more than she loved Christ."

"Oh, no," lamented Madeline. "Poor Evan. If only he had listened to us. And Maude? It's hard to imagine."

Alice gasped when she recognized the smiling short lady in a light blue dress, following her angel, weaving her way toward her through the crowd. They fell in each other's arms, weeping.

"Oh, Alice, what a lovely young lady you have become." The short lady sobbed.

"Grandma Violet!" Alice exclaimed, surprised. "You sound just the same as when I heard you in Evan's valley."

"Evan's valley? Where was that?"

Alice laughed happily. "Sorry, Grandma. It wasn't you. It just *sounded* like you."

"You always were a bit forgetful." Violet laughed.

"Grandma, what was it like to be ...dead?"

"Dead? It doesn't seem as if I've been dead. It was just like taking a short nap. Remember when Jesus raised the maiden from the dead, then later, Lazarus? He said they were only asleep. That's what it was like for me—a five-minute deep sleep."

Everyone met their closest friends and loved ones, but only a few were able to meet Jesus personally because of the vast sea of humanity surrounding him. Once loved ones had been reunited, it seemed to them as if Jesus' voice rang out to the outer realms of space. "My beloved children, we shall now begin the long journey home, where I shall welcome each of you personally. Well done, my good and faithful friends! Enter into my joy."

Moments later the distance of immeasurable space hid the convulsed ugliness of earth and it appeared to be a beautiful planet once more. The small circle of the world quickly shrank behind them as they soared through the universe, and painful memories of all its suffering and sin faded.

Madeline and Owen beamed with delight at as they gazed around them during their flight to heaven. The universe was not dark and forbidding. In a strange but comforting way, it seemed like home. Distant galaxies were swirls of color and silver streams of glorious light that moved gracefully. Some galaxies paraded past like enchanting kaleidoscopes. At first they appeared as distant bright balls, but as they came closer, their beauty pervaded space in every direction. Some colors were entirely new to them. Patterns and motions such as they never dreamed existed floated by. Often, a sun would pass by and they could not look at it its brightness for long. Encircling these suns, glorious planets of different colors and sizes appeared briefly and then were left behind. Some looked so beautiful and enchanting, Madeline felt sure they must be inhabited. She longed to visit their inhabitants and tell them personally how much Jesus meant to her and what it was like to be rescued from a hellish, doomed planet. She longed for her turn to meet Jesus when they arrived at his home, heaven.

"How big is the universe, Gilactus?" Madeline asked her angel, remembering his name.

Gilactus was amused. "How big? Much greater than the imagination of man can picture. By the way, we are just passing into the realm of Orion."

"How big is it compared to the distance earth's telescope could measure?" probed Madeline, wanting to know more.

"I don't know," replied Gilactus.

"You are an angel but you don't know where it all ends?" asked Madeline respectfully.

"Who said that God's creation has an ending? You are using earthly measures," replied Gilactus, grinning.

The concept of the possibility of a universe without end silenced Madeline into deep contemplation, and she exchanged looks of wonderment with Owen.

Madeline and Owen looked intensely into each other's eyes and embraced.

"Madeline, you were so beautiful on earth that the Lord hasn't needed to change your appearance," said Owen tenderly. "But there's a special loveliness within you now. I don't know what to expect in heaven except that it will be wonderful beyond description. I can't even *imagine* how good it will be. I'm glad we've got each other to share eternity with."

Madeline smiled the warmest and most beautiful smile Owen had ever seen. It seemed as if Jesus, eternity, and happiness smiled at him through her.